The Edge of Darkness

Vaseem Khan is the author of two bestselling crime series set in India: the Baby Ganesh Agency series, and the Crime Writers' Association Historical Dagger-winning Malabar House novels set in 1950s Bombay. Vaseem was born in London but spent a decade working in India. His first standalone thriller, *The Girl in Cell A*, was published in summer 2025. Vaseem is also the author of a series of mystery novels featuring Q, the iconic character from the James Bond franchise, beginning with *Quantum of Menace*, published in autumn 2025.

Also by Vaseem Khan

The Malabar House series

Midnight at Malabar House
The Dying Day
The Lost Man of Bombay
Death of a Lesser God
City of Destruction

The Baby Ganesh Agency series

The Unexpected Inheritance of Inspector Chopra
The Perplexing Theft of the Jewel in the Crown
The Strange Disappearance of a Bollywood Star
Inspector Chopra and the Million Dollar Motor Car
(Quick Read)
Murder at the Grand Raj Palace
Bad Day at the Vulture Club

Standalone novels

The Girl in Cell A

The Edge
of Darkness

Vaseem Khan

HODDER &
STOUGHTON

First published in Great Britain in 2026 by Hodder & Stoughton Limited
An Hachette UK company

The authorised representative in the EEA is Hachette Ireland, 8 Castlecourt
Centre, Dublin 15, D15 XTP3, Ireland (email: info@hbgi.ie)

1

A CIP catalogue record for this title is available from the British Library

Hardback ISBN 978 1 399 74785 1
Trade Paperback ISBN 978 1 399 75213 8
ebook ISBN 978 1 399 74787 5

Typeset in Adobe Caslon by Hewer Text UK Ltd, Edinburgh
Printed and bound in Great Britain by Clays Ltd, Elcograf S.p.A.

Hodder & Stoughton policy is to use papers that are natural, renewable
and recyclable products and made from wood grown in sustainable
forests. The logging and manufacturing processes are expected to conform
to the environmental regulations of the country of origin.

Hodder & Stoughton Limited
Carmelite House
50 Victoria Embankment
London EC4Y 0DZ

www.hodder.co.uk

This book is dedicated to old friends in India, whose memories so often provide the genesis for these novels.

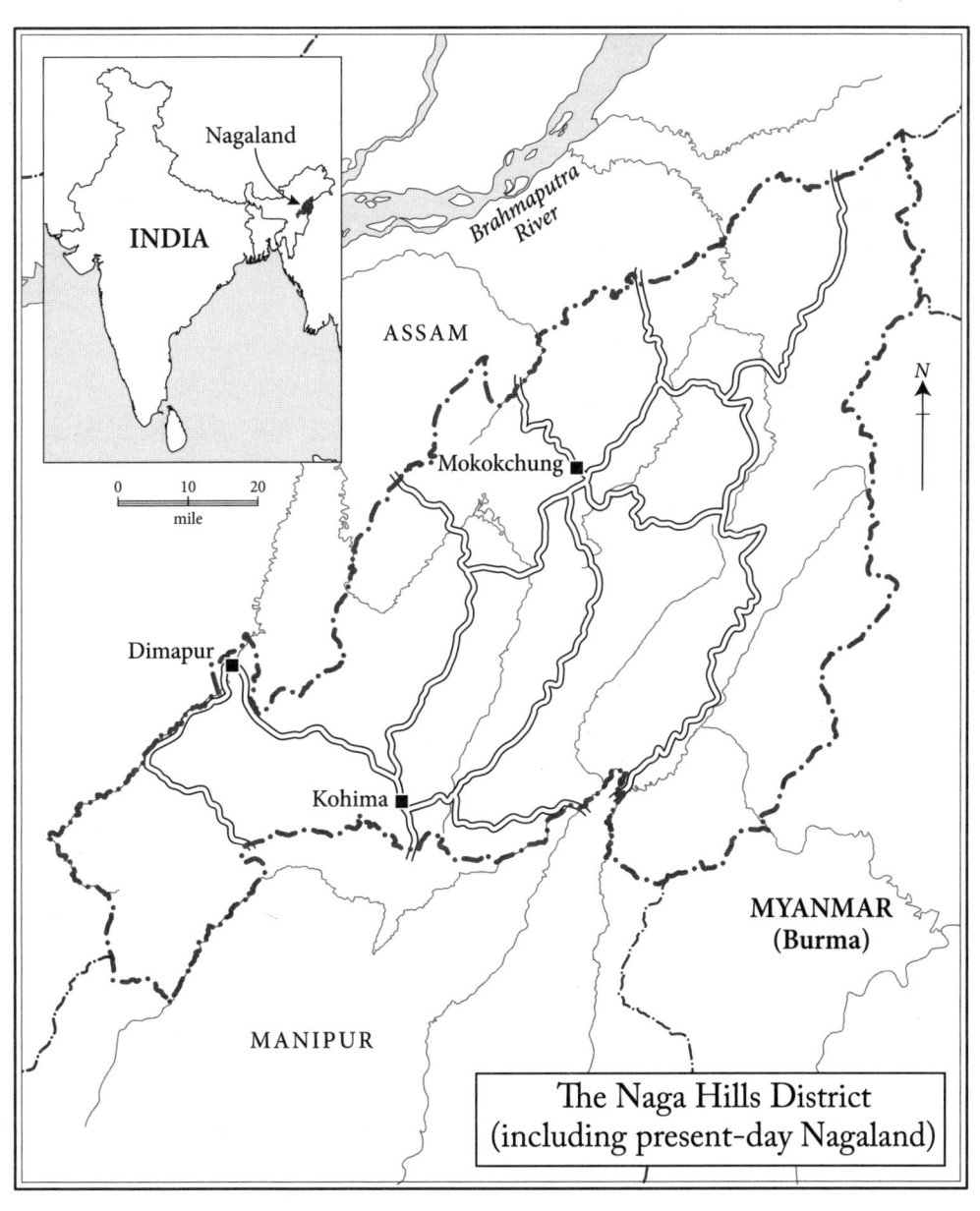

The Naga Hills District
(including present-day Nagaland)

I

The Naga Hills District, Assam Province, 1951

The shriek came from the darkness between the trees, a howl so plaintive it returned her instantly to the streets of Bombay. A typical evening in India's glamour capital, punctuated by the yells of fruitsellers, the shouts of rickshawwallahs, and the tortured cries of those discovering too late that not everything that glittered in the city of dreams was gold.

But she was a long way from home now.

'It's a capuchin. Whole troop of them, by the sound of it.'

Persis turned from the wooden railing to find the American, Oren Rake, approaching, cigar in hand. Rake, a cadaverous man in his late forties, with dark hair, greying in iron streaks, had the weathered quality common to men who had spent time in the tropics, battling the elements. In India that was a fight most men were bound to lose. The saner ones tended not to step into the ring at all.

But you couldn't explain that to a foreigner.

Rake stopped beside her, the floorboards of the hotel's rear veranda creaking softly beneath his feet. A tall man, well over six feet, and powerfully built. He wore a bush suit, in olive green, together with a revolver, holstered at the hip, as if he had swaggered out of a saloon in a low-budget western. She could smell his odour, a unique blend of a woody aftershave and his own rutting-stag musk.

Persis watched him fumble in his pocket for a cigar cutter, snip the cigar, then light it. The tip glowed dully.

'So you're a cop?'

Was she? She couldn't be sure any more. Banished from Bombay, sent three thousand kilometres eastwards to the very edge of the country, to lose herself in these godforsaken hills, she was finding it difficult to reconcile past with present.

Persis Wadia, India's first female police detective.

How hollow those headlines now seemed! And how vainglorious the expectations such words placed upon her.

And yet. There was little doubt that she had earned her spurs. The cases that she had investigated back at the Malabar House station in Bombay – beginning, just over a year ago, with the murder of a prominent English diplomat – had catapulted her to national attention, a star at the tender age of twenty-eight. The fact that the station was populated by a contingent of the force's most unwanted had done little to slow her rise. Her subsequent fame had brought out the best – and worst – in her fellow citizens. Plaudits from those who considered her apotheosis in line with the country's post-independence march on progress; brickbats from those horrified by the notion of women abandoning their traditional posts and overrunning the manly edifices of the new regime.

Persis had put on a steely front. Having lost her mother as a child, she had been raised by her father – a man who would have made Attila the Hun seem a geisha by comparison – never to take a backwards step. But sometimes the strength it took to deal with prejudice – and idiocy – was beyond her.

'Do you suppose I'm wearing this uniform for fun?'

Rake's grey eyes, the colour of ash, held fast; then he set his elbows on the railing and leaned out into the night.

Beyond the perimeter wall the hillside ran steeply down into the jungle, a dense mass of trees that whispered thickly into the near distance. Sounds emerged from the shadows, not just the gibbering of monkeys, but the whine and whirr of insects, the eerie song of flying lizards, and the rustling of bats. Above, the sky was a velvet dome, stars gleaming with crystal-bright urgency. If there was a solitary compensation to being here, Persis thought, it was the startling beauty of the night heavens.

'We haven't been officially introduced. My name is Oren. Oren Rake. I run a mining outfit, a few hours north of Kohima.'

'I know who you are, Mr Rake.'

'Please. Call me Oren.' He flicked ash over the railing. 'I have a place in Kohima, but I spend most of my time out in the hills. These days, when I venture south, I tend to stay here, at the Victoria. It's a little isolated, but that's no bad thing. Kohima's a real frontier town, now. You never know if you're going to make it out alive.' He flashed an easy grin.

Did she agree with him? Perhaps. Kohima was one of only two or three towns worthy of the name in the Naga Hills region, and the site of the police station to which Persis had been seconded. The place was growing fast, but with growth came the anxieties – and politics – of modernity. Following independence, the local Naga population had split into those who favoured continuing as part of the new India – with all that entailed – and those who wanted to go their own way.

Greater Nagaland. *Nagalim.* An independent nation for the Naga people.

The very idea had caused the prime minister, sitting in faraway Delhi, to choke on his morning grapefruit. The Centre's response had been swift and urgent. Nehru had made it clear that there was as much chance of India letting go of the Naga Hills as there was of a tiger giving up a coolie clamped in its jaws. Soldiers had been despatched. Furious headlines had railed against the ungrateful eastern tribes out in the misty hinterlands beyond the 'chicken's neck', that narrow pass that connected mainland India to the semi-tropical tea-growing regions of the north-east.

For Persis, still finding her feet in the region, it meant navigating a place where, increasingly, death and rhetoric had become opposite sides of the same coin.

'How long have you been out here?' Rake's gaze remained on the jungle.

'Just over a month.'

'And what brought you here?'

What could she tell him? That any notion of choice in her presence here was laughable? That the powers-that-be had decreed her banishment, for reasons that she still found baffling? Her thoughts returned to Bombay, the sights and sounds of a city that, in spirit and aspect, remained a million miles from these forbidden and unknowable hills. Bombay, with its chaotic traffic, its thunderous advance on destiny, its overpowering *essence*. A city that had inspired a thousand songs, a thousand films, and a thousand stories, including her own.

Though, of late, her life had taken the sort of unexpected twists that even Bombay's mercurial film directors might have balked at.

Living through the turmoil that had marred the end of the Raj had taught her that life was neither predictable nor fair. Since joining the force, the trials and tribulations of being the Indian Police Service's only woman, at the mercy of male superiors – and peers – who often treated her as an abhorrent infection rather than a colleague, had only served to sharpen her defensive reflexes. But you couldn't keep a good woman down. Not if she was standing over you with her foot on your neck.

Perhaps the American sensed her hesitance. 'Well, whatever it was, I doubt you were sufficiently prepared for *this*.' He nodded into the jungle. 'They say the forests are haunted by dead soldiers.

Englishmen and Japs. The Naga believe each star in the night sky is a warrior fallen in battle. They love a good death here.'

Rake's assertion was not so far from the truth. Could anything have truly prepared her for the intrigues of a land all but cut off from the rest of the world? A Shangri-La of sunless forests and highland villages, mired in myth and war?

'*He's* out there, somewhere. Baba Dao. The great revolutionary. Apparently, his name means "father of daggers".' Rake examined the glowing tip of his cigar. 'They say he's vowed to kill every last one of us. Foreigners, I mean. That goes for mainlanders, too.'

She was saved from having to respond by the arrival of the night porter. The youth – barely into his twenties and dressed in a white dinner jacket monogrammed with the letters HV – Hotel Victoria – was flushed, eyes wide. 'Madam. The manager has requested your presence.'

'Where?'

'Mr Sinha's room. We have a problem.'

Persis followed the young man – she recalled that his name was Peter Jadonang – through the hotel, up several flights of stairs to the topmost floor. The floor was taken up entirely by the suite rooms of Mohan Sinha, the region's governor. Sinha had been sent to the Naga Hills district by Prime Minister Nehru a year earlier. In that time, the man had made it his mission to stamp out the incipient rebellion. But for every fire he put out, he appeared to have started two more.

She had seen Sinha around Kohima, always with an armed escort, met him only the twice, the first time a day after she had arrived in town. Sinha had summoned her to his office at the commissioner's residence, eager to make the acquaintance of the country's only female police officer, a celebrity in her own right.

The governor had wanted to hear about Bombay. Bright lights, big city. He had spent almost the entirety of his life in Calcutta, Bombay's dour older sister, had once dreamed of travelling the well-trodden path to India's city of dreams, pursuing a career in film. But his father, a wealthy businessman, had had different ideas.

In that first meeting, Sinha had struck her as a man consumed by his own legacy. He had talked incessantly about his intent to pacify the region – by any means at his disposal – and then to advance upon Delhi as a conquering hero. He was a chain-smoker, with a penchant for expensive suits and French perfume. Rake thin.

It had taken her a while to see beyond the dandyish veneer to the political animal within. Sinha was an important man. He had made a name for himself in Bengal, the country's richest state, where he controlled a large voting bloc. During the war years, that fame had grown, as he had pitched himself headfirst into the communal rioting that had erupted in Calcutta and her environs. Somehow, he had emerged from the carnage unscathed, and with a vociferous base at his beck and call. More than one commentator believed that the wily, Oxbridge-educated politico had the chops to make it all the way to Delhi, possibly as a successor to Nehru. In time.

Perhaps the prime minister had sensed this, forcing his hand in sending Sinha to the crucible of the Naga Hills. Here, it was assumed, Sinha would either prove his mettle or be swallowed by the jungle and forgotten.

She found the hotel manager, David Keishing, pacing the floorboards outside Sinha's door like an expectant father.

'What's the problem?'

'Mr Sinha isn't responding,' said Keishing.

'It's late. Perhaps he's asleep?'

'No. He never sleeps before midnight. Peter goes in to collect his dining cart each evening at this time. He has never not opened the door before.'

'Fine. So open it. Why am *I* here?'

Keishing, a short, round-faced Naga in a grey morning suit, patted his hands together nervously. In the tropical heat, the suit seemed both an extravagance and wildly incongruous. The man was practically swimming in his own perspiration. Persis knew that the uniform – along with much of the Hotel Victoria's starched aspect – was dictated by the establishment's idiosyncratic proprietor, Apeni Ao.

'Mr Sinha is a powerful man. If I break into his room without permission . . .' He left the thought unsaid.

'But you think *I* should do it?'

'You are a police officer.'

'*I'll* do it.'

Persis turned to find Rake breathing down her neck. The American had followed her from the hotel's rear veranda. 'Mohan is a friend. I'd hate to think anything's happened to him.'

He stepped forward, but Persis stopped him with a raised hand. 'If I need your help, I'll ask for it.'

She turned to the door, examined it, then tensed herself. Focusing her energies, she aimed a kick at the lock, then another, and another. When she eventually burst through, she realised that the inner bolt, now displaced from its mooring, had been drawn.

She found herself in a spacious living room, a sofa arrangement – complete with a marble-topped coffee table – to one side. On a sideboard, a gramophone took pride of place. One wall was taken over by a portrait of Queen Victoria, set side by side with an image of Gandhi. The queen was po-faced. Gandhi appeared to be smiling at a joke only he understood.

She caught sight of her reflection in a gilt-framed oval mirror.

She had arrived back late from Kohima that evening, and had ventured out on to the hotel's rear veranda, still in her khaki uniform, a moment of respite before the business of showering and changing for dinner. Minutes later, Oren Rake had interrupted her solitude, and then the night porter, Peter, had arrived to summon her. Her cheeks were dusty from the ride back from the city, and her nostrils twitched at the pungent note of sweat rising from her clothing. With her cap removed, her hair, thick and black, wound behind her head in a plait. She knew that she favoured her mother, dark eyes and features that men found attractive. At the police academy, she had expended as much energy batting away unwanted advances as she had in the gymnastics hall. In the years since, there had been only two genuine interactions with the opposite sex, one a brief liaison with an older man who had walked out on her, abruptly and without explanation, only to send her a card to his wedding a month later; the other, the unhappy state of affairs with Archie Blackfinch, a train wreck that had been slow in the making, but threatened to derail them both.

She shook away the thought, returned to the room.

Doors led off on all sides.

The others crowded in around her shoulders. 'Don't touch anything,' she said.

Persis stepped through the door to her left and into a formal dining room. A mahogany dining table ran the length of the room, its surface mirror-bright with polish. On the table was a folded newspaper and a plate harbouring the remains of a meal, a glass half-filled with amber liquid set beside it. At the foot of the table stood one of the hotel's wheeled dining carts, draped in a white cloth. Atop the cart was a bottle of whisky, and a steel cloche on a sterling-silver tray. A window in one wall was inset with mosquito mesh. Visible behind the mesh: a succession of iron bars.

Her nostrils twitched. Oren Rake's unique musk made itself known, settling around her shoulders like a fox fur.

A cry of alarm sent them swiftly back into the living room.

Persis followed Rake and David Keishing through another door and into a master bedroom. The cry had come from the en suite attached to the bedroom. She saw Peter framed in the doorway. The boy's face had paled; horror twisted his handsome features.

Persis walked past him and into the bathroom.

What she saw there sent her stomach into freefall.

2

The journey from Bombay had taken a week.

Her father had come to the station to see her off, a rare afternoon away from the bookshop. She had followed in his wake as he had commandeered his wheelchair around the station like a tank, cleaving a passage through the press of sweating bodies: passengers, coolies, beggars, snack vendors, eunuchs, railway staff, and the occasional shellshocked foreigner caught up in the madness.

It had been a month since Persis's posting papers had come through, informing her that she was being transferred from the familiar chaos of Bombay's Malabar House station to the far north-east, a place she had not only never visited, but one that was so far removed from the India that she knew it might as well have been the dark side of the moon.

Her father, Sam Wadia, had been less than sympathetic. 'You're being punished. Perhaps you deserve it.'

It was a sore point between them.

Sam, having once supported Persis's desire to join the force – to howls of protest from around the country – a woman in the Indian Police Service? Why not train chimps to serve in the army? – having stood – or, rather, sat – by her through the various trials and tribulations of her early cases – cases that had made her name, splashed across the country by newspaperwallahs intoxicated by the idea of India's first – and lone – female police inspector – had now decided that her new posting was the result of Persis's demonstrable lack of tact.

Which was rich coming from a man who could engineer a fight with his own shadow.

To be fair to him, Persis had sensed that, beneath Sam's critique, her father was worried. But he wasn't about to undermine her with talk of the dangers she might be set to face.

Her aunt, Nussie – her late mother's younger sister – on the other hand, had never been one to hold back on that particular topic. 'It's nothing but wild jungle out there,' Nussie had protested. 'Full of savages and madmen.'

'Sounds a lot like when you and Papa are in the same room,' Persis had muttered.

'I'm glad you think this is funny. You know you can always quit, don't you?' Nussie's tone was brittle. Another old battle.

But quitting was the last thing on Persis's mind. If her superiors thought they could get rid of her by sending her to the country's least savoury posting, they were sorely mistaken. You couldn't make a camel sit by beating it. Or so Birla, her sub-inspector back at Malabar House, had once told her. She wasn't certain that this was true – Birla's homespun wisdom had often been found wanting – but, camels not being readily to hand at the station, she had never been able to put the matter to the test.

The train rattled east across the plains for the best part of two days, stopping overnight in Calcutta. Kipling's Calcutta, as she had heard many of the Britishers who ventured into her father's bookshop back in Bombay refer to it. As if the city – and, by extension, India herself – was somehow an invention of their forebears. Persis had recently travelled to the old colonial capital in pursuit of another case, a white man accused of murdering a nationalist Bengali lawyer. The trip had almost resulted in her death.

The journey continued northwards from Howrah Station on the Kamrup Express, rattling through dust-hazed coalfields, before threading a path through the Siliguri Corridor, that narrow spit of land, never more than a dozen miles in width, that mazed into the country's north-eastern region. The so-called 'chicken's neck' was flanked, on the one side, by Nepal and, on the other, by the newly created eastern wing of that other blood-birthed child of India's Partition: Pakistan.

The train halted in Siliguri, a stop necessitated by a change of drivers and the onboarding of military supplies and personnel, and then a further day east, travelling at a snail's pace along narrow-gauge tracks, rising up with the land and passing through places that Persis had only ever read about in books, their names incantations against her ever-increasing sense of dislocation: Cooch Behar, Goalpara, Guwahati.

On this final leg she was joined at her dining table by an Englishman named Asquith – 'As in the former prime minister' – dropping into the seat opposite her without asking.

Persis had been too stunned by the man's audacity to protest.

Asquith, a small man, balding and potbellied, swaddled in a crisp white linen suit and tie, turned out to be excellent company, at least for himself. It was not only impossible to get a word in edgeways, but any words that Persis might have ventured were bludgeoned aside by Asquith's nonstop barrage. Under ordinary circumstances, she would have set the man straight, but, for all his bluster, Asquith at least seemed to possess some knowledge of the region's political affairs.

Persis knew nothing of the Naga Hills district of Assam save the little she had gleaned from a book her father had pressed into her hands on the day she had departed: *The Naked Nagas* by Christoph von Fürer-Haimendorf. The book's subtitle had been telling: *Head-Hunters of Assam in Peace and War*. Not that that had seemed to faze her father.

For three decades, Sam Wadia had run Bombay's oldest bookstore, the Wadia Book Emporium, a favourite of both ordinary mortals and celebrated Bombayites alike. Persis and Sam lived above the shop, in an apartment graced by her dead mother's Steinway, her father's second, recently married wife, and a Persian tom named Akbar who expected to be waited upon, hand and foot, with little in the way of gratitude offered in return.

Growing up surrounded by books had offered Persis some solace for losing her mother at the tender age of seven. Watching her father haunt the bookshop from behind his granite counter, hunkered down in his wheelchair – a legacy of the accident that had cost Persis's mother her life – had been an education. Sam claimed that he was a people person. The problem was that the only people he appeared to like were those that came into the shop, bought books, and never opened their mouths to ask questions or, heaven forbid, exchange pleasantries. According to her father, no one could accuse Sam of rudeness. Not if they ever wished to set foot in the shop again.

Asquith pulled a handkerchief from his trousers. 'Have you ever been this way? No?' He patted his brow with the folded square of cotton. 'Misty hills. Forgotten forests. Lost tribes and strange rituals. Reminds me of an H. Rider Haggard novel.' A louche grin. 'They say there are Naga out in the deeper hills still hunting heads. Take this Baba Dao fellow. The locals claim he orders his insurgents to not only bring back heads, but to boil them so that he can display them in his hut.'

Persis had read about the custom, long prevalent among the many tribes of the Naga Hills. The British had made a concerted effort to wipe out the practice. It was said that they had only partially succeeded.

'And the political situation?'

'An absolute mess. The insurgency is giving Nehru sleepless nights. I blame Gandhi, of course. The man practically gave the Naga his word that they could have their own country once independence materialised. A pipedream, of course.'

'Not for the Naga,' said Persis.

'A bunch of half-naked savages? What would they do with their own country?' Asquith reached into his pocket, placed a pistol on to the table. The weapon was so small it resembled a toy. Persis almost laughed. 'They say the Kamrup has been held up on several occasions. Insurgents are particularly active along this stretch of the line. But you have nothing to fear, dear lady. I'm an excellent shot.' He leaned in, voice falling to a whisper. 'And if you would feel safer with me standing guard in your compartment tonight, I would be more than willing.' His lips stretched into a smile.

Persis returned the smile with one of her own. And then she reached into the bag at her side and set her own revolver on to the table. 'Government issue,' she said, brightly. 'Did I forget to mention that I'm a police officer?'

3

'His head is missing.'

Persis assumed that the hotel manager's words – as unnecessary as they were – had been forced from his mouth by terror.

A body lay in the bath. A body without a head.

The copper bathtub, standing on clawed feet, with handrails running along both sides, took up centre stage in the room. The dead man's arms flopped over the sides. On one wrist, sacred threads could be seen. The water in the tub, barely covering the man's nudity, was pink with blood. A few spots of blood had fallen on to the floor tiles at the head of the tub.

Persis took a deep breath. 'I think we can rule out suicide.'

Oren Rake gave her a sharp look.

'Where is it?' breathed Peter, the night porter.

Persis looked at him. 'What?'

'The head? Where is it?'

A quick survey revealed no sign of the missing head. She noted that the bathroom's solitary window, set high into one blue-tiled wall, was barred.

'I need you all to step outside.' She ushered the men out of the bathroom, back through the suite, and into the corridor.

Only Rake offered up a protest. 'What do you intend to do? Perhaps I can help?'

'This is now a police matter, Mr Rake. You can help by staying out of my way.'

'Mohan was a friend. The idea that someone did this to him . . .' Rake's expression darkened.

Persis directed herself to David Keishing. 'I need you to call Dr Andrews in Kohima. Tell him that someone has died at the hotel and I need him out here to certify death. Don't tell him who the victim is.'

'The man's clearly dead,' said Rake. 'You don't need a doctor to tell you that.'

'It's procedure,' responded Persis. To Peter she said: 'Is Apeni Ao here?'

'Yes.'

'Fetch her.'

The boy's eyes widened a fraction. 'Now?'

'Yes. Wake her up. And fetch Sinha's aide too.'

She watched the two men leave, then turned back to Rake. 'There's no need for you to remain here.'

Rake frowned. 'I'll stay if it's all the same to you.' She watched him re-light his cigar, take a long puff, as if to steady himself. 'Why did you tell Keishing to keep Mohan's identity from the doctor? There are no secrets out here. By morning everyone in Kohima will know. By afternoon it will be across the wires. Nehru will have to respond. It's going to be brutal.'

'You think this was the work of insurgents?'

'Who else?'

'The door was locked. The windows are barred. How did the killer get in?'

Rake paused, cigar in the air. 'A technicality.'

Persis suspected it was going to be a good deal more than that.

She waited in uncomfortable silence, watching Rake smoke. Minutes later, the hotel's proprietor, Apeni Ao, arrived, flanked by Peter Jadonang and a tall white man rubbing sleep from his eyes.

Looking at Ao, Persis found herself once again reminded of a hummingbird. The woman, in her sixties – though she could easily have passed for any age from fifty to a hundred – was tiny, so small that she could have comfortably worn children's clothing. As it was, the hotel's proprietor wore a sarong-style skirt with a Western blouse, the skirt in navy blue, the shirt a shade of off-white. Her face, creased with age, was shorn of make-up, and her hair, usually pulled back into an immaculate bun, bore the hallmarks of someone who had been raised from slumber in urgency.

The man at Ao's shoulder appeared to have dressed in equal haste. He wore plain trousers and a white shirt, notable for the lack of a tie. His hair, blond and thick, was without its customary application of Brylcreem and flopped over a broad forehead. Blue eyes squinted behind round-framed spectacles.

This, Persis knew, was John Templeton, Mohan Sinha's personal aide.

'What's going on here?' The words burst out of Templeton like panicked sheep.

Ignoring him, Persis directed herself to Ao. 'I have bad news. Mohan Sinha has been murdered. His body is inside. I have called for Dr Andrews from Kohima so that the death may be certified. I'm going to search Sinha's suite. I thought you should be informed.'

'Murdered? What nonsense!' Templeton was looking at her as if she had lost her mind. He blinked rapidly, then tried to move around her and into the suite.

Persis stepped across to block his path. 'I would rather you remain outside. At least until I complete my search.'

'Get out of my way.'

Her jaw tightened. 'Don't make me ask again.'

'Inspector.'

Persis pulled her eyes from the Englishman and looked down at Ao.

'It is important that we see Sinha's body,' said the older woman. 'I'm sure you can understand that? Once we have done so we will return outside and allow you to do your work.' The words were said calmly and without any edge of authority.

Persis relented. 'Follow me. Don't touch anything. And prepare yourselves.'

She led them through to the bathroom.

As Templeton caught sight of the body, a cry escaped him. His legs buckled and he fell back against the wall, sliding down to his knees.

Apeni Ao's eyes remained on the grim spectre of the headless corpse. Finally, a small shake of the head and what sounded like a muttered prayer. Persis could sense the woman's inner turmoil. She could only imagine what was going through Ao's thoughts.

Myths surrounded the owner of the Hotel Victoria, as thick as flies. Some said Ao had been born in the distant hills bordering Burma, that she had escaped a brutal upbringing at the hands of her father, the chieftain of a particularly aggressive Naga tribe, that she had run away to the southern half of India, worked as a courtesan in the Chowmahalla Palace in Hyderabad. The old soaks in the bars of Kohima claimed that Ao had stolen the treasure of the Nizams, and had then returned to the Naga Hills to build the Hotel Victoria, a tribute to the woman she admired above all others: Queen Victoria of England. Ao had never married, and had no children. The hotel was everything to her, and she ruled it with an iron fist.

By virtue of its fort-like position atop a hill just kilometres from the town of Kohima, the Hotel Victoria had once attracted wealthy and powerful clientele. But with the advent of independence, the Naga Hills district had become an unsafe place to conduct business – whether of a political or commercial nature. As a consequence, Ao's establishment had lost much of its regular clientele. Nevertheless, it continued to provide a certain surety against the vicissitudes of fate – and the predations of the native insurgents who harboured a particular hatred for the politicos despatched by Delhi to tame them.

Persis could only imagine the repercussions for the hotel of Mohan Sinha's murder.

'How can you be sure it's him?' said Ao, eventually.

The thought *had* occurred to Persis. 'I'm working on the assumption that it is. It's easier than believing that someone broke in here just to leave behind a headless corpse.'

'The rings.'

Persis looked at Templeton, still collapsed on the floor.

'The rings on his right hand. They're his.'

She turned back to the body. Three rings graced the fingers of the right hand where it flopped against the side of the bath.

'Are they valuable?'

'An emerald, a sapphire, a black opal. Yes. They are valuable.'

'Then we can rule out robbery as a motive.'

Templeton stared at her, then rose awkwardly to his feet. 'What happens now?'

'We wait for the doctor, Andrews. Meanwhile, I'm going to search Sinha's rooms. And then I'm going to need to talk to everyone who was in the hotel this evening, beginning with you.'

Templeton looked as if he was about to protest, but then decided against it. 'I'll be in the bar.' She watched him walk out.

Turning to Ao, Persis said, 'How well did you know Sinha?'

The woman paused before speaking. 'When he came to the Naga Hills a year ago, he moved into the commissioner's residence, in Kohima. It was only after the first assassination attempt that he decided he needed somewhere safer. I offered him a suite here. He moved in a few months ago, placed armed guards around the hotel, and has been here ever since. Frankly speaking, I had hoped that his presence here might recover the hotel's fortunes. A high-profile guest, an encouragement to similar visitors. The hotel is on its knees. We have few guests now.' Her mouth tightened into a grimace. 'This killing will hit me hard, Inspector. Sinha's murder might just signal the death knell for the Hotel Victoria.'

4

Five weeks earlier, Persis's train had shuddered to a halt at Dimapur Junction, where the railhead ended.

Dimapur, the ramshackle gateway town leading into the Naga Hills interior and once the capital of the thirteenth-century Dimasa Kingdom – a people that had traded with the Chinese Ming dynasty – sprawled along the banks of the Dhansiri River. The town had been leased to the Naga Hills district in 1918 by the Assam Province of British India for the purpose of building a railway line spearing into the uncharted forests east of the city. That heady ambition had met with the brute reality of engineering in the tropics; many a British foreman had given up in disgust, sent packing by a combination of heat, malaria, and the unwillingness of the natives to play ball with their own subjugation.

Persis had been met on the platform by Peter Jadonang, a fresh-faced porter from the Hotel Victoria.

Taking her suitcases, he had led her through the sleepy station to a waiting jeep.

Kohima lay almost eighty kilometres further into the interior, along a road that quickly became a jolting purgatory, winding through dense forest, and obstructed by clanking buses, obstinate bullocks, and the occasional military vehicle ferrying troops so young they resembled choirboys.

As the slow hush of the forest wound itself around Persis's throat, the reality of her predicament began to creep over her.

Persis was a city girl. She had grown up in Bombay, lived nowhere else. The city – with its noise, colour, and penchant for high drama – was a part of her, and she a part of it. Now, just over a year into her tenure as the country's first female police inspector – a year in which she had tackled several high-profile cases – she found herself relegated to a hinterland so far removed from the ambitions that had driven her to the police service in the first place that she may as well have dropped off the face of the earth.

She was still struggling to work out how it had happened.

Malabar House, Bombay's smallest police station, had seemed the obvious place to send her following her graduation from the academy. It was where the rest of the Bombay force's misfits were banished, a collection of officers who had disgraced themselves, their uniform, or the men that held sway over their careers. Persis's crime had been no less egregious: she was a woman interloping in a man's world.

Nevertheless, she had settled in, champing at the bit to prove herself. Malabar House served not just as a place where careers were sent to die, but as a convenient dumping ground for cases of a sensitive nature. Cases that no one else wanted; no one in their right mind, at any rate. But that was the point of Malabar House. The senior echelons of the service considered the station's inhabitants lacking in the very qualities of self-preservation that indicated stable mental faculties. They also considered them eminently expendable.

In actively solving several such cases, Persis had disproved her superiors, attracting both admiration and censure. But the rewards of success were fleeting. Her status within the service remained contentious, and her penchant for speaking her mind tended to upset those who didn't like to be upset. Following her last case – that of a young man who had died in the attempt to assassinate the country's new defence minister – died at Persis's own hand – her commanding officer, Roshan Seth, had been transferred to the Naga Hills.

Persis had protested vociferously, so vociferously that, just weeks later, her own posting to the district had been authorised.

She was left with a simple choice. Leave the force or agree to the move.

Seth had assured her that the posting would be temporary. 'They're punishing you. A slap on the wrist. You're too good an officer for them to let you go. Besides, they *need* you. You're a symbol now. A symbol of the brave new country they're so keen on running into the ground.'

Seth's cynicism had always seemed to her his most endearing quality, a view shared by few others. But there was a grain of truth to the man's words. Persis's elevation had struck a chord with many in the country, mainly women, but others too. What could be more progressive than giving a woman a uniform and a gun?

Right now, Persis would have loved aiming that gun at those who had sent her eastwards.

Thoughts of Roshan Seth ignited memories of Malabar House. The tiny basement in which the station's handful of staff had been housed – inside a corporate building on John Adams Street, a busy thoroughfare near the southern tip of Bombay – had become a second home, her fellow officers a family, of sorts. She thought of them now, with mixed feelings. Oberoi and Fernandes, the two other inspectors at Malabar House; Oberoi as handsome and as arrogant as a peacock; Fernandes, a dark and morose man shouldering the burden of his own bad luck. Birla and Haq, the station's sub-inspectors, the one as thin and as slippery as a lie, the other the size of a collapsed barn and with roughly the same demeanour. The ragged peon who sat dozing by the door waiting to be bellowed into action. The trio of semi-pedigreed dogs who loitered in the first-floor lobby and occasionally wandered downstairs to sneer at those even lower on the totem pole.

And then there was Archie Blackfinch, a regular visitor to the premises.

A hand gripped her heart, gave a hard squeeze.

The Englishman was never far from her thoughts. She settled on her last memory of him – holding *his* hand at the hospital, looking into his eyes, words lining up anxiously behind each other in her throat. Blackfinch had been injured in the encounter with the political assassin that Persis had shot dead just months earlier. Since that time he had languished in a coma at the Breach Candy Hospital in Bombay.

If there was one thing above all others that wrenched at her when she thought of her home city, it was the Englishman's predicament, and the complex equation that held them trembling in a sort of magnetic field, balanced at the point where attraction met repulsion. A criminalist by training, Blackfinch had been in the country for well over a year, deputed from the Metropolitan Police Service in London, helping establish Bombay's first forensic science lab. During that time, he had distinguished himself by his three-legged inability to navigate the city's political labyrinth, all the while demonstrating the sort of forthright lack of tact that Persis found both definitively English and, to her intense consternation, beguiling. The man was cut from a similar cloth to herself, albeit possessed of all the elan of a stuffed boar.

With a shake of the head, she sent the handsome Englishman tumbling back into the darkness.

She couldn't afford to dwell on Blackfinch now.

The jeep arrived at the town of Kohima, then skirted around it, taking a trail up towards the neighbouring hill, some four thousand feet in elevation. The heat seemed to rise with the land, until it cloaked her like a hot towel. They passed a burned-out wreck, the skeleton of an army truck, a reminder of the fact that this forested backwater had now become both a political and literal battlefield. From the surrounding jungle came the shrieks and gibbers of monkeys.

When the hotel finally hove into view, it sat her back in her seat.

Perhaps the sight of a colonial building rising out of the jungle should not have seemed incongruous to her. India's cities were defined by their variegated architecture, a hodgepodge of Hindu, Islamic, and, most poignantly, European expressiveness. Calcutta's neoclassical torso. Bombay's Victorian hips. New Delhi's regimented lines.

The Hotel Victoria was surrounded by a fifteen-feet high whitewashed wall, topped by iron spikes, and two feet of barbed wire. A phalanx of armed guards manned the gate looking bored enough to point their weapons at each other and put themselves out of their collective misery.

Beyond the gate, the hotel rose to five floors, a vision of regal white showcasing large bay windows and a central, twin-colonnaded porch. Subsequent explorations had revealed interior proportions and fittings that might have embarrassed a French palace: vaulted ceilings, pile carpets, peacock-patterned flock wallpaper, chequered flooring, a monogrammed staircase, and rooms stuffed with enough vintage furniture to crowd out a museum. A formal dining room, a billiard room, a swimming pool, and a library rounded out the hotel's amenities.

Clearly, no expense had been spared.

To Persis, the place seemed an elaborate joke. But she couldn't imagine who the joke was aimed at.

'Come, madam,' Peter had said, as she had stood in the lobby for the first time, looking around in astonishment. 'Let me show you to your room.'

5

Andrews arrived in a lather of sweat and irritation. A large man, red-faced and jowly, with damp white hair and a white beard, like an angry Santa Claus.

He barrelled into the room, stiff-legged, a scuffed leather medical bag swinging by his side.

The others – Apeni Ao and the American, Oren Rake – rose to their feet from the sofas in the suite's living room. Persis had ordered them to leave, but they had been singularly disinclined to do so. The hotel manager, David Keishing, and the night porter, Peter Jadonang, had already been sent on their way. The fewer people disturbing the crime scene, the better. If there was one thing Persis had learned from Archie Blackfinch, it was this.

Andrews loomed over Persis. His breath was a living thing, sharp with the stink of alcohol. 'I was asleep.'

'And now you're not.'

'I had company.' He didn't elaborate. She had heard that Andrews was fond of the local women. She doubted the feeling was mutual. But some men preferred affection paid for by the hour. And some had no choice in the matter.

She followed him as he clumped through to the bathroom, Ao and Rake close behind. The sight of the body momentarily gave the doctor pause. Persis thought he might make a fast quip, but he didn't.

She watched him lean down into his bag, remove a pair of latex gloves, stretch them on to his hands. 'I'm going to drain the tub.'

'Do you have another pair?'

'Help yourself.'

Persis bent to the bag, pulled out a pair of gloves. Straightening, she saw Andrews had already leaned his bulk over the tub to pull the plug. They stood back, watched the water swirl away, leaving a rim of pink around the tub.

Andrews looked around, walked to a shelf, took down several towels, laid them out on to the tiles beside the bath.

'I'm going to need a hand.' He positioned himself at the head of the tub, beside a pair of golden taps, waited for Persis to move towards the man's feet. 'Ready?'

Persis's inclination was to reply with a terse 'No.' No, she wasn't ready to heave a naked headless man from a bloodstained bathtub, and probably never would be. But that was the job. Death, in all its gruesome splendour.

The body weighed next to nothing. As they lowered it on to the towels, Andrews let go several inches above the floor, allowing the corpse to smack dully on to the covered tiles. So much for respecting the dead.

Persis looked on as the man bent to examine the corpse.

'Can you positively identify him?'

The doctor pointed at a scar on the back of the dead man's hand. 'I treated him for that cut a month ago. And there's this.' The finger moved to the right shoulder where a complicated cicatrix embossed the skin. 'A childhood accident. It's him.'

Persis heard Ao mumble something behind her. The hotel proprietor's last hope – that perhaps the body might be of someone other than Sinha – had vanished. Oren Rake said nothing.

Andrews hauled himself to his feet. Peeling off his gloves, he threw them back into his bag. 'There are no signs of any injury save the obvious one. Until I conduct a full autopsy, I can only assume he was killed by the act of decapitation.'

'There's no sign of blood in the other rooms.'

'In which case he must have been killed inside the tub. The blood was allowed to drain away, and then the killer propped him up, filled the tub, and left him there.'

'Why?'

'I'm afraid that's *your* domain, Inspector.' He picked up his bag. 'I need a drink.'

With Andrews out of the way – and Ao and Rake finally despatched – Persis directed herself to the task of searching the dead man's suite.

She began by covering Sinha's modesty with a towel. Andrews hadn't seen the need for such a gesture, but Persis considered it a necessary courtesy, not least because she had no wish to be confronted by the erstwhile governor's headless nudity each time she ventured near the man's corpse.

She began with the bathroom.

Aside from the body, there was little else to find. Sinha's bath-robe lay in a heap to one side of the room. She had no idea whether he had removed the robe himself or whether his killer had done so. There was no blood on the garment, so it had to have been discarded before the man's head had been parted from his body.

The bedroom seemed larger each time she set foot in it. She compared it to her own room, down on the second floor, smaller and far less grandiose. You could comfortably have stabled horses in Sinha's bedchamber. The bed that dominated the space was large, teak-framed, and surrounded by a mosquito net. Figurative sculptures had been carved into the bedposts, with armorials on the pelmet rail. On the headboard, a scene from a battle – complete with ranked elephants – had been worked into the wood.

The bed appeared slept in, the covers rumpled. She imagined the emaciated politician lost inside its white-sheeted expanse, tossing and turning in dreams.

A quick examination of the floor-to-ceiling wardrobes revealed only Sinha's fondness for good tailoring. And shoes. The man had more shoes than the average Bollywood starlet, including a pair that looked as if they had been fashioned from snakeskin. Persis had rarely met a man confident enough to parade around in snakeskin shoes.

She walked through to the living room.

A brisk search of the space revealed nothing. A selection of records were stashed below the gramophone, mainly big band staples. A bookcase held a range of reading material: classics, adventure stories, detective novels, legal tomes, a stack of *National Geographic* magazines. She wondered at the journey these books had made all the way out here.

She continued on to the dining room.

The six-seater dining table seemed inhabited by ghosts. A folded newspaper, *The Statesman*, made a stark statement against the table's polished mahogany. The headlines focused on Nehru's plans for land reform, a vision that was being received by the country's feudal tsars and newly disenfranchised royals about as well as an invitation to the guillotine in revolutionary France.

She bent closer to the abandoned plate she had seen earlier. The leftover meal appeared to consist of chickpeas and boiled rice. Simple fare for a complicated man.

She sniffed at the crystal tumbler beside the plate. Whisky.

She made a mental note to have the contents of the plate, the glass, and the whisky bottle atop the dining cart preserved and sent for analysis. Though precisely where such an analysis might be conducted escaped her. This was Kohima, not Bombay.

. The thought once again brought up the spectre of Archie Blackfinch.

During his time in India, the Englishman had overseen the inception of Bombay's first fully equipped forensic science lab, repeating that minor bureaucratic miracle in several other cities. Persis had worked closely with him on a handful of prominent cases. Tall, dark-haired, handsome – in his own lean and bespectacled way – something about Blackfinch had worked its way under her skin. They had begun an ill-judged liaison, a relationship – if such it might be called – that had grown more awkward by the day. It was one thing to work with the old enemy, quite another for a woman who had blazed her way through the last days of the Raj to associate herself with such a figure. If their personal entanglement ever became public knowledge Persis could expect the axe to fall swiftly on her career.

There were many things the service might tolerate, but embarrassment on a national scale was not one of them.

The point had recently become moot following her discovery that Blackfinch was—

'Madam.'

She turned to find a white couple hovering in the doorway. The man was of medium height, short dark hair plastered on to his head as if with a trowel. His bearing was starched, as was his dress, a waistcoat and tie, despite the fact that the hour was close to midnight. A plain wooden cross, dark in colour, garlanded his neck, prominently displayed atop his clothing. A thick moustache and watery grey eyes gave him the look of a lost mariner.

The woman was younger, attractive, with striking, copper-coloured hair, teased into ringlets. She too was severely dressed, with a long dark dress that ran up to conceal her throat.

The pair must have been suffocating in the heat.

Persis knew them as Christopher and Florence Danvers, an American Baptist couple stationed at the hotel. She had met them in passing, judged them instantly as religious obsessives, and steered clear of them ever since. The pair had ventured out to Kohima some months earlier, intent on pursuing the godly mission of converting the natives to Christianity. Persis suspected they might have missed the boat. Their predecessors had done such a fine job on that front over the past century that almost nine tenths of the local populace had embraced the word of Christ, in one form or another.

Whether Christ had embraced them was another matter. Had he been around, the Son of God might have been somewhat put out to discover that many of his new subjects still indulged in their age-old animist customs, not to mention the occasional bout of headhunting.

'We heard a commotion from our room, and came to investigate.' The woman had spoken. 'Is it true? Is Sinha dead? Murdered?'

'Yes,' said Persis. 'This is now a crime scene. I must ask you to step outside.'

Lines appeared on the man's brow. 'Do you know who killed him?'

Persis hesitated. 'No. Not yet.' Was there a hint of relief in his face? She saw his pale eyes scan the room. 'Are we safe?'

'Safe is a relative term out here.'

The woman spoke again. 'Has someone said a prayer over the body?'

'Sinha was a Hindu.'

'Yes. But he's still entitled to God's mercy. May I?'

Persis swallowed her instinctive retort. She knew, from past interactions with those of a religious bent, that argument was pointless. This was India, after all, where the miasma of religion – of every possible persuasion – curdled the very air.

She led the Americans through to the bathroom. Florence Danvers stopped as she caught sight of the body. A small breath hitched in her throat. And then she seemed to recover herself. Her voice was unnaturally loud in the silent room. 'May Christ who died for you admit you into his garden of paradise. May Christ, the true Shepherd, acknowledge you as one of his flock. May he forgive all your sins, and set you among those he has chosen.'

The recitation delivered, she turned hazel eyes to Persis. 'No man's life should end in such a manner. We will be downstairs, with the others, should you need our counsel.'

With the American couple gone, Persis returned to the dining room.

Quickly, she examined the contents of the dining cart. The bottle of whisky was a brand she recognised, Black Dog, a favourite of her father's, who seemed to knock it back as if it was no more potent than lemonade. The first time Persis had tried it, she had woken up three hours later, unable to feel her legs.

She lifted the white cloth. On the cart's lower tray stood a further selection of branded alcohol bottles, wine and spirits, at various stages of having been emptied.

Clearly, Sinha was a man who enjoyed his drink.

She wondered briefly if the politician had been addled when the murder had taken place. Surely, such a gruesome death would have initiated bloodcurdling screams. Despite being up on the hotel's topmost floor, someone would have heard.

Unless Sinha didn't scream at all. In which case he must have been comatose. Or rendered unconscious. She made a mental note to check with Andrews once the autopsy was complete.

Her final search was of Sinha's office.

She knew that the politician did much of his work at the commissioner's residence in Kohima, but as the violence had escalated in recent months, he had taken to hiding out in the hotel on occasion. She knew that it chafed him to do so. Sinha was a man who liked to be seen by those over whom he held sway.

The room was sparse, with a large desk, a solitary filing cabinet, a ceiling fan, and not much else. A telephone sat on the desk, alongside a blue-veined notepad and an inkstand. A large canvas of a red-throated Blyth's tragopan, the region's native pheasant, looked down on the desk from the wall opposite. The bird looked mildly depressed, perhaps at the notion of sharing a space with a man capable of outdoing it in elaborate courtship displays. Sinha's courtship was with the locals and was of the type that stated, in no uncertain terms, 'love me or I shall shoot you'.

On the desk, an ashtray housed the half-burned remains of what looked like a photograph. The charred wedge of card, scalloped along its one remaining edge, showed a woman, seated, finely dressed. Only a portion of her face remained, but she appeared pale-skinned, possibly white, though it was hard to be certain. She was sitting next to a man – clearly Sinha, albeit a younger version, grinning broadly, moustache waxed and hair shining as brightly as the polish on his shoes.

She turned the photograph over.

On the back were the words: *Calcutta, 1923*, written in a close hand. Below was another word, abutting the destroyed edge of the photograph: *Sin*. The photo seemed to have been recently placed in the ashtray. She could only assume that Sinha had burned it earlier that evening. Why?

She pulled open the desk's drawers, found only one other item of significance, tucked inside a Gideon Bible. A blank envelope, inside which was folded a typed note. The note read, simply:

Nagalim will never be yours. Leave now. Or die.

The sentiment seemed unequivocal. A death threat. By insurgents.

Insurgents? She heard her father's voice: *One man's insurgent is another's freedom fighter.* During the independence years, the British had called the Indians marching in the streets many things, but freedom fighters was not one of them.

She transferred the charred photograph and the note to her pocket, then riffled through the filing cabinet, but found little to shed light on the killing.

She stepped back into the living area. A moment to consider the situation, and then she walked back into the office, picked up the telephone. Dialling reception, she asked for a security guard to be sent up from the front gate.

The man arrived, looking mildly perplexed.

Persis explained the situation, then said: 'No one is to enter these rooms without my express permission. Do you understand?'

And then she turned and made her way down to the bar on the ground floor.

6

She saw immediately that the hotel's entire contingent – as far as she could make out and excepting the security staff – had congregated in the bar. The hotel manager, David Keishing, stood at the shoulder of Apeni Ao, sitting on a burgundy Chesterfield in the centre of the room.

The American couple – Christopher and Florence Danvers – sat rigidly at a wooden table on the far side of the room, as if keen to station themselves as far away from the bar as possible, where the doctor, Andrews, flopped on a stool. Oren Rake loomed behind the wooden counter, acting as barman, splashing whisky into a pair of tumblers. Peter Jadonang hovered beside him, twitching nervously, clearly uncomfortable at the sight of the American serving his own drinks.

Sitting in a bucket-shaped armchair in a corner by himself was Sinha's aide, John Templeton, also clutching a glass, into which he stared morosely.

One other person was in the room, leaning over Florence Danvers's shoulder, whispering something in her ear, a tall, young woman, dark-haired and olive-skinned. Persis had yet to make her acquaintance but knew that this was Maria Fontanelli, an Italian journalist staying at the hotel. Fontanelli had only arrived a fortnight ago, brought to the north-east by God knew what.

The woman was dressed in high-waisted trousers in black-and-white check with a succession of heart-shaped buttons marching down one hip. The trousers were paired with a short-sleeved blouse in crêpe de chine, V-necked and sporting a Peter Pan collar. Her sharp features were set off by the lightest layer of make-up. To Persis, she looked the very epitome of European chic.

Her eyes ran over the bar and its occupants.

In her time at the Hotel Victoria, she had rarely ventured here. She drank little and when she did, she preferred to do so alone and in suicidal ill temper, like the Russian writers her father so admired. She was also less than fond of the décor. The bar's determination to stay true to the hotel's Victorian ideals meant that taste had left the building early on in the design process. The wood-panelled walls gleamed with polish, the panels interspersed with flocked wallpaper bearing scenes from what appeared to be an opium addict's nightmares; a chandelier hung from a lofty ceiling, so large and bowed by its own extravagance it looked as if it might crash down on them at any moment. The heads of animals, mounted on wooden plinths, stared glassily over the space: sun bears, monkeys, a boar, a lemur, and a tiger. None of them looked particularly happy with their allotted role in the hotel's furnishings.

An ankle-thick carpet lay underfoot, a strange choice for the tropics, Persis thought.

She saw that the room's bay windows had been left open, allowing the sweltering, post-monsoon heat to swagger into the room and take a seat at the bar. She could feel perspiration trickling down her spine.

Expectant faces turned towards her.

She realised that she would have to choose her words carefully. Perhaps she should have telephoned her commanding officer, Roshan Seth? But she knew that Seth was usually dead to the world by this time, having drunk himself into a stupor. If there had been any hope that banishment to Kohima might cure him of that particular ill, such hope had been marched to the nearest wall and handed a blindfold and a cigarette soon after his arrival in the Naga Hills district.

'Mohan Sinha is dead,' she began. 'He was murdered in his suite earlier this evening. Dr Andrews has arranged for the body to be transferred to the morgue at Kohima Hospital.'

'Is it true that his door was bolted from the inside?' She saw that it was the American, Florence Danvers, who had spoken.

'Yes.'

The woman exchanged glances with her husband. 'How is it possible? How could anyone get into a locked room and murder him?'

'I don't know.'

'Well, what *do* you know?'

The outburst had come from Sinha's aide, John Templeton.

Persis focused on the man. 'I know that whoever killed Sinha is in this room.'

Templeton blinked furiously behind his spectacles as the others straightened in indignation.

Rake set down his whisky, leaned over the bar. 'You're not seriously suggesting one of us had a hand in Mohan's death?'

'I don't believe in the supernatural, Mr Rake. The facts are simple. The Hotel Victoria is on a hill, situated behind a high wall, and surrounded by guards, doubly so since Sinha moved in. Sinha was murdered in the past hours. No one came in from the outside. Ergo his murderer has to be someone who was in the hotel during that time. That means one of the individuals in this room. Excepting Dr Andrews and myself, of course.'

'That's mighty generous of you,' said Andrews, lifting his glass in mock salute.

Apeni Ao rose to her feet. 'Inspector, I appreciate your desire to solve this crime swiftly, but I cannot allow you to drag my guests into this.'

Christopher Danvers broke in. 'Has it occurred to you that the fact that the man is missing his head indicates that his killing was the work of insurgents? Headhunting is still practised out here, Inspector.'

'Unless one of *you* is an insurgent, I highly doubt it.' She could feel the note that she had found burning a hole in her pocket. 'There will be an official investigation. Each of you will be questioned. Until we determine the killer's identity, you are all suspects. I must ask you to remain here, at the hotel, until further notice.'

Oren Rake released a bark of laughter into the room. It raced around, knocking things over, then vanished through a window. 'By what authority?'

'Mine,' said Persis.

'Not a chance,' said Rake. 'I have business in Kohima. And then I must return to my mine. Unless you're going to arrest me, I'm afraid I'm going to decline your generous offer.'

Persis ground her jaw. She realised there was little point in arguing with the man. The truth was that her authority here was minimal. 'Should you choose to leave the region it may be considered an admission of guilt.'

'Don't worry. I won't go far. Haven't you heard? There's gold in them thar hills.' Rake picked up his glass, flashed her a sardonic smile, then threw it back.

'How do you wish to proceed?' Florence had risen to her feet.

'I will need to interview each of you, individually.'

'I'm afraid that will have to wait until tomorrow,' said her husband, also getting to his feet. 'We have had a long day and are both exhausted.'

'I must insist.'

'We answer to a higher authority than yours, Inspector. Florence and I have an important engagement with the Naga Hills Baptist

Church Council tomorrow. We must prepare ourselves.' He wrapped a hand around his wife's elbow and began to steer her away. Persis saw the woman resist for a moment, and then fall into line. Something flashed momentarily in Florence Danvers's eyes. Anger? Resentment?

Curious.

She watched the couple leave the room. It was futile attempting to stop them. Rake had been right. Her ability to command these people was non-existent. Not without clear evidence of guilt.

She turned to the others in the room, addressed David Keishing. 'What time did Sinha return to the hotel?'

Keishing glanced at Ao. The woman nodded. A tongue flicked over his lips. 'Around eight.'

'And what time was his evening meal delivered to him?'

'At nine thirty. Mr Sinha was a man of routine. Peter makes a point of being on time each evening.'

Persis turned to Peter Jadonang. 'Did you see or hear anyone in his room when you delivered the meal?'

The boy's face seemed troubled. 'No. There was no one.'

'How did Sinha seem to you? His demeanour?'

'He was his usual self. Preoccupied.'

'Did he say anything to you?'

'No.' A hesitation. 'He gave me some money.'

'Why?'

'He was a generous man. I had told him once that it was my dream to go to the big city, to find work there. Perhaps even Calcutta. He tipped me regularly, to help me save for such a time.'

'What did you do next?'

'I returned to reception. I was there until I came back to Mr Sinha's room at eleven.'

'Can anyone vouch for you during that time?'

'I can,' said David Keishing. 'We were at the reception desk together. Madam Apeni joined us, to go over the books. We sat in the office behind the reception.'

'The three of you were in sight of each other?'

'Yes. At least until Madam Apeni went up to sleep at around ten thirty.'

'Do you usually meet at such a late hour?'

Ao smiled wanly. 'It's the only time quiet enough for us to do so. Our staff strength is much reduced these days. We are all required to take on extra duties during the day. Even me, Inspector.'

'Did anyone else come into the hotel during that period?'

'Yes,' said Keishing. 'You did.'

Persis heard Andrews laughing quietly in the silence. She could feel heat rising to her cheeks. 'I meant anyone other than myself or the other guests.'

'No. Though there was a telephone call from Sinha to reception at around nine forty. He wanted me to relay a complaint to the cook that the meal she had prepared for him was over-seasoned.'

'Where *is* the cook?'

'She left after making Sinha's supper. He is generally the last to eat. He rarely eats in the dining room.'

Persis herself had only eaten in the dining room on occasion. She found the formality oppressive, not to mention the possibility of having to engage with her fellow diners. The horror of an actual *conversation*.

Nine forty. Which meant that Sinha had been alive ten minutes after Peter had delivered the evening meal.

'I've had enough of this.'

Persis turned to see Oren Rake make his way from behind the bar. The man's temples glistened with sweat. 'If you need me, you know where to find me.'

He marched out of the room. As he left, a pair of Naga arrived, made a beeline for Andrews. 'Sir. We have brought the ambulance.'

'It looks as if Sinha's chariot is here,' said the doctor. He slugged back the rest of his whisky, wiped his hands on his trousers, and got to his feet. 'I'll carry out the autopsy in the morning. You're welcome to join us, Inspector.'

'Us?'

'Myself and Sinha. I'm sure it will be as much fun for him as it will be for me.'

Her eyes followed the man as he lurched from the room ahead of the ambulancemen.

She turned to Ao. 'I must search the hotel. I'll be looking for the murder weapon and Sinha's missing head. It must be done now. I'll need some of the hotel's security detail to help. And access to every room.'

Ao nodded. 'You shall have it. I will organise the guards for you now.' The old woman rose to her feet. 'Inspector, I cannot tell you how important it is that you find Sinha's killer quickly. This is about more than my hotel. The situation here is volatile. There is no predicting how Nehru will react. If more troops come to the hills, more violence will ensue. Do you understand?' The words were delivered gently but Persis could feel the pressure of the sentiment behind them bearing down on her. She watched Ao leave the room, Peter and David following her out.

'And then there were three.'

Persis turned to face the Italian, Maria Fontanelli. 'We haven't met.'

'No,' said Fontanelli. 'But I know all about you, Inspector. I've greatly enjoyed reading about your exploits. Wherever you go, headlines follow.' Her English was excellent, made mellifluous by a musical accent.

'I'm told you're a journalist?'

'For my sins.'

'What brings you out to the Naga Hills?'

'I could ask you the same thing.'

'I— Officers routinely accept postings outside their home regions.'

'I doubt many choose to venture from Bombay to the bright lights of the Naga Hills.' There was a hint of amusement in the woman's voice.

'You haven't answered my question.'

'I go where the story takes me. The unrest out here is a story. And now I have an even bigger one.'

'You mean Sinha's murder?'

'What else would you call it, if not a story?'

Persis knew it would be futile to ask the woman to restrain her journalistic ardour. She had dealt with newswallahs before. Their monomaniacal approach would have embarrassed a rutting bull. Such encounters always left her with the need to disinfect herself.

Fontanelli appeared to have read her thoughts. 'We're not *all* evil. Just as not every police officer is corrupt, lazy, and incompetent.' She glanced at the slender watch on her wrist, then back at Persis. 'I propose that we work together. You keep me informed as to the progress of your investigation and I – I will restrain myself from sensationalism.'

'I don't work with journalists.'

'Pity. I have the feeling you'll need all the help you can get.' The woman beamed brightly, before breezing out of the room with a final: '*Ciao, Ispettrice.*'

Persis found herself alone with John Templeton, who had barely lifted his head from the depths of his glass since she had entered the room.

Her words, and the subsequent departure of the others, had singularly failed to penetrate his cocoon of misery.

She walked across the room and dropped into an armchair opposite the Englishman.

Tiredness was finally beginning to play its insidious song. She was almost glad that the others had been so uncooperative. The thought of interviewing each of them after a long and gruelling day held little appeal. A good night's rest would leave her sharper, better able to formulate and conduct multiple interrogations.

Nevertheless. Finding herself alone with Templeton was an opportunity she could not pass up. Plunging straight in, she said: 'How long have you worked for Sinha?'

The Englishman maintained his posture of the damned. The silence stretched. Persis was all but ready to give up on the man when, finally, he spoke. 'I began working for him in 1948, a year after independence. He had just joined the cabinet of the chief minister of Bengal and was in search of a new aide. I'd spent several years with the Indian Civil Service in Calcutta. I'd met him during the course of my duties and considered him a rising star. I volunteered myself for the role.'

'Wasn't that a risky proposition? Giving up a cosy civil service post?'

'Not really. The ICS said they would hold a position open for me should I change my mind. Sinha gave me no reason to do so.'

'Even when he was assigned to the Naga Hills?'

'Even then.'

'Why didn't you leave in 1947? Go back to England?'

'This is my home. I came out here in '31, the year after I graduated from the University of Manchester. I fell in love with the country. Frankly, I can't imagine going back to England. I have no one left there. No one alive, at any rate.'

Persis had heard similar sentiments. Brits who couldn't stomach the thought of returning to the Old Country, with its depressing climate and even more depressing financial prospects. She realised that Templeton was older than she had at first thought. The man didn't look a day over thirty, let alone in his early forties. 'And here? Do you have family in India?'

'No.' An emphatic declaration.

'What about Sinha? Does he have family?'

'A wife. Two children. They live in Calcutta. I've been in touch with them. They won't be coming out here. When your investigation is concluded, I will arrange for Sinha's body to be sent home and he will be cremated there.'

Persis shifted in her seat. 'Why did he come out here? To the Naga Hills.'

'You seem to think he had a choice.' He clutched his glass tightly. 'Nehru sent him here. Some say the PM disliked Sinha, that this was a punishment posting.'

'But you don't agree?'

He leaned forward, eyes burning. '*Sinha* didn't agree. He thought Nehru was testing him. Sinha had aspirations to higher office and Nehru knew it. The Naga Hills were a stepping stone to the Cabinet.'

'*If* Sinha had managed to rein in the insurgency.'

'Yes.'

Persis allowed a beat. 'What kind of man was he?'

'Committed. Intelligent. Willing to take risks.'

'A good man?'

'Good? What does that mean any more? A million died during the Partition years, countless millions in the war. I suspect there are many in India today bloodied up to the armpits who consider themselves "good men".'

'I'm interested in *your* opinion.'

Something squirmed beneath his skin. 'I think he was a man who didn't shy away from making hard decisions. He had a mandate and he executed it in a hostile environment.'

'And that made him enemies?'

'Enemies came with the territory. Literally.' He lifted his glass to his mouth, took a gulp.

Persis pulled out the note she had found inside the Bible in Sinha's desk and handed it to the man. She watched as he fumbled it open, scanned it from behind his spectacles.

'I found this in his desk. Did he mention it to you?'

'No.'

'What do you make of it?'

He flipped the note on to the coffee table. 'Not much. He was always receiving death threats. The insurgents made no secret of the fact that they hated him.'

'Why?'

He looked at her incredulously. '*Why?*'

'I'd like to hear it from you.'

'Because he represented the Centre. He stood for everything they're fighting against. Sinha was here to suppress the insurgency and tie the Naga Hills firmly to India. He made no concession to their desires for an independent Naga nation.' He seemed to deflate. 'I guess they finally made good on their threats.'

'Where were you during the time between Sinha retiring to his room and his death?'

She had asked the question without forewarning, to gauge his reaction.

Templeton frowned. 'You can't possibly think that I had anything to do with this?'

She waited him out.

'I was in my room, Inspector.' His tone had stiffened.

'Alone?'

45

'Yes.'

'Asleep?'

'No. I was listening to the radio. The World Service. I read a book. I tried to sleep. But sleep is hard to come by, out here.'

A thought occurred to her. 'Sinha's bed was crumpled. Did he usually nap after returning from the office?'

'No. He was an insomniac. He never slept before midnight.'

'Perhaps the hotel staff forgot to make the bed?'

'Impossible. Apeni Ao is a stickler. Besides, Sinha expected his suite to be meticulous at all times.'

She wasn't certain why the unmade bed bothered her, but it did. She reached into her pocket and took out the partially charred photograph she had found in Sinha's ashtray. 'Does this mean anything to you?'

He examined the picture with a frown. 'No.'

'Why would Sinha burn this picture? Why now? This evening, I mean?'

'I have no idea.' He rose abruptly to his feet. 'It's been a long day.' Without another word, he marched from the room.

'Was it something I said?' muttered Persis.

It was almost two a.m. by the time she returned to her room, peeled off her uniform, showered, and fumbled her way to her bed.

Her last act of the evening had been to lead a search of the hotel, employing the hotel's retinue of security guards. They had begun in the basement wine cellar and made their way upwards, every space, every room – including those of her primary suspects – searched. The search had been cursory, at best, her fellow guests indignant, her team of searchers better suited to standing around all day smoking and drinking cups of tea than any form of police-work. Their combined efforts had failed to turn up either the victim's head or the murder weapon. Another mystery. Either they had missed something in the search – quite possible, given the resources at her disposal – or the objects in question had been spirited away and disposed of. But how?

Exhilaration and exhaustion battled inside her.

For the past month, she had slowly felt her feet sinking into the mire. Any notion that she might have entertained that the Naga Hills district would serve as a challenge rather than an endurance test had evaporated within days of her arrival. The weeks since had passed in a blur of mind-numbing monotony. The cases that landed at the tiny station in Kohima were routine: disputes between neighbours, stolen gewgaws, lost goats. Death was a way of life in the hills; but murder – of the type that necessitated a police investigation – was rare. The killings that had begun to make daily news – of Indian soldiers on the one side, native insurgents on the other – fell under the purview of the local army set-up. Roshan Seth and his team – if team was not too grandiose a word for the handful of lost souls haunting the local police station – were rarely invited to the party.

She was too wired to sleep.

Sliding off the bed, she walked to a sideboard, and poured herself a glass of wine.

Her stomach rumbled. She had eaten earlier, in Kohima, but that was a good seven hours ago. She wondered if the hotel's kitchen might be persuaded to rustle up something at this late hour, then remembered that, like a member of the gentry upended by fate, the Hotel Victoria was going through a period of reduced circumstances. It ran on a skeleton staff and most of the rooms remained empty. The cook had gone home.

She might be able to persuade the night porter, Peter, to make her a snack, but the boy looked as if he had had enough trauma for one evening. Ask him to prepare her a sandwich and he would probably end up slicing off his own finger.

She considered picking up the telephone, attempting to connect to Bombay. But her father would be asleep by now. And there was no guarantee the phone would be working. Power cuts were routine out here. Not simply because the state of basic amenities in the region would have made residents of a Bombay slum shake their heads, but because the insurgents had lately begun to adopt that tried and tested tactic of guerrilla warfare the world over, namely, blowing up the local infrastructure.

She set down the phone and returned to the bed.

The book by her bedside – an Agatha Christie novel – made encouraging, come-hither noises, but she was too tired to indulge the grande dame.

The events of the evening swirled around her thoughts. She wondered, briefly, if she had become inured to horror. By the cases she had worked, the parade of the dead. A man had had his head removed from his body. In any other context it was a vision of the macabre that would linger, not merely for the duration of an investigation, but long into the future.

But she wasn't just anyone. She was a police officer. A woman who had looked into the abyss, time and again. She had lost her mother aged seven. Death had come calling early and left its mark. The killing of Mohan Sinha – in a manner that, on the face of it, seemed impossible – was no more than a thrown gauntlet.

She recalled, now, her *second* meeting with the man. A humid evening out on the hotel's rear veranda. Venturing there, she had found the politician sitting in a cane chair, smoking a cigarette. Unusually, he was alone. For a moment, neither had said a thing.

Sinha had looked at her, then looked back out into the night. 'It's human nature to romanticise that which we don't understand. Out there is a wilderness, a way of life completely alien to people like you and me. City dwellers. Children of a civilised world. What do you think they make of *us*?'

She had no idea how to respond to this. A full moon shone luminously in the sky above. A night bird exploded in the treetops below.

'We arrive out here,' Sinha continued, 'intent on showing the Naga how the world works, how it *should* work. And pretty soon we encounter the brute realities of the very nature we believe makes them children to us. They hate us. Not because we seek to suppress them, but because they can no more understand us than we them. Our only meeting point is death.'

He rose to his feet, flicked the cigarette out over the railing and into the darkness.

Turning to her, he had held her a moment with liquid eyes. 'You're a beautiful woman, Inspector. Would you care to join me in my suite?'

She had demurred, curtly. He had accepted with a knowing smile, as if, perhaps, this was only a temporary setback, a lost battle with the war still to be won.

As Persis drifted slowly into sleep, several questions occupied her thoughts, mosquitoes batting against her mind's netting.

Who had killed the politician and why?

How had they got into a locked room to carry out the killing?

And a final macabre thought before the darkness enfolded her: *Where was Sinha's head now?*

7

The capuchins were on top form.

A symphony of shrieks, screeches, and mocking howls dragged Persis from sleep with the sun cresting the treetops. Morning in the tropics. An assault on the senses, heightened by the feeling that, out here, at the edge of the known world, reality flickered between earthiness and a pale version of paradise.

She ducked into the shower, then pulled on her spare uniform. Briefly, she considered wandering out on to the balcony, but saw that several of the monkeys had massed along the rail, glaring at her through the window. Brown streaks on the glass demonstrated their ire. She had learned, the hard way, that the capuchins had extraordinarily good aim. She had no idea why they had taken a dislike to her, but their continued antipathy only added to the feeling that she didn't belong here.

She finished dressing, checked her revolver, set her cap on her head, then went downstairs.

The breakfast room was empty, save for the serving staff, who stood around looking at each other like debutantes at a ball breathlessly awaiting a handsome cavalry officer and now faced with his buck-toothed country cousin. Persis knew that on the pecking order of the hotel's guest roster she registered a distant last. She was only here because her anticipated lodgings in Kohima had been swept away by a late monsoon mudslide just days before her arrival. Ever since, she had been billeted at the Victoria, a not unwelcome development as far as she was concerned, given the volatile state of affairs in the district.

An enormous portrait of Queen Victoria loomed over the ranked soup tureens and silver serving trays. The monarch looked as if she had indulged in a fair few hearty breakfasts herself, though the food had clearly failed to please her, judging from her expression of constipated disdain.

Persis ate quickly – a simple bowl of kedgeree – glad of the opportunity to be alone with her thoughts. The day unfurled before her. Her first port of call: the stationhouse in Kohima, to update Roshan Seth on developments. No doubt her commanding officer had already received word of Mohan Sinha's death. She couldn't imagine he would consider it anything but another kick in the mouth.

Roshan Seth had once commanded a senior position in the Bombay Police Service, a man of whom great things were expected. And then independence had arrived, a changing of the guard, and mutterings that Seth had perhaps been a little *too* accommodating when the British had been in charge. An accusation with no legs, but plenty of teeth, razor-sharp and quick to sink themselves into Seth's backside. His once promising career had been marched to the gallows, a noose placed around its neck, and a trapdoor sprung. His actual body, regretfully still capable of forward momentum, had been banished to the twilight zone of the Malabar House station. And there he had remained for the past four years, left to shepherd a flock that most would have willingly herded over a cliff, whilst slowly losing himself in a bottle.

There was no doubt in Persis's mind that Seth would entrust the Sinha investigation to her. Roshan Seth, of all people, knew her capabilities; she had demonstrated them often enough during her short time at Malabar House. Besides, the only other ranking officer at the Kohima station was a young Naga, James Angami, a man who had no real experience to draw upon.

Precisely *how* the investigation proceeded would, to a certain extent, depend on the politics of the situation. Mohan Sinha had been Delhi's man. His murder was a challenge to Nehru's authority – assuming it had come at the hands of insurgents. No doubt the prime minister would demand a swift resolution. Persis could only hope that *swift* did not translate into *bloody*.

Reports of suppression in the region had been trickling out to the mainland ever since independence back in 1947. The soldiers stationed here, constantly on alert against attacks, fearful of death lurching out of the jungle, needed little encouragement to exercise their superior military might. If the expenditure of bullets was a marker of their angst, so were the number of unfortunate monkey and bear corpses left in the wake of their jungle patrols, possibly mistaken for natives. Or perhaps the local wildlife had simply become convenient targets for men plagued by an excess of nervous energy. And perhaps *that* explained the antipathy of the capuchins outside her balcony.

The idea that she now found herself in the eye of the storm, perhaps the only one capable of holding back a wholesale slaughter, left her with a profound feeling of disquiet.

Having eaten, she made her way up to Sinha's suite, checked that a guard was still on the door, then entered to take a last look around.

Natural light hazed into the cluster of rooms, subtly altering the atmosphere. In the bathroom, the ring of pinkish residue around the tub served as a gory reminder of the body that had lain there just a few short hours earlier.

Death. A ringing note in the silence. A creature whose appetite could never be satisfied. What was man in the face of such a beast? What was left when the beast had devoured the soul? A handful of memories and the illuminated pointillism of a life, each dot soon scattered to the winds, a swirl of fireflies in the darkness, one by one winking out, until all was lost to the void.

She left the suite, headed back to the lobby, thoughts of the dead man following her as she trudged down the carpeted steps.

8

The road to Kohima wound downhill through thick bamboo forest before beginning its rise up the flank of the adjacent hill. In the near distance: the haze of the blue mountains, as early British explorers had once named them.

Once again, Persis, a lifelong denizen of the concrete antheap that was Bombay, was struck by the alien nature of the landscape. Mile upon mile of enchanted jungle, a verdant terrain of impassable highlands, shadowed valleys, and leech-infested rivers. Not a level plane in a thousand miles. Hidden beneath the jungle canopy were the centuries-old bamboo-and-thatch villages of the Naga tribes, now set beside the contemporary ruins of WW2 army bases and downed fighter planes, a silent and incongruous collision of the modern and ancient worlds.

Before arriving here she had read about the fabled city of Shambala, a place of esoteric knowledge and ancient wisdom said to have inspired James Hilton's Shangri-La. A paradise on Earth. Many, believing Shambala to be a real place, had ventured east in search of the city, to China, Tibet, and finally to the eastern reaches of India. Hitler himself had sent several expeditions. All had met with disappointment.

Perhaps, Persis thought, because of a simple failure of imagination.

Shambala did not exist, not in any earthly sense.

But out here, in the Naga Hills, was another lost kingdom, one that, quite possibly, would have preferred to remain that way.

*   *   *

The police station, a relatively recent addition to Kohima's ramshackle collection of brick-and-timber homes and weathered government buildings, had been converted from an old cowshed. On hot summer days, the ghostly stink of manure wafted through the single-storey, tin-roofed concrete structure, even though no cows had been stabled in the vicinity for at least a decade. But those that worked in the station could not be dissuaded. If a building could be said to have a soul then the soul of the station resided with its former bovine residents.

A low retaining wall, pockmarked with bullet holes, surrounded the stationhouse.

What exactly lay behind the bullet graffiti, Persis had yet to discover. The station was too far from the site of the battle that had earned Kohima its place in history – alongside the unwanted title of 'Stalingrad of the East'. A local had told her that the bullet holes were the work of insurgents. Another had told her that a disgruntled Naga, whose wife had left him for a man who had once worked in the former cowshed, had taken his ire out on the stationhouse. Having met several of the locals, Persis sided with the latter explanation.

She parked the jeep, then walked into the station compound, where several chickens scratched at the dusty earth. A rooster stopped its pecking to confront her with a belligerent look.

Inside, she found Constable Joshua Binny smoking a cigarette at a wooden desk, sitting beneath a slowly turning ceiling fan. Binny's sandalled feet were up on the desk, arms behind his head, face turned to the heavens as if contemplating the mysteries of the universe. He nodded as Persis entered, but otherwise made no move to right himself.

Persis refrained from comment.

Binny was another of those Naga of indeterminable age, the type who seemed to reach the age of sixty and then *never age another day.* His face looked like a cabbage left too long in the sun. The man hadn't so much entered the policing profession, as fallen into it; it had been a hard landing. Persis wasn't certain that Binny had ever worked an honest day in his life. But he had certainly managed a few dishonest ones.

But beggars couldn't be choosers, as her father had pointed out to her on the telephone. Kohima wasn't Bombay. You took what you were given and made the best of it.

The station team comprised four, not including Pearl, the sociopathic Naga cleaning woman who came in once a week, armed with a sweeping brush, a mop, and a rusty dao. Quite why she needed the Naga short sword to carry out her duties Persis did not know, but no one had yet had the courage to ask.

Aside from Persis and Binny, the station's official roster included Roshan Seth and a young Naga sub-inspector: James Angami. Between them they held responsibility for the four thousand souls that comprised the city of Kohima. Four thousand living souls, and almost as many dead ones, buried in the war cemetery up on Garrison Hill or slowly rotting into the soil of the surrounding jungle.

Persis walked to the office at the rear of the stationhouse, where she entered to find Roshan Seth in discussion with Angami.

The sight of Seth filled her, as it did each time she set foot in his office, with both gladness and an intense sense of disorientation. Gladness, in that a familiar sight so far from home was invariably reassuring. Disorientation because, to see Seth here, as if transplanted by a whirlwind from his office at Malabar House and deposited behind another desk that served only to remind him of his own failures, gave the lie to the notion that she had been sent here for any other reason than to mock her.

Seth, in his familiar khaki uniform, waved her into a seat. She saw that James had stood. The young man – she thought of him as young, but he was only a year younger than her – vibrated with unholy zeal. She knew that he had graduated from the academy with flying colours. She knew that he was ambitious and driven. She knew that he thought of her as something of a mentor, or, at the least, a shining example of what an outsider to the force might achieve. James, as a Naga, had cast himself in a similar light.

She eased into the proffered rattan seat, slipped off her cap, and ran a sleeve over her brow. The heat was abominable, the creaking fan above Seth's desk doing little save to ensure that the hothouse atmosphere was shuffled democratically around the office so that all corners were equally unbearable. Beside her, James folded silently back into his own chair. The man seemed not to sweat, she noticed. Not a hair out of place. High-boned, clean-shaven cheeks and hooded eyes. A meticulous attention to his appearance. A handsome man.

The door opened behind them and Constable Binny wandered in, to take a position against the office's rear wall, cigarette poking out of the side of his mouth.

Seth wasted no time in getting down to business. 'Sinha's murder has opened a real can of cobras. Shroff has taken charge of the district, issued a security alert. More troops are on their way.'

Persis knew that Colonel Hiten Shroff was the military commander based in Kohima. Shroff had replaced his predecessor a year earlier, after the man's right ear had been blown off in an insurgent attack, along with his left ear, and pretty much everything in between. The colonel's subsequent actions in the region had led to a sharpening of tensions. Technically speaking, Shroff answered to Mohan Sinha, the region's political supremo. But with Sinha out of the picture, and a replacement yet to be named by Delhi, Shroff had taken the opportunity to temporarily elevate himself to the throne.

'He's asked to see you, later today, at five p.m.,' continued Seth. 'At the officers' club.'

'Why?'

'Because I've told him that *you* are heading up the investigation into Sinha's killing.'

Persis found herself hesitating. The prospect of being grilled by the colonel held little appeal. She had been here long enough to know that there was no getting away from the region's suffocating military presence. In the wake of the post-war insurgency, visitors to the Naga Hills district – be they Indian or otherwise – required special authorisation. Military checkpoints blocked passage into the area. In all but name, the hills languished under an army protectorate.

Seth placed his elbows on the desk. 'Tell me what you have so far.'

Quickly, she went over the night's proceedings, the discovery of the body, the search of Sinha's rooms and the hotel, the basic timeline of the man's death, and the discussion with his aide, John Templeton. She described the other guests, each now a suspect.

'A locked room?' James Angami's smooth brow crinkled. 'How is that possible?'

'The door was bolted from the inside. The windows were barred. There were no hidden entrances. No one could have got inside.'

Seth seemed incredulous. 'Are you telling me the man cut off his own head then somehow made it vanish? That's a trick I'd pay to see.'

'He didn't cut off his own head. I have no idea how the killer got into Sinha's suite. Yet. But it has to be one of the other guests.'

Seth's moustache twitched beneath his long nose. 'And what would be their motive exactly? Why would a foreigner wish to murder Sinha? Why would his own aide want to kill him?'

'On the face of it, none of them had a reason to want Sinha dead. But the facts say otherwise. I'm going to start digging into each of their backgrounds today. Perhaps someone will let something slip.'

'We're going to interview them?' James seemed to relish the idea.

'We?' Persis stared at the younger officer.

'Yes, *we*,' said Seth. 'The situation is too volatile for you to go charging off alone. You'll be working with James.'

She turned back to Seth. 'He has no experience with a case like this.'

'Neither did you, once upon a time. Or did you think police officers on this side of the country hatch fully formed from the egg?'

An earlier Persis might have railed longer, ignored Seth, gone her own way. But recent events had tempered her. She had learned, the hard way, that hubris led invariably to a fall.

She took out the typed note she had found in Sinha's desk and the charred partial photograph.

The two men examined the artefacts. Even Binny drifted over for a look. His eyes widened fractionally as he read the note. 'There you have it,' he said, dropping his cigarette to the floor and crushing it beneath a well-worn sandal. 'The insurgents did it. What more proof do you need?'

But something about the man's tone jarred. Persis frowned. 'You don't think the note is genuine?'

Binny grinned. 'The Naga involved in the insurgency aren't in the habit of sending notes. They tend to shoot first and worry about writing letters later. Those that can actually write.'

Persis stared at the man. But Binny was already lighting another cigarette that had somehow magically appeared in his hand. A voice in the outer room turned the constable's head. Without a further word, he left, closing the door behind him.

Seth was speaking. 'What are your next steps?'

She returned her attention to her commanding officer. 'Andrews is conducting the autopsy this morning. After that, I'm going to track down Christopher and Florence Danvers.'

'The missionaries?'

'They don't call themselves that.'

'Then what, pray tell, do they call themselves?' Seth's tone could have stripped plaster from the walls. If there had been any plaster to begin with.

'Does it matter? They're in town this afternoon, meeting with the Naga Hills Baptist Church Council. I'll speak to them at the church.'

Seth scowled. 'Fine. Maybe you can ask them how God plans to get us out of this mess.'

Persis glanced at James. She knew that the sub-inspector was a devout Christian. Seth's dismissive approach to the Christian conversion of the Naga must have grated. Not that James had made his irritation known.

Sensing her scrutiny, the junior officer juddered into speech. 'I know the pastor who runs the church. He's a friend of the family. Perhaps he can help.'

'James, can you step outside a moment?' said Seth. 'I need to speak with Persis.'

The man stiffened. For a moment, Persis thought he might argue. But obedience was too deeply ingrained. He nodded, got to his feet, and left the room.

Seth reached into a drawer, pulled out an unlabelled bottle. Taking a steel glass, he poured himself a generous measure. 'The thing about rice beer,' he said, 'is that it tastes terrible, but at least it doesn't leave you unable to remember where you are. Or, for that matter, *who* you are.' He took a gulp, made a face, then set down the glass. 'Are you sleeping any better?'

'Not really.'

'Me neither.' He sighed. 'I'm sorry, Persis. You're paying the bill I left behind.'

Seth's apologies had grown old. But the man continued to feel obliged to make them. A part of her felt sorry for him. Seth's star had fallen so far – through no fault of his own – that any possibility of resurrection had long since vanished. To a certain extent, it had been Persis's own efforts on various high-profile – and politically sensitive – cases that had put noses out of joint and led to Seth's current banishment. The feeling had been that Seth had failed to keep his young ward in check. Malabar House was a backwater, the tiny station a holding pen for the force's unwashed and unwanted. Roshan Seth – and his team – were not meant to create waves.

Perhaps it would have been better for Seth – for them both – if his wife had come out here with him. But when Seth had asked her if she wished to accompany him, the woman had replied, simply, 'Why in the world would I want to do *that*?'

Persis thought she might like Mrs Seth, if she ever got the chance to meet her.

'You're going to have to tread a fine line with this one.' Seth had fixed her with a sober look. 'Shroff is going to use this as an excuse to ramp up his operation in the hills. There's going to be terrible trouble. Whatever you do, don't take sides.'

She raised an eyebrow. 'Exactly how many sides are there?'

'You know what I mean. We have to work with these people. Sinha called them savages. But they're not that. The British taught them Christianity. The Japs showed them brutality. And now, we, the Indians, are trying to remake them in our own image. Citizens of a republic they never asked for or wanted.'

'That's not true for all. Some of the Naga *want* closer ties with the mainland. They crave modernisation. Many fought for Indian independence because they believe in a united country.'

'Perhaps. But if Sinha's death is anything to go by, I suspect such voices will soon fall silent.'

'Then you *do* think the killing was the work of insurgents?'

'I do,' said Seth.

'And how do you think they got into the hotel? They couldn't have flown over the walls. And then through a locked door.'

'Look around you, Persis. We're in a place where myth and magic still hold sway. The impossible is entirely probable.' She watched him lift his beer back to his mouth.

'Have you heard from Malabar House?' Why had she asked him that? What she really meant was: have you heard from Archie Blackfinch?

'No. And I have no desire to do so.'

Unbidden, her mind conjured up an image of the Malabar House station when she had first arrived there, languishing in early-morning torpor: Birla and Haq marking time at their desks with twists of pungent fried snacks they'd bullied out of a local street vendor, waiting to be jolted into action by one of the station-house's cadre of inspectors. Perhaps Hemant Oberoi, one of those very inspectors, on the telephone with another of his fancy women, convincing her – and himself – that he would soon be shot of this ignominious posting. Or George Fernandes, a hulking presence at his own desk, fretting over his young son, constantly battling illness; Fernandes, who had only landed at Malabar House because he'd shot the wrong man, a mistake, he argued, that *anyone* could make. Last, and invariably least, Roshan Seth, once a prince, now lower than a pauper, drinking his way through the darkness behind a locked door at the very back of their basement office.

They said you only learned to truly appreciate something when you had lost it. Persis had never quite been part of the team. But with each passing day she felt the absence of her former colleagues more acutely, ghosts that had once haunted her, and had now abandoned her to her fate.

9

A cloud of flies lifted from the carcass of the dead dog.

The dog appeared to have been run over in the street, its dying testament to the cruelty of fate a forced evacuation of its bowels. The fact that the body lay just yards from the gates to the local hospital seemed to Persis a particularly trenchant indictment on the vicissitudes of life in the hills.

The Kohima Civil Hospital – recently renamed as the Naga Hospital – had begun life as a ten-bed dispensary back in 1905, staffed by missionaries with medical experience, and treated by locals – those who had yet to be convinced of the charms of the new faith sweeping the hills – largely with suspicion. The Naga might well have been devils for collecting heads, but that was good clean fun, a rite of passage for young men and an accepted strand in the tapestry of tribal heritage. But the white medicine men that worked inside the hospital, the procedures they performed on unsuspecting natives ... that was a whole other kettle of skulls.

During the war, the hospital's capacity had swelled. Many a soldier had breathed his last inside the clinker-brick edifice, staring up at whitewashed ceilings, wondering, perhaps, what cruel jest of the gods had brought them to die in such an alien land so far from home.

They found Andrews down in a basement room, prepping the body of Mohan Sinha for its post-mortem. The familiar smell of formaldehyde invaded Persis's nostrils. They said that if you worked enough murder cases you became used to it. Whoever had said that probably needed a different hobby.

Sinha's headless corpse was stretched out on a slab in the centre of the room, his modesty covered by a white loincloth. There was something bathetic in the sight, a sense of descent from the sublime to the ludicrous. Twenty-four hours earlier Mohan Sinha had been the most powerful man in thousands of square miles. Now, he was a mutilated vessel of flesh, a sight to strike horror in his friends, satisfaction in his enemies, and pity in those who didn't care much either way.

A late-middle-aged Naga woman in a white nurse's uniform was helping Andrews into a bottle-green apron. The man's girth – and the woman's sparrow-like size – made the operation a clumsy affair. Andrews muttered under his breath, but seemed disinclined to rebuke his assistant. Possibly for fear of the consequences. The ability of older Naga women to reduce even the most fearsome of their menfolk to quivering lumps of tribal jelly had been well documented.

'Shall we begin?' said Andrews, once he was ready. Without waiting for an answer, he turned to a trolley on which were ranked the various instruments of his particular brand of torture. Picking up a scalpel, he lumbered back to the corpse, then bent to his task, beginning by opening up the chest with the familiar Y-shaped incision.

Persis stole a glance at James Angami's face. This was the sub-inspector's first post-mortem. She knew that he would have been put through his paces at the academy, but there was something wholly different about an autopsy in a live murder case.

The younger officer seemed to sense her scrutiny, turning his head to meet her gaze with an unblinking stare of his own.

She looked away, felt a sudden flare of heat along her throat.

* * *

Almost two hours later, Andrews was washing his hands at the sink.

He spoke over his shoulder, patches of perspiration making a map of murky continents on the back of his shirt. 'As I said yesterday, there are no defensive wounds on the body. Death, as best as I can determine, came from the severing of the head from the torso. Once the head was severed, oxygen transport to the brain was interrupted. Sinha would have lost higher brain function within seconds.' He finished washing his hands and picked up a towel.

'Can you determine the weapon used to kill him?'

'A bladed weapon, of course. A long straight edge. Broad.'

'A dao?' said James.

'Quite possibly. The cut is clean. I don't believe it was a serrated blade. The edge would have been incredibly sharp to get through the neck without hacking at it.'

'Someone who knew what they were doing,' Persis surmised, mentally adding: And if the weapon *was* a dao, it would provide more support for those who already believed the killer to be a Naga insurgent.

'I would hope so,' said Andrews. 'No easy thing, sawing off a man's head.' He set the towel down. 'The toxicology analysis will take a few days. I don't have the facilities to do a thorough job here. I'll have to send the samples to Calcutta.' He raised a finger to forestall Persis's incipient protest. '"Patience is bitter, but its fruit is sweet." Aristotle.'

Persis wanted to tell the man that Aristotle probably didn't have a murder to solve when he had said that.

'He's a lot smaller in the flesh,' observed James.

'Well, yes,' said Andrews. 'A whole head smaller.'

The quip earned a sharp look from the young policeman. Andrews seemed unrepentant. Droplets of sweat sparkled in his bushy eyebrows. 'It might be worth considering the psychology of the act,' he said. 'If the killer wanted simply to end Sinha's life there were other, easier means. Why do it this way?'

'Are you suggesting there was something symbolic in the killing?' said Persis.

'I'm suggesting that this is a land where symbolism matters. I don't know if your killer was an insurgent or not. But I do know that whoever cut off Sinha's head did so to make a point, even if only to themselves.'

IO

Persis's next port of call was Kohima's oldest church.

Here, she hoped to speak with the American Baptist couple, Florence and Christopher Danvers.

Her own relationship with religion had always been a fretful affair, taking its cue from her father. Sam's approach to God had always been ambivalent. At times he was willing to concede that, indeed, there might be a greater power out there, a power beyond the ken of man, because – in his words – people were idiots and idiots could not be responsible for the manifest splendour of the revealed cosmos.

Sam's attitude to the overtly *godly*, however, was a different matter.

Indians had fifty words for faith, all of them interchangeable with the word madness. There were more religions on the subcontinent – both homegrown and imported – than you could shake an olive branch at. Faith, in all its permutations, wrapped itself around every aspect of daily life, and many matters pertaining to the next one. For some, such dogmatic adherence to ecumenical lore provided stability and a means of belonging to something greater than themselves. For others, religion fomented factionalism and strife, blighting lives and trapping the powerless – for there was no faith yet invented by man that did not involve a hierarchy – into millennia of doctrinal servitude.

The Partition riots that had seen a million dead in the final years of the independence Struggle proving – if her father had ever needed proof – that all religions contained, within their unyielding dogmas, the seeds of their own destruction.

Perhaps it was no surprise then, that Sam Wadia harboured a particularly virulent hatred of missionaries.

Persis remembered one occasion, several years earlier, when a robed man had come into the bookshop intent on delivering to her father his particular version of the Good News. Ten minutes later, Sam had thrown the book at him. Literally. The thousand-page tome – a treatise on post-independence tax regulations in the agricultural sector – had concussed the poor chap to such an extent that he had not only forgotten the creed that he had been vociferously proselytising just moments earlier, but also his own name.

The Church of St John the Baptist comprised a squat and elongated building covered by a red-tiled roof and fronted by a central bell tower. The bell tower, framed against a sky of purest blue, soared above the church's surrounding structures, a pair of cobblers, who, it was said, had been engaged in a bitter feud for over a decade. The Shoe War, as it had become locally known, had witnessed several casualties, with various gentlemen-about-town banned from one or the other establishment for the crime of fraternising with the enemy.

The chapel's whitewashed façade glimmered in the late afternoon sun, casting a diamond-bright radiance back into the street.

Persis and James approached on foot. The church was set close enough to the hospital, along the town's principal thoroughfare, for them to have walked the short distance between the two in mere minutes. The street was quieter than usual, the broiling midday heat holding many hostage indoors. Those that had business that could not wait scurried along both sides of the dusty road seeking scraps of shadow like soldiers dodging sniper fire.

Persis's uniform was soaked by the time she reached the church's arched front doorway. She had given up fretting about the state of her attire. Being lathered in perspiration seemed the natural state of affairs here. She glanced at her colleague who had momentarily stopped to cross himself and mutter something under his breath. He caught her looking and turned away.

They stepped into the church.

The interior, a cramped space crowded with ranks of wooden pews and lit by natural light falling in from sash windows, was only marginally cooler than the street outside. Persis saw several midday worshippers sweltering in the aisles. An elderly man in a dark suit turned his head. Tribal tattoos crawled over both his cheeks and across his forehead. The sides of his head had been shaved, leaving behind a tuft of dyed black hair at the crown, giving him the look of a badly sheared sheep.

A hymn was being played on a piano. Stone steps led up to a raised platform where several young Naga were mangling the words with a nasal local inflection. A wooden pulpit rose to one side, a reading desk at its base. A King James Bible lay open on a lectern, like a shot bird. Behind the choir, a teak cross loomed from the wall.

'May I be of assistance?'

They turned to find a short white man, rotund beneath his robe, waddling towards them. His head was entirely bald and an aggressive shade of pink. A clerical collar, tightened around a bullfrog neck, seemed all but set to shoot off under the intolerable pressure. The man blinked. 'James? Is that you? We haven't seen you here for a while.'

The sub-inspector shot a sidelong glance at his senior officer, then turned back to the approaching minister. 'Pastor Matthews. I – I've been busy.'

'Too busy for God?' The pastor waggled a disapproving finger. 'It's a good thing God is never too busy for you.' He beamed at Persis, the smile transforming his features, putting her in mind of a giant baby. 'You must be the new inspector I've been hearing about. A woman! My word, whatever will they think of next? Female priests?' His features collapsed into mirth.

Persis bit down hard on her tongue. Her fingers twitched beside her revolver. 'We're here to see Christopher and Florence Danvers. I understand they're meeting with the council.'

Matthews looked surprised. 'Why yes. They are. What exactly is your interest in them?'

'I'm afraid that's police business.'

The man seemed unimpressed. 'You're inside a church, Inspector. Nothing is hidden from God's eyes.'

'We're making routine enquiries,' said James. 'In relation to last night's incident at the Hotel Victoria.'

'By incident, I take it you mean Mohan Sinha's brutal murder?' Matthews crossed himself. 'May he rest in peace. Though, I suspect peace in the afterlife is something that may well elude our erstwhile governor.'

'Why do you say that?' said Persis.

Matthews stuck out a belligerent lower lip. 'Because Mohan Sinha was hardly a man of peace, Inspector.' He expanded no further, instead turning on his heel. 'Follow me.'

They tracked after him as he wobbled his way into the interior of the church, along a narrow hallway, and through to a small conference room at the rear of the premises.

As they entered, Christopher and Florence Danvers looked up from a large table. Florence's expression was one of surprise. Christopher Danvers rose clumsily to his feet, face turning a shade of puce. 'What the hell do you think you're doing? We're in a meeting.'

'You were too tired to speak with me yesterday,' said Persis. 'So we will speak now.'

Danvers looked as if he might choke on his own outrage. Persis saw his wife lay a restraining hand on his arm.

'This is highly irregular, Inspector.' Persis focused on the man who had spoken, the third person in the room, the individual the Danvers had been meeting with. A slim, neatly pressed gentleman in a linen suit. Persis saw that he was of mixed ancestry: half white, half Naga. Just enough of each to be despised by both. That was how it often went with those whose genetic heritage condemned them to a cold welcome around two campfires, at least in Persis's experience. Indians often seemed hellbent on punishing those of their countrymen who, through no fault of their own, evinced bloodlines of their former conquerors.

The man stood up. 'My name is Simon Ruivah and I am the chief secretary of the Naga Hills Baptist Church Council. What is this about?'

Persis explained why they were there.

Ruivah looked troubled. 'Yes. I was informed this morning of Sinha's death. A horrific tragedy and one that, no doubt, will have enormous repercussions for the region.'

'In what way?'

'Come now, Inspector. You've been here long enough to understand the delicate balance between the various forces vying for power in the Naga Hills.'

'By forces, you mean the central government, the army, local India loyalists, and those demanding Naga independence. And then there's you, in the middle of it all.'

'The church is a neutral entity. Our aim is solely to promote the message of peace, and to mediate where appropriate.'

Persis refrained from pointing out that, if history was anything to go by, the sort of mediation religious orders provided often came at the point of a sword.

'At any rate, your enquiries are clearly of great import. I will leave you all to discuss the matter.' Ruivah turned to the Danvers. 'We will continue our conversation at a later time.'

Persis watched the man leave, dragging Matthews along in his wake. Turning back to the Danvers, she saw that Florence had retaken her seat while Christopher Danvers was still standing and seething. 'Have you any idea how long it took us to set up this meeting?'

'No,' said Persis, and took a seat.

Danvers had clearly been expecting more, an opportunity for him to give vent to his outrage. But the enemy's refusal to engage left him spluttering. He looked helplessly at his wife, and then his knees seemed to give way, and he collapsed back into his chair.

James sat down beside Persis. A ceiling fan moved above them, ruffling the collar of his dress shirt.

'You certainly know how to make an entrance,' began Florence. 'How can we help you, Inspector?'

'As I stated last night, it's my belief that Mohan Sinha's killer was a guest of the hotel—'

'Ergo we're suspects?' interrupted Christopher. His sallow features were once again animated.

'Let her speak.'

The American subsided and Persis was struck, once again, by how easily the older man was bullied into submission by his wife. It was becoming clear that not only did Florence Danvers wear the trousers in the Danvers household, but she was also the brains of the outfit. Her husband appeared to have as much agency as a ventriloquist's dummy.

Florence's gaze was still on Persis. 'I assure you, we had nothing to do with Sinha's death. We will help in any way that we can. Ask your questions.'

'Sinha was killed between nine forty and eleven. Where were you both during that time?'

'As we stated yesterday, we were in our suite. Together.'

'A husband and wife alibiing each other rarely holds up in court.'

'But we aren't in court, are we?' A faint smile flickered over Florence's lips.

'What are you doing here? In the Naga Hills?'

'God's work,' blurted Christopher, belligerently. A hand rose to tap the wooden cross around his throat, dangling atop his clothing from a chain of wooden beads. 'The only vocation that truly matters.'

'How long have you been here?'

'Just over two months,' said Florence.

'Based at the hotel?' James had spoken for the first time.

'Yes.'

'Because Sinha refused to give you permission to travel further.' Persis watched for a reaction. Christopher Danvers didn't disappoint. 'The man was a bureaucrat. A Napoleon with a pen.' He seemed on the verge of saying more but was once again brought to heel by a glance from his wife.

Florence turned to Persis. 'You have to understand that the status of missionaries here is hazy. After India became independent, all foreign missionaries were compelled to leave the Naga Hills district. It's taken a lot of persuasion for Christopher and I to even get this far.'

'And then Sinha told you: this far you shall go and no further. That must have been . . . frustrating. To come all this way, and then to be blocked at the final hurdle.'

Florence offered up a wan smile. 'Missionaries are nothing if not patient. Have you any idea how long the American Baptist mission has been working in the Naga Hills?'

The truth was that Persis had known little about the potency of the Baptist incursion into Naga territory until she had arrived in the region. The Naga, she now knew, had lived undisturbed for centuries in their secret fastnesses, out in the jungles of the northeast. Western anthropologists, never shy of letting facts get in the way of a good story, would later suggest that they had arrived in the region from China or Nepal or Tibet or, in some of the wilder flights of fancy, via Polynesia. The Naga themselves had many origin myths, but none that might verifiably be traced back to a particular part of the world. They lived in independent and intensely aggressive village societies, perched atop forested hills, ever willing to wage war on one another for the slightest trespass. Scholars had compared them to the city-states of ancient Greece, though such a comparison, Persis thought, might well have raised the likes of Plato and Socrates from their tombs to launch vociferous protest.

What was fact was that a mass conversion to Christianity had taken place from the late nineteenth century onwards, a process that had managed to finally unite the Naga tribes – as much as communities who would gleefully raid each other's villages in search of heads *could* be united. The first Baptist missionaries to the region had realised that to bring such disparate peoples together they required a common tool; they gave this to the Naga by translating the Bible into the local language. Suddenly, Jesus was alive in the hills, traipsing about in two-thousand-year-old sandals, converting the locals from their animist leanings to the true word of God.

Persis changed tack. 'Why did you choose to stay at the Hotel Victoria?'

'Where else would we stay?' said Christopher.

'I would have thought you might wish to be closer to your flock? In Kohima. And in less grand lodgings than the Victoria. What would Christ make of such extravagance?'

The American's eyes tightened at the corners. 'You can mock us, but let me ask you this: have you ever saved a human soul? I don't mean physically, I mean the light within a person, a light that can only enter the gates of heaven via Christ and His Word?'

'I'm not a Christian,' said Persis. 'I have my own god to appease. And whether any of us make it into heaven is debatable.'

'To answer your question,' interjected Florence, 'we're staying at the Victoria for reasons of safety. We were told that insurgent raids into Kohima were on the increase.'

'And yet you have no qualms about going out into the jungle to meet with those same insurgents?'

'Our business isn't with the insurgency,' snapped Christopher. 'We have no truck with war and warmongers. Ours is a higher calling. To bring the light of truth to the heathen.'

She resisted the urge to remind him that, over the millennia, the bloodiest wars had been instigated by the demagogues of faith. Invariably men, though it always amazed her how rarely *that* was mentioned.

James spoke up. 'So it's just a coincidence that you chose to stay in the same hotel as Mohan Sinha? The man who held the power to grant you a permit to travel into the interior?'

A vein throbbed at Christopher Danvers's temple. Persis had the impression that the man would make a terrible card player.

'When was the last time you spoke to him?' James continued.

The American seemed momentarily confused by the question.

'We spoke with Sinha a couple of days ago,' answered Florence smoothly.

'And what was the outcome of that discussion?'

'He agreed to give us our permit. He was due to sign off on it this week.'

Persis frowned. 'Why didn't you tell us this right away?'

'You seemed to want chapter and verse of our time here, Inspector.'

'We had no wish to harm the man,' said Christopher. 'Quite the opposite. We needed Sinha alive and well.'

'Unless, of course, you're lying,' said James.

The man's face puffed up like a bullfrog's. His wife spoke hastily into the jagged silence. 'Why would we lie? Why would we kill the only man who could give us the permission we need to carry out our work?'

'Perhaps Sinha was particularly intransigent?' said Persis. 'Perhaps you hoped that by getting rid of him he might be replaced by someone more amenable? Perhaps one of you – or both – went to his room last night to reason with him. Matters became heated. The next thing you know you have a dead man on your hands. What do you do? Two foreigners, known to be at odds with the victim? You couldn't afford to be implicated in Sinha's murder. And so you decided to deflect suspicion. By making it look as if locals were responsible.'

'Preposterous,' seethed Christopher.

'My husband is right,' said Florence. 'We are people of faith. "Thou shalt not kill". And what exactly do you think we did with the head? How did we get into a locked room? We're missionaries, not magicians.'

Persis allowed the uncomfortable silence to fester, then took out the photograph fragment she had found on Sinha's desk, pushed it across the table. 'Does this mean anything to you?'

The couple passed it between each other. 'No,' said Christopher.

Persis could detect nothing in the man's tone to indicate that he was lying. But then, it was only in books that detectives could so readily read a man's mind. In reality, practised liars could tell you that the sky was black in the middle of the day without batting so much as an eyelid.

Florence Danvers rose to her feet. 'I'm sorry, Inspector, but we have work to attend to.' She summoned up a wan smile. 'I understand that you have a job to do and that you must proceed with your investigation. But we had nothing to do with Mohan Sinha's death. I wish you Godspeed in finding his killer.'

II

The sun had begun to drop towards the horizon by the time they emerged back into the street. There were few street lamps in Kohima; what artificial lighting there was consisted largely of lanterns, a flickering cascade of fireflies illuminating the rabbit warren of alleys and narrow lanes that mazed around the fledgling city.

Persis realised that her stomach was rumbling. 'I need something to eat.'

James hesitated as if debating with himself, then said, quickly, 'My grandmother has invited you to supper.'

She stared at him. Her deputy's ears had reddened. 'Why?'

'She wants to meet you.' He coughed to conceal his awkwardness. 'I'm sorry. She's been asking for a while. She won't take no for an answer.'

A dog howled in the silence. A passing rickshawwallah hollered at a man standing by the side of the road. 'In that case,' said Persis, 'I would be delighted to accept.'

Driving through the labyrinth of narrow streets, she was struck, once again, by how badly put together Kohima appeared. A town thrown together from bits of old wood, corrugated iron sheeting, crumbling bricks, random lumps of concrete, and the occasional glint of modern engineering that looked as out of place amongst the general chaos as a nun in a police line-up.

They drifted past the schoolhouse, the general store, and the local market. An olive-green army truck was stationed by the telegraph office, flanked by a tank and an armoured jeep. A soldier in military fatigues, a turbaned Sikh twice the size of the average Naga, leaning over a Sten gun, watched them as they drove by in a cloud of dust.

The market, in the relative cool of the pre-twilight hours, was busy, a riot of colour and noise, locals haggling over lamb and goat and chicken and practically anything that could move or crawl on God's earth. If there was one thing Christianity hadn't managed to subvert it was the Naga willingness to eat anything and every-thing, up to and including the myriad insect species of the jungles they inhabited. Or so she had heard.

Persis had yet to risk some of the more exotic dishes. Constable Binny was particularly keen on her trying out frogs' testicles swimming in butter. She hadn't realised that frogs even *had* testi-cles. And if they did she was happy for them to remain where nature had intended.

Lately, however, she had begun to suspect that Binny was making fun of her, and that, perhaps, her attitude stemmed from a mixture of parochialism and ignorance. Most Naga appeared not to eat anything more offensive than badly seared steak.

The Angami home was approachable only by foot, along a narrow and winding path that led up from the street below; you didn't have to be a mountain goat to get there, but it might have helped. The single-storey dwelling made a bright note in a dull symphony, its wash of lilac paint contrasting vividly with the grey-faced homes that sputtered along the track on either side. Persis looked up. A further cascade of homes climbed upwards, broken by occasional earthworks that gave the hill the look of having sprouted a particularly scrofulous disease.

She was struck, once again, by how far she was from the archi-tectural sophistication of Bombay, even if, in recent years, that sophistication had been tempered by the exigencies of unbridled growth. In the city of dreams, slums now sat side by side with the edifices of empire, like beggars making themselves comfortable beside princes.

They were let into the house by James Angami's grandmother, a sprightly and vivacious woman who put Persis in mind of Apeni Ao, the proprietor of the Hotel Victoria. She wondered if there was a factory deep in the hills producing elderly, birdlike Naga women, with the strength of bullocks and the capacity to bear war and husbands with equal perseverance.

The home itself was a testament to the versatility of bamboo. Bamboo chairs, a bamboo table, a bamboo sofa, a bamboo lamp-stand, bamboo sideboards. If it was possible, Persis suspected, James's grandmother would have worn bamboo socks.

Her name was Esther and she clearly took great pride in both her home and her grandson. Having seated them at the table, she wandered back into the corner of the room where various pans were bubbling away on a stove. Persis didn't have the courage to ask what was in them.

'It's chicken stew,' said James, as if reading her thoughts. 'I told her you were squeamish.'

'I'm not squeamish. I just prefer to eat things that won't fight back.' She rose to her feet. 'I'd like to wash up.'

'Of course.' James pointed at one of two doors leading off the living room.

Persis walked into a bathroom, closed the door, then leaned over the sink.

What was she doing here? Her reflection held no answers. It was bad enough, she thought, finding herself out in this strange land, populated by people who seemed utterly alien to her, but to end up in the home of her junior officer, breaking bread, implied the beginning of an intimacy that she found intensely uncomfortable. Back at Malabar House, she had kept her fellow officers at arm's length. The one man she had let inside her guard, Archie Blackfinch, had ended up betraying her.

She could not – would not – risk that again.

A splash of cold water returned her to her senses. She towelled herself off, then made her way back to the table.

Her gaze wandered around the room, snagged on a garlanded picture of a middle-aged Naga couple – both in Western dress – on the wall. 'Your parents?'

'Yes.'

'How did they die?'

James looked momentarily startled, as if it hadn't occurred to him that she might ask this. 'My ancestors were born deep in the hills. But my grandparents were educated by missionaries. My parents moved to Kohima soon after they married. My father joined the Indian Civil Service as a clerk, Assam division. Five years ago, he was murdered. Here in Kohima. My mother drowned herself three months later.'

Persis masked her surprise. Seth had failed to mention this. And, in the month that she had known her deputy, she had failed to ask. The thought embarrassed her . . . What did one say to such a thing? 'Is that why you left the army and joined the police force?'

She knew that James had fought in the war. It was about all that she did know.

His expression changed. 'I enlisted aged eighteen. My parents were set against it, but I wanted to get out of Kohima. I wanted to see the world beyond these hills. The irony is they sent me right back here.'

'You fought in the Battle of Kohima?'

'Battle?' A snort escaped him. 'It was a slaughter.' He nodded at a painting of Jesus on the wall, a blond, blue-eyed saviour bathed in a messianic halo. 'My grandmother believes the soldiers that died up in the hills walk with Jesus.'

'You don't sound convinced.'

'If they're walking anywhere near Jesus, I hope they're wearing body armour.' The muscles of his face hardened. 'The things I saw up on that ridge, the ways men found to kill each other ... They say God made man in his image. If that's the case, then I'm not sure I'd ever want to meet Him.'

Persis allowed a beat. 'Did you investigate your father's death?'

'I did. He was stabbed to death outside a bar. No witnesses, none that will admit to being there. And that's all I've ever been able to find out.'

She saw how much it cost him to admit his failure, in this, a task that he had taken as a grail quest, a penance, perhaps, for abandoning his parents to join the army. She found her lips moving of their own accord. 'My mother died in a car accident when I was seven. It took twenty years for my father to admit to me that she died because *he* had been at the wheel.'

Their eyes met and something wordless passed between them.

They were brought out of their mutual reverie by the scrape of Esther's bamboo sandals. The old woman set two large bamboo bowls on to the table. A spicy aroma, thick enough to choke a horse, attacked Persis's nostrils.

They chatted as they ate. For the first time since arriving in the region she found herself relaxing. Meals at the Hotel Victoria had always been guarded, undermined by the place's artificiality. And dining with Roshan Seth had reminded her too much of Bombay and all that she had been forced to leave behind.

'Don't eat too much, James,' said Esther. She looked at Persis. 'He can't handle spice. It goes right through him. In one end and out the other. Whoosh!'

'Nanna!'

Persis fought the urge to smile.

'Tell me, dear, why did you join the police service?'

Persis felt her deputy's eyes on her. 'I wanted to show them that I could. To show them I was as good as any man.'

Esther clapped in delight. Trapped stars sparkled in her eyes.

They talked for a while, Esther curious about Persis's life in Bombay. 'James tells me you lost your mother when you were a child.'

'I did. But she left me with more than just memories. She taught me to play the piano, for one. Badly. She taught me to think for myself, to make my own decisions. My mother was a sophisticated woman, born to be a socialite, until she eloped with my father. She came from money. She married for love.'

'Always for the best, dear. At least that way, your mistakes are your own.' The woman's face crinkled. 'It must still be strange for you, wearing that uniform. James tells me there are many who want you to take it off.'

'People hate change. Especially when it threatens them.' A fierceness rose inside her. 'I fought through the Quit India years. I have as much right as anyone to serve my country.'

They moved on to discuss the case. 'There's not much sympathy for Sinha,' said Esther. 'Not that I would wish such a death on anyone,' she added hurriedly, as her grandson opened his mouth to protest. 'But he's alienated many Naga by trying to enforce Nehru's edicts.'

'Is Indian control any different to when the British were here?' said Persis. 'Or the missionaries who converted the Naga to a foreign faith?'

She heard James choking on his stew. But Esther did not look away. 'The missionaries offered us salvation. They did not seek to rule us. As for the British ... They gave us a way out of the hills. My son worked for the civil service because he wanted to, not because he was forced to.'

Persis could have said much more, about the invisible bonds of colonialism, about the thousand and one ways that Indians had been forced to live as second-class citizens in their own country, the lucky few ennobled – and enriched – by their British overseers, as and when it suited the imperial agenda. But she said nothing.

There was nothing to be said.

Later, as she helped the old woman with the dishes, Esther placed a hand on her arm. 'It's fine to feel vulnerable, child.'

She stared at the woman, then looked away. 'I don't want them to know. That I'm not always as sure of myself as I pretend to be. They would use it against me.'

'My grandson thinks the world of you ... He's a handsome man, don't you think?'

A spike of alarm rose inside her. She buried her hands in the sink.

'It's about time he settled down.'

Persis risked a glance, caught the sly smile curling the older woman's lips.

The worst of it was, she couldn't disagree.

Her sub-inspector *was* a handsome man.

12

War had left its mark on Kohima.

The place's claim to fame, as Persis had learned early on, centred around a Japanese attempt to advance into India through Burma, hacking their way through the dense jungle that blanketed the eastern reaches of the subcontinent. Originally intended as a spoiling manoeuvre against the British troops based at Imphal, the Japanese commander of the offensive, perhaps buoyed by endless cups of sake and a sociopathic belief in his own destiny, had decided that the attack might persevere beyond simply the Naga Hills region, forcing its way down on to the Indian plains, there to be followed by a triumphal march on Delhi. India would be taken, the British undone, and he could go back to Tokyo a hero, with an elephant tucked under each arm.

Things hadn't quite panned out that way.

In April 1944, a column of soldiers from the Japanese Fifteenth Army worked their way up from Imphal to the Kohima Ridge, where they were met by troops from the British IV Corps. The resulting battle, sixty-four days of mayhem, left ten thousand dead, and the region devastated. The fighting had been particularly fierce around the then deputy commissioner's bungalow, which stood on the hillside at a bend in the road, housing, among other things, a private tennis facility, much abused by the commissioner and his white-shorted – and knock-kneed – British visitors. The Battle of the Tennis Court, an encounter that would later invite comparisons to the massacre at Verdun, saw the combatants dug into slit trenches so close they were able to lob grenades at one another.

Ultimately, the Japanese were beaten back due to a tactical miscalculation. They ran out of food. Many later died of starvation as they withdrew back into the jungle. The general in charge of the offensive had been invited to commit seppuku. Politely declining the opportunity to disembowel himself, he had instead chosen to mount a defence of his actions at a court martial in Tokyo.

Soon after arriving in Kohima, Roshan Seth had walked Persis up to the cemetery on Garrison Hill, housing a thousand Allied war dead, together with a stone memorial for the nine hundred Sikh and Hindu casualties whose corporeal remains had been given to the holy fire. She had stood in the harsh glare of the midday sun, looking at the rows of neat white crosses, and felt a darkness creep over her, the shades of the dead whispering in her ear, demanding some measure of sense be distilled from that which no rational philosophy could explain.

But war had not had its fill of the region. In the aftermath of independence, a new war had erupted. A civil war. Standing beside her commanding officer, she had silently wondered just how many more graves would end up populating these rugged hills before all was said and done.

The journey to the Kohima Officers' Club from James Angami's home took less than twenty minutes and passed in almost complete silence. Persis glanced at her junior colleague, who seemed to still be recovering from the trauma of having his naked baby pictures forced on to his superior officer by his grandmother.

A strong military presence greeted them outside the club, including several tanks lined up to greet visitors with a nostril's-eye view of their main gun muzzles.

Persis and James were confronted at the entrance to the compound by a large young soldier clearly bristling with a desire to give some-one smaller than himself a good thrashing. They were asked to state their business, then forced to submit to a search, the young corporal snarling at them like a gorilla in heat. Their weapons were confiscated, their protests overridden, and then they were led inside.

To one side of the walled compound, soldiers milled at the entrance to a timber-framed barracks. The barracks, once populated by British officers – *white* officers – now housed Indian soldiers under the command of Colonel Hiten Shroff, the region's military chief, and now, with Sinha's death, the de facto overseer of the Naga Hills district.

Persis could feel eyes boring into her back as they were marched on towards the club's main building. Her status as novelty had begun to wear thin back in Bombay; but, out here, a woman in uniform stuck out like a sore thumb.

The Kohima Officers' Club: an expansive maroon-painted bungalow with a gabled roof, a colonnaded porch, and a pair of well-groomed Buddhist pines stationed primly to attention either side of the front entrance. In days gone by a British flag would have hung from the flagpole rising from the roof; now an Indian tricolour drooped in the windless humidity.

To Persis, the club resembled a temple, of a faith that had fallen on hard times.

On either side of the bungalow, a pair of recently added watch-towers rose into a darkening sky.

She craned her neck upwards.

At the top of each tower she could make out a brace of soldiers, armed with machine guns. Perhaps it was her imagination, but they seemed twitchy, looking down at her with mournful faces. She imagined that standing a post in an exposed crow's nest in the middle of an insurgency wasn't exactly a plum assignment.

They were escorted into the building, along several corridors, and then into the colonel's office.

Shroff turned out to be a squat man, in a khaki uniform, with boots so shiny they could have dazzled a blind man. He was younger than Persis had assumed – barely into his forties – with dark hair cut short, and severely parted, and a sublime moustache. Here, thought Persis, was a man who took his facial hair – and by virtue of the fact, himself – seriously. A man in love with his own mythos.

'Inspector, thank you for joining me.' Shroff did not bother to stand. He sat behind a large desk, covered in papers, but did not offer a seat to his visitors. His dark eyes fixed on James. Persis answered the unspoken question. 'This is Sub-Inspector Angami. He is assisting me with the Sinha investigation.'

Shroff's expression gave nothing away; but his silence spoke volumes. Persis knew, from Roshan Seth, that the colonel was no fan of the Naga. His stance, since arriving in the region, had been anything but conciliatory. If Sinha had been Delhi's man in the hills, Shroff served as Nehru's hammer. There was good reason that the colonel lived behind barricaded walls. If there was one man the insurgents would have wished to send into the afterlife more than Sinha, it was the region's military commander.

'Sub-Inspector, please step outside.'

Persis sensed her deputy stiffen. 'Colonel—' she began, but Shroff held up a hand. 'This is the army, Inspector, not the police force. Orders are not questioned. They are obeyed.'

A hot flush scalded her insides. *Orders? Obeyed?*

Before she could speak, she heard James turn on his heel and march stiffly out of the room.

She turned back to Shroff. 'That was unnecessary.'

'You can take the savage out of the jungle, but you cannot take the jungle out of the savage.' Shroff reached into a drawer, took out a bottle of whisky and a solitary glass. 'There's nothing like good Scotch. Got a taste for it during my time at Sandhurst.'

Persis wrestled with her anger. There was no point in antagonising Shroff. With Sinha's passing, the colonel was now the most powerful man in the region. If he wished it, he could have her removed from the investigation, or, indeed, the hills district entirely.

Shroff sipped at his glass. 'I understand that you've already made progress?'

'Yes.'

He frowned, raised an expectant eyebrow. It slowly dawned on her that the man was waiting for her to complete her acknowledgement. 'Yes, *sir*,' she ground out.

'And what have your efforts determined?'

She brought him up to speed. She considered holding back the threatening note from Sinha's desk – *Nagalim will never be yours. Leave now. Or die* – but then decided that it was too important a piece of evidence to keep from him, particularly given that she had already revealed its existence to Sinha's aide, John Templeton.

Shroff listened in silence, his hard, dark eyes revealing nothing. 'An impossible murder? But the very fact that Sinha is dead suggests that the killing was anything but impossible. And the absence of the head – not to mention this warning note . . . Is it not obvious that this is the work of insurgents?'

'There were no insurgents in the hotel that night.'

'Can you be certain of that? Baba Dao has sympathisers in places you would least expect.'

'Are you referring to the Danvers?'

'Missionaries have a long association with the local tribes.'

'My understanding is that the Danvers had been waiting for Sinha to issue them a permit to the interior. They claim he had just agreed to approve such a permit. In which case, they had no motive to kill him.'

Shroff frowned again. 'Any permit into the hills must come across my desk, so that I can notify the checkpoints. Sinha was in the habit of letting me know as soon as he made any such decision. I received no such word.'

'Are you saying that the Danvers are lying?'

'If they are, it would mean Sinha continued to refuse them. And that *would* give them a motive for murder.'

'Killing Sinha doesn't exactly help them. Besides, I doubt that murder would sit well with the tenets of their faith.'

'Did the Partition years teach you nothing, Inspector? Throughout history, men have killed for their gods. Why should the Danvers be any different? Perhaps they murdered Sinha in the hope that his replacement might be more amenable to their demands.'

'Aren't *you* Sinha's replacement?'

'Only temporarily. Nehru will send a politician to the hills soon enough.' The way he said *politician* – in roughly the same tones a landlord might say *cockroach* – suggested that the colonel was far from enamoured of the prospect.

She looked on as he raised himself from his seat, walked briskly to a map spread across one wall. The map depicted the Naga Hills district in its entirety, with a constellation of red flags marking villages dotted throughout the terrain. 'Have you any idea what is going on in these hills? Sinha knew. Nehru didn't send him out here on a whim. Twenty years ago, Mohan Sinha was stationed here. The Naga made it clear then that they had no wish to be part of the India we were fighting for. These are the people Sinha was dealing with. Disloyal. Ungrateful. Treacherous.'

Persis's thoughts reeled. Until that moment, she had had no idea that Mohan Sinha had been in the region before. To her knowledge, the man had arrived in the Naga Hills just a year prior to his death. The revelation of his previous time here instantly threw a new light on her investigation.

Shroff tapped the map, indicating the ridge above the town of Kohima. 'Up on that hill two failing empires fought each other into the mud, over territory that neither had any claim to. The British and the Japanese are now gone. India belongs to Indians, now and forever.' He turned to her. 'Many died for this land. We won't give up a single square inch, Inspector. Not to the Naga, not to anyone. I owe that to our martyrs.'

Persis found her voice. 'Many Naga fought in the war. Many fought for independence.'

'The Naga were enamoured of the British. And enamoured of the Christian faith. How can we trust a people willing to forget their own creed?' A wildness flamed in his eyes, a madness that Persis recognised: the mania of the fanatic. With Sinha's killing, something had been set loose in the colonel that had been waiting a lifetime for its moment.

Despite the heat, her insides shuddered.

The colonel's eyes continued to drill into her. 'The insurgents – or their sympathisers – be they the Danvers or others – killed Mohan Sinha. *That* is the conclusion I expect you to reach. Do we understand each other?'

13

She found James waiting for her in the inner compound, pacing the lawn outside the officers' club bungalow, seething like a schoolboy jilted on prom night.

An apology formed on her lips—

'Why didn't you leave with me?' His attempt at a low hiss reverberated off the distant hills. She saw a group of nearby soldiers turn their heads.

She swallowed the apology. 'Have you finished?'

He glared at her. She sensed the vast reservoir of resentment inside him. His desire to prove himself in the teeth of animosity. In that moment, she saw herself in him, a mirror to her own raging ambition upon joining the service.

The colonel's adjutant arrived to frogmarch them out of the compound, turning on his heel as soon as he had deposited them outside the walls.

They stood in the lee of a tank. A brace of soldiers lounged against the hulking vessel, machine guns hanging from their shoulders, watching them with interest, as if they might unexpectedly burst into song.

She briefed her deputy on her conversation with the colonel.

James absorbed her words. 'Do you think the fact that Sinha was here two decades ago has a bearing on his murder?'

'I don't know. But it's not something we can ignore.' She hesitated, considering the wisdom of her next words. 'There's another possibility that we cannot discount. Sinha's death has given Shroff carte blanche to stamp his authority on the region.'

It only took a second for James to understand her meaning. 'You can't possibly believe that the colonel somehow orchestrated Sinha's murder?'

Out of the corner of her eye, she saw a handcartwallah approach on the far side of the street, the cart piled high with coconuts and melons. The geriatric fruitseller looked too old to be pulling such a load. 'I don't know. But we need to keep it in mind as we proceed with the investigation.'

The handcart came to a stop, and the elderly Naga began to limp over to the soldiers by the tank, slipping a bag of coconuts from his shoulder. His melon-like face spread into a toothless grin. 'Coconut milk! Coconut milk!'

Persis saw one of the soldiers straighten. 'Stay back, old man. This area is out of bounds.'

The coconut seller ignored him, reached into his sack, pulled out a coconut.

Persis's gaze narrowed. There was something wrong with the coconut. It was too small, too dark. She saw the old man's face transform, eyes flatten into sheets of glass. His hand blurred over the object in his hand, and then his arm pulled back, and he launched the object towards the tank.

Time slowed. An instinctive cry escaped her. She willed herself to move, but her body was gripped by paralysis.

Seconds later, the grenade exploded, lifting the tank from its treads, and blowing both soldiers – and James Angami – towards her in a roaring sheet of flame.

14

The baby-faced doctor wore a white coat several sizes too large, as if he had recently regressed to boyhood. The impression was enhanced by the look of stern expectation directed his way by the nurse at his side. The look suggested that he was a toddler and she his nanny, supervising his first tottering steps into infancy.

To Persis, the man looked barely old enough to have passed through puberty, let alone medical school.

She was sitting on the edge of a hospital bed, having just finished being examined. Her skull felt as if it had been used as a drum, and she fancied that she could still hear a ringing in her ears. But, all things considered, she had come out of the explosion relatively unscathed. 'How is . . . James?' she croaked. The answer seemed to matter more to her than it should, more than she could put into words.

'Incredibly fortunate. He was saved from the worst of the blast by the . . .' The boy-doctor's voice tailed off, '. . . the others.' He wiped his hands nervously on his coat.

Persis knew that the soldiers who had been manning the tank were dead. She knew this because she had seen both corpses on the ground, one with the legs blown off. One of the legs, still attached to a booted foot, had landed beside her head.

The doctor had slipped into a posture of frightened mournfulness. She wanted to tell him that the dead were not to be feared. The dead could be grieved, pitied, even envied, but never feared. For in the act of dying they lost power over the living, save the power accorded them by those they left behind. For many years Persis had allowed her dead mother to exert such a power over her. But with the first murder that had fallen into her path, and the warrant that she had accepted for bringing justice to the soul of that mortal flesh, she had realised that she must learn to let go. It was the only way to prevent the darkness grinding your soul to dust.

'Inspector, we must stop meeting like this.'

She turned to find Andrews at her shoulder. The hospital's chief medical officer nodded at the young doctor. 'Off you go, Ravi. You have rounds to finish.'

'Yes, sir.'

She watched the medic scuttle away, accompanied by his child-minder nurse.

'May I invite you for a drink? You look as if you could use one.'

'I want to see James.'

'He's not going anywhere.' He ushered her out of the room, along the corridor, and into a cramped office.

She watched him shrug off his white coat – revealing braces and a sweat-stained, checked shirt that, by all rights, should have been indicted as a crime against humanity – and then conjure up two cups of tea. She was both relieved and disappointed that he hadn't offered her something stronger.

'Darjeeling,' said the doctor, setting a surprisingly dainty pair of porcelain cups on to the desk. 'There's one thing to be said for the north-east – we have access to the finest tea in the world.' He removed a flask from his pocket and poured a measure into his cup. He angled the flask at her, but she shook her head.

Andrews crash-landed in a chair on the far side of the cluttered desk, waving her into the seat opposite. She watched him excavate a pipe from the pocket of his white coat, light it, then set it theatrically into the corner of his mouth the way Sherlock Holmes might have done.

He puffed away, examining her with a direct gaze from under his bushy white eyebrows. 'Death is very much at home out here,' he said, eventually. 'Take it from me. I served in Kohima during the war. Tended to the casualties ferried back here each day. Too many for a chronically understaffed hospital to handle. I saw young men die needlessly, victims of mankind's hubris. Now I see the same hubris creeping over the hills. Men killed by insurgents; men killed by the army. What was it Gandhi said? An eye for an eye leaves everyone blind?' He cradled his tea. 'You have your work cut out. Sinha's death may not have been on the battlefield, but it might as well have been.'

She felt the sudden urge to tell him everything. The motor of her voice started up and she heard herself rehashing the meeting with Shroff, the colonel's insistence that she reach his desired conclusion, namely, that Sinha had been murdered by insurgents.

'Sinha's absence has created a power vacuum,' said Andrews. 'Shroff is simply using it to his advantage.'

'Doesn't anyone care about the truth?'

Andrews released a guffaw. 'Truth! In a place such as this?' He scratched at his cheek, puffed on his pipe. 'There are some saying that evil spirits were responsible for Sinha's murder. Given the circumstances of his death.'

'You'd have to be a pretty motivated ghost to chop off a man's head and walk through walls with it.'

'Aye. But they're a strange people, the Naga. Christians and pagans, all at once. And once they get something into their heads, it's the devil's own job to get it out again.' He chuckled.

'You like them, don't you?'

'I admire them. The Naga are a law unto themselves.' He picked up his teacup. 'The British tried to tame the hills. They only partially succeeded. What chance has Nehru got?'

*   *   *

She followed Andrews as he led her through the hospital.

They entered a cramped ward occupied by hollow-eyed men, sitting or lounging on white-sheeted beds, many of them frail, all of them twitchy, sallow, and haunted. 'Opium addicts,' said Andrews, matter-of-factly. 'It's become quite the scourge in recent years. There are wolves in these enchanted forests.'

A young man – he couldn't have been more than a teenager – followed her with his otherworldly gaze as she made her way along the ward. His head seemed too large for his bony frame. He looked as if he hadn't slept in a month.

They passed through several more wards before Andrews ushered her into a private room lit by bright lighting that bounced from the walls.

James stood on the far side of a hospital bed, half turned away from her, pulling on his dress shirt. She saw, with a sense of mild astonishment, that tattoos made a tessellated pattern along his upper back and shoulders. The effect reminded her of snakeskin.

She knew, vaguely, of the reverence with which tattoos were held in Naga society, but had thought that Christianised Naga had long abandoned the practice.

James jerked at her entry, froze. Their eyes met. A moment of embarrassment at his semi-nakedness, and then he pulled on the rest of his shirt and buttoned it all the way to the top as if he were a nun and she a barbarian intent on ravishment.

The shirt was torn in several places and looked as if it had been singed in a fire.

Persis saw too that his right cheek was swollen. She was taken back to the instant of the explosion, James's body hurtling towards her, his face colliding with her shoulder, the back of her head striking the earth, darkness descending.

They were both lucky to be alive. Had the grenade landed a dozen yards closer to them, had the tank – and the two soldiers stationed beside it – not taken the brunt of the blast, then neither she nor her deputy would be standing here, facing each other in acute discomfort.

She recalled the aftermath of the explosion, surfacing from a momentary unconsciousness to find the street overrun by troops pouring from the compound. She had pushed herself to her elbows, ears ringing from the blast, twisted her neck to see soldiers standing over the bullet-ridden corpse of the coconut seller. Coconuts had fallen from the man's bag, and rolled around on the bloodstained earth.

Colonel Shroff had arrived moments later, made his way first to the fallen soldiers, to kneel by their bodies. His ashen face had spoken volumes.

He had turned to her, walked over, and helped her to her feet. '*This* is what we are dealing with, Inspector. Perhaps now you understand?'

Andrews crowded into the room behind her, breaking the spell. 'How do you feel?' he said, directing himself towards James.

'Like an elephant kicked me around for fun.'

'Could be worse,' said Andrews, briskly. 'You could be stretched out in my morgue like the poor bastards blown to kingdom come.' He reached into his pocket, produced the flask, waved it at the younger man.

'I don't drink,' said James, stiffly.

Andrews stared at him. 'That knock to the head must have been worse than I thought.' He stashed the flask, then said, 'You're fine to be discharged. Some bruising and a little scorched skin. And you'll need a new uniform. You're a lucky young man.'

'What about the coconut seller?'

Andrews looked at Persis. 'What?'

'The man who threw the grenade. The insurgent.'

'What about him? He's dead. And in Shroff's custody. Though what sort of questions he expects a dead man to answer, I do not know.' He sighed. 'The violence is spiralling out of control.'

James spoke into the sudden silence. 'One of the nurses told me the colonel has announced a new push into the interior.'

Andrews nodded glumly. 'He's going to use this incident to renew his efforts to find Baba Dao. Hah! The man couldn't find his own arse if I sewed it to his face.'

Persis wondered how much Andrews had had to drink. His face was florid, but that seemed par for the course. His accent had broadened in line with his animation.

She saw that James was looking at her. 'What do we do now?' He seemed momentarily lost, as if the ice had cracked below his feet and he faced the prospect of plunging into freezing-cold depths. A brush with death tended to have that effect, Persis reflected.

'We do our job,' she said. 'We find Sinha's killer.'

15

She returned to the hotel to find that the guard strength at the gates had been doubled. A case of corrective action after the horse had not only bolted, but cantered joyfully around the countryside, then died standing up in a field.

She went straight to her room, stripped, and headed into the shower.

The blessedly cool water sluiced the day from her. She washed her hair twice, convinced that the residue of the explosion still clung to her. Not to mention blood and gore from the bodies of the murdered soldiers.

Having dressed – in a sleeveless, pale-green cotton dress – she made her way down to the dining room. She had no appetite, but the prospect of being alone in her room held little appeal. She needed human contact, anything to stave off the darkness of the past hours. The bodies of the dead men, symbols of the hatred that had infected this region, haunted her, left her hollow and afraid.

The dining room was deserted save for a solitary diner.

John Templeton spooned listlessly at a bowl of soup. As she approached, he snapped to attention, lifted a napkin to his mouth, then stood to meet her.

Words exploded from her. 'Why didn't you tell me Sinha had worked in this region before?'

Templeton's brow crinkled in confusion. 'How is that relevant to his murder?'

'Nothing can be discounted at this stage.' She reined back her irritation. 'What did he do here, back then?'

'It was well before I knew him. We've never spoken about it. But a record of his work in the district will be stored at the commissioner's residence. It's where all bureaucratic records for the Naga Hills are kept.'

'In that case, I will need you to meet me there tomorrow. Shall we say ten a.m.?'

He blinked at her like a mole dug up out of the earth. 'You can't simply order me to do your bidding. I don't work for you.'

'You don't work for anyone, any more.' She leaned in. 'I met with Shroff this evening. I presume you've heard of the attack at the officers' club? He's given me a free hand with this investigation. Would you prefer to talk to *him*?'

Templeton's lips pursed. His hands mangled a small invisible animal. And then he nodded. 'Very well. Ten a.m. You'll pardon me if I don't join you for dinner.' She watched him stalk away. It was becoming a *pas de deux* between them.

'Madam.'

She turned to find the young porter, Peter Jadonang, looking at her. 'Madam Apeni has requested that you join her.'

She followed him out of the restaurant, then down two flights of stairs, along a series of corridors, through a small wooden door, and into a cool, low-ceilinged space with a stone floor. On one side were racks of wine bottles, on the other a row of about a dozen enormous wooden barrels. The hotel's wine cellar. Persis had begun her fruitless search of the premises here the night before.

Apeni Ao stood beside a barrel that was taller than she was. She smiled as Persis approached, then turned a spigot set into the face of the barrel before her and filled a glass. She held it up to Persis. 'We fill our own barrels.'

Persis hesitated, then accepted the glass of red. The wine was plummy, and sharper than she had expected. Palatable. But only just.

'Any good?' asked the hotel's proprietor.

'No. Not really.'

Ao released a laugh, a tinkling sound in the confined space. 'Well, I cannot fault your honesty.' Her expression became grave. 'I understand you were present at today's attack on Shroff's compound?'

'Yes.'

'You were lucky to survive. But at least you now understand how fragile the situation is here, why we must have order.'

'You sound like the colonel.'

'Shroff is Nehru's creature. But his sentiments are not entirely wrong. We have a common goal and that makes us bedfellows, uncomfortable though the thought might be.'

'A common goal? Tell that to the insurgents. To Baba Dao. To the families of the dead soldiers.'

'War breeds orphans,' said the old woman philosophically. 'The dream of a united Nagalim cannot be fulfilled while we are in conflict with the central government. Independence – at least of the type Baba Dao and those who follow him wish for – is a mirage.'

'Didn't many once think the same about freeing our country from the British?'

'The British were foreigners, a cancer eventually rejected by the body. But how can an arm ask for independence from the shoulder to which it is attached? Mohan Sinha was an Anglophile, like myself. Yet we both participated in the Quit India movement. We shared a vision for the Naga Hills. A future of hope, free of our colonial past. A future in which we take our rightful seat at the table in the new India.'

Persis looked down at the glass in her hand.

'When the forest blooms there is no more beautiful place in the country,' Ao continued. 'And yet, towns such as Kohima languish in shadow. A mass of boarding houses, drinking joints, and brothels. A rabbit warren of open sewers that flood downslope in the monsoon. Have you ever lived beneath a river of shit, Inspector? I assure you, it is not pleasant.'

'Bombay's not so different,' countered Persis. 'Every time it rains our roads are filled with potholes bigger than the egos of politicians.'

A crooked smile split the old woman's features. 'What the Naga Hills district needs is investment. Investment that can only come from the mainland. But who would wish to invest in a region blighted by conflict? Sinha's murder has set back our cause by years.'

'Do *you* think Baba Dao was behind his killing?'

'I do.'

'Could his influence have extended to one of the guests at the hotel? Convinced them to carry out the murder? The Danvers, for instance?'

The hotelier pondered the question, then said, 'I don't know. And if I did I would be loath to say. I take my duty to my guests as a sacred trust. Would you ask a priest to betray the secrets of the confessional? ... I don't envy you your task, Inspector. And remember this: Baba Dao is more myth than man.'

'You don't believe he's real?'

'Oh, he's real alright. But his legend has been carefully curated to radicalise Naga youth who should know better. Meanwhile, to the Centre, he has become a convenient bogeyman, a symbol of forces in the Naga Hills they believe are rampantly unpatriotic. Bear that in mind.'

*   *   *

Back in her room, Persis asked the switchboard to connect her to Bombay.

It was pointless keeping anything from her father. Having pretty much raised her on his own, Sam was preternaturally attuned to her moods; the man had a bloodhound's ability to sniff out a story. Throughout her adolescent years, a raised eyebrow and a stern pause would leave Persis overcome by a violent urge to confess everything, like a woman strapped to a chair watching an inquisitor lovingly caress instruments of torture. She had no doubt that Mohan Sinha's gruesome murder would have made headlines around the country by now. It was only a matter of time before her father figured out she was up to her neck in the affair.

When he came on the line, she launched into a summary of the past twenty-four hours. As she finished, a maw opened up over the line. It was an age before her father replied. 'So you almost got yourself blown up? What have you planned for an encore? Having yourself fired out of a cannon?'

'You're overreacting.' As soon as the words were out of her mouth she wished she could push them back in.

But her father displayed uncharacteristic restraint. 'You're alive and unhurt. That's the main thing.'

She sensed his disappointment. Or perhaps it was resignation?

Sam broke the awkward silence. 'I received a call. From the hospital. From Maisie.'

The floor fell away beneath her feet. Her insides hollowed.

'Did you hear what I said?'

She forced air into her lungs. 'I did. Is – is Archie okay?'

'He is. Relatively speaking. He's still in a coma. No change there.'

A gush of relief washed over her.

'Don't you want to know what Maisie wanted?'

'No.' She put down the phone. For a second, a vision of her father's shocked face hovered above the telephone. It took every ounce of her strength not to call him back.

She walked out on to the balcony.

Moonlight poured over the treetops like cream. Stars crowded the sky. The army of hateful capuchins had retired for the night; she was grateful for small mercies.

Not for the first time since arriving out here, she felt herself caught inside a trap, the nature of which remained unclear. She missed the familiar absurdities of home. The soothing night sounds of Bombay: psychotic taxiwallahs, screeching fishwives, the occasional mugging. A scream welled in her throat; she pushed it down, buried it beneath the chaos of unwanted feelings that thoughts of Archie Blackfinch invariably engendered.

It was for the best. Any further entanglement with the Englishman was not only ill advised but a recipe for disaster. At the least, it would throw her off balance. And she needed a clear head to navigate her way through the labyrinth she now found herself in with the impossible murder of Mohan Sinha.

Blackfinch would have to wait.

16

Persis had rung her deputy as soon as she had awoken, asking him to meet her at the commissioner's residence in Kohima at ten a.m.

She arrived at ten minutes before the hour, found both James Angami and John Templeton awaiting her, the newly reconstructed bungalow that made up the commissioner's office – and one-time home – on Garrison Hill looming over their shoulders.

She knew that, in its previous incarnation, the residence – and the formerly attached garrison quarters – had been blasted to smithereens in the fierce fighting during the Battle of Kohima. In the years following the war, the original building had been rebuilt – at least, in part – and now served as a regional administrative HQ. Mohan Sinha had worked from these offices, and, for a while, had lived here, in the attached residence, until the constant threat of assassination had persuaded him to move to the relative security of the Hotel Victoria.

How false that security now seemed.

Persis's gaze roamed over the bungalow. The building's design reflected the British fetish for recreating a little part of the Old Country wherever they planted their flag. Architecture that aggrandised the merits of empire, the sort of colonial building designed to hammer locals into subservience like nails banged into planks of wood. Bombay had a surfeit of such buildings. As a child, Persis had marvelled at their maroon-and-concrete grandeur. As an adult, participating in the independence struggle, that admiration had been tempered by the notion that such buildings advanced statements of intent that no longer felt comfortable to Indians seeking to reclaim their heritage.

She saw too, that, like the officers' club lower down in the town, the commissioner's residence was highly fortified, with a rough-hewn outer wall, sandbags piled at its feet. The fortifications gave the otherwise regal edifice a furtive, badly disguised look, like a Russian aristocrat on the run from Bolsheviks.

Templeton led them into a large reception where besuited Indians sat on tan Chesterfields wilting beneath ceiling fans. Some of them looked as if they had been sitting there since the dawn of time and would remain there until the world was consumed by flame. She supposed that Sinha's death was merely a minor perturbance in the lives of lifelong bureaucrats. The day-to-day governance of a region meandered on even when the governor of that region had, quite literally, lost his head.

They followed Templeton into the building's interior and to the desk of a youngish Naga that he introduced simply as Samuel. The round-faced – and round-bellied – youth was dressed in a cream-coloured suit and a tie that appeared to be garrotting him. A nose you could plough a field with graced a smooth-skinned face, marred only by a moustache that looked like a failed horticultural experiment. Unfortunate features aside, Samuel quickly understood the task at hand, rising to the challenge with the enthusiasm of a frisky terrier.

'What you are looking for will be in our records room,' he announced, leading them onwards into the depths of the building. 'Fortunately, most of those records were removed from the old storeroom for safekeeping before it was destroyed during the war.'

Minutes later, they had been led into a small space crowded with ancient wooden filing cabinets, the sort that looked as if they might crumble to dust just by looking at them. '*Un*fortunately, the cataloguing system leaves much to be desired. It's one of the tasks on my list. There are never enough hands.' He grinned apologetically.

'I'm afraid I must leave you to it,' said Templeton. 'I have work to attend to.'

'I'd like to talk to you once I'm done,' said Persis.

He seemed displeased with the notion, but nodded. 'I'll be in my office.'

It took them several hours to find anything useful.

Sifting through the files in each cabinet – records that appeared to have been filed by a drunken illiterate – they found tiny insects crawling out at them, and clouds of dust assaulting their nasal passages.

'What exactly are we looking for?' asked James.

'Anything to do with Sinha's time here some twenty years ago.'

They waded through endless minutes of endless meetings, minuted at times by typewriter, at times by handwriting so illegible it might as well have been ink flicked randomly on to paper. They scanned local reports, land agreements, legal disputes, building ordinances, purchase orders, expense filings, account ledgers, and administrative chits by the bushel.

The day had drifted into afternoon by the time James broke the silence. 'I think I have something.'

Persis set down the manila folder she had been examining and walked across to him.

He held out a paper. She took it, saw that it was the frontispiece to an ethnographic survey of the Naga Hills – dated January 1930 – a survey commissioned by a Mohan Sinha, Special Advisor to the Tribes and Backwards Classes of the Naga Hills District.

So that was what Sinha had been doing here. He had served as the ruling British authority's liaison in the region, mapping the local tribes. That explained why Nehru had sent him back, two decades later, a successful politician seemingly banished to the nation's troubled hinterland. She doubted that Sinha would have been happy with the assignment. But, sometimes, a job well done could work against you.

Together, they went through the remaining records, hunting for Sinha's work in the role of special advisor to the Naga tribes. They found records pertaining to the extensive survey he had carried out, population censuses, economic reports, and information that bordered on intelligence assessments: the military capability – and disposition – of the various tribes that made up the hills.

'Look at this.' James handed her a folder. Inside was a newspaper article, dated 1929, detailing a rebuttal to a 'Naga memorandum to the Simon Commission'.

'What am I looking at?'

'Back in 1929, a group of prominent Naga calling themselves the Naga Club wrote to the Simon Commission, a delegation sent to India by the British government to examine potential constitutional reform. They detailed their objection to a post-colonial, independent India that included the Naga Hills. They wanted the British government to acknowledge that when the British finally left India, the Naga would be strongly opposed to their homeland being merged with India.' He looked at her. 'Every Naga knows about the memorandum. It set the tone for the idea of an independent *Nagalim*. The British responded to the document by declaring the Naga Hills an "Excluded Area". This angered mainland Indians fighting to get rid of British rule. Sinha expressed some of their views in his rebuttal to the memorandum, namely that the Naga could not possibly govern themselves. They were too divided, too dependent, too poor to pay for their own administration.'

She scanned the article. 'His response is scathing. He seems to regard the Naga as children, asking for a freedom that was neither practical nor thought through. His tone is patronising. I suspect he would have angered many.'

'Undoubtedly.'

'Which means that when he returned here, two decades later, there may have been some who harboured a grudge.'

They continued searching. An hour later, Persis unearthed a packet of photographs in an envelope wrapped in an elastic band. She flicked through the photos, dozens of black-and-white shots of Sinha's interactions with the many tribes of the Naga Hills. One photograph snagged her eye. It showed Sinha, dressed in a crisp suit, standing beside several tribal leaders – in traditional outfits and holding native weapons – daos and spears. Standing beside Sinha was a tall white man in a safari suit, instantly familiar.

Oren Rake. The American miner.

His hair was darker and his face not as lean as it now was. But Rake's brooding and gruffly handsome aspect was unmistakable. What was he doing in a twenty-year-old photograph with their murder victim? She knew that Rake had been mining the hills for years, but why had he failed to mention that his relationship with Sinha went back all the way to the politician's original deployment to the region?

'Here, take a look at this.' James stepped across and handed her a letter, typed. Stapled to the letter were several sheets, constituting a report. Much of the report had been redacted.

Persis scanned the letter and the attached paperwork. Together, they made up a complaint by the Naga Club about the death of a young Naga named Aaron Koza in early 1930. Koza had died in police custody. The police claimed he had died by his own hand. The circumstances of Koza's death were unclear – too much of the report had been redacted. But, from what little remained, it was obvious that Mohan Sinha had been approached to deal with the matter. His response had failed to satisfy the member of the Naga Club who had initiated the complaint, a man by the name of Bartholomew Sema.

'And this.' James handed her another document. The document detailed Sinha's transfer to another branch of the Indian Civil Service, and his subsequent move back to Calcutta. The transfer took place within two weeks of the date on the final letter in the documentation regarding the death of Aaron Koza.

Persis raised an eyebrow. 'It looks as if Sinha's superiors were none too happy with the way he handled this young man's death.'

'Agreed.'

'Do you know anything about the case itself? Have you heard of Koza?'

'No. I was just a boy then.'

'It may be nothing, completely unrelated to Sinha's killing. But it's worth following up. Good work.'

They returned to their labours, stopping only for a quick meal in the dining room. They ate quickly, discussing various theories, discarding them as quickly as they arose.

'I still don't see how anyone could have got into a locked room,' said James.

'Nevertheless, someone did.' She met his eye. 'Your tattoos, do they mean something?' And in her mind's eye: the muscled contours of his naked torso. She looked down at her plate.

It was a moment before James replied. 'We walk a strange tightrope out here. On the one side we have India and the modern world. On the other the traditions we grow up with. My parents were committed Christians. But that didn't mean they had forgotten their roots. Our tattoos pay respect to our ancestors, to the old ways. In the old days, warriors would be tattooed for each head they took.' He gave a wry grin. 'More importantly, they speak to our deep connection with nature and the kingdom beyond the visible. They are part of our collective identity, a common language. They tell our story.'

17

They completed their task deep into the afternoon.

Persis left her deputy to tidy up, and went in search of John Templeton.

She found him in an office at the rear of the premises. Templeton had a stack of files at his elbow and appeared to be methodically working his way through them, pen in hand.

'What do you know of the Naga Club? And Mohan Sinha's involvement with them?'

Templeton set down his pen. 'A bit before my time, Inspector. As far as I can make out the Naga Club was formed by a group of Naga who served together in the First World War, in theatres beyond India. When they returned to the hills, they banded together to set out their desire for a separate Naga homeland in the eventuality that the British would be ousted from the subcontinent.'

'And they wrote to the Simon Commission back in 1929 expressing that view.'

'Yes.'

'But Sinha stood against that view, and responded publicly to that effect.'

'Correct. And his view has never deviated. He believed in a united India. Then, and now.'

'But it's not inconceivable that he made enemies back then?'

'He was an administrator towing the party line in a region beset by unrest. Enemies, as I have already said, came with the territory.'

She changed tack. 'What do you know of an Aaron Koza?'

His brow furrowed. 'I haven't come across the name.'

She explained the case, showed him the paperwork. 'There's not much information here. Someone has gone to great pains to redact the details. Did Sinha ever mention him?'

'No.' A pause. 'How is this relevant?'

'I'm not sure that it is. But I want to chase down the details.'

'Then I suggest you ask those behind the complaint. The members of the Naga Club. Though, of course, they're not called that any more.' She waited for him to elaborate. 'In 1945 the Naga Hills District Tribal Council replaced the Naga Club. A year after that they became the Naga National Council. For a while, the NNC dropped their demand for complete independence, instead arguing for autonomy within a post-colonial India. But after the war those demands became secessionist. In 1947, the NNC declared their own independence from Britain, a day before India officially became independent. They had the notion that they could carve out their own nation, out here in the north-east.' His lips twisted. 'Inevitably, violence ensued. The problem with the Naga is that they don't know when they're beaten.'

'Where can I find this Naga National Council?'

'They maintain offices here, in town.'

She jotted down the address on her notepad. 'I have some questions for you. Personal ones.'

His face became wary.

'How would you characterise your relationship with Sinha?'

He seemed taken aback. 'What do you mean? He was my boss. I worked for him.'

'Did you ever disagree?'

'No. He made the decisions. I was his aide.'

'Was he unhappy with your work?'

'No.' The word came out with a hint of vehemence that raised her antennae. He seemed to realise this, added, 'We had a good working relationship.'

'But no personal relationship? You didn't socialise?'

'Not really. I mean, we ate together on occasion,' he added, limply.

'Did you find it awkward, taking orders from an Indian?'

'Your question says more about you than it does about me, Inspector.' She waited. 'It was my choice to stay in India after independence. I have never had an issue with the country or its people. Not every Englishman was Clive of India.'

'You said that on the night Sinha was killed you were alone in your room.'

'Yes.'

'But no one can verify that.'

'That's what alone means.' He checked his watch. 'If there are no more questions, I have work to attend to.'

'Just one last question ... Do *you* sympathise with the Naga cause?'

He blinked behind his spectacles. 'No. Of course not. And calling it the *Naga* cause is a misnomer. Many Naga have no desire for independence.'

'And Baba Dao?'

'What about him?'

'I showed you the note that I found in Sinha's office. "*Nagalim will never be yours. Leave now. Or die.*" You seemed to dismiss it. So I ask you again, could Baba Dao be involved in Sinha's murder?'

'Baba Dao is a guerrilla leader intent on causing as much disruption as he can. Sooner or later the authorities will capture him and he will be made an example of.'

Persis persisted with her line of questioning. 'Do you think he could have influenced one of the guests at the Hotel Victoria? Somehow convinced them to murder Sinha on his behalf?'

His eyes widened. 'That scarcely sounds probable.'

'But not entirely implausible.'

He said nothing, face troubled.

She stood. 'There are only two facts of which I can be certain. Mohan Sinha *was* murdered that night. And there were only five of you in the hotel at the time whose movements I cannot account for at the time of the murder. We'll talk again.'

18

The Kohima station broiled in the late-afternoon heat.

Seth was behind his desk, James seated opposite him. The commander swilled ice around a glass of what looked like water but could just as easily have been something stronger. 'I should stick an apple in my mouth and crawl inside an oven. It would be cooler than this.'

Persis took off her cap, sat down beside her deputy, then brought Seth up to speed on the investigation. He listened impatiently, fidgeting in his seat. When she had finished, he said, 'I thought it might be different out here. A quiet backwater. No one hounding me for results, threatening to do unspeakable things to me should I fail. Instead, I've got the country's senior-most police commissioner calling me from Delhi demanding to know why I haven't solved an impossible case in a matter of minutes. Meanwhile, Shroff is ramping up for World War Three. How do you think Baba Dao and his merry band of insurgents will respond once the colonel starts bulldozing his way around the jungle? "Father of knives". Hah! If I were ever to be given a nickname I would want it to be "father of boredom".' A grimace. 'And now here you are telling me we're no further forward in figuring out what actually happened to Sinha.'

'It's a complex investigation. It will take as long as it takes.'

He fixed her with a jaundiced eye. 'Let's just hope I haven't been sacked or blown up by an insurgent's grenade by the time you get around to solving it.'

Persis turned to James. 'Something Templeton said – or rather didn't say – has been bothering me. I have the feeling that there might have been trouble in paradise.'

'I don't understand.'

'I think his relationship with Sinha might not have been as harmonious as he maintains. I want you to dig into his background. Until a few years ago, he worked for the Indian Civil Service in Calcutta. Start there.'

James nodded, pulled a notebook from his pocket, scrawled inside it. She realised that the notebook was a new addition to his arsenal, wondered if he had seen her do the same and decided to emulate her. The thought ignited an unexpected blush of vanity.

Seth broke into the sudden silence. 'Makes you think, doesn't it? If you're right, one of your guests at the Hotel Victoria somehow got into Sinha's room and cut off his head. Someone who, in any other context, we might consider "civilised".' He sighed. 'A quiet life. Is it too much to ask?'

She left Seth's office, found Constable Joshua Binny at his desk in the outer office, rolling a thin cheroot with the practised concentration of a watchmaker. A chicken sat on the desk observing his labours with an expression of cocked interest.

As Persis loomed over him, Binny raised his head, then slowly lumbered to his feet.

'How long have you been a cop in Kohima?'

'Well, that would be a long time now. Why do you ask?'

'Did you know that Sinha was out here some twenty years ago?'

He raised an eyebrow. 'No. But then, my memory is not what it once was. And I spent several years stationed in Dimapur.'

'He worked for the British, served as some sort of special advisor to the local tribes. He was only here for a short while; perhaps that's why you don't recall him.'

He shrugged. The chicken clucked gently.

Persis realised that short of picking the man up by the ankles and banging his head on the floor she was unlikely to jog his memory. 'I have a task for you. While he was here back in 1930, Sinha was approached to deal with the death of a local by the name of Aaron Koza. Koza died in police custody. I presume that a report of the incident would have been made. Where would we find records from back then?'

Binny pulled at his ear. 'All the old records will be here.' He nodded at a door at the rear of the station. 'The problem is there was a fire at the old stationhouse. Not to mention flooding on several occasions. And then there are the rats, of course. We saved what we could.'

She had the sudden urge to scream. But it seemed pointless. 'Have a look anyway.'

'Yes, madam.'

As she turned away, she stopped, looked back. 'Do you realise there's a chicken on your desk?'

'Yes, madam.'

'Dare I ask why?'

'I think she likes me.'

19

In Bombay, a one-armed man juggling melons would scarcely have attracted a second glance. In a town as new – and as starved of street theatre – as Kohima, a small crowd had gathered.

The juggler, a wizened homunculus resplendent in ragged shorts and a sweat-stained silk shirt, grinned toothlessly at his audience, all the while flinging his train of melons higher and higher, solitary hand a hummingbird blur, cracked voice providing a running commentary.

Behind the man's shoulder rose a ferocious-looking building, built seemingly of timber, with a gabled roof topped by a pair of enormous crossed daos made of wood.

Persis parked her jeep across the road, just yards from the master of melons.

The address John Templeton had given her for the Naga National Council had brought her to the centre of town, and a busy thoroughfare that flattered to deceive. Lined with hastily erected office buildings, it petered out quickly into a run of cheap boarding houses, bars, and eateries. The NNC building stood out on the street, a peacock nestled in the midst of a line-up of crows. Its architectural extravagance extended to a fresh coat of paint and a sentry in tribal costume dozing on a wooden stool by the door.

As Persis approached, an automatic reflex actuated his knees, catapulting him to his feet. He brandished his spear and muttered a few words in Nagamese.

Persis ignored the theatrics and walked past him and through the open doorway.

Inside, she discovered a young woman sitting behind a long wooden counter. Persis explained the reason for her visit and was asked to wait as the receptionist vanished through a door behind the counter.

She allowed her eyes to wander around the room. The walls of the reception bore blown-up photographs of Naga – both in tribal dress and in modern outfits – in the company of non-Naga, both white and Indian. Many of the photographs had been taken out in the hills and reminded her of the photograph of Oren Rake and Mohan Sinha standing together in a tribal setting some two decades earlier.

The receptionist returned and Persis was duly led through the premises to an office bearing a brass plaque with the legend *Deputy Chairman, Naga National Council.*

Inside, she was met by a small, middle-aged man dressed in herringbone tweed. The suit's jacket hung on a coatrack, but the tie was pinned neatly to a pristine white shirt by a gold tiepin. 'Inspector, my name is Levi Rengma. I understand that you are heading up the investigation into the death of Mohan Sinha?'

'Murder.'

'I'm sorry?'

'The murder of Mohan Sinha. Not death.'

He offered a wan smile. 'Quite. Do have a seat. Would you like something to drink? Tea, perhaps?'

She thought about declining, then changed her mind. 'Something cold?'

In short order, two glasses of lemonade arrived. Rengma made a show of sipping at his, then said, 'What is it that you think I might be able to help you with?'

'Tell me a little about the NNC.'

Rengma settled into his seat. This was an amiable start to what might prove a difficult conversation. 'The NNC evolved from the original Naga Club, a group of Naga patriots who saw the opportunity for a united Naga nation once the British were sent on their way. Our mission is simple: to fight for the independence of the Naga Hills.'

'Fight? By any means necessary?'

'I take it you are insinuating that we were somehow involved in Sinha's murder? I'm afraid I must disabuse you of that notion. We are a peaceful organisation. Our principles are Gandhian. We seek regional autonomy through non-violent means.'

'And yet, an armed struggle, led by Baba Dao, has been ongoing for several years. The insurgents are fighting for the NNC's cause, a cause diametrically in opposition to Sinha's remit here. You would have me believe there was no animosity? No ill will?'

'I did not say there was no animosity. I dare say that few Naga will shed tears for Sinha. But the NNC has never advocated for an armed struggle against the Centre. Nor did we wish for Sinha's removal. His killing achieves nothing. Delhi will simply send someone else. Indeed, Sinha's murder has provided the perfect excuse for a ramped-up military operation in the region. One might almost say that whoever killed the man did Nehru's government a favour.'

Persis said nothing.

Rengma reached into his desk, took out a packet of cigarettes, lit one. 'You're from Bombay, aren't you? I've followed your story in the newspapers. India's famous woman police officer. When I heard that you were coming to the Naga Hills I was astounded. What could a well-known officer such as yourself want out here? I surmised that perhaps you had fallen foul of powers with the ability to determine your destiny – quite probably through no fault of your own. *That* is the position we Naga find ourselves in.'

He sighed. 'I suppose it is difficult for someone from a city as cosmopolitan as Bombay to understand. But the Naga have a distinct identity. India will swallow us, change us, until we become unrecognisable to ourselves.'

She bristled at his words, at the implied insult to the city of her birth. He realised his misstep. 'I have offended you. That was not my intent. But you, like Mohan Sinha, represent the Centre. You could not possibly understand our struggle.'

'Do you condemn the insurrection?'

He offered her a bloodless smile in reply. 'That is a very clumsy question and you do not strike me as a clumsy woman. For the record, I condemn all violence in this conflict – on both sides. Off the record: I may not approve of Baba Dao's methods, but he's fighting our fight.'

'By killing innocents.'

'There are no innocents in war, Inspector. Have you any idea what is happening out in the hills? The reports are supressed. But word gets back to us. Shroff's soldiers have killed innocents. Torture is commonplace. Is it any surprise that the insurgents respond in kind?' Smoke rose around the man's hooded features.

'Do you know who he is? Baba Dao?'

'No. And if I did, I would not tell you.'

'Delhi has labelled him a terrorist. If they find him, they'll make an example of him.'

'Death comes to us all. What better way to die than fighting for your homeland? We Naga have a saying: "a small bird can give birth to an eagle". The hills are small, but in Baba Dao we have given birth to an eagle.'

'Why are you so convinced that being part of India will be detrimental to the Naga?'

'If history has taught us anything it is that whenever a dominant culture imposes its will on a smaller populace, it is the latter that is inevitably destroyed. Annihilation by assimilation, that is the choice we face.'

Persis reached into her pocket, unfolded the report she had discovered pertaining to the death of Aaron Koza, explained what she was looking for.

'I am afraid this is before my time,' said Rengma. 'But, reading between the lines, it is obvious what has happened. Aaron Koza paid the price for dreaming of an independent Naga nation.'

'You believe he was murdered for his political views?'

'He wouldn't be the first.'

'What can you tell me about the man who made the complaint following his death? Bartholomew Sema?'

'The name is familiar. As I recall, he was one of our founding members.' Rengma picked up a telephone, spoke animatedly with someone on the other end. Setting the receiver down, he crushed his cigarette in an ivory ashtray set beside the telephone. 'That was our archivist. I have asked him to check our records for Sema's whereabouts. He retired years ago and I am not certain where he might be.'

Some twenty minutes later, the archivist arrived and handed Persis a chit on which was scrawled an address.

'Mokokchung,' she read aloud.

'It's a good way north of Kohima.' Rengma's lips pursed. 'I hope Sema will be of help to you if you do find him. Sadly, there are many Aaron Kozas now. Young men caught up in the violence. Punished for sins they have yet to commit. India mourns for Mohan Sinha. But who mourns for the Aaron Kozas of the world?'

20

Driving up the winding hill road back to the Hotel Victoria, Persis became conscious of the dramatic silhouette made by the hotel against a low-hanging moon. A photographer's dream.

She slid the jeep to a halt, stepped outside, allowed the jungle silence to settle over her. Leaning against the vehicle, she closed her eyes, and focused on the case. A confusion of facts marched along the forest floor of her mind like army ants, devouring everything in their path. She forced herself to impose order, channel the marching ants into straight lines.

What did she know? What did she *need* to know?

Mohan Sinha, the politico in charge of the Naga Hills region, had been murdered inside a locked room at the Hotel Victoria. His head – and the murder weapon – had yet to be located, despite an extensive search of the premises. It had been all but impossible for anyone outside the hotel to have entered the place around the time of the murder, narrowing the cast of suspects down to the hotel's guests and staff. The skeleton crew of staff had strong alibis. The guests less so.

John Templeton, Oren Rake, Christopher and Florence Danvers, and Maria Fontanelli. The circumstances suggested that one of them had murdered Sinha. The question was: why? And, indeed, how? It was rare for a murder investigation not to be able to determine the exact means by which a killing had taken place. It added a measure of the surreal to an already complex investigation.

Persis's short but eventful experience on the force had taught her that, in any given crime, motive was the key. What motive could any of these individuals have had to murder the regional governor?

The Danvers claimed that Mohan Sinha had, following a lengthy delay, finally given them permission to take their Baptist mission into the hills. But Colonel Shroff had refuted that idea. Were the Danvers telling the truth? And, if not, did the refusal of a permit constitute a compelling enough motive for murder?

And Oren Rake, the American miner. Why had he failed to mention the fact that he had known Sinha some two decades earlier, during the man's previous tenure in the region? Back then, Sinha had served as a special advisor to the Naga tribes. A young local named Aaron Koza had died under contentious circumstances; Sinha had been approached about the matter but had clearly mishandled the situation, and, as a consequence, been sent packing back to Calcutta. Did the Koza affair hold any significance in Sinha's death more than twenty years later?

She focused next on the journalist, Maria Fontanelli. On the face of it, the Italian had no reason to wish Sinha harm. She had arrived in the hills to report on the ongoing insurgency. The fact that she now had a far more explosive story on her hands was surely only a matter of coincidence. The woman was ambitious, but not even the most ambitious reporter would create their own headlines by murdering their subject.

Lastly, there was John Templeton, Sinha's aide. The man seemed genuinely upset by his employer's death. But looks could be deceiving.

And there was other evidence. The charred photograph she had found in Sinha's suite, of a young woman – possibly white – in a much younger Sinha's company. What was it doing there? Why had it been burned – presumably by Sinha – on the very evening of his death? Who was the woman? With only half of her face remaining an identity would be difficult to determine. On the back of the photo: *Calcutta, 1923* and the cut-off word *Sin—* A reference to Sinha, of course. Perhaps the woman's name too had been scrawled on the card, now burned away?

There was also the note inside Sinha's desk, the death threat. Could the note have come from Baba Dao, leader of the insurgency, a man who had made it his life's mission to oppose the Centre? Might he have convinced one of the guests at the hotel to act as his proxy? To murder Sinha in his name? The missing head seemed a tangible link to a Naga killer. Then again, that might be a distraction, an attempt by the real killer to deflect scrutiny by clumsily pointing towards a tribal perpetrator?

And, finally, there was the unmade bed. A minor detail but one that continued to bother her. She had confirmed with the hotel staff that the bed had indeed been made that morning. John Templeton claimed that Sinha was not the kind of man to nap after returning from work – so why was the bed in disarray?

There was enough here to occupy a team of investigators. But all she had at her disposal was an inexperienced sub-inspector, and an aging constable whose desk served as a chicken roost.

She got back into the jeep and continued up the hill.

21

Having showered and changed, Persis made her way to the dining room where she found Maria Fontanelli seated at a table set before the room's longcase clock.

'May I join you?'

'Of course. I've only just sat down.'

They ordered. 'Wine, madam?' the waiter asked, picking up a bottle.

Persis nodded, watched the glass as he poured.

'I should warn you, the wine is from the hotel's cellar,' said Fontanelli. 'It's not great. But one has to show willing.' She beamed brightly. 'So . . . how is your investigation going?'

'You don't really expect me to speak about the case?'

'Isn't that why you sat down here? So you can ask *me* questions? It's only fair that there's a certain quid pro quo.'

'That's not how this works. You're a suspect in my investigation. *I* ask the questions. You answer. We can do it here, or I can take you to the stationhouse.'

The Italian tossed back her head to let loose a mellifluous laugh. Light bounced from a long stretch of olive-skinned throat. Fontanelli's black hair was cut short, to the shoulders, and her green eyes crinkled in mirth. She wore a white satin blouse with dagger collars above jodhpur-style trousers, looked ready to step on to the set of a film about the wayward daughter of a ruthless shipping magnate. 'I've never been a suspect in anything before. Fire away.'

'Let's start with the night of Sinha's murder. Where were you that evening, from nine forty to eleven?'

'I had dinner here, and then I went to my room. I had a story to file and I was up late working on it.'

'What sort of story?'

'A background piece. A romantic vision of the Naga Hills, prior to the British arrival. A lost civilisation, untouched by the outside world. That sort of thing.'

'The Naga weren't lost. They knew exactly where – and who – they were.'

'And then the Europeans arrived and everything went to hell. I've heard it all before, Inspector. I'm a journalist. I don't make the news. I report it.'

Persis picked up her glass. 'Were you alone in your room?'

'Not many eligible males in the vicinity. So, yes.'

'Did you have any previous interactions with Sinha?'

'No. Though I had been trying to get a meeting with him ever since I arrived out here.'

'Why?'

'Why do you think? I wanted to interview him. He's the man at the heart of everything. Or was.'

'Did it bother you that he refused to meet with you?'

'He didn't refuse. He was too busy. Which, reading between the lines, meant that things weren't going too well and he had no desire to expose himself to a journalist.'

'You're referring to Sinha's attempts to quell the insurgency?'

'Insurgency is the term your government uses. But to many Naga their call for independence is a political movement.'

'Baba Dao doesn't appear to be canvassing locals with political rhetoric. He prefers throwing bombs around.'

'A man who understands the power of a headline. Now, if I could just get an interview with *him* ...' Her eyes blazed. And then she noticed Persis's expression. 'You don't approve? I'm a female reporter trying make a name for herself in an industry dominated by men. Very few things make the front page. Sex. Scandal. Murder. Sinha's killing, the insurgency, Baba Dao – these are the things our subscribers pay to read about. I would have hoped that you, of all people, could understand that.'

The waiter arrived with their food, a pasta dish for Fontanelli and a poached haddock for Persis. She suspected the fish had made its way up to the landlocked interior from Calcutta.

'I had nothing to do with Sinha's death,' said the Italian, picking up a fork, 'I needed him alive. Though, I grant you, his murder has proved a boon. I filed a story yesterday that had my editor on one knee begging to marry me. How often is a reporter present at ground zero when something like this happens?'

The woman's zealousness troubled Persis. 'You do realise a man has lost his life? In the most horrendous circumstances?'

'In the most *incredible* circumstances. A locked room murder! The staple of mystery fiction.' She skewered an olive, popped it into her mouth. 'Tell me, do you have any theories about *how* the killing might have been carried out? My readers would love to know.'

Persis picked up her own cutlery, attacked her fish. 'Where are you from in Italy?'

'Cortona. It's a small town in Tuscany. We've been around since the time of the Romans.'

'Family?'

'I'm an only child. My father is a baker.'

Persis met the woman's gaze. 'I lost my mother when I was seven.'

'I know. I read it in a profile piece. And your father runs a bookstore.'

'Yes. In the same way that a knight runs a castle. He views customers as the barbarian horde.'

'Sounds a lot like *my* father. A customer once made the mistake of insulting his focaccia. My father chased him along the city walls with a crossbow.'

'You said you'd been deputed from elsewhere?'

'I'm based in Calcutta. I write for the *Gazette*.'

'When did you come to India?'

'Some six weeks ago.'

'Why India?'

'Why not? I've always loved the idea of travelling through the east. Following in the footsteps of Marco Polo.'

Persis swallowed a mouthful of fish, then set down her fork. 'Did you see or hear anything that evening that might have a connection to Sinha's death?'

'I'm afraid not.'

'Did you see him in the hotel that day?'

'No. As I'm sure you know, he wasn't in the habit of mingling with the rest of us. Almost always ate in his room.'

'I suppose you'd tried knocking on his door? In pursuit of your interview?'

'Once. When I first arrived. But I was gently rebuffed by his aide, and warned not to try again or I would be sent packing from the hotel.' Fontanelli draped an arm elegantly over the back of her chair, raised her fork with her other hand. 'Kohima will soon be crawling with my peers. Each one in search of a story. Don't you think it would be better to have at least one of us on *your* side?'

Persis lifted her wineglass, took a large mouthful. The longcase clock chimed the hour. She focused on Fontanelli's expectant look. Something about the woman's face seemed abstractedly familiar. A thought tapped on the side of her brain demanding to be let in . . . The moment passed. 'I'm not used to needing anyone on my side.'

'Everyone needs an ally. And in a place like this . . . Well, let's just say I've always believed in that old adage, "two heads are better than one". Especially when they're female.'

Persis smiled, and picked up her fork.

It was as she was climbing up to her room that she was blindsided by another thought that had long been struggling to make itself heard.

When she had first searched Mohan Sinha's suite, the bed had been unmade. She had asked herself why? Now, she felt she had the first glimmer of an answer.

On the night of his murder, Sinha had arrived at the hotel late in the evening and gone to his room. Around an hour later, his evening meal had been brought up to him. Had he decided to nap during that hour? It seemed highly unlikely, a man renowned for being an insomniac. Besides, his aide claimed Sinha *never* napped. So then why was the bed unmade?

There was only one other explanation that made sense.

She continued up the stairs to Sinha's suite.

The guard sitting on a seat by the door rose awkwardly to his feet.

'Has anyone tried to enter these rooms since I put you on the door?'

'No, madam.'

She stepped into the suite, closed the door behind her. She stood a moment, passing her eye over the inert space. Nothing had changed since she had been in here previously. Stillness, and that strangely numinous feeling of disquiet that was the hallmark of any place where death had arrived unannounced and in violent temper.

She walked into the bedroom, began to search again, unsure of exactly what she was looking for, or what she might have missed the first time around.

Fifteen minutes later, she struck gold.

As she held the new evidence in her hand, a sense of shock reverberated through her. She was faced, once again, with the realisation that an investigation could turn on the simplest of discoveries, and that it was often not divine revelation, but a gradual accumulation of the mundane that led to the telling insight.

What was now obvious to her was that one of her suspects had lied.

And, in any investigation, the arrival of a lie often signalled the beginning of the road to resolution.

22

The road to Oren Rake's mining operation speared north out of Kohima, a fifty-mile stretch that, on a good day, would take three hours, ascending the flanks of a succession of ever higher and more remote hills, a terra incognita of deep jungle where not only did eagles fear to tread, but hid inside their eyries gibbering in terror at the prospect. Monsoon damage, the depredations of contractors, and the recent activities of insurgents made the winding route an obstacle course, and not one for the faint of heart.

Not that a small thing like a dangerously cratered road surface flowing beside a deadly drop seemed to faze her second-in-command, thought Persis.

She had handed over driving duties to James Angami who, for reasons best known to himself, had taken this as a sign that he had been selected to drive at Le Mans. Persis, holding on to the jeep's grabrail with a white-knuckled grip, looked out of the open window, teeth clenched, as her deputy raged into every hairpin bend, skirting ever closer to the tarmac's edge. Below, rusting metal corpses wedged in the branches of hillside trees made the world's ugliest Christmas decorations. She wondered if the skeletons of lost drivers had been left to rot down there, whether their passengers too had made the mistake of placing their trust in maniacs.

The morning had already proved eventful. Having been tasked with digging up more information about John Templeton, James had telephoned the Indian Civil Service office in Calcutta where he had been informed by a Saeed Malik – Templeton's former boss – that not only had John Templeton displayed an exemplary record during his years there, but no doubt would do so again now that he was returning to the fold.

'He's already found himself a post?' said Persis. 'With Sinha's body not even cool? So much for loyalty.'

'You misunderstand. According to Malik, Templeton had been in touch weeks *before* Sinha's death about returning to the ICS. When I explained the situation to the man – namely that Templeton was a suspect in Sinha's killing – he seemed taken aback. Reading between the lines, he now believes that Sinha had decided to let Templeton go.'

'Why would Templeton keep that from us?' Persis mused. There might well be an innocent explanation for the Englishman withholding such information, but she doubted it.

She next explained to her deputy the new evidence she had discovered during her impromptu search of Sinha's bedroom the night before. That she had had no opportunity to pursue that line of enquiry had been due to the fact that the suspect in question had been missing from the hotel. Both last night, and that morning.

'Do we need to put out an alert?' James asked.

'No. Not yet. Our suspect has no intimation of the new evidence. I doubt they've gone on the run. And we don't want to warn them off. I suspect they'll be back at the hotel soon enough.'

'You're taking quite a risk.'

'That's the job, isn't it?' Persis turned back to the open window. The new lines of investigation would have to wait. For now she had decided to press on and speak to another of those who had been present in the hotel the night of the murder: the American, Oren Rake, self-professed friend of the late and, seemingly, unlamented Mohan Sinha.

* * *

An hour later, the mine sprang out at them following a sudden bend in the road, a broad steel gate framed by a high archway from which hung a creaking signboard painted with the words: RAKE MINING CORPORATION.

A solitary guard sat beside the gate, picking at his teeth with a pocketknife.

They presented their credentials and the reason for their visit. The guard pointed with the knife, directing them inwards.

The jeep juddered along a bumpy access road until they arrived at a parking area crowded with dump trucks, flatbed haulers, and other mining vehicles. A flat-roofed office building rose from the earth beside the lot, surrounded by several rickety satellite buildings that looked as if they had been assembled by a hurricane.

Inside the office, they were met by a small Naga man in work shorts and a sweat-stained white shirt. He introduced himself as Adam Zhimomi and told them that he was the site manager. He wore a hard hat and a peppery beard. His eyes were sleepy and something about his movements seemed off. Persis wondered if they had disturbed the man after a long shift. Perhaps he had been enjoying a noon siesta before resuming his duties?

'We're here to see Oren Rake,' she said.

'Mr Rake is in shaft five. He will be some time.'

'In that case you'll have to take us to him.'

Zhimomi looked uncertain, but then an inbuilt deference to authority appeared to seize him, and he nodded, turning to lead them towards the mine proper.

They walked several hundred yards along a dusty road that curved around the side of the hill. A truck rumbled by and out of sight.

When they finally emerged on to the mine plateau, they found themselves standing on an apron of churned dirt, decorated with heaps of slag, on which were parked several more trucks. Around the site she noted the presence of heavy equipment and machinery that she could make nothing of: hooks and pulleys, rusted chains like the rigging of a ship, and other complicated mechanisms. In the near distance: a series of wooden huts, a temporary village erected for the site's workforce.

The truck nearest to them was mobbed by labourers loading coal by hand by means of enormous bamboo baskets. Persis was surprised to discover that the loaders were women, dressed in ragged saris, their faces coated in dust. Behind them, a succession of mine shaft openings made gaping mouths in the hillside, as if a drunken giant had decided to punch holes in the mountain.

Aside from the low rumbling of the truck, there was a strange soundlessness to the vista. Persis had the sense of a crime being committed and all involved doing their best to maintain a silence lest they alert the authorities.

Zhimomi led them up a winding dirt path towards one of the shafts.

At the entrance, Persis found herself hesitating. She looked behind her, saw the women had stopped their work and were watching her, ashen-faced acolytes following an Incan princess as she climbed stone steps to a sacrificial altar.

She followed the others into the shaft. Seconds later, the darkness had swallowed them.

Zhimomi led them to a pit lift.

Soon they were descending into the bowels of the earth.

Persis glanced at her deputy's face. James seemed unconcerned by their entry into the underworld. She wondered again at his time in the army. The things he had seen. The violence he had participated in. What did that do to a man?

The lift shrieked to a halt at the bottom of the shaft.

They spilled out into a lantern-lit darkness. Zhimomi allowed them a moment to gain their bearings, and then led them through a maze of tunnels crawling with Naga mine workers – men and women – bent double in the cramped conditions, blackened wraiths hacking at the coalface with pickaxes or pushing wheeled coal tubs up steep inclines or hauling eighty-pound baskets of hewed coal on their backs. Modern machinery was notable by its absence. This was coal mining as it had been done at the turn of the century: brute force and expendable human materiel. A sense of outrage slithered around her insides, at the notion that *anyone* should be forced to endure such an existence simply to put food on the table.

They found Oren Rake standing with another Naga, studying plans. The tall American looked like a giant in the tunnel, head practically scraping the tunnel roof, a fairy-tale ogre in a hard hat. Persis was surprised to discover that he spoke fluent Nagamese. And if he, in turn, was shocked to find the policewoman in his subterranean domain, he hid it well. 'Inspector. Why am I not entirely surprised to see you here?'

'I'd like to talk to you. About the night of Mohan Sinha's death.'

'And it couldn't wait?'

'I told you not to leave the hotel. You ignored me.'

'I have a business to run. I had nothing to do with Mohan's death and I don't know anything that might help you.'

'You said he was your friend. I'd have thought you would wish to assist us in any way we saw fit.'

He looked down at her, gaze hawkish. 'Step this way.' He led them to a tunnel mouth further along, lit by a solitary lantern hanging from a timber support. As he approached, Zhimomi spoke up. 'Sir. That tunnel isn't safe. The roof beams have rotted through. We haven't replaced them yet.'

'It's only for a few minutes.'

The four of them entered the tunnel, Rake and his site manager, Persis and her deputy. She saw that James's face had taken on a starched aspect. With a flash of insight, she realised that, like her, he had never been in the mines, had never seen his fellow Naga toiling in this hellish environment. In the event, it was the sub-inspector who spoke first, the words propelled out of him. 'How do you justify working them in such conditions? Why aren't they using modern tools?'

Rake seemed taken aback by the unexpected attack, but rallied quickly. 'Have you any idea what it costs to bring heavy equipment into the hills? I use the tools to hand. Men and muscle.'

'And women,' said Persis.

The American raised his chin. 'Yes, I use women. The government made it lawful during the war. They couldn't get enough coal to power the war effort. I give these women opportunity. I put money in their pockets. You, of all people, should be able to appreciate that.'

She bristled at his wrongheadedness. 'How many die down here? In the dirt and the darkness?'

'Yes, we lose people. Flooding. Gas fires. Roof falls. Mother Nature is a fierce adversary. But here's the thing. The more of them I lose, the more turn up here begging for work. Back in the States the unions are killing the mining industry. Damned Commie agitators. But here, I can do whatever the hell I want.'

'As long as you keep the coal flowing.' James's bitterness was a wasp in the darkness.

'Now you're catching on.'

'And how did Mohan Sinha fit into this?' said Persis.

'He represented the Centre. Whatever I needed – bureaucratically speaking – it was his job to provide.'

'Is that why you were at the Hotel Victoria?'

'One reason, sure.'

'Did you meet with him that day? The day of his death.'

'As a matter of fact, we met at his offices. In Kohima. A very productive meeting. We discussed opening up another mining operation, a few clicks east of here.'

'Are you certain he was cooperative? My understanding is that the Centre has been less than keen to allow foreigners to operate in the hills. Attitudes have changed since independence.'

Rake narrowed his eyes. 'I built this operation from nothing. I'm not about to let the Indian government steal it out from under me.'

'Did Sinha try to steal it from you?'

'Mohan Sinha was my friend. We had an understanding.' His lips twisted into a cobra smile. 'If you're sniffing around for motive, you won't find one.'

'Did you see Sinha later that evening? At the hotel?'

'I did not.'

'Where were you between nine forty and eleven?'

'I got back to the hotel around seven, had a shower, then a drink in the bar, then something to eat. And then I went back to my room. And then, later, as I recall, I was out on the veranda with you.' A beat. 'I had no reason to want the man dead. You're barking up the wrong tree.'

'You say Sinha was your friend. Did he confide in you? Did he ever mention the Danvers?'

'The Danvers?' He grunted. 'He didn't much care for them. They'd been hounding him for that damned permit. He was taking his time signing off on it.'

'Why?'

'Because the Indian government is highly suspicious of Baptist missionaries. They think they're working to set the eastern tribes against them.'

'Do you think Sinha suspected them of sympathising with the insurgency?' James had spoken up.

'I have no idea.'

'Could they have murdered Sinha on behalf of Baba Dao?' persisted Persis.

Rake snorted. 'The Danvers are missionaries, hardly assassins. Besides, the insurgents are an uncoordinated rabble. Shroff will snuff them out soon enough. Killing Mohan was a big mistake.'

'The Danvers are fellow Americans,' said Persis. 'Yet you seem to have a low opinion of them.'

'Not my kind of Americans. I'm afraid God and I have never seen eye to eye. Anyway, it's not the Danvers you should be looking at. It's that aide of his, Templeton. I'm a good judge of men, Inspector, and *there's* a man I wouldn't trust even if he told me my name was Oren.'

'Why?'

'Something Mohan said. About not recognising him for what he was.'

'What did he mean by that?'

'I don't know. He clammed up after he'd said it.'

She glanced at James, then said, 'Did you know that Sinha had, in all likelihood, decided to dismiss Templeton?'

'No. But it doesn't surprise me.'

Persis looked away, her gaze swallowed by the pitch-black maw of the tunnel as it stretched away into darkness. When she looked back she saw that Rake was watching her curiously. 'You knew Sinha when he was out here two decades ago. Why didn't you mention it?'

His cheek twitched. 'Yeah, I knew him. What of it?'

'*How* did you know him?'

'He was sent out here by the British as some sort of liaison to the tribes. I'd already been out in the hills a few years. I knew the tribes. He asked me to show him around. And so I did. We hit it off.'

'He was removed from the hills following the death of a young native named Aaron Koza.'

Rake's face betrayed nothing. 'Am I supposed to know who that is?'

'A Naga boy who died under mysterious circumstances back in 1930. A complaint was sent to Sinha, as tribal liaison. Did he ever talk to you about Koza? Then? Or more recently?'

'No.'

'Sinha's mishandling of Koza's death might have had him sent back to Calcutta. You say he was your friend. And yet he never discussed it with you?'

'I told you I've never heard the name before.'

She took out the half-burned photograph she had found on Sinha's desk. 'Does *this* mean anything to you? You knew Sinha when he was much younger. Who is the woman he's sitting with?'

He looked down at the picture. 'I have no idea who the woman is. But, yeah, that's Mohan.'

She allowed a beat, then: 'What kind of man was he?'

'He was a tough sonofabitch. You wouldn't think so to look at him. But the man made his bones in Calcutta politics. I've seen snakes run for cover down there.'

'Was he close to anyone else? Did he confide in anyone?'

'Mohan was a loner. Oh, he was married, did the dutiful thing. Had a couple of kids. But he spent a lot of time away from home, if you catch my drift. He liked female company. Just not always his wife. Frankly speaking, he didn't much trust women. Can't say I blame him.'

She raised an eyebrow. 'You're married?'

'Divorced. She took the house. I took my life back.' His guffaw was a rifleshot in the darkness.

A voice hailed them from the mouth of the tunnel. 'Excuse me,' Rake said.

She watched him stride abruptly out of the tunnel, brushing past her deputy, who turned to follow.

She found herself replaying the American's words. Could he be trusted? The man seemed cagey, overly confident of his answers . . . A sound turned her head. She peered deeper into the darkness inside the tunnel, found herself moving unconsciously towards the sound. Another sound now, deeper, threatening . . . She realised that the sound wasn't coming from up ahead, but above.

Everything happened in a rush.

She heard the site manager, Zhimomi, cry out: 'Madam!' A moment later, he crashed into her, bearing them both along the tunnel, an instant before the roof came down on them.

The last thing she would later remember seeing, outlined in the tunnel mouth, was James Angami, staring open-mouthed, as she was buried beneath the mountain.

23

'We have to get back in there!'

Dust swirled in the air, as thick as swarming midges.

James coughed into the darkness. The world was still spinning. Falling debris had struck him; he was bleeding – a constellation of cuts and grazes marked his face and arms – but he had escaped the worst of it.

'Are you insane?' Rake was breathing heavily beside him. 'This entire section is unstable. It could come down at any moment. We need to get out and let it settle. Then we shore it back up. That's going to take time.'

'I'm not leaving without Persis.'

'If she's still alive, we're not going to be much use to her if we're buried down here with her.'

Another rumble sounded above them. A shiver of dust rained down.

James peered desperately into the wall of rubble before him, seeking an entry point. Feeble light from a single unbroken lantern picked out misshapen lumps of rock and timber stanchions interred in the mass. His heart hammered against his ribcage; terror – not for himself, but for Persis – clanged between the walls of his skull.

A hand pulled at his arm.

He looked at Oren Rake with eyes stretched wide in uncertainty.

'For Christ's sake, man. I've been doing this my whole life. You have to trust me.'

*   *   *

Archie Blackfinch was sitting at his dining table pontificating, in that mildly overbearing way some Englishmen had, on the imperatives of history. The gravitas of his impromptu lecture was somewhat undermined by the fact that he was in a dressing gown, and slightly out of breath, talking too quickly, perhaps out of a sense of panicky bewilderment at her unexpected appearance at the door to his apartment.

A blazing row with her father had sent Persis spinning out of her home; not knowing where else to go, she had turned up out of the blue, suitcase in hand. Blackfinch, caught in the headlights, had stuttered his way through a chorus of platitudes, then agreed to her spending the night.

And then, to her astonishment, he had slipped a record on to the gramophone and asked her to dance, completely forgetting that he could dance about as well as a camel with wooden legs, one of them sawn off at the knee. Having wrestled their way through several numbers, they had sat down again, an electrical charge crackling between them, stars crowding in at the window, passing the popcorn around, and settling down to see what might happen next.

What had happened next was that Blackfinch had turned to her and said—

Her eyes snapped open.

She floated inside an impenetrable darkness, glutinous enough to bind limbs and dull the beating of her heart. Slowly, the sound of her own breathing emerged.

She became aware of the fact that a body was draped across her. Her lips stumbled into action. 'Archie?'

The body released a low animal moan.

This wasn't Archie Blackfinch. Consciousness returned fully, with a screech of tyres.

Persis jerked into motion, heaved the body aside, then sat

143

upright. A fit of coughing overtook her, violently vacating the dust from her lungs.

She stood up, into pitch black, took a fingertip inventory of herself.

She could feel blood seeping through a gash in the fabric of her shirt, a throbbing at the back of her skull. Her hair, her face, her mouth were coated in dust. But, otherwise, she seemed intact.

She dropped to her feet, reached out in the dark, hands feeling their way around the formless shape she had cast aside … Zhimomi, the site manager. And he was alive.

Her searching hands discovered a torch dangling from the man's work shorts.

She fumbled it from him, and switched it on.

The sudden glare forced her to blink, swept her back to her feet.

Panning the torch around, she saw immediately the fallen mass blocking the entrance to the tunnel. Her heart fell away. She sensed, with an instinct born to all animals, that she was in grave danger. The roof fall should have killed her. That it had not was merely an exercise in cruelty. There was no way out through the blockage, not in any reasonable timeframe, and not with the tools at their disposal. They would suffocate in here, or find themselves buried beneath another rock fall.

As if to underline her assessment, a rumble sounded above her. More dust fell, hurling her into another bout of coughing.

Panic slipped its leash. A moment of blindness, the heart and mind eclipsed by naked terror.

She swung the torch around, examined the rest of her surroundings, saw that the tunnel at her back moved off into darkness. Where did it go? A way out or a dead end?

She bent down and hauled Zhimomi to his feet, slapped his face, once, twice, thrice. The man slowly swooned back into semi-consciousness. 'Where does this tunnel go?'

But the Naga was incoherent.

Another rumble. No time to waste.

Persis slipped his arm around her neck, then began pulling him towards the open tunnel mouth.

A memory now.

Aged seven, just a month after her mother had died, when the night demons still came to visit.

She had awoken into an unnatural darkness, another of the frequent blackouts that plagued Bombay in the turbulent years when men were marching in the streets and the British were slowly losing their minds.

She had cried out for her father, heard him clumsily roll in on the wheelchair he was still getting used to, following the crash that had killed her mother.

'Hush now, Persis. There's no need for fear.' He had led her to the window, pointed to the tiny slum that had sprung up behind their street, the twinkling dots made by kerosene lanterns and clay lamps. It was a day before the festival of lights overtook the city, a celebration of the vanquishing of good over evil. 'In the darkest night,' her father had told her, 'light is a prayer.'

Persis stumbled along the tunnel, torch held out before her, dragging Zhimomi along, the site manager's feet marking a stumbling rhythm on the packed earth. The man was still not fully back with the living and she wondered if, perhaps, he had sustained a serious injury. It dawned on her that the Naga had probably saved her life. At the last instant, he had thrown himself at her, bearing her out of the way of the worst of the rock fall and taking the brunt of it upon himself.

What nameless instinct had made him do that? For a complete stranger?

The same instinct, perhaps, that propelled her own search for truth, that made humans better versions of themselves.

The tunnel stretched on, a serpent of grey stone, tons of rock held up by the flimsiest-looking stanchions. At any moment, she expected to be buried, like the pharaohs of old, beneath a mountain of stone.

They arrived at a tunnel section flooded with water. The water slopped over her ankles. She couldn't tell how deep it might get.

But there was no choice.

She waded in, and was soon up to her waist in inky black liquid. She held the torch above the water, struggled to keep Zhimomi moving forward. A burble escaped his lips, words that meant nothing.

After what seemed an age, she waded out on to dry earth. Her relief was short-lived. Something was wrong with the tunnel ahead. The floor, the walls, appeared to be … moving. And then she understood what she was looking at, and terror gripped her shoulders in icy claws, stopped the motor of her breathing.

Rats. Hundreds and hundreds of rats.

Rats. Her mortal fear … But now here was Mrs Narlikar, a regular at her father's bookshop, a devout Hindu who would always arrive fresh from the temple, smelling of incense and sandalwood, with lotus flowers in her hair. 'Rats are not our enemies, Persis. A rat is the vehicle of Lord Ganesha. In Rajasthan there is a temple where rats are worshipped, where devotees permit them to crawl over their feet, and feed them saucers of milk.'

Yet, set against Mrs Narlikar's iron-like faith: the anti-ideologies of the *Encyclopaedia Britannica*, which Persis had read cover to cover in her teenage years, sitting alone at the back of her father's bookshop, on the battered sofa that her mother had installed and Sam Wadia had wrecked. The *Britannica*, with its stories of the Black Death that had wiped out a third of Europe's population, bodies piled high in the streets, pyramids of corpses, the like of which Persis would not see outside the covers of a book until Partition's murdered multitudes.

She closed her eyes.

Forward, Persis. There's no way back.

Whose voice was it? Roshan Seth's? Her father's? Archie Blackfinch's?

She opened her eyes, lowered her head, and charged, screaming at the top of her lungs. The carpet of rats jerked to life, rats bolting in all directions, squeaking in terror.

Persis pounded her way through, felt them crawling over her feet, clinging to her legs. She almost fell as her foot slipped on a writhing body as large as a small cat.

And then, flying from the walls, they came at her. Rats landing on her back, her shoulder, a rat clawing at her hair, hissing into her ear.

She screamed, and now there was no longer any pretence. She was no longer India's first female police inspector, a pioneer, a woman who feared nothing. In that moment, all was forgotten – courage, dignity, self-possession – sacrificed upon the altar of sheer, undiluted terror.

She dropped Zhimomi to the floor, whirled around in the dark, flailing madly with the torch, with her fists, her shrieks mingling with the chittering of the panicked rats.

The madness rose to a crescendo . . . and then was gone.

The rats had vanished.

Persis stood there, heart threatening to erupt from her chest, the silence echoing harshly along the tunnel like a raven's caw.

An eternity seemed to pass.

Finally, she reached down, pulled Zhimomi to his feet.

Together, they moved on.

An age later, they arrived at the base of an iron ladder set into the tunnel wall.

A narrow beam of daylight, falling from above, glimmered at the top of the ladder.

A way out.

Persis set her head against the ladder and wept.

24

'How are you feeling?'

The doctor looked even younger than she remembered.

Persis ignored him, and turned back to the sink. The woman facing her in the square of mirror above the running tap looked as if she had been in a schoolyard fight. Her khaki dress shirt was caked in dirt, blood darkened her collar, and the state of her hair suggested she had been dragged through the jungle by her heels.

Mirrors never lie. But, just this once, she wished *this* mirror might murmur a reassuring half-truth, tell her that none of this was her fault. In the space of just over a year on the force she had been beaten, strangled, and shot at; not to mention almost blown up, burned alive, and buried beneath a mountain. As stars of misfortune went, this was practically a small galaxy. She suspected that even seagoing Jonahs, responsible for down-ing a dozen ships, would edge away from her should she find herself sitting next to one of the luckless creatures in some dockside bar.

She soaked a cloth and wiped the dust from her face and throat.

Behind her the young doctor cleared his throat. 'Cheating death twice in two days. You should take a turn in our local casino.'

Persis turned off the tap, then swung around to face him. 'How is Zhimomi?'

The doctor – his name was Ravi, she recalled – made an attempt at looking grave, the effect undermined by the adolescent acne scarring his cheeks. 'He's suffered a severe concussion. His brain is orbiting somewhere out beyond Neptune. But he'll live. Thanks to you. What you did, dragging him through the mine . . . that was incredible.'

'He saved me first,' she muttered, not meeting his eyes. She had never been comfortable with praise. Praise was easy to give – and receive – but hard to live up to.

'Of course, his lack of . . . coherence may not just be the effects of the rock fall.'

'What do you mean?'

'He's an opium addict. Couldn't you tell?'

Persis recalled Andrews saying something about an epidemic. 'Do you get a lot of addicts at the hospital?'

'We've seen a surge in the past couple of years. They say opium is coming in through China, addicting the tribals. A Chinese plot to undermine our hold over the region.'

Persis said nothing. A parallel thought had just struck her. She knew, from living in Bombay, that addiction was the most democratic of monsters; it rarely restricted its appetite to one section of the population. If the tribals were succumbing to the depredations of the drug, why not others? Why not those in power, those whose daily life was a tightrope of anxiety and danger? A man like Mohan Sinha, perhaps.

'Well, as I say, you're very fortunate,' continued the doctor. 'Nothing more than cuts and bruises. The nurse will see to them.' He beamed at her. 'Let's hope we don't have occasion to meet again. Third time isn't always a charm.'

She went looking for Andrews, the smell of iodine wafting ahead of her along the hospital's bustling corridors.

She found the doctor with a patient, berating the man for

various health-related misdemeanours, including chronic abuse of the liver. Pot and kettle, she thought.

She waited until he had finished, then pulled him to one side. 'Has the toxicology analysis on Sinha's body come through from Calcutta?'

'Not yet.'

She frowned. 'Don't they understand how urgent this is?'

'Aye. They do. Fat lot of good it does. Law unto themselves, the Bengalis. If I ask them to hurry up they're as likely to spend hours lecturing me on the evils of haste.'

'It occurred to me that Sinha might have been an opium addict? Could that explain why he didn't scream? Perhaps he'd drifted into a stupor when his killer struck.'

'Opium doesn't usually have such a strident effect. And just because no one heard him scream, doesn't mean he didn't.'

'Perhaps he overdosed?'

Andrews scowled. 'It's possible, I suppose. But if Sinha was an opium addict, he did a damned good job of concealing it. I certainly didn't notice, and I saw the man fairly regularly.'

Persis refrained from voicing her thoughts. Namely, that it wouldn't surprise her that the Scotsman had failed to note such a thing. The man appeared to operate on whisky fumes at the best of times. 'What's the name of the testing centre you sent the samples to?'

'It's pointless, Inspector. They won't answer to you. And, frankly, the last thing I need is a kamikaze cop ruining the very fragile relationship I already have with them.' Andrews checked his watch. 'I have to go. But I'll make another call later today. Shoo them along.' He stopped at the door. 'You're a brave woman. Risking your neck to save Zhimomi. If it had been me, I would have left him there.'

Persis watched him go, frustration balling her hands into fists.

She had never been good at waiting. Or working through the chain of command . . . A possible solution occurred to her, setting her feet in motion. Five minutes later, she was standing before Ravi, the adolescent doctor. 'Where do you send your toxicology samples to? In Calcutta?'

He told her. She scribbled down the address, thanked him, then turned towards the door.

25

'You look as if a house fell on you.'

Roshan Seth sat at his desk, eyeing his subordinates in the way a man might examine a pair of lepers that had inveigled their way into his daughter's wedding.

'It's been a rough day,' said Persis.

'And what have you learned, other than the fact that police officers have no business fooling around inside coal mines?'

She went over the case as she saw it. 'I still maintain it has to be one of the five guests staying at the hotel the night Sinha was killed. I've now spoken to them all.' She raised a hand, ticked off each suspect on her fingers. 'Maria Fontanelli, a journalist from Calcutta, here in search of a story. She appears to have no motive to want Sinha dead. Quite the opposite. She needed Sinha alive. He *is* the story – or was.'

'Perhaps she lost patience? Decided to conjure up her own story. "Mysterious murder of hated politician".' Seth threw up his hands before Persis could protest. 'It's a theory. I didn't say it was credible.'

'And then there's Sinha's aide, John Templeton. We now suspect that he had been given his marching orders by Sinha.'

'Why?'

'No idea. I haven't spoken to him yet. But, if it's true, it *would* give him a motive.'

'Again, not exactly a credible one. If we all went around murdering bosses who gave us the boot, we'd be knee-deep in corpses.'

'Perhaps it was something else,' interjected James. 'A motive we're not aware of. Or perhaps we're underestimating the depth of feeling here. A white man dismissed by an Indian he had served loyally for years? Perhaps Templeton felt betrayed.'

Persis ticked off another finger. 'And then there's Oren Rake, the mining boss who claims to be an old friend of Sinha's. Though he forgot to mention that he'd known the man when Sinha was out here some twenty years ago. He claims that all he did back then was chaperone Sinha around the tribes – our victim was some sort of tribal liaison appointed by the governing authority at the time. But Sinha was replaced in a hurry – following a complaint about the death, in police custody, of a young Naga named Aaron Koza. The perception appears to be that Sinha did little to respond to the complaint, and that this caused local upset. He was summarily yanked back to Calcutta. But Rake says he knows nothing about the affair.'

'What relevance does this Koza case have to Sinha's killing?'

'Possibly none. But I think it's a lead worth following up.'

'And there's nothing in the police files about this?'

Persis twisted in her seat to look at Constable Binny. The man was at his customary station, leaning against the wall by the door. He shivered to life. 'Afraid not. I took a look at the files in our storeroom. Nothing.'

'Why am I not surprised?' muttered Seth.

Persis felt a stab of disappointment. But it was no more than she had expected. 'It might not matter. I'll be travelling to Mokokchung tomorrow to track down the man who sent in the original complaint to Sinha, back in 1930.'

'Sounds like a wild-goose chase to me,' said Seth. 'You'd be better off targeting your efforts on the present day. Does this Oren Rake have a motive to have wanted Sinha dead?'

'None that I can find.'

Seth seemed to consult an internal genie, before responding. 'Here's a possibility. A mining operation can only operate in the hills with a government licence. That licence would have to be signed off by Sinha. What if that licence was being withheld? What if Rake and Sinha fell out?'

Persis opened her mouth to object, then changed her mind. 'A situation very similar to the Danvers's. Except that Sinha and Rake appear to have known each other a very long time. And Rake claims they were friends.'

'Friends fall out all the time. And the machinery of government can ride roughshod over the closest ties.'

Persis hesitated. 'Yes. I suppose that's possible. At any rate, it's worth checking out.'

Seth raised an elegant eyebrow. 'You sound surprised that I might have had an original thought.'

She coloured. 'I didn't mean—'

He waved her objection away. 'I earned my stars long before you were even at the academy. But now I'm sitting out here, in the middle of nowhere, with chickens in my stationhouse.'

Persis pressed on. 'There's something else.' She described her second search of Sinha's bedroom, the new forensic evidence she had unearthed.

'Why in the devil didn't you start with that?' said Seth irritably. 'Call me presumptuous, but this is more than enough to drag in your suspect for questioning.'

'My suspect, as you put it, is presently absent from the hotel.'

'On the run?'

'I don't know.'

Seth sat back. 'The Naga Hills are a small place. I wouldn't want to encounter either the tribals or Shroff's men out in the jungle, not in the current situation. Not that we can expect any cooperation out of the colonel. He's made it clear he wants to pin Sinha's murder on Baba Dao.' He shook his head. 'Make it a priority to bring in your suspect for questioning.'

'Very well.'

'I take it you still haven't solved the *how*? How in the world did our murderer get into a locked room to kill Sinha?'

'No,' said Persis.

Seth's mouth twisted into a grim line. 'What are you going to do now?'

'Now? Now I'm going to take a long, hot bath.'

26

She was as good as her word.

Arriving back at the Hotel Victoria, she staggered straight to her room, drew a bath, stripped, and fell gratefully into watery oblivion. Sitting in the tub, a glass of wine by her side, she closed her eyes and attempted to banish the macabre presence of Mohan Sinha, whose headless corpse she had discovered in another bathtub and who now seemed intent on squeezing in beside her.

The near-scalding water brought relief to her aching muscles. Her bruises sang; cuts and grazes joined in, an acapella of tiny voices that, collectively, served to remind her that the case was exerting a toll on both her body and mind.

Her thoughts became painfully bright. The jungle slithered into the room, vines reaching for her, tying her into knots.

There were too many variables, too many aspects to the investigation. She felt like a woman walking across a five-lane motorway, cars hurtling at her from both directions. If she wasn't careful, she would be flattened, another casualty of this dubious paradise at the edge of the world.

She closed her eyes and sank beneath the water.

Still wrapped in a towel, she called Bombay.

The telephone in the bookshop was picked up not by her father, but by a voice she thought she recognised. 'Mrs Flanders?' She could not hide her astonishment. The only explanation for a customer handling Sam Wadia's telephone was for the world to have ended.

'Persis? Is that you, dear?'

'Where's my father?'

'He's out in the street remonstrating with a man in a bullock cart.'

Words failed Persis.

'I believe the man is demanding that he be paid for delivering an item of furniture that your father insists is neither in the condition that he expected to find it nor, indeed, the item that he had ordered. It's quite the discussion. A small crowd has gathered. Sam seems to be in his element.'

A smile tugged at Persis's lips. Her father was never happier than when he was on a crusade. She wondered what the 'item of furniture' might be. Sam was notoriously tight-fisted and his idea of replacing worn-out fixtures was generally to wait until they crumbled to dust. She hoped it wasn't the sofa at the back of the bookshop.

Much of her childhood had been spent curled up on that particular item of furniture, hiding from the loneliness of her adolescent years. An only child, motherless, with few friends, she had made the bookshop her refuge, the characters of the books therein a cast of friends that had remained loyal throughout the years. Back then, the shop catered to a large British clientele and so English classics had become her favourites. *The Hobbit. The Wind in the Willows. Mary Poppins.* She was particularly fond of *National Velvet*, and the novel's young female protagonist, Velvet Brown, whose refusal to take no for an answer had provided Persis with the inspiration with which to face the injustices of the world. Velvet's mother had swum the English Channel, a fact few remembered, but which raised bittersweet memories for Persis of her own mother, whose forthright ability to shape life to her desires had left an indelible impression on her daughter. It was her mother who had taken over the bookshop after Sam's father had perished. It was she who had fashioned it into the enterprise it would go on to become. If there was one thing Sanaz Wadia had taught her daughter before her untimely death, it was to never let others dictate the rules.

Persis missed her terribly.

'Oh, hello!' said Mrs Flanders, brightly. 'A constable has arrived. Would you like me to fetch Sam, dear?'

'No,' said Persis. 'I wouldn't want to spoil his fun.'

Down in the dining room, she was astonished to discover Florence and Christopher Danvers, sitting at a table in the corner, heads lowered over their evening meal. The only other inmate was Maria Fontanelli, on the far side of the space. The Italian raised an elegant hand, fluttered a wave in the policewoman's direction, beckoned her over.

But Persis had eyes only for the Danvers.

She walked to the Americans' table, loomed over them. They looked up from their conversation to stare at her.

'Where have you been?' said Persis.

Florence Danvers spoke first, her tone mild. 'We stayed with an acquaintance in Dimapur last night. We had work there. Why?'

'I told you not to go anywhere.'

Her husband's expression hardened. 'We have a mission here, Inspector. God's work doesn't stop just because you order it to.'

Persis took a deep breath. 'I must speak with you both. In an official capacity.'

'Whatever you have to say you can say here,' said the man, stiffly.

She thought about arguing, and then realised it would be an exercise in futility. So be it.

She looked around, pulled across a chair from the nearest table. Lowering herself into the seat, she locked eyes with Florence Danvers.

'I decided to search Sinha's suite again. I discovered something I had missed the first time around. Trapped between the mattress and the headboard of Sinha's bed.' She reached into her pocket, slipped out a small paper bag. From the bag, she excavated several long hairs. Copper-coloured. She set them on to the white linen of the table. 'These belong to you, don't they? What were they doing in Sinha's bed?' Persis pressed on before the woman could answer. 'You were sleeping with him.'

A silence dropped between them, as concussive as an exploding landmine.

The American stared mutely at her, then whispered: 'You're mistaken.'

'I can easily organise a forensic comparison,' said Persis, pointing at the woman's head. She glanced at Christopher Danvers, expecting fury, but the man's expression was curiously placid.

'What do a few strands of hair prove?' said Florence.

'I have enough to arrest you. To take you to the station and interrogate you. To lock you up. Unless you begin talking. *Now.*'

The woman's face grew still. 'It's not what you think.'

'What I think is that you slept with my murder victim on the evening that he died. Tell me that's not true.'

A cloud passed over Florence's handsome features. 'Mohan Sinha was an opportunist. For the past two months, he kept us hanging, refusing to issue the permit we need to enter the hills. Without a permit we would have no choice but to return to America, our purpose unfulfilled. We have invested everything in this venture. Spiritually, financially, emotionally. I don't expect you to understand.' A glance at her husband, who sat rigidly in his seat, staring directly ahead. 'I went to Sinha's room that evening. I wanted to make one last effort to convince him. Appeal to his better nature. I should have known better. He made me an offer. Sleep with him. Sleep with him and he would issue the permit.' Her cheeks trembled. 'And so I did. God forgive me, but I gave in to him. I was desperate. *We* were desperate.'

'But he didn't give you the permit, did he?' said Persis.

'No. After we had . . . finished, he told me he needed more time to think. It was the way he smiled . . . I reacted badly. I was angry. But it was just words. I didn't kill the man.'

'Not then. We know he was alive when you left him because his evening meal was delivered shortly afterwards. But later that night, you – or perhaps your husband – returned to his suite.' Persis turned to Christopher Danvers. 'I'm presuming that you knew what had happened? Between Sinha and your wife?'

'Florence told me. When she returned from his rooms. And yes, in that instant, I was furious. But I did nothing.'

'You expect me to believe that you *didn't* confront Sinha that night? A man who had forced your wife into a degrading act, and then failed to grant the permit he had promised her in return for debasing herself?'

His face reddened. 'As the Bible tells us, "Avenge not your-selves, but rather give place unto wrath. For it is written: 'Vengeance is mine, sayeth the Lord.'"'

Persis felt the touch of a hand. She looked down to see that Florence had reached out to place a hand over her own. 'We were angry, Inspector. We loathed Sinha. But we didn't kill him. Such an act would have ended our mission, with or without a permit. Do you understand?'

The urge to arrest them both shuddered through her, as acute as any drug-ridden palsy. But would a few strands of hair suffice? No court would convict on such flimsy evidence.

'What time did you go to Sinha's room?'

'Not long after he returned from his office in Kohima. Around eight thirty.'

'How long were you with him?'

'Thirty minutes. No more. I wanted to get out of there as soon as I could.'

Her husband spoke up: 'Sooner or later, all sinners must answer to God.'

Persis wasn't certain if he meant Mohan Sinha, his wife, or himself.

In the end, she left them with a warning. 'Leave town again without my permission and I will alert every authority in the region. You will be arrested on sight. That's if they don't shoot you first.'

The Danvers stiffly nodded agreement, then retreated from the dining room, their meal uneaten.

Persis made her way across the room to Maria Fontanelli.

'You seem to have a strange effect on people, Inspector. They're forever walking out on you. Please, won't you join me?'

Persis ordered. As she waited for her meal to arrive, she found herself parrying journalistic thrusts from the Italian. Fontanelli's curiosity was a hound on the hunt. Persis threw her a few crumbs, but the bulk of her investigative efforts she kept veiled from the inquisitive newswoman. Headlines would have to wait. Besides, she was a long way from resolving the case. And the fact remained that, whether Fontanelli thought of herself as such or not, she *was* a suspect in the murder of Mohan Sinha.

They talked of their early careers.

Fontanelli described her first months in an Italian newsroom. 'I was the only woman on the journalistic side of the house. The older hacks' eyes almost popped from their skulls the day I walked in. And the younger ones decided it was open season. I spent most of my energy fighting off unwanted advances. Sometimes literally.

I once had to hit a guy over the head with a desk lamp. His mother came in to complain the next day. He was forty-five years old, married, with four kids. *Idiota!*'

Persis knew the feeling. She remembered a hairy moment at the academy when a trio of her peers had drunk themselves into a stupor and burst into her room late one night, intent on mischief. Perhaps they had forgotten that she excelled in hand-to-hand combat. A costly lapse. One had ended up with a broken nose, one with three broken fingers, and one found himself flying headfirst out of the window. Thankfully, she had been billeted in a ground-floor room.

Fontanelli burst out laughing and called for more wine.

'What sort of stories did you cover back in Italy?'

'Fashion. Food. Housekeeping. It's not as if I had a choice. I got my break when I chased up a story on my own time, following the lives of several prominent fascists after the war. In the countryside, there were mass purges. Blackshirts were rounded up and killed by the thousand. But in the cities, they hid in plain sight, or were given amnesties. Men who had committed war crimes walking around among the great and the good, taking communion, going to football games – it was a surreal situation. I wrote a piece about one such man. My editor had the courage to publish it. Unfortunately, the article ruffled feathers in the corridors of power. My editor was sacked and I was forced to leave Rome.'

'Why did you come out here? To India? To the Naga Hills.'

'As I told you before, the insurgency is a story.'

Well, thought Persis, at least the woman was consistent. Did the fact that she was out here in search of a story make her more or less of a suspect? Perhaps she considered Mohan Sinha a fascist? Might that have been a motive for her to want to murder the man, fuelled by an internal rage at the wickedness of men in general?

As an explanation for murder it lacked substance. Persis couldn't see the charming Italian suddenly hacking off a man's head simply because she disagreed with his ideology.

Fontanelli poured another glass of wine, looked at the bottle. 'I'll say this for our host. She keeps a fine cellar.' She picked up her glass, took a sip. Her lips curled. 'Well, *fine* might be an overstatement. But she certainly is an incredible woman.'

'Apeni Ao?'

'Yes. I'm going to do a piece on her. Though, understandably, she's reluctant at this precise moment. She seems to think Sinha's death might sink her hotel once and for all. I believe she's relying on you to perform some sort of miracle.'

'Even if I do find out who killed Sinha, it won't save this place.'

'Oh, I don't know. Notoriety has always been good for business. But no one likes an unresolved mystery. We want to know that the ghosts haunting our rooms have been laid to rest.'

27

As she walked up the marbled staircase, Persis's thoughts returned to Florence Danvers.

The woman had admitted to being in Sinha's room just prior to his death, admitted that she had slept with him in order to gain the permit that she – and her husband – so desperately craved. And then the man had reneged on their deal.

She could hear Roshan Seth's voice in her head, demanding that she arrest the Americans immediately. Something held her back. She had no way to be certain, but some element of Florence Danvers's testimony didn't quite ring true. But, for the life of her, she couldn't work out where the falsehood lay. She needed more time.

Besides, if the Danvers *were* arrested, lawyers would no doubt become involved. Possibly even the American consulate. The pair were foreign nationals. In order to arrest them for a crime, particularly one as grim as this, the burden of proof to be met was set higher. A meaningful interrogation could not proceed without definitive evidence of wrongdoing. They couldn't simply be hung upside down in a cell and caned on the soles of their feet until they confessed, a much-maligned, but tried-and-tested interview technique in many police districts around the country.

In the meantime, there were other suspects to question.

*   *   *

She made her way up to John Templeton's room.

It was time to confront the Englishman with the information that her deputy had discovered, namely, that Mohan Sinha may have been set to dismiss his aide.

Persis knocked. Several moments passed, and then the door swung back to reveal Templeton, dressed in a claret-coloured silk robe, blinking myopically at her from behind his round-rimmed spectacles.

'May I have a moment?'

He seemed set to refuse, then simply nodded, and turned back into the room, flopping into a chair by the desk.

She followed him in, taking in the space with an evaluating gaze. Her first impression was that the Englishman lived like a monk. There was nothing on the side units or the desk, no photographs, no knick-knacks, no personal memorabilia. Nothing to indicate that the space had been occupied for several months. On the face of it, John Templeton seemed as intriguing as a mallard.

'How can I help you, Inspector?'

A whisky glass trembled in his hand. She saw that his blond hair had flopped over his forehead, and that his robe was tied loosely around him. There was a louche quality to the man at odds with the way he had previously presented himself.

He raised his glass. 'Where are my manners? Would you like a drink?'

'No.' She decided to plunge straight in. 'It's come to our attention that Sinha intended to dismiss you from his employ.'

A puff of air escaped him, as if a fist had landed in his solar plexus. 'Who told you that?'

'That's not important. What's important is how you reacted to the news.'

He gaped at her. 'You can't think I would harm the man simply because he . . . he wished to make a change.'

'So you admit that he gave you notice?'

'I admit nothing. Besides, it's moot now, isn't it? The man is dead. And not by my hand. I shall soon be returning to Calcutta, putting this . . . unpleasantness behind me.'

'Unpleasantness. That's one way to describe your boss having his head cut off.' She continued to hold him with a grim look. 'I take it you won't be staying on? Waiting for Sinha's replacement?'

'Whoever fills Sinha's shoes will arrive with his own people. Besides, there's nothing left for me here. Mohan Sinha was more than my employer. He was . . . my friend. I would never have harmed him, Inspector. He meant the world to me.'

Perhaps it was the strange intimacy of the words, the sudden slump in his shoulders, the catch in his voice. A door had opened, into the Englishman's soul, and Persis was given the opportunity to peer briefly in . . . A thought ignited inside her head, blazing with the brightness of an exploding sun . . . Could she have misjudged the relationship between the buttoned-down Englishman and his erstwhile employer? Might Sinha have meant more to Templeton than she had supposed?

She recalled Oren Rake's words, in reference to Templeton: *Something Mohan said. About not recognising him for what he was.*

Undoubtedly, if such an affection existed, it was one-sided. Sinha's penchant for womanising had been well established. No doubt Templeton had come to terms with that long ago – how else could he have worked with the man for so long? But how would the Englishman have reacted when it became clear that the man he worshipped intended to repay his years of dogged faithfulness by giving him the boot?

The notion, arriving unexpectedly as it had, filled her with wonder. A leap of conjecture, to be sure, but she felt certain that there was an element of truth to it. She had now only to press home the insight, to strike hard and fast until the man gave up something concrete.

But John Templeton's moment of vulnerability had passed. He set down his glass. 'If that will be all, I must retire. The day has left me exhausted.'

As a way of drawing a line under the meeting, the statement seemed definitive.

'I went to see Oren Rake, up in the hills. Tell me, does his mining operation require a government licence?'

'Of course.'

'And Sinha would be in charge of authorising such a licence?'

'Not exactly. Such licences are awarded by the central government.'

'But Sinha would have had great influence over such a decision? As the man in charge out here, in the hills district?'

'Yes.'

'Was Rake's licence due for renewal? Or was there a reason that Sinha might have wished to revoke it?'

Templeton considered the question. 'Now that you mention it, yes. The licence *was* up for renewal. And it wasn't altogether certain that it would be renewed.'

'Why not?'

'Because we are now several years past independence. Nehru has only recently presented his five-year plan, a programme of economic development that aims to make India self-reliant, modernising key sectors such as agriculture, education, and the heavy industries. In that scenario, there isn't much room for an American to continue to own and operate a large coal mine anywhere in the country.' He paused. 'Do you think Rake could have . . .?'

'Perhaps. Then again, he's not the only one with a motive to have wished Sinha harm.'

He squinted at her, then raised his palms, before turning them over, and ushering her towards the door.

She had barely entered her room when the phone rang through from reception. A call from Bombay. But it wasn't her father. The voice on the other end was clipped, British, and female. 'Maisie Blackfinch here. Am I speaking with Persis?'

Astonishment welded her lips shut.

'Persis? Is that you?'

She slammed down the phone, heart racing, fighting for calm. But some emotions couldn't be put into a box. They pushed open the lid and came howling forth, laying waste to all that they touched.

Archie Blackfinch had been the most straightjacketed man Persis had ever met. An Englishman so governed by the rules of civility, of an old-fashioned formality, that he could have doubled as a statue in Bombay's law courts. When they had first met, she had found his starched persona intensely irritating. His fussiness-to-the-point-of-distraction, his penchant for delivering unasked-for disquisitions – often on the most obscure of topics – the politics of newt-mating, the dangers of sword swallowing – that left her with the overwhelming desire to punch him in the face each time he opened his mouth.

And yet.

Somewhere along the way, a transformation had taken place. He had revealed himself to her, and in so doing, had demanded a reciprocal act of revelation. It had happened without her conscious involvement; by the time she had realised what was going on, it was too late.

Blackfinch was an intelligent, handsome man. A wearer of badly fitting suits and scuffed shoes. Spectacles that he kept taking off to wipe on a shirtsleeve. A man of razor-sharp intelligence married to the social aptitude of a camel. A good man, dogged in the pursuit of justice. His presence had come to electrify her; the closeness engendered by working together, the meeting of two minds – and hearts – born on opposite banks of a vast river of historical and political circumstance, nevertheless finding common cause. And then, later, the crossing of a Rubicon that could not easily be uncrossed.

And yet.

The leap seemed too great. In post-war India, the notion of an Indian woman – one already balanced on the edge of a precarious public pedestal – falling into a romance with a white man, an Englishman … The very thought of it had become a burning moral dilemma that threatened to derail her.

And then, when she had finally decided to act, to surrender to the imperatives of the heart, the ground had fallen away beneath her feet.

When they had met, Blackfinch had told her that he was a divorcee. A rash marriage, entered into in haste, and quickly abandoned. He had claimed that his feelings for Persis overshadowed all; that their eventual coming together had peeled away any lingering tentacles of that failed marriage.

And so it had been a shock when his wife, Maisie, had turned up in Bombay, following Blackfinch's shooting at the hands of a political assassin.

It transpired that the word *divorce* held a different meaning in Archie Blackfinch's lexicon.

The couple were estranged, but no divorce papers had been signed. Technically, the Englishman was still a married man. And now, as he lay in a coma at the Breach Candy Hospital in Bombay, recovering from an assassin's bullet, his wife had come to reclaim him.

In a sense, Persis's banishment to the Naga Hills had come at the perfect time. It was probably a good thing for Blackfinch that three thousand kilometres lay between them.

Once again, she felt the anger rising, threatening to overwhelm her. A white-hot rage, tempered by sorrow, and a bottomless self-pity. Feelings that splashed back and forth over her heart, at times scalding, at times freezing.

Almost two months after being shot, Blackfinch had yet to emerge from his coma. His wife remained at his bedside. Persis had thought there might be space for her too, but it had swiftly become clear that three was not only a crowd in the Englishman's hospital room, but a particularly ripe and unpleasant gathering.

But what could she do? The hopelessness of the situation had been one reason that she had acquiesced to the Naga Hills reassignment. Distance might not cure Blackfinch – or cure her of him – but it gave Persis's bruised heart somewhere to hide, and time to grieve.

She shook her maudlin thoughts away, poured herself a whisky.

Sitting at the room's desk, she looked again at the photograph of Mohan Sinha taken as a young man, sitting with a white woman at a table in what looked like a nightclub.

She turned to the back. The words *Calcutta, 1923*. And the cut-off word: *Sin—*

She focused closely on the latter. As she examined the word, she became conscious of something that she hadn't noticed earlier: the inordinate amount of space between the *n* in *Sin* and the burn line that had destroyed the rest of the photograph . . . Revelation seized her . . . *Sin* was a *single* word. She had assumed that the letters had simply been the first three letters in a truncated *Sinha*, but now she saw that she had erred. And if the word was simply *Sin*, what could it mean? Were there more words to follow? If so, what were they?

And now, a second revelation. She remembered, from the case that had recently taken her to Calcutta, reading a newspaper piece, a profile of one of the oldest nightclubs in the city. Sin City.

Could that be it? *Calcutta, 1923, Sin City.*

She considered the notion from all angles, and then returned to the phone and asked to be connected to James Angami, in Kohima.

'How are you feeling?' he asked, as she came on the line. His voice, the image of him, momentarily scrambled her thoughts. Unbidden, she found herself setting the man beside an image of Blackfinch. How different they were! And yet each, in his own way, caused an unwelcome swirl of emotions inside her . . .

'I'm fine . . . I need you to do something tomorrow.'

'Tomorrow? I thought we were going to Mokokchung?'

'I am. You're not. I want you to go to Calcutta, instead.'

Silence drifted down the line. 'Calcutta?'

'The photograph that we found in Sinha's room – I think it was taken at a nightclub called Sin City. I want you to go and do some digging.'

'The photograph may have no connection to Sinha's murder.'

'He tried to burn the photo on the evening of his death. Why?' She allowed a trace of steel to enter her voice. 'In case I was less than clear, this isn't a choice.'

An intake of breath. 'No. Madam.'

She was about to put down the phone, when something else occurred to her. 'While you're there, I want you to track down the forensic analysis lab that Andrews sent Sinha's toxicology samples to. Give them a kick in the rear.' She reeled off the address.

'Anything else?'

'That's enough for now.'

A beat. 'You do realise that it's over a day to Calcutta? And a day back.'

'In that case, you had better set off early in the morning.'

She set down the receiver, picked up her whisky glass, and walked back to the bed.

Perhaps she could have handled that better. Men found it difficult taking orders from her. She understood that. Didn't mean that she had to pander to it.

If James Angami's feelings were hurt because she refused to coddle him, so be it.

Sometimes, you had to bang heads to get the job done.

Even if they were handsome heads, of men you had come to—

She shook away the thought, gulped at her glass, and settled down to sleep.

28

She knew that it must be a dream because the cab driver had been handsome and polite and had opened the door for her, greeting her pleasantly with a bow at the waist, instead of spitting betel juice on to the ground by her feet, as was the usual manner of welcome among Bombay's taxiwallahs.

In the dream, she had asked the driver to take her to the Breach Candy Hospital, where Archie Blackfinch awaited, awoken from his slumber, freed from the shackles of his past, and now ready, willing and able to resume what had begun between them in misadventure, proceeded in a peristalsis of confused emotions, and, seemingly, ended in calamity. In the dream, Archie was whole again, smiling in that smug little-boy way of his. 'Where have you been, Persis?'

'Me? I've been right here. It's you who were lost.'

And now: mere inches apart, the heat of their bodies flowing from one to the other and back again. Archie looking down at her, a living flame dancing in his eyes. She could feel her heart swelling, pushing against the walls of her chest. *How unbearably handsome he was!* 'Persis,' he began—

A noise dragged her back to the land of the living.

For a moment she lay there, blinking into darkness. Her mouth felt sour, her head cloudy. Perhaps she shouldn't have had that second whisky? Or the wine at dinner.

Darkness crowded the window. It was well before dawn.

What had awoken her?

There it was again. A noise, just at the edge of hearing ... She hauled herself to her elbows, reached for the Victorian lamp by her bedside, a heavy, standing affair, the kind that would need two men and, quite probably, an elephant to move.

A circle of light bathed the bed.

She rubbed sleep from her eyes, sat fully upright, and squinted into the gloom puddled in the corners of the room—

There. A movement, where there should be none. Her uniform lay on the floor where she had kicked it off. And it was ... *moving* ... Gods! How much *had* she had to drink last night? As if to reproach her, a bolt of pressure stabbed upwards from her bladder.

She slipped out of bed, the terrazzo marble cool on her bare feet.

She stepped towards the bathroom ... and froze.

A head had poked out from below the trousers of her uniform. A black and gold striped head, with a forked tongue. A snake.

She recognised the species instantly. A banded krait, one of the most venomous on the subcontinent. Feared the length and breadth of the country. A killer. *How had it found its way into her room?*

No time for that now.

The snake had registered her presence, was slithering towards her.

Her thoughts went to her service revolver. But the gun lay inside her desk, cut off from her by the advancing animal. Fear made a knot in her throat.

She needed a weapon. But there was nothing to hand.

The snake's tongue rasped, the noise obscene in the pre-dawn silence.

She knew that banded kraits were nocturnal hunters. She knew that the krait's venom was highly neurotoxic, leading to vomiting, excruciating pain, respiratory failure, and diarrhoea. It was this last prospect that terrified her the most. Dying was bad enough. But for her corpse to be found by others, her nightgown soiled by the evidence of her terror ... Unthinkable.

The krait closed the gap between them. A few more feet and it would be within striking distance.

Her panicked brain propelled her limbs into motion.

She reached for the bed, grabbed the mosquito net where it was still rolled up on to the frame, yanked it down, and threw it over the snake.

Tangled up in the netting, it writhed on the floor, tying itself into knots.

Persis stepped behind the bed lamp, rocked it violently back and forth until it capsized, then stood back to watch as it crashed on to the snake, crushing its head beneath its marble midsection. Moments later, the krait fell still.

Her legs gave way and she collapsed on to the edge of the bed. Her heart galloped wildly. Her body was drenched in a clammy sweat.

And now her earlier thought returned: how had the snake entered her room? With the doors and windows locked?

The obvious answer reared up inside her. Someone had put the snake here.

She followed the logic of the thought to its inevitable conclusion. Someone wanted her out of the picture, wanted to stop her from proceeding with her investigation. But who?

Any one of her principal suspects – Oren Rake, John Templeton, Maria Fontanelli, and Florence and Christopher Danvers – could have found a way into her room and left the snake here.

The act indicated a desperation bordering on madness.

If nothing else it confirmed her initial instinct on that first night when she had come face to torso with Sinha's corpse; namely, that there was a killer loose in the hotel. A killer who had killed once and clearly had no compunction about killing again.

And now, *she* was in the firing line.

29

When the British first ventured into the Naga Hills, they had gone in, as they invariably did when visiting any place further than the coast of Bournemouth, armed to the teeth.

Rumours of aggressive locals, ravenous tigers, poisonous snakes, and fist-sized insects – not to mention several lost expeditionary forces, swallowed whole by the jungle in the manner of Rome's legendary Ninth Legion – had planted themselves firmly in British heads, until the very idea of being posted to the north-eastern hills incited a quietly gibbering terror in the staunchest of sola topi-ed warriors.

In the latter half of the nineteenth century, the Assam Rifles had arrived in Mokokchung and built a stockade on DC Hill, a base from which to strike out into the eastern forests. The town had grown up around the military outpost, gradually becoming the most important urban conurbation in the northern half of the Naga Hills district.

And it was to Mokokchung that Persis headed the following morning, the drive from Kohima to the northern city taking six hours, through relentlessly rugged terrain. By the time she arrived, just as the sun had wheeled past the noon hour, she had had her fill of intoxicating views and stretches of road so lonely it was a wonder humans had lingered long enough to piledrive an arrow of tarmac through the jungle.

The night's events slithered around her thoughts.

Before leaving that morning, she had spoken with the hotel's owner, Apeni Ao, and the manager, David Keishing, summoning them to her room to show them the dead snake. Keishing had been aghast, Ao coldly furious. The last thing the old woman could afford was another death on the premises, particularly that of the officer investigating the gruesome murder that might yet shut down her beloved hotel.

With some effort Persis had reined in her own anger, seeking a neutral tone. 'How could someone have got into my room?'

Keishing looked morose. 'I am afraid it would not be so difficult. We can only afford to operate a handful of staff now. Often, whoever is at reception is called away to attend to a guest. We hold spare keys to all the rooms in a rack behind the counter. It would be simple enough to take a key to your room, then later place it back.'

Ao shook her head. 'I am sorry, Inspector. We have failed you.'

Persis turned to Keishing. 'I want every key to my room. I will return them when my investigation is ended.'

As she navigated her jeep up the steep slope leading into Mokokchung, the town opened up before her, an orderly collection of tidy streets, colourful buildings, and lawns so well tended that they could only be the legacy of the British, whose near-sociopathic love of manicured topiary had driven generations of Indian gardeners to distraction.

Persis knew that the town was the stronghold of the Ao clan – Apeni Ao's forebears – renowned for their love of festivals, singing, and a no-nonsense approach to lopping off the heads of their enemies. The festivals and singing had survived the conversion to Christianity – the Ao had been the first of the Naga tribes to be seduced by the new faith. As far as headhunting went, the Ao, like many, claimed to have retired the practice to the realm of past misdemeanours, revived now only in myth and song. Whether that was entirely true was beyond the bounds of both Persis's knowledge and the scope of her investigation.

It didn't take long for her to find her way to the home of Bartholomew Sema, the man who had sent in the original complaint to Sinha about the death of Aaron Koza back in 1930.

The home, a spacious, cream-coloured, L-shaped bungalow, set with a sky-blue roof and shuttered windows, stood on a patch of lawn so virulently green it looked as if it had been coloured by a dye made from crushed caterpillars.

Persis's knock was greeted by an elderly woman with the face of a squashed prune. 'Yes?' The woman stared at her with what seemed to Persis an unwarranted hostility. She suspected that it wasn't every day that cops came calling at the Sema residence, and certainly not a woman dressed in khaki. She explained her mission.

The woman's face dissolved into sadness. 'I am afraid you're five years too late, Inspector. My husband is no longer with us.'

A fist of disappointment struck Persis in the gut.

The woman seemed to register her angst. 'The name you mention, this Aaron Koza, I vaguely remember my husband talking about the case. But my memory is not what it once was.'

'Anything you can recall would be useful.'

'I'm afraid that I can't be of much assistance to you . . . But I know someone who might be able to help.'

The offices of Mokokchung Timber took up two floors of a three-storey building in the very centre of the hilltop town, one of a handful of officious-looking edifices bordering a cobbled square. Sandwiched in between the offices were satellite enterprises: eateries, a couple of bars, a church, a tailor, a barber, and, for the sake of variety, a hole-in-the-wall shop selling chickens in bamboo cages.

As Persis parked her jeep in front of the chicken shop, the birds looked out at her from between the bars of their cells, as forlorn as any retinue of human inmates locked away in Bombay's infamous Arthur Road Jail.

She walked into the ground floor of the timber enterprise, and, in short order, was seated before Edward Sema, logging entrepreneur, and thirty-eight-year-old son of the late Bartholomew. Briefly, she explained the situation.

Sema, an overweight, round-faced man, balding patchily at the crown, wore a shirt stretched so tightly around his more-than-ample stomach it looked set to explode from his frame in a confetti of cotton. The shirt was complemented by a fat red tie that barely made it to his navel and looked as if it belonged on a schoolboy. The lenses of his spectacles were half an inch thick.

The office was broiling. Electricity had yet to make its way up to Mokokchung, and the absence of a ceiling fan had left Sema lathered in sweat. Not that the man seemed to notice. Persis watched him pick up a pencil, an end gripped between the thumb and forefinger of each hand, and flex it as if intent on snapping it in half. 'Yes, I remember my father talking about Koza. The boy's death bothered him enormously.'

'Do you recall the facts of the case?'

'As a matter of fact I do. My father spoke about it often, you see, and with great passion. Aaron Koza was a young man caught up in the troubles of the time. Back then, my father – and others – had established the Naga Club to promote the cause of Naga independence. The response from the British – and the Indians who worked for them – men like Mohan Sinha – was strident.'

'Your father spoke of Sinha?'

'He did. Sinha was sent to the hills as a tribal liaison. At first, the Naga Club tried to work with him. But it quickly became clear that he had been sent to the hills to undermine the Naga separatist movement.' He set down the pencil. 'Aaron Koza was part of a radical student faction in Kohima, active in pushing our cause. He had studied in Calcutta. An educated tribal, you might call him.

'According to my father, one day, Koza was simply scooped up by the local police. For questioning.' The man's eyes dulled. 'Twenty-four hours later, he was dead. The police released a terse statement declaring that Koza had died by his own hand. A suicide. But word soon began to spread that the poor boy had been beaten to death. What added fuel to the fire was the fact that the body was never returned. The authorities cremated it, quickly, and without permitting the family to either see the body or attend the cremation.' A pause. 'My father felt responsible. It was the Naga Club's message that Koza had taken to heart, his fierce advocacy on behalf of Naga independence that led to his arrest. My father wrote to Mohan Sinha.'

'What did he want from him?'

'He wanted the truth to come out, and for those responsible to be punished. He demanded a full-scale investigation. He wanted justice for Aaron Koza.'

'Who *was* responsible?'

'I'm afraid that I cannot tell you. The police refused to name the officers who had been present at his interrogation. An official report was subsequently unforthcoming. Hidden behind red tape and the auspices of "national security".'

'But a report must exist? Somewhere?'

'*Somewhere* is the key, Inspector. The same somewhere where all lies vanish. A lost kingdom guarded by the lions of politically sanctioned misdeed.'

Persis pondered the man's words. 'Do you think there might be a link between Koza's death and Mohan Sinha's murder?'

Sema frowned. 'Twenty-one years have passed since Aaron Koza died. Who would want to exact vengeance for his death now? And why blame Sinha? Blame Koza's actual killers.' He flashed a grim smile. 'Someone has gone out of their way to make it look as if a Naga is responsible for Sinha's death.' He picked up the pencil again and pointed it at the window. 'Do you see that tree on the far side of the square? We call that the head-hanging tree. Once upon a time, Ao warriors would decorate its branches with the bloodied skulls of their enemies. Thankfully, such practices have vanished from the hills.'

'Have they? Many seem to believe that Baba Dao is keen on reviving the old ways. That he may well have been behind Sinha's murder.'

A fleeting expression of anger contorted Sema's features. 'Myth-making is in our blood, Inspector. Baba Dao – whoever he is – is simply using our fondness for storytelling against us.'

'You don't believe in Dao's struggle?'

His reply was emphatic. 'No, I do not. I believe that our future lies *with* India, not independence.'

'I can't imagine your father would have been pleased with such a sentiment.'

Sema raised his chin. 'My father, like many, lived inside a noble dream. The idea that, somehow, the Naga tribes might unite to fashion a thriving, modern society out in the hills, with no help from the Centre. He was a student of history. During his war years, he had read about Vercingetorix, the Gaulish chieftain who united the French tribes against Caesar. My father thought he could do the same with the Naga. What he conveniently chose to forget is that Caesar ultimately slaughtered the Gauls and subjugated their once proud nation.'

A commotion from the square outside raised them from their seats.

Standing at the window, Persis looked down on to the heads of a crowd of animated locals, drawn from their offices, standing as one to watch the arrival of a cavalcade of tanks.

*   *   *

'Inspector,' said Colonel Shroff, rising from behind his makeshift desk. 'What brings you out to Mokokchung?'

'I might ask you the same thing, Colonel,' said Persis. 'Except that I have just witnessed your tanks roll into town and your man with a megaphone declare martial law.'

'Hardly martial law,' said Shroff, mildly. 'A temporary curfew.'

'And what happens to those who refuse to obey your curfew?'

A hard glint flashed in the soldier's eyes. 'Only enemies of the state have something to fear by the imposition of law and order.'

'Who decides who is or is not an enemy of the state?'

Shroff retook his seat. 'Your commanding officer has been keeping me abreast of the investigation. But I've always preferred field reports directly from the horse's mouth.'

'The problem isn't the horse,' said Persis. 'The problem is whether you want to hear what the horse has to say.'

Shroff steepled his hands, waiting.

Persis hesitated, then quickly sketched out the course of her enquiries, the various avenues she had been pursuing.

The colonel listened intently. When she had finished, he said, 'And Baba Dao? How do your efforts link him to the murder?'

'I don't know that that they do.'

The skin around his eyes tightened. 'I thought I had made myself clear. Insurgents are behind Sinha's death.'

She struggled for calm. 'I'm a police officer. I go where the evidence takes me. At this time, I have nothing to link Baba Dao to the crime. Nor any other Naga, insurgent or otherwise.'

Shroff's jaw twitched. 'You haven't been here long enough to understand them. To know them for what they are.'

'And what exactly is it that you think *they* are?'

'Ungrateful.'

Persis felt a flush of heat. 'This is their land.'

'There is no *their*. We are one nation. Anyone who seeks to undermine that is a traitor. And there is only one fate for traitors.' And in his eyes Persis saw that strange fanaticism she had witnessed in her countrymen throughout the Quit India years, an unstoppable force that had, to begin with, taken the British by the scruff of the neck and marched them out the door, before turning inward, to cut a swathe of destruction across the subcontinent, Indian upon Indian.

But Shroff hadn't finished. 'Baba Dao is out there. I *will* find him, even if I have to burn down every village from here to Burma.' He pressed forward in his seat. 'Sinha was murdered on the orders of Baba Dao. Find the evidence. Or I'll find someone who can.'

'And if I don't?'

'Then, Inspector, you may discover that there are far worse places for a young policewoman to end up in than these godforsaken hills.'

30

Her journey back to Kohima was interrupted by an upturned donkey cart.

Persis dismounted from the jeep to help the unfortunate farmer right his vehicle and gather up his cargo of melons, many of which had rolled on to the grassy verge. Others had split messily on the tarmac, luring a legion of creatures from the jungle out on to the road: lizards, macaques, snakes, and all manner of insects.

Behind them, the sun had dipped sharply, crowning the surrounding forest in a corona of gold. The cart owner cast nervous glances at the shadows between the trees. 'Leopards, madam,' he explained.

She glanced at the man. His enormous moustache spread boldly outwards from either side of his nose like the wings of an albatross. Persis suspected the facial hair alone would scare off most predators.

With the cart loaded, a second obstacle arose. The donkey had settled into the middle of the road and appeared in no hurry to resume its duties.

Persis watched the farmer cajole, plead, threaten, then eventually beg the beast to cooperate. The donkey swished its tail, exhibiting as much interest in its owner's demands as a hangman in the pleas of a blindfolded convict on the scaffold.

Finally, Persis took out her revolver and marched over to the animal. The man saw her approach and lifted his hands to ward her away. 'No, madam!'

Persis pushed him aside, raised the revolver in the air, and fired.

The donkey shot to its feet, squirting a stream of terrified excrement on to her boot.

She watched it gallop off down the road, the farmer in hot pursuit.

Setting her revolver back in its holster, she looked down at her steaming foot.

An apt metaphor for the state of her investigation, she thought.

By the time she had reached her room and taken off her uniform, it was past nine.

She showered, dressed – in loose white trousers and a collarless burnt-peach blouson with an embroidered neckline – then went downstairs. The dining room was empty.

She ordered, glad of a moment's respite.

The food arrived quickly, a thick lentil and potato broth. As she ate, the case kept intruding, in time to the rhythm of her spoon on the bottom of the bowl.

Each day seemed to bring yet more complexity to an already labyrinthine investigation. Ever more leads to be followed up. Before walking into the dining room, she had checked at the reception counter for messages, had discovered several from Seth. She knew that she owed her commanding officer an update, the increasingly frantic tone to his notes hinting at the pressure he was under to deliver a result.

But a result was no nearer now than it had been several nights earlier when she had walked in to find a headless Sinha in his bathtub.

Roshan Seth, like everyone else relying on her, would simply have to wait.

With the meal ended, she picked up her wine glass, and went in search of the hotel manager.

She found Keishing in his office behind the reception counter. 'Have any of the guests been acting strangely today? Any who asked specifically about me?'

An expression of confusion crossed his swarthy features. 'Madam?'

'If one of my fellow guests was responsible for last night's snake, they might well have wanted to know whether I had survived the night unscathed. An oblique enquiry, perhaps?'

Understanding bloomed. He hesitated, then plunged: 'Madam Danvers enquired about you.'

'Did she say what it was regarding?'

'No, madam.'

'Is she in her room?'

'I believe the Danvers are dining with a friend tonight, in Kohima. They left the hotel earlier.'

'Did they take their luggage with them?'

'No, madam.'

Persis placed a hand on the counter. 'In that case, give me the spare key to their room.'

Keishing had protested, of course. But Persis was not to be denied.

She made her way up to the Danvers's suite and knocked. When no answer came, she used the spare key and slipped inside.

The suite was roomy, larger than her own, though not as large as Sinha's. She had searched it quickly once before, when looking for Sinha's missing head and the murder weapon. But that had been a quick frisk, under the gimlet eye of Christopher Danvers.

There was method to searching a room, a lesson she had learned during her training at the academy. Given that she had missed vital evidence in her initial search of Sinha's suite – namely, the stray hairs belonging to Florence Danvers – she was determined to take even greater pains this time around.

She began with the bathroom, fingering her way along the couple's simple and inexpensive toiletries. In the bedroom, she took extra care with the bed, before moving to the wardrobes. The Danvers's taste in clothing was, like the rest of their lives, ascetic. Hard-wearing fabrics in a range of funereal blacks and greys. Not quite sackcloth, but Persis wouldn't have wanted to walk around in Florence Danvers's dresses, not in this heat.

A pair of suitcases at the bottom of the wardrobe turned out to be empty.

Which left only the desk.

She went through the drawers with infinite care, and was disappointed to discover nothing of note, certainly nothing linking in any way to her investigation.

She padded back to the bed, sat down.

What had she expected to find? Revelatory evidence that would crack the case wide open, linking the Danvers directly to Sinha's murder? Or, perhaps, to Baba Dao?

Her gaze alighted on a painting of Jesus, framed in glass, arms spread wide, beseeching the masses. Something about the painting was sending a signal to the back of her brain ... It was slightly askew. Most would not have noticed, but to Persis the tiny misalignment felt at odds with the sterile neatness of the rest of the room.

She walked to the picture, lifted it from the wall, brought it back to the bed.

Slipping her penknife from the pocket of her trousers, she carefully worked the blade around the edge and popped off the back, revealing several folded sheets of paper hidden between the painting and the slim wooden backing.

She unfolded and scanned the sheets – there were three of them.

A wave of disappointment moved through her.

They were written in a language she could not decipher. She suspected it was Chinese, but could not be sure.

Why would the Danvers have hidden these documents away? Why did they have documents written in Chinese in the first place?

Questions that would have to wait.

She returned the picture to the wall, glanced around the room to ensure that there were no immediate signs of intrusion, then left.

As she arrived at the reception counter, intent on returning the Danvers's room key, the telephone rang.

She watched Keishing pick up the receiver, listen, and then turn to her, surprise writ large over his flattened features.

'Madam. It's Dr Andrews. He has asked for you to come to Kohima. Urgently.'

31

The bridge lay on the outskirts of town, a weathered stone arch built by the British to cross a fast-moving brook that snaked down the flanks of Garrison Hill. With the arrival of the annual monsoon, the brook would transform into a raging torrent, thundering on to rocks below, sweeping along with it organic detritus discarded by market traders, the wistful tokens of prospective lovers, and the occasional careless drunk. During the war years, tanks had rumbled over the bridge's stonework, to the accompaniment of marching infantry.

Persis arrived in her jeep, still dressed in her trousers and blouson.

Andrews was waiting for her at the foot of the bridge, trussed in a black tuxedo. 'I was at a bridge club dinner when the call came in,' he explained. 'A passing motorist stopped to relieve himself over the bridge. Saw the body. Almost joined it down on the rocks. Follow me.'

She fell into step behind the older man as he began to navigate a cumbersome path downslope, picking his way over rocks and enormous tufts of grass jutting out at odd angles like the heads of angry trolls. Halfway down to the riverbed, Andrews slipped, stumbled, fell to earth. For an instant, she thought he might tumble forward, like a circus clown, rolling head over heels all the way down to the bottom. But he flung out a hand, grasped a convenient rock, and held fast. Odysseus in a storm.

Cursing, he heaved himself to his feet, smacking dirt off his trousers. 'I'm too old for this,' he muttered, pulling a handkerchief from his pocket to wipe the dirt from his palms.

Five minutes later, they arrived at the bottom.

The river was no longer in spate, a month having passed since the monsoon rains had departed the hills. Rock and gravel lined the bed, the rocks weathered smooth by the action of generations of fast-moving water.

A body lay spreadeagled before them, face down, male, dressed in a suit, one arm flung forward, as if pointing the way ahead. Blood matted the rear of the skull. A smear of blood was visible on a large rock beside the head.

Clutched in the body's other hand, pale under the moonlight, Persis saw an object.

It took a second for her to recognise it for what it was, and then to realise that she had seen it before. A mahogany cross, of the type Baptists favoured, simplistic and without the image of Christ carved into the wood.

The last time she had seen such a cross, it had been hanging around the neck of Christopher Danvers.

Andrews moved closer to the body. 'I haven't had a thorough look yet, but safe to say that he was killed by the fall.'

Persis dropped to her haunches. Reaching out, she dug both hands under the body and, with considerable effort, turned the corpse over, on to its back.

She continued to crouch, listening to the sounds of the night, a chattering rhythm that rose, beat by beat, to a crescendo inside her head.

Stretched before her, staring dully into space, was the body of John Templeton.

32

'Isn't it obvious?' said Andrews. 'The man killed himself. Drove to that bridge and flung himself over the edge. A swan dive into oblivion.'

It was the following morning, and Persis was back at the hospital mortuary. Andrews had just completed his post-mortem of John Templeton's body. The Scot was in a foul mood, haunted by a hangover from his previous night's bridge club festivities and his late-night exertions dealing with the Englishman's corpse. He thumped around his domain as if the man's demise had been a personal affront designed to inconvenience him.

'What makes you say that?' said Persis.

Andrews gave her the evil eye. 'The man's car was parked beside the bridge. There were no signs of anyone else having been out there. He fell forty feet, cracked his skull open on the rocks below. I would have thought that a seasoned police officer could join the dots without my help.'

'How can you be certain the damage to his skull isn't the result of a blow from an assailant?'

'I can't be certain. Just as I can't be certain that an elephant can't fly by flapping its ears. But I have enough sense to look at the facts and draw the obvious conclusion.'

'Which is?'

'Templeton killed Mohan Sinha. A man he worked for and was, presumably, loyal to. But then guilt set in, eating away at him until, finally, it got the better of him. Couldn't live with himself. And so he took the coward's way out.'

'Why? Why would Templeton kill Sinha?'

'I don't know, Inspector. Am I expected to do *all* of your work for you?'

Persis hesitated. She had no desire to share with the Scot the fact that Sinha had, in all probability, dismissed Templeton from his post, and that this might have been the motive for the Englishman to commit murder. She had even less desire to share her other conjecture, about Templeton's hidden feelings towards his boss. But the words bubbled on to her tongue of their own accord. 'How well did you know him? Templeton, I mean?'

Andrews grunted. 'I met him a few times, of course. Usually in the course of treating Sinha. Templeton was always hovering around. Always fussing. It was a wonder he didn't wipe the man's bottom for him. Hell, maybe he did.'

'Did Templeton have a woman out here? Someone he met with regularly?'

The question seemed to take him by surprise. 'Not that I knew of. Come to think of it, the man seemed a bit of an ascetic. Some men are like that. Regard life's sybaritic pleasures as positively barbarian.'

She picked her next words with care. 'Do you think Templeton might have . . . harboured feelings for Sinha?'

'Feelings? What do you mea—?' He stopped as realisation struck him with the force of an anvil dropping on to his skull. He dragged fingers through his beard. 'Why didn't I see it? It's a wonder how blind a man can be if he chooses.' He looked squarely at her. 'An *affaire de coeur*? Yes, that might just make sense. A man dotes a little too heavily on his boss. Years of running around after him, pining in the shadows. One day, he makes his feelings known. Hoping against hope that his long-repressed emotions will be met with understanding. Instead, Sinha is repulsed. And so the monster is loosed.'

The scenario seemed plausible. Might this be the answer? Might Templeton's apparent suicide have settled the matter of Mohan Sinha's death? But why would Templeton have gone to the elaborate effort of cutting off Sinha's head, and staging the killing to look as if the murderer had entered a locked room? How had he managed that anyway?

Another thought was bothering her. 'And what of the cross in Templeton's hand? Christopher Danvers's cross?'

Andrews shrugged. 'Why don't you ask Danvers?'

'The Danvers are missing. I checked their rooms this morning and they haven't returned to the hotel since leaving it yesterday. No one seems to know exactly where they are.'

'I guess that's one similarity between you and Colonel Shroff – with all your authority and your fancy uniforms you still can't make people dance to your tune.' He thrust out a belligerent chin. 'You don't know for certain that the cross belongs to Christopher Danvers. There are thousands of such crosses in the hills. Practically every Naga has one. And even if it does belong to him, perhaps he *gave* it to Templeton. For the betterment of his Christian soul.' He sniffed. 'You have your answer, Inspector. Now wrap up this case so that we can bring some semblance of order back to this benighted region.'

33

Before heading to the stationhouse, Persis turned her jeep towards the town's mercantile quarter. She had a specific destination in mind, guided by the sheets of paper she had discovered hidden in the Danvers's room and presently burning a hole in her pocket.

A week after arriving in Kohima she had managed to tear the sleeve of a favourite dress; the garment had been sent to a tailor recommended by the staff at the Hotel Victoria. A detail of that transaction had stuck in her mind: the tailor in question was Chinese.

The man's story had become the stuff of local legend.

Born into a family of imperial Chinese tailors, Ronald Lee – as he now styled himself – had ventured westwards from his native Kunming some three decades earlier, trekking across Burma and into the easternmost reaches of the British Empire in India in search of fame and fortune. He had found neither.

Nevertheless, and contrary to the rumours that had almost sent him racing back to Kunming, he had discovered that, far from being in a hurry to chop off his head, the warlike locals appeared keen to welcome him, a novelty to their hilly domain. And so, he had decided to stay.

Several years later, his fledgling tailoring business had taken off when he had found favour with the district's deputy commissioner, a stiff-necked Brit from the Home Counties renowned for his walrus moustache, his ability to smash a cricket ball into the upper atmosphere, and his adherence to the precept that clothes maketh the man. In due course, Lee's impeccably cut suits became must-haves for any gentleman of breeding called upon to spend time in the eastern tropics. It was said that a Ronald Lee suit could rival a Savile Row fit, elevating a man with the skeletal elasticity of an orangutan to the manly silhouette of a Clark Gable.

Persis entered the tailor's premises to find a large cat settled on the counter, sporting an eye-patch. The cat returned her stare boldly from its one working eye; clearly, a creature that had lived eight lives to the full, and mortgaged the ninth to the hilt. An old woman sat behind the counter, so wizened and immobile that, at first, Persis thought she might be a mannequin. Smoke drifted from a calabash pipe set into the side of her mouth.

'I'm looking for Lee,' said Persis.

Long seconds ticked by, and then the woman plucked out the pipe and aimed it towards a black curtain fencing off the rear of the space.

She found Ronald Lee in the back room, shearing a sheet of cloth with a pair of enormous scissors seemingly designed to snip tree trunks in half. Lee was short, dumpy, and the possessor of a square chin, reminding Persis of pictures she had seen of the Italian dictator, Benito Mussolini. Dyed hair, black as tar, flowed back over a boxy skull. His pale cheeks were red, and a sheen of sweat stood out on his forehead.

Persis introduced herself, then said, 'I need your help.'

Lee looked her up and down. Then down and up. 'Yes, madam. *That*, I can see. But do not worry. I have just received a fabulous new bolt of red silk—'

'Not that kind of help.' She explained her errand. Pulling out the Danvers's mysterious sheets of paper, she unfolded them, and held them out to Lee.

The man took the papers, passed a quick eye over them. 'Yes. This is Chinese.'

'How long will it take you to translate?'

'Not long at all,' he said. 'This is a list, Inspector. A most intriguing one.'

34

The stationhouse was deserted. At least of its human residents.

Persis entered to find Constable Binny's avian admirer settled on the roof of the steel almirah that served as the station's evidence locker. The bird appeared somnolent in the broiling afternoon heat, head tucked into neck, eyes lidded.

She filled a glass from a metal water pot by the door, drained it, then filled another.

Walking to her desk, she slipped off her cap, ran a forearm across her brow, then sat down. The electricity appeared to be out again, stilling the ceiling fans. The heat placed its hands around her throat, squeezed gently.

The silence was oppressive. Unlike the Malabar House station back in Bombay, the Kohima stationhouse was frequently left unattended. Hostage to the rhythms and exigencies of life in the hinterland. Not that it seemed to matter. As Seth had told her on the day she had arrived, 'It's irrelevant whether we're here or not. No one trusts the police anyway.'

She believed otherwise. Had to believe. Humankind, no matter where and how it flourished, had an innate need for law and order. For justice. Otherwise, what was there but savagery? Those who wore the uniform served as a living manifestation of that need.

The hen clucked gently in her half-sleep.

Unbidden, her hand went to the telephone on her desk.

Moments later, a familiar voice came on the line. 'Malabar House station. What do you want?'

'I see you've been working on your bedside manner.'

'Persis?' Birla's voice carried with it a sense of astonishment, as if perhaps, he had never expected to hear from her again.

Of all her colleagues at Malabar House, Pradeep Birla – one of the two sub-inspectors housed there – had been the most accepting of her presence. The man was shiftless and unreliable and had spent most of his career moving sideways in a manner that would have made crabs seasick. But, at this moment, the vision of his dark pockmarked face filled her with an unexpected gladness.

'How goes it in the jungle?' Birla continued. 'I see you've made headlines again.'

'Death does seem to follow me around.'

'In that case, don't hurry back.' They shared a grim laugh. Birla had been in the thick of it with her on several recent cases. The man's sentiment was probably only half said in jest.

'Who's running the station now?'

'No one. They haven't announced Seth's replacement. Oberoi seems to think he's in charge. Strutting around with a broom up his backside.'

She could well imagine it. Hemant Oberoi, the son of a wealthy industrialist, had joined the force on a whim. Or possibly to annoy his father. And had then stepped into the proverbial manure by dallying with the daughter of a man even more powerful than Oberoi Senior. His banishment to Malabar House was temporary, but he prowled around the basement office like an exiled general, waiting to be set free to lead his legions in conquest.

'What are the others doing?'

'Oberoi is out on an investigation with Haq. Some Nariman Point banker decided to smother his wife with a pillow. And then shot himself in the mouth. Somehow, he missed.'

'Fernandes?'

'He's with your apprentice. At the gun range.'

'Seema?' Persis pictured the young girl from the slums who had recently become a fixture at the station. Seema Desai had won a place on an apprenticeship programme, inspired by Persis's example. After a rocky start, the girl had proved herself with an informal role on a recent investigation, so much so, that Persis had subsequently found her part-time work helping her father in the bookshop. Seema had taken to the role with the fervour of a bull elephant. Much to Sam's consternation.

'Fernandes has given her a weapon?'

'Two minutes in Oberoi's company and she wanted to shoot something. Apparently, the girl's a natural. Can already hit a fly at a hundred paces. Preferably one sitting on Oberoi's face.'

'Fernandes is hardly the judge of a good shot.'

'You can't hold it against him just because he shot the wrong man. Could have happened to anyone.'

George Fernandes was a good man. She knew that. He had ended up at Malabar House through one of those crushing accidents of fate, chasing a suspect through a crowded Bombay market, shooting the man dead, and then discovering, to his horror, that his bullet had found the wrong target. A part of her was glad that it was Fernandes and not Oberoi who had taken over Persis's mentorship of Seema. Another part of her felt a twinge of envy. Seema was still a long way from applying to the police academy, but Persis had hoped to be the one to steer her to that moment.

'Why are *you* in the office?'

'Someone has to man the fort,' said Birla. 'How goes it with your case? The headless governor. You've outdone yourself there.'

She was reluctant to discuss the investigation. Instead, she imagined herself back at her old desk, one of several jumbled haphazardly around the office, her ancient typewriter, the rickety wooden chair, and the dented filing cabinet in the corner. She became acutely aware of just how much she missed the station-house, and the life that she had begun to fashion there. For good or ill, Malabar House had captured her heart, and she found herself drawn back to it, salmon to birthing stream.

'I have to go,' she said.

'Well, keep in touch. And don't go losing *your* head. I hear they're quite hard to find again.'

After the call, she continued to dwell on the conversation and her own reluctance to confide in Birla about the investigation.

She saw the case as a chessboard, each piece representing suspects and strands of the investigation. John Templeton, now dead. Florence and Christopher Danvers, missing, perhaps hiding out somewhere, maybe even in town. Oren Rake, a man whose very livelihood might be at stake. And Maria Fontanelli, padding across the board like a big cat, on the hunt for a story.

Her thoughts drifted back to Mohan Sinha. What secrets had died with the man?

Some twenty years ago, he had served briefly in the region. A young Naga had been killed during his tenure as advisor to the tribes. How, if at all, did Aaron Koza fit into the puzzle?

And then there was Baba Dao, spinning a dark web over every-thing. Might the Naga revolutionary be behind Sinha's death, as Colonel Shroff – and others – suspected? The ultimate puppet master? If so, then who, among the hotel's guests, had served as his puppet?

She knew that she had reached that point in the investigation when the lines of evidence, like a compass needle finally finding true north, should be aligning to steer her in the right direction. Yet all was confusion. All she knew for certain was that the case had sunk its fangs into her.

Fangs. She thought again of the snake, how, but for the speed of her own reactions, she might well be inhabiting a first-class berth in Andrews's mortuary, stretched out alongside Mohan Sinha and John Templeton.

Snakes. Grenades. Mine collapses. How many brushes with death could she survive before her luck ran out?

Her eye caught on the door at the back of the office, leading into the storeroom.

Restless, and in need of a distraction, she got up and walked over to it. Entering the room, she was confronted by a tumult of old furniture: broken chairs, desks, table lamps, and a battered sofa that looked as if donkeys had kicked it around for sport. At the very back of the space stood a series of filing cabinets, three rows deep.

She knew that Constable Binny had already searched the cabinets, looking for the original police report into Aaron Koza's arrest, which she presumed had been prepared by someone at the old Kohima station. Binny had told her that his search had been unsuccessful.

But the man was hardly the most reliable investigator Persis had worked with. A chicken was sitting on his desk, for heaven's sake!

Besides, searching the files gave her something to focus on.

Picking her way through the maze of junk, she decided to begin with the cabinet closest to the door. She opened the topmost drawer ... and then bellowed as a grey shape leaped out at her, landing on her shoulder, before hurling itself from there to the floor.

A mouse.

If it wasn't rats, it was mice.

She allowed her heartbeat to return to normal, then resumed her search.

Within minutes she realised that the task was going to take longer than she had thought. The files were in no discernible order, hundreds and hundreds of reports catalogued as if stuffed into a barrel and thrown over a cliff.

A cold fury rose inside her.

She had always believed that flogging was too good for those who considered paperwork an inconvenience. Meticulous attention to paperwork formed the backbone to any successful organisation – the British had ruled an empire practically on the strength of their ability to make people fill out forms, in triplicate. And, of course, shooting them when they didn't. This prerequisite went double for the police service, where reports served as the touchstones from whence justice might be dispensed – or innocence determined – long after the initial offence had taken place.

It took her several hours to impose a sense of order on the files before her. There were almost three decades' worth of records, over a thousand cases. In Bombay it might have been ten – or a hundred – times as many.

She made piles of files based on the date typed – or scribbled – on top of each folder, flinging them on to heaps corresponding to each year. She would leave it to Binny to tidy up the mounds later on, and file them properly. Many of the files displayed fire or water damage. Or the cheese holes made by boring insects.

When she finally found records for 1930, the year in which Koza had been arrested, she slowed down, went through them with greater care.

Another thirty minutes passed . . . and then, finally, she had it.

The manila folder trembled in her hand.

She opened the file, found a photograph of a young man glued to the inside cover. Aaron Koza. Intense, dark features; a head of Brylcreemed hair; a white shirt; clean-shaven.

The eyes seemed to drill into her; she was forced to tear her gaze away.

The report began with a typed cover page, setting out the date – 15 March 1930 – the arrested man's name and particulars, and the old stationhouse's address.

She turned the page.

For a moment, she stared at the file in stupefaction.

The bulk of the report had been torn out. The jagged edges of the sheets stared up at her.

A dull rushing sound, like steam, sounded in her ears.

And then she stood, and went back to her desk. Taking a handkerchief from her pocket, she soaked it with water from her glass, and set it over her face. Leaned back in her chair.

Why was the report missing? Who had torn out the pages? *When* had they been torn out?

If Koza's plight had captured her imagination before, now it blazed inside her thoughts, a full-blown inferno.

She pulled the handkerchief away and looked down at the folder, opened it, checked it again, as if, perhaps, the act of hiding behind a dampened cotton sheet had somehow restored sanity to the world, and the missing pages had magically reappeared.

But the world, as she had discovered over the past year, was rarely a sane place.

And for a policewoman operating at the very edge of darkness, easy answers were as hard to come by as a rich man's journey through the eye of a needle.

35

The door swung back and Roshan Seth marched into the office.

He stopped as he caught sight of Persis, crooked a finger at her, then turned and headed for his office.

Once inside, he stalked around to the far side of his desk, violently pulled open a drawer, excavated a bottle and a glass, and poured himself a drink. She watched him take a large swallow, then begin pacing figures of eight behind the desk. 'I've been to see Shroff's new deputy, a Major Liaqat Khan. He's just rolled into town at the head of what looks like an entire battalion, up from Calcutta. It appears that the major will soon be joining Shroff in the interior. They're going to set the hills alight, smoke Baba Dao out. Crush the rebellion, once and for all.'

Persis took a seat, set down the manila folder she had found in the storeroom, and said, 'And the Centre has sanctioned this?'

'Would it matter if they hadn't? Who can stop Shroff from doing exactly as he pleases out here? Sinha's death has given him a free hand. Nehru will look the other way – all in the name of national security.' Seth set down his glass with a thump, then lowered himself slowly into his seat. His glazed eyes drifted to a point somewhere beyond the stationhouse. 'I thought it would be different out here. I thought I could leave the old hatreds behind, the politics, the infighting. I should have known better.'

Persis allowed him a moment, then said, sharply, 'We still have a case to solve.'

Her commanding officer roused himself from his personal Slough of Despond, picked up his glass again. 'You were right. You said all along Sinha's murder wasn't the work of insurgents. Not that Shroff – or anyone else – wants to hear that.'

'Are you referring to John Templeton?'

'I am. Andrews filled me in this morning.'

'So you subscribe to the theory that Templeton murdered his boss, then killed himself in a fit of guilt?'

'Why am I sensing that you're not convinced?'

Persis lined up her thoughts. But Seth spoke before she could get a word out. 'I should tell you that Shroff has already heard of Templeton's suicide. His theory – the theory he wishes us to officially endorse – is that John Templeton was in the pay of Baba Dao. He murdered Sinha at Baba Dao's behest. Another foreigner intoxicated by the insurgent cause.'

'I don't buy it. And I suspect you don't either.'

Seth gave a hollow laugh. 'What does it matter what either of us believe?'

'There's something else.' She told him about the snake in her room. 'Someone tried to get me out of the way. That should tell us something.'

'You can't be certain the snake didn't find a way into your room all by itself. In case you hadn't noticed, we're surrounded by jungle. Besides, even if a human agent *is* responsible for the snake, Shroff will argue that it was Templeton's doing, attempting to stop you from pursuing your investigation. When his attempt failed, he realised the game would soon be up, and so he decided to top himself.'

'That doesn't make much sense.'

Seth threw up his hands. 'Fine. So perhaps Templeton didn't kill himself. Perhaps Baba Dao gave him a helping hand off that bridge. Perhaps our insurgent friend was tying up loose ends.'

'Why would a man hidden away deep in the jungle, a man who openly challenges the might of the Indian army, care about "loose ends"?'

But to this Seth had no reply.

'There are other things. Loose ends of my own.' She led him through her recent findings, the Aaron Koza case, the fact that Florence Danvers had been in Sinha's room the night he had died, that she had slept with the man in order to persuade him to approve the permit she and her husband so desperately craved. 'And then there's the cross found in Templeton's hand. I'm convinced it's the same one I saw around Christopher Danvers's neck.'

'And you have evidence of this?'

She hesitated. 'No.'

'Why would the Danvers kill Templeton?'

She felt suddenly unsure of her footing. 'If we assume that the Danvers were responsible for Sinha's murder – perhaps Christopher Danvers killed the man after discovering his wife's infidelity – and we further assume that somehow Templeton found out, and that he threatened to reveal what he knew – then it's not inconceivable that Danvers somehow lured Templeton out to that bridge. A scuffle ensued, Danvers threw Templeton over the side, and lost his cross in the process.'

'What exactly would Templeton hope to gain by blackmailing the Danvers? They're a missionary couple, not millionaires.'

Persis had no answer to this. 'Nevertheless, I'd like to bring them in for questioning.'

'I told you to arrest them after you found the hairs in Sinha's room. You spoke with them, but let them go. Why?'

She had known that Seth would eventually circle back to this. 'I didn't think they were responsible.'

'You didn't then, but you do now?'

'I – I'm not sure. But there's something else I'd like to ask them about.' She took out her notebook, handed Seth the sheets of paper she had discovered in the Danvers's room.

'What's this?'

'Documents I found hidden in the Danvers's suite at the Hotel Victoria.'

'Is this Chinese?'

'Yes.'

'Presumably, you don't expect me to decipher this?' His tone could have cut through lead pipe.

'I've had it deciphered. It's a list.' She took several more sheets from her notebook and passed them over. 'Here's the translation.'

Seth scanned them. His moustache twitched. 'This is a list of military supplies. Weapons. Clothing. Field kit.'

'Yes.'

The room seemed to contract. 'What do you think it means?' he said, finally.

'I don't know. But if Shroff were to hear of this . . .'

'It wouldn't change a thing. Shroff is hellbent on destruction. Nothing is going to deflect him from his path.' He cradled his jaw with a hand, eyes still on the sheet before him. 'Forget the Danvers. This case has enough complications as it is.' He cut off her incipient protest: 'Tell me about this Koza business. Surely you don't think *that* has anything to do with anything? A twenty-one-year-old case?'

She tapped the manila folder she had discovered in the storeroom. 'I found this out back. The police report filed following Koza's arrest. The key pages detailing who was present at his interrogation – and exactly what was said – have been torn out. Why?'

'Who cares why?' Seth's frustration appeared ready to boil over. 'Why would Koza's death have anything to do with Sinha's murder two decades later?'

'I don't know that it does. But I want to follow it through.'

He placed his elbows on the desk and leaned in. 'Persis, you don't seem to understand what it is that I am trying to tell you. Colonel Shroff is now in charge of this region. We are under military rule in all but name. He wishes us to draw a line under the case. If we go against him, we are, effectively, challenging both his personal authority and the mandate he has been given by the Centre. What do you think will happen – to us both – in such a scenario? ... No. Don't answer.' He blew out his cheeks, seeking calm. 'I am ordering you to write up the case, pin Sinha's murder on John Templeton, and let that be an end to it.'

'And if I say no?'

His shoulders seemed to sink. He sat there like a disappointed orangutan. For a long moment, he simply stared at her. And then something else seemed to occur to him. 'Where is James?'

'In Calcutta.' She explained, tersely, that she had sent the sub-inspector off to investigate the half-burned photograph she had found in Mohan Sinha's room, and to hurry up Sinha's toxicology analysis.

Seth frowned. 'And when were you planning on telling me this?'

'I was in Mokokchung all day yesterday.'

'More loose ends?'

Persis lifted herself from her seat. 'There is *one* thing I agree with. I should write all of this up. Just in case, heaven forbid, we decide to do some actual policework around here.'

The station's only working typewriter was so old it looked as if it belonged in a museum.

Persis heaved it over to her desk, slipped a sheet of paper into the platen, and rolled it into position.

She took a deep breath, allowed the anger to steam out of her ears, and composed her thoughts. Finally, she began to type.

The noise of the clacking keys awoke the hen from her slumber. She perked up atop the almirah, then flapped down to the floor. Strutting over to Persis's desk, she watched the policewoman with a beady eye, then leaped up to settle herself on the desk's edge.

Persis stared at the beast. Her instinct was to shoo the bird away. But there was something strangely soothing about having the chicken sitting there. Absurd.

She went back to her report, detailing every aspect of the case, each discovery, each line of investigation. She knew that she should have typed up her notes at the end of each day, as had been her modus operandi back at Malabar House, but time had been in short supply over the past few days, particularly when each day had brought another leap into the unknown, accompanied by a side order of a brush with death.

Time passed. Her belly began to rumble. She glanced at her watch, realised that it was almost evening. She wondered briefly if James had reached Calcutta yet. The journey should have taken thirty hours or so, but the trains here were notoriously unreliable. She wondered if the trip would now turn out to be for nothing. Seth's insistence that she draw a line under the case disappointed her. Perhaps he had simply issued the instruction on instinct, or to place it on record should higher powers later demand answers of him.

Could she blame the man?

Bludgeoned by fate, Roshan Seth had already lost all that had once mattered to him: a career, purpose, ambition. Perhaps all the commander could do now was to survive, to hang on, as best he might, to the unravelling threads of his existence.

But Persis had never backed away from a fight. And though it might yet prove to be the case that John Templeton had murdered Mohan Sinha – and subsequently killed himself – the fact that so many loose ends remained meant that she could not permit herself to simply tie a neat bow around the case and hand it over to Colonel Hiten Shroff. Sinha, for all his faults, deserved justice. And if John Templeton's death had not been by his own hand, then the Englishman too deserved her consideration.

Besides, whatever else she might conclude about the circumstances behind Sinha or Templeton's deaths, there was one thing that continued to defy explanation: *how did the killer get into a locked room?*

The thought sat her back in her seat. She closed her eyes, and sent her mind spiralling through the ether to the Hotel Victoria.

Disembodied, she hovered above Sinha's suite, placing herself there on the night of his death. She observed the politician at his dining table, newspaper spread before him, pouring wine from a bottle taken from the dining cart, sitting down to eat his meal.

She walked in his shadow as he went to the bathroom. She watched him undress.

And then ... was this the moment that he had been overpowered by his assailant?

In all likelihood, yes. There was, after all, no sign of a struggle anywhere else in the apartment.

Once subdued, the politician had been manhandled into the bathtub, and then the gory work of removing the head had begun. And finally, a hand around the tap, water pouring in, and the decapitated body left to float in grim repose.

How had the murderer got into the locked suite?

Perhaps it was her assumptions that were at fault. What if the murderer hadn't entered the room? What if the murderer had been waiting *inside* the room? Hiding inside a wardrobe? Under the bed? But if that were the case how in the world did he then get out again, leaving behind a door locked from the inside?

She focused once again on the suite as a whole, wandered from room to room.

Hovering over the dining table, she looked down on the half-eaten meal, the newspaper spreadeagled on the table . . . A flicker of something. A piston moving slowly inside her brain . . . It was almost there. An idea of how it might have been done.

And then it was gone.

A grunt of annoyance escaped her. She had all but had it.

She glanced at the hen, who seemed to share her disappointment, clucking in sympathy.

Sighing, Persis bent back to the typewriter to finish her report.

36

Back at the Hotel Victoria, Persis found Peter Jadonang at the reception counter.

'Have the Danvers returned?'

She fully expected him to reply in the negative, but instead he nodded. 'Yes, madam ... What I mean is that *Mr* Danvers has returned. He went up to the library. I served him coffee there.'

'No sign of Mrs Danvers?'

'He did not mention her, madam.'

She took the stairs to the first floor, walked along a carpeted corridor, and through a pair of darkwood doors into the library.

The place had the look and feel of a Victorian gentlemen's club. Floor-to-ceiling bookshelves crammed with leather-bound volumes; glass cases crowded with esoteric objets d'art and the carcasses of small animals; a scattering of comfortable armchairs in which it was easy to imagine side-burned martinets of empire gently dozing, hard-spined tomes propped on their stomachs.

There was only one person in the library, and it wasn't Christopher Danvers.

Maria Fontanelli rose from a maroon Chesterfield, a book in hand. Persis caught a flash of gold lettering. *Alice in Wonderland.*

Fontanelli noticed her look, smiled. 'It seemed appropriate ... Were you looking for me?'

'No. Christopher Danvers.'

'Yes, he was in here. Left just as I came in. I believe he went up to his room.'

Persis began to turn away.

'I hear you've identified the killer. In fact, I hear he took a dive off a bridge in Kohima.'

Persis felt the muscles of her face tighten. 'John Templeton is a suspect in Sinha's killing. No more.'

Fontanelli stepped closer. 'In my business, narratives have a way of taking on a life of their own. John Templeton, an Englishman in post-Raj India, working for an Indian, decides to murder his employer, and then kills himself. Why? At the behest of Baba Dao? Or is the motive personal?' A smile split her features. 'First rule of journalism. Reduce the large to the small. Focus on the human element. I could dine for a month off the bylines alone.'

'It's usually the human element that's the first to feel the heat when the large, as you put it, makes itself known. Shroff is on the warpath. The Naga Hills are going to be a dangerous place for a while.'

'Where you see danger, I see opportunity. War zones are where journalists make their names.'

'War zones are also where journalists get killed. I'd hate to be the one writing to your mother.'

For the first time, Fontanelli's mask slipped. Her smile vanished. A tongue flicked out to touch her bottom lip. 'Tell me, that photograph you showed me, Sinha as a younger man, did you get anywhere with it?'

'Not yet. Why do you ask?'

A beat. 'We're not so different, Inspector. Journalists are detectives, in our own way. We also hate loose ends.'

Standing outside the Danvers's room, Persis hesitated, recalling her uninvited entry of the day before.

But this was no time for doubt.

She thumped on the door, then stepped back.

Seconds passed, and then the door opened. Christopher Danvers stood there, dressed in a suit. Persis's eye went immediately to the front of his shirt. The wooden cross was missing.

'I'd like to talk with you. It's urgent.'

She thought the man might protest, but instead he simply stepped back into the room and ushered her through. She heard the door snick shut behind her. A flutter of panic raced up her spine. Turning, she faced the florid American. Her hand stayed close to her holster. 'Where's Florence?'

He turned aside her question with one of his own. 'What is it you want to talk to me about?'

'Last night, John Templeton's body was found below a bridge on the outskirts of Kohima.'

'So I've heard.'

'Did you also hear that we found a wooden cross in his hand? Exactly like the one you usually wear.'

He blinked. 'What are you suggesting?'

'Where *is* your cross?'

A frown. 'I don't know. I seem to have misplaced it.'

'When did you realise it was missing?'

'I'm not sure exactly when . . .' He stopped. 'Why would I want to harm Templeton? I barely knew the man.'

'Templeton was Sinha's aide. His confidant. Perhaps you blamed him for failing to help you obtain the permit you wanted from Sinha.'

'That's ridiculous.'

'Or perhaps he discovered that *you* killed Sinha. Perhaps he threatened you. Tried to blackmail you.'

'You're making no sense. I had nothing to do with Sinha's death. And even if Templeton *had* threatened me, what exactly could I have given him? I'm a missionary. I have no worldly chattels.'

'Are you really?' said Persis, softly. 'A missionary? Is Florence?'

The American's eyes narrowed. 'What's that supposed to mean?'

She pulled the sheets she had taken from their room from her pocket, held them out. His gaze remained on hers, then dropped to the sheets. Immediately, she saw his eyes widen. 'Why would a pair of American missionaries be in possession of a list of military ordnance, written in Chinese?'

He appeared to have lost the power of speech, entranced by the papers in her hand.

'Where is Florence, Christopher?'

He seemed to revive. His shoulders straightened. A strange light glistened in his eyes. 'Florence? You won't find Florence, Inspector. Florence is gone.'

Alarm trilled inside her. 'What do you mean? Have you harmed her?' She stepped forward. 'What have you done?'

A smile twisted his features. But he said nothing.

The silence stretched. And then, without warning, the door burst open in a blur of noise and colour. Within seconds, the room was full of soldiers, armed and aggressive. They surrounded the American. 'Christopher Danvers, we are here to take you into custody.'

Persis stared at the soldier who had spoken. 'On whose orders?'

'Colonel Shroff.'

'On what charge?'

'I am not at liberty to say.' He nodded at his men.

The last thing Persis saw, as Danvers was bundled from the room at a double-trot, was the American's face. There had been no shock, no anger. Merely a dull resignation.

As if he had been expecting nothing less.

* * *

She found Apeni Ao in the dining room.

'Do you know that Shroff's soldiers have just hauled away one of your guests?' She explained the situation.

The woman said nothing, merely seemed to compress further in her seat. 'What would you have me do? In the past week, two of my guests have died, at least one of them brutally murdered. And now another is arrested by the military.' Sadness leaked from her tiny frame. 'This truly is the end, Inspector. I cannot see the Hotel Victoria surviving this. I am already mortgaged to the hilt. I can barely service the debt as it stands. I cannot even sell the place. Who would buy a scandal-hit property such as this?'

Persis said nothing. There was nothing to say.

She had only been in her bedroom five minutes, when the phone rang.

It was Maisie Blackfinch.

Persis hesitated. Every instinct told her to ignore the call. But for how long could she run?

'Yes?'

She heard the woman clear her throat. 'Persis. I seem to keep missing you.'

'No. I simply had no wish to talk to you.'

She heard an intake of breath. 'Well, that's refreshingly direct.'

'What do you want?'

'I thought you might like to know how Archie is doing.'

She wanted to tell the woman to go to hell and to take Archie Blackfinch with her. But she couldn't. Her traitorous heart was thumping two-fisted at the inside of her ribcage, bellowing to be heard.

'He hasn't pulled out of his coma. The doctors remain hopeful. They think he could snap out of it at any moment. But, frankly, I've stopped believing them. His vital signs are fine. He just seems . . . disinclined to wake up.'

'He's not asleep.'

'I know.' A snap in the woman's voice. 'At any rate, I've come to a decision. I'm going to take Archie back to London. Have him looked at by specialists. We have the best doctors in the world. In London.'

Wingbeats of panic around her ears. Words crowding into her gullet. 'You can't—'

'I'm his wife,' said Maisie, cutting her off. 'His welfare is *my* responsibility. I gave him every chance to recover out here. It's time for a change.'

The floor seemed to be sinking beneath her feet.

'I just thought you should know.'

'Fine,' said Persis, and put down the phone.

A haze had drifted in front of her eyes. Her stomach seemed to have curled in on itself. She felt her way to the bed, sat down on the edge.

Blackfinch's face floated before her. Smiling crookedly, sunlight glinting off his spectacles. She remembered his scent, the warmness of his breath, the physical heft of him, moving above her.

She lay back, stared up at the ceiling.

The idea that he would vanish, back to the far side of the world. That the possibility of seeing him again might be extinguished, once and for all.

A resounding terror fell upon her.

It was several seconds before she realised that the sound of weeping was her own.

37

Dreams plagued her throughout the night. Twice she awoke in a coil of bedsheets, Lancashire cotton soaked damp with perspiration, hair matted to her forehead, a nameless terror on her lips. Sleep came and went. Monsters snarled at the edges of conscious thought.

When she awoke for the final time, morning had edged slyly towards afternoon. The police officer in her was horrified; another, saner part of her felt a measure of relief. Days of mental and physical punishment, of near-death escapes, had taken their toll.

She was human, after all.

She lay there, head turned, blinking at coins of sunlight patterned on to the wall by the window blinds. The world beyond was eerily quiet. The monkeys were silent. She found it disorienting. Absurdly, she missed them.

She rose, showered, dressed in another freshly laundered uniform, then picked up the phone and asked to be connected to the Kohima stationhouse. Roshan Seth answered on the seventh ring.

She explained the situation to him, the events of the past twenty-four hours. The arrest of Christopher Danvers, the fact that he had vanished into military custody.

'We need to get him out. I need to talk to him.'

Seth's laugh sounded like a dying seal. 'Why don't you ask me to move Jerusalem to a less contentious location while I'm at it?'

'In that case, we need to find Florence Danvers before the army catches up with her.'

'And how exactly do you propose we do that? Shroff has flooded the region with soldiers. What do *I* have? James is in Calcutta. And I wouldn't trust Binny to find his own shoes if they were glued to his feet. Which leaves you and me. Kohima is small, but not *that* small.'

Persis considered the situation. The night's fitful rest had left her feeling surprisingly calm, ready for the challenge ahead. 'There are only so many places she could have gone.' A thought suddenly scraped across the front of her brain. 'Why was Christopher Danvers arrested by the *military*?'

Silence.

'A few hours after I showed you the military ordnance list I'd found in the Danvers's room, soldiers arrived to arrest him.'

The silence stretched to breaking point. Finally, Seth spoke. 'Fine. Yes, *I* phoned Major Liaqat Khan and told him about the list. It's clearly a military matter, out of our jurisdiction.'

The urge to rail at him ballooned into her throat. But he cut her off before she could speak. 'The Danvers have been lying to you from the start. Whatever they are, they're not missionaries. I'm a patriot, Persis. I won't apologise for that.' The line went dead.

She stared at the receiver in her hand, then set it down, gathered herself, and headed downstairs. A few months ago, she might have allowed her rage to get the better of her. But time – and experience – had tempered her. Seth had acted according to his lights. Or to serve his own convenience. Either way, there wasn't much she could do about it now.

As she passed reception, she was stopped by an apparition limping towards her, a dark and wounded ghost that took her back to the razor-edged dreams of the night before. A momentary shock ran through her; she found herself frozen to the spot. And then the apparition spoke. 'Madam, I have been waiting for you.'

She blinked away the vision. The man before her was no spirit. This was Oren Rake's site manager, Adam Zhimomi. The man who had saved her life in the mine; and who, in turn, she had rescued from their joint entombment.

'What are you doing here?'

'I must show you something.'

'What are you talking about?'

'I cannot *tell*. I must show. Please come with me.'

'Where?'

'Into the jungle.'

'Why would I do that? Why would I trust you?'

'Because I have the answers you seek. Because I am tired of the lies.'

Her eyes remained on the man, with his crumpled white shirt, his smudged trousers, his haggard, peppery-bearded face. His features appeared to have aged in the past two days. He looked like a man who had awoken from a deep slumber, only to find himself on a conveyor belt headed towards a wood chipper.

'Wait here,' she said. She walked around the counter and found the hotel manager, David Keishing, sitting inside his office wrestling with a stapler. The stapler appeared to be winning. She explained the situation to him. 'If I'm not back within four hours, inform Roshan Seth at the police station.'

Keishing looked troubled. 'Are you sure this is wise? Given all that is happening?'

'I don't know,' said Persis. 'What I do know is that I need answers. And Zhimomi claims to have them.'

They were stopped at a checkpoint on the eastern edge of town.

A pair of armed gorillas in military fatigues barked at them in an extended duet, then ordered them to alight from Zhimomi's jeep. Persis took out her ID. 'I am investigating the murder of

Mohan Sinha. Colonel Shroff has expressly ordered me to find a link to Baba Dao. To do so, I need to visit the interior.' It was close enough to the truth.

The colonel's name set them on edge. They glanced at each other as if God had been mentioned, and they had been told He was on his way to carry out an inspection.

'Would you like to send a message to the colonel telling him that you have prevented me from carrying out his orders?'

She might as well have asked them if they would have enjoyed slapping a lion in the face.

Moments later, they were on their way.

38

The car – an imported white Buick, as sleek and as grand as a yacht – entered the city early on the morning of the second day after he had set off. James Angami offered up a silent prayer, and rolled his neck. It cricked like a bolt being ratcheted into place. He had been travelling for the best part of two days, had long ago stopped listening to his body's myriad complaints. What was the point?

The train from Kohima had been delayed for over twelve hours at Siliguri – an insurgent raid had made off with a section of track, leaving behind a trussed-up and severely concussed railway employee who would later swear blind that he had been trampled by a herd of wild horses.

Fed up of cooling his heels, James had finally ventured out of the station, and found a driver willing to take him to Calcutta. The man, a Bengali, was a native Calcuttan and, as the sub-inspector had quickly discovered, a belligerent loudmouth – it was generally considered the case that the two went hand in hand – and proceeded to spend the best part of the following day holding forth on the failings of his father, a respected industrialist, who, it transpired, had turned up at his local mosque for Friday prayers a week earlier, pulled a revolver from his pocket, and shot himself in front of a flock of the faithful.

Why he had done so remained a mystery.

Having died intestate, he had left behind a seven-sibling rivalry for his worldly goods that appeared set to not only sever family relations, but cut them into small pieces, and scatter the pieces on to a bonfire. 'The only ones getting rich from my father's wealth will be the bloodsucking lawyers,' the man lamented, in a soulful dirge that lasted almost the entire length of the drive.

But now, finally, they were here . . . Calcutta!

James hadn't been in the city since passing through on the way to boot camp, almost a decade earlier. A young man full of the excitement of the first-time-away-from-home adventurer. A young man full of himself. The glory of war had lent a bounce to his step, a mood mirrored by the great metropolis. Wartime Calcutta had been a city transformed by the influx of tens of thousands of soldiers, men in uniform willing to fritter their army salaries on wine, women, and whatever passed for song among the locals. In this, they were in keeping with the city's vision of itself, an indulgent metropolis that had once served as the capital of the British empire in India.

Raised from a pestilential, tiger-infested swamp by British engineers, the city that had once sat on the subcontinent's breast like a jewel – only to be dulled when the centre of power moved to Delhi – had regained some of her old swagger. Calcutta had always been more than the sum of its parts, at once a bawdy comedy, a licentious romance, and a place of monstrous splendour, Raj-era decadence vying with the soot-and-slums reality of the modern, rapidly industrialising city. A city that strived to be all things to all men. To some: India's city of joy; to others – such as Rudyard Kipling – Calcutta born and bred – the 'city of dreadful night'.

What Calcutta thought of Kipling was unprintable.

Having alighted near the Chitpur Railway Station, James thanked his host, then hailed a cab to the Sin City nightclub.

His thoughts turned to the case, and from there to Persis.

Strange woman. Intriguing, enigmatic, committed. But distant.

He had heard the rumours, of course. The men she had killed – in the line of duty. Not that killing seemed to faze her. The run-ins with the force's top brass – the latest of which had led to her banishment to Kohima. And the secret – perhaps not-so-secret – affair with an Englishman, a ripe mango of a scandal-in-the-making. An Englishman that, if the smoke signals were true, was currently lying in a hospital bed reduced to the status of drooling vegetable by a would-be assassin's bullet.

His own reaction to her presence was telling.

Not that he could express such a feeling. Aside from the fact that she was his superior officer, nothing about the woman communicated an indication that she would welcome such interest. She was the type who could garrotte a man's ardour with a single look, before kicking the corpse of his infatuation into a ditch.

And yet. Each time she settled her gaze on him, he felt his heart speeding up. Moments when he fought for composure around her.

Something had passed between them. He was sure of it. An unspoken sense of . . . kinship? Understanding? Attraction? A semi-coherent signal all but strangled by her past and his own reticence. And the shadow of a comatose Englishman.

The question was: *what could he possibly do about it?*

39

Adam Zhimomi stopped the jeep along a deserted stretch of road, thick jungle on both sides, bamboo rising high above the road, a river of blue sky caught between palisades of green.

Persis tensed. Her hand strayed instinctively to her revolver. Not that a revolver would be of much use against a coordinated ambush.

But Zhimomi ignored her, disembarking from the vehicle, and limping to the side of the road. She looked on as he began to push bamboo stalks out of the way. She saw that the stalks had been lashed to a wooden latticework, itself fashioned from bamboo, creating a makeshift gate that permitted the illusion of freestanding vegetation, whereas, in fact, it concealed the entrance to a dirt road.

From the jeep, the entrance was all but invisible.

Zhimomi returned, drove the jeep inside, then got out and closed the gate behind them.

The jeep wound uphill for another hour, following a tortuous dirt path. Persis saw that vehicles had come this way regularly enough to flatten vegetation into the earth, but little else had been done to ensure the integrity of the road. Potholes bounced them along; the jeep's axle cried out like a prisoner on the rack.

Zhimomi finally brought the vehicle to a halt. He beckoned her out, then led her through a bamboo thicket, pushing his way through with his bare hands. They emerged at the edge of a large field, spread over the hillside. The field was carpeted in tall flowers, heart-shaped, with waxy, blue-purple leaves and yellow stamens. As Persis looked on, Zhimomi slipped a knife from his pocket. A jag of alarm speared at her . . . but then the man leaned down, and hacked at the nearest flower. Sap flew into the air, and with it a distinctive, pungent smell.

Opium!

Persis marvelled at the vast expanse of the field. She had seen pictures of poppy fields before, but never the real thing. The scale of it took her breath away.

'This is one field,' said Zhimomi, his tone flat. 'There are others.'

She turned to look at him, remembered how the doctor who had treated Zhimomi after the mine incident had told her that the man was an addict.

'The hills have many mineral treasures: coal, oil, zinc, tin, even gold. But the most profitable crop is opium.' His face contorted. 'Opium has infected the jungle. We were children. We did not know. Now it has us in its grip.'

'Whose field is this? Oren Rake's?'

But he had already turned away, beckoning her onwards.

They skirted the edge of the field, coming upon a screen of trees. Zhimomi stopped behind the trunk of a towering pine, ushered her closer. Persis crept up behind him, looked over his shoulder, past the tree's trunk to a series of low wooden sheds sitting in a large square of cleared earth. A water-tower rose on stilts from the centre of the cluster. Several vehicles, including a motorcycle, could be seen parked in the lee of the largest of the buildings on the very edge of the clearing. The area seemed deserted, but Zhimomi's attitude indicated that this might not be the case.

'This is where the flowers are processed,' he whispered. 'We slice open the seed pods, allow the gum to bleed out. We dry the gum, then roll the dried resin into balls, ready to be transported for sale.'

'Where is it sold? To who?'

But Zhimomi seemed overcome by a sudden fear. He squinted towards the far side of the collection of buildings. 'We must leave.' His voice was low and urgent.

'Not yet,' said Persis. She bent low, then made her way to the nearest building. Staying in her crouch, she eased along to an open window, raised her head to peer into the interior.

A vast, gloomy space stretched away from her. Oil drums could be seen stacked around the edges, the centre of the room taken up by trestle tables on which were arrayed dozens of large wooden trays. In the trays were ranked thousands of resin balls.

She tried to imagine the wealth on display. Wealth that came at the expense of misery. How many lives had been ruined by the drug? How many deaths occasioned because of it?

'Hey, you!'

Her head jerked around. A man stood at the corner of the adjacent shed, staring at her as if a rare and strange creature had materialised before him.

Persis swung around to Zhimomi ... But the Naga had vanished.

She cursed, tensed herself to make a run for it, when the newcomer shouted again, this time brandishing a revolver: 'Stop!'

She twisted around, dived for the floor just as a bullet bit into the wall beside her, scattering wooden splinters in all directions.

Rolling forward, she leapt back to her feet, and ran around the side of the shed as more bullets came her way. She snatched at her revolver, reached back around the corner, and fired off a volley of shots. Shouts came back by way of reply, followed by more shots.

She heard another voice join the first, then another. At least three, possibly more.

She was outgunned, and with a limited supply of bullets. How long could she hold out? Not long enough.

Desperately, she looked around.

About thirty yards away, shielded by the building, were the vehicles she had seen earlier.

No choice. She had to go. *Now!*

She stuck the revolver around the corner again, fired off three more shots until the revolver clicked empty, then turned, and ran.

Seconds later, she was peering into the larger vehicles, hunting for any sign that keys might have been left on the dashboard or in the ignition.

Nothing.

She stepped over to the brace of motorcycles, a pair of Royal Enfield Bullets. No time to think.

She straddled the nearest bike, hit the starter, heard the engine thrum to life, and, with a final look over her shoulder, roared off towards a dirt road leading into the poppy field . . . only to find a jeep coming towards her from the opposite direction.

She swung the bike into a tight curve, kicking up a spray of dirt, and bucked the machine towards the nearby line of trees. Shouts chased her, and then the sound of the second bike roaring after her. More bullets cracked into the air. She ducked low over the Enfield's fuel tank, raced towards the trees.

Moments later, she was swallowed by the forest gloom.

She weaved the bike through an obstacle course of tall trees, greenery flashing before her eyes, branches whipping at her. Revving the engine, she watched the needle spin frantically on the gauge; the bike roared ahead. The sound of her pursuer dwindled behind her.

She tore deeper into the forest. She had no idea where she was headed; her mind was aflame with a single overriding thought: the need to place as much distance between herself and the bike behind as she could.

It seemed an eternity later that she found herself easing off on the accelerator.

Had she lost her pursuer? She couldn't be sure; couldn't dare to hope—

A log sprang at her from beneath a cover of fallen leaves. She hit it full on with the front tyre, went careening over the top of her handlebars, somersaulting through the air. A strangled shout escaped her, a fraction of a second before she thudded into the trunk of a Nepal alder.

The lights went out.

40

The taxi dropped him off outside the club.

He paid the driver, watched him screech away in a storm of dust and fumes.

Turning to the building at his back, James spent a moment taking in the less-than-imposing façade.

Sin City was clearly fighting a losing battle against the ravages of time, decay, and a sharply fading popularity. The place looked as if it had been bombed during the war and then bombed again afterwards, for good measure. Repairs seemed to have been made in as cheap and slapdash a manner as would allow the doors to reopen. Perhaps they should have stayed closed. To the sub-inspector's eyes, the club resembled the sort of ratty gin joint that Kohima had in abundance, rather than the type of establishment where British and Indian mavens had once danced the night away.

He walked through the front doors, found himself in a poky, unmanned reception, and carried on through a set of swinging double doors to a parqueted main hall, tables and chairs stacked along the walls. In the centre of the hall was an elderly man slouched over a mop, moving across the floor at roughly the pace of tectonic shift. The mop appeared to be the only thing holding the old Methuselah upright.

'I'm looking for the manager of this place,' said James.

The janitor revived from his torpor, straightened, and pointed his mop towards the rear of the hall.

The manager, closeted in a tiny office at the back of the club, turned out to be a Frenchman named Maurice Deschamps, a man who looked as if he had lived out the club's credo, sampling not only every sin known to man, but several he had himself invented. Thin to the point of emaciation, his face resembled that of a Punchinello puppet, with a hooked nose and thinning hair the colour of mud scraped back over a bullet-shaped head. A feeble moustache was waxed into place above razor-thin lips. A collared shirt, open at the neck, revealed a sweaty expanse of coiled brown chest hair, like furred bedsprings.

James explained his errand, then held out the photograph Persis had found in Mohan Sinha's office.

'This is the politician whose head was taken from his body?' The words, spoken in a French accent, were accompanied by a slicing motion across the throat.

'Yes.'

'And you Indians say we French have taught you nothing.' His lips cracked into a mirthless smile. He registered James's confusion. 'The lessons of the French Revolution, *n'est ce pas*? Guillotine the head. The rest will follow.'

'The picture?' prodded the policeman. 'Do you recognise the woman?'

Deschamps waved a dismissive hand. 'I bought this club just before the war. I am afraid I cannot help you.'

Disappointment welled inside the younger man. Had he come all this way for nothing?

The Frenchman picked up a bottle by his elbow, poured a glass. 'Have a drink, *mon ami*.'

'I should go.'

'Yes, you may go. But then you would not speak with Mr Priyam.'

James frowned. 'I'm not sure I follow.'

'Mr Priyam has been here since the club was built. If anyone remembers your mystery woman, it will be him.'

41

Something was licking at her face.

Her eyes flickered open. Persis blinked, looking up at a haze of green. She turned her head. A tree frog focused into view. Its bulbous eyes observed her dispassionately. Had it just run its tongue over her?

She pushed herself on to her elbows. The frog darted away.

Pain ignited between her shoulder blades. Images leaped into her head: the chase, the crash, arcing through the air to strike a tree. She was glad that she had hit the tree with her back and not with her skull. Had the latter been the case, the frog might well have been called upon to deliver her eulogy.

She carried out a quick inventory. She had lost her gun and her pocketknife. But the rest of her seemed to be intact. No permanent damage. At least no more than she had already sustained over the past days.

And then she saw that her left lower trouser leg had turned dark. Investigating, she discovered a gash across the shin, bleeding gently into the cloth. Cursing, she slipped off her belt, pulled a handkerchief from her pocket, wound it around the cut, then tightened it into place using the belt.

Standing, she found she could walk well enough by ignoring the bolts of pain shooting up through her leg. A minor chord among the aria of aches that now seemed to constitute her body.

She circled the area, quickly found the bike. It had slipped into a shallow ditch, as if perhaps, it had known that its useful life was over and all that remained were burial rites. A quick look convinced her that there was no point wasting time on it.

She stood a moment, back against a trunk, examining her surroundings.

She had no idea where she was, how far into the forest she had come. She couldn't even be certain which direction she had come *from*. At any other time, the presence of so many trees, such lush environs, might be a tonic for the soul. But she was a lifelong city dweller, a creature of brick and concrete. In her current predicament, she was not only a fish out of water, but a fish bludgeoned over the head by fate, with a cat waiting in the wings.

A bird called out. A crossfire of jungle sounds erupted into the silence.

She willed herself into motion. The only thing she could do was to keep moving, and hope that she stumbled upon one of the many roads that crisscrossed the hills.

Waiting in this isolated spot to be rescued was not an option.

Sooner or later her pursuers would find her.

The canopy did little to alleviate the murderous heat. Nevertheless, she was grateful for the occasional shafts of light that speared down through the roof of leaves above her head to help her pick her way through the forest-floor gloom.

Time passed.

Her head sang. The gash on her leg throbbed, gently at first, and then thrumming inside her skull like the sound of a broken engine. Her tongue felt rubbery. Thirst clawed at her throat.

Did that tree look familiar? She was sure that she had seen it before.

Panic began to permeate the haze of her thoughts.

As a girl she had loved adventure stories, particularly tales of real-life survival. Men – and women – lost in remote wildernesses, battling nature – and the odds – to return themselves to civilisation and safety. In such stories, salvation had seemed inevitable. Plod along, one foot in front of another. Persevere. Eat the occasional tree snake. The fates might put you through the wringer, but, ultimately, you would be rescued.

But what about the *other* stories? What about the stories of men and women stranded in the wild that never made it? The ones killed by heatstroke, or thirst, or rock falls? The ones torn apart by wild animals. The ones who curled into a ball and just . . . died. No one wrote about them. No one wanted to hear about their ignominious ends.

Persis kept walking.

She wondered what her father was doing. No doubt he was sitting behind his counter in the bookshop, watching some old woman with a beady eye, on the off chance that she might sneak a volume of *Reader's Digest* into her handbag. Her father lived for the moment when he might catch one of those old bats at it.

And Archie Blackfinch. The Englishman's wife's words came back to haunt her. The thought of Archie being lifted into the belly of a plane – or a ship – and parcelled back to England, a comatose dummy with neither choice nor awareness of his predicament.

She knew that she should let him go. After all, what could she offer him? What could he offer *her*?

But that was the point, wasn't it? Love was an equation that made little sense.

Love. Hah! He wouldn't know love if it came and punched him squarely on the nose.

No. That wasn't right.

He had told her that he loved her. She distinctly remembered him saying the words. It was she who had failed to reciprocate. Why?

Perhaps, instinctively, she had known that something wasn't right, that he was hiding a grisly secret that would make the whole thing inherently unworkable.

Damn you, Archie Blackfin—

She tripped, stumbled forward, and rolled down a sudden declension in the ground.

When she righted herself, she saw that she was at the foot of a track leading up towards a cave mouth. The cave winked at her from an outcrop of grey rock rearing from the hillside.

A feathered spear stuck up out of the earth beside the cave mouth.

Alarm trilled through her, undercut by an overwhelming sense of relief. The spear was the first sign of humankind in what seemed like hours. And there might be water inside the cave. Trickling through the rocks. The thought alone constricted her throat.

She scrambled her way up to the cave, hesitated at the entrance, and then fell inside.

42

Mr Priyam, it turned out, was the club's accountant, a man as lugubrious as Frankenstein's monster.

He was a big man, sitting in a chair that seemed too small for him, round-shouldered, and perfectly bald, with white hairs shooting out of his ears, and dark, sinister eyebrows. His face – and form – looked made for thuggery; and yet his voice, a low basso rumble, was calm and measured.

Having listened to James's story, he slipped on a pair of half-moon spectacles and examined the photograph. Instantly, a change overcame his features.

'This is Sophia,' he murmured.

'Sophia?'

'Sophia Pierri. She worked at the club for several years, back when I was still the assistant bookkeeper.'

'What did she do here?'

'She was a hostess. A very popular one. Everyone loved her.'

'How did Mohan Sinha know her?'

'In the worst possible way. He used to come in here regularly. Back then, we were a haunt for many of the movers and shakers in town.' A grimace. 'He became infatuated by her. And she by him. Sadly, she did not see through him until—' He stopped.

'Until?'

'Until it was too late.'

James watched the old man's gaze drift into the past. 'They began a relationship,' Priyam continued. 'Sophia fell pregnant.

When she informed him, Sinha refused to have anything more to do with her. She was forced to leave the country in disgrace.'

'Where did she go?'

'She returned to her home town. In Italy.'

'Italy?'

'Yes. Did I not say? Sophia was Italian.'

'Do you know what happened to her?'

His lower lip folded upwards. 'She wrote to me, some years later. Just the once. Told me she had married. An Italian. A local baker. She had taken his name and he, in turn, had given his name to her child. Sinha's child.'

'What was the child's name? Can you recall?'

A beat, as memory was summoned. 'Maria. Maria Fontanelli.'

43

Persis stepped further into the cave ... A shape shot out at her, small and dark, zigzagging across the cave floor. She flung herself to one side; her foot rolled on a stone, and she pitched forward, crashing into what felt like a pyramid of stones. Her gull-like bark echoed off the walls.

And then she saw her assailant outlined in the cave mouth, barrelling out into the open. A boar. Relief washed through her. She choked out a laugh.

Her eyes adjusted slowly to the gloom.

She was sitting on the floor, surrounded by ... grinning skulls.

The realisation entered her with a dull horror.

She was inside a shrine. A shrine of bleached bone.

She had read about this sort of thing, caves where Naga from the olden times would leave the skulls of their ancestors. Holy places. Venerated. Preserved.

What would they make of her desecration, if they happened to stumble upon her?

A feverish terror rattled through her. Her emotional resources were all but depleted. But she had common sense enough not to sit here and wait for—

Noises filtered in from just beyond the cave mouth. The sounds of several people. Was it the Naga of this cave? Or had the men from the opium field found her?

Or was she simply losing her mind? At this point, she wasn't willing to bet against the latter.

She braced herself. There was nowhere left to run.

A voice drifted into the cave. 'Please come quietly. They really don't want to hurt you.'

Time stood still. Her head wobbled on her neck. She recognised that voice.

Impossible. What could *she* possibly be doing here?

A woman walked into the cave, hands raised, her silhouette backlit against the cave mouth.

'Persis? Are you OK?'

'Yes,' said Persis, faintly. There seemed no other sane response.

Florence Danvers stepped closer. 'In that case, I must ask you to come with me.'

44

The policeman in charge of the Manicktala station on Canal West Road had been unexpectedly helpful.

James had walked in, asked to use a telephone to make a call to Kohima. The politics of policing on the subcontinent being what they were, there was an equal chance that his request would be granted or that he would be thrown back into the street, if not the station's drunk tank. To be fair, you would have to be at least mildly intoxicated to request any sort of assistance from a police station in India's city of joy, unless that assistance involved relieving you of surplus cash in your wallet.

But the commanding officer, an Atul Bijoy, had turned out to be a jovial sort. A Bengali who clearly enjoyed more than his share of sweets, he had invited James to make his call, then further invited him to share a meal. Without waiting for an answer, he had snapped his fingers imperiously, sending a constable scurrying off to fetch rice and chicken from a local restaurant.

'Tell me, James, is it true that the door was locked from the inside?'

James suspected that Bijoy's helpful attitude stemmed more from a macabre sense of curiosity, than from any camaraderie of khaki.

'Yes,' he said. 'Sinha's suite was locked. We're still trying to work out how the killer might have entered.'

'I do so love a mystery,' beamed Bijoy. 'And a headless corpse, to boot. Delightful!'

James wasn't certain that 'delightful' was the first word that sprang to mind at the thought of Mohan Sinha's gruesome murder; but he had enough tact not to voice his concerns. 'The telephone?'

'Of course, of course.'

James expected the man might leave him to it, but Bijoy, like a Calcuttan mother-in-law on her son's wedding night, had every intention of keeping abreast of affairs as they developed. The younger man had no choice but to get on with it.

But they were both to be disappointed.

The call revealed only that Persis had left the hotel that morning and had yet to return.

James set down the phone. He would try again later. He *had* to let Persis know about Maria Fontanelli.

His thoughts focused on the implications of the revelation. The Italian had lied. She had told them that she was a journalist, sent to the Naga Hills in search of a story. But the truth was that *she* was the story. Mohan Sinha's illegitimate daughter. The daughter of a woman seduced and then abandoned by the murdered politician. It seemed a safe bet that Fontanelli had come to India to confront her father.

Had she been in his room that night? And if she *had* confronted him, had decades of rage – at her mother's abandonment, at her own grief of never knowing her true father – spilled out from her, spiralling into violence?

James knew that he should call Roshan Seth. Inform his commanding officer and have him make the arrest. But as his hand moved once more towards the phone, he froze.

He couldn't do that to Persis. To himself. This was *their* case. It was their arrest to make.

Ambition and duty. Rivals that rarely saw eye to eye.

He made his decision. Maria Fontanelli wasn't going anywhere. There had to be a reason the woman had stuck around after Sinha's killing. She was waiting for something. James had read about murderers who returned to the scene of the crime. Something warped in their psyche. Or simply a desire to observe, gleefully watching the authorities run around like headless chickens while the killer stood not yards away.

45

The blindfold transformed the forest floor into an obstacle course. Trailing roots. Stones sticking up out of the earth. But stubbornness was a hard habit to shake. It was only after the third time that she had been sent sprawling that she accepted the offer of Florence Danvers's hand.

They walked on in silence, broken by occasional bursts of chatter from the phalanx of Naga accompanying them. Persis had seen enough before the blindfold was put on to know that some of them had been dressed in tribal fashion, while at least one wore Western clothing.

'That gash on your leg will need seeing to.' Florence's voice seemed to thrum through her hand and along Persis's arm.

Persis said nothing for a while. A bird cawed in the canopy high above. 'You're not a missionary, are you?'

'No.' A beat. 'Though I *am* a believer.'

'In what?'

'Politics by other means.' The American's voice was bright and brittle.

'Is that what they're calling spying, these days?'

The woman said nothing.

'There can't be many American missionaries in India wandering around the blue hills with a list of military ordnance written in Chinese. Let me guess . . . CIA?' Persis turned her head. Light filtered in around the edges of the blindfold.

'I'm afraid I couldn't possibly confirm or deny.' They walked on. 'But let's assume, for the sake of argument, that you're in the right ballpark . . . I suppose you might have questions.'

'Only one. Why?'

It took a moment for Florence to respond. 'Conflict between India and China has been brewing ever since independence. Both nations have long laid claim to the Aksai Chin region to the north. While the British were here, *armed* conflict was, by and large, avoided. But the dynamic has now changed.'

'Why do the Americans care?'

'The tyranny of geopolitics, Inspector. This is a region in flux. The insurgency in the Naga Hills keeps the Indian government distracted, off balance.'

'And the American government wishes to support the insurgency by facilitating the provision of Chinese arms to the Naga? To Baba Dao?'

'Well, it wouldn't exactly be prudent – or smart – to offer *American* arms to Baba Dao. Plausible deniability, Inspector.'

'I don't see how you're going to be able to keep this quiet. Your husband is in custody.'

'He's not my husband.'

Persis almost chuckled, a cynical laugh. 'No. Of course not.'

'Though I am rather fond of him.'

'So fond of him that you left him behind to face the music when you ran for the hills.'

'That was *your* doing, not mine. I'm afraid your investigation into Mohan Sinha's death was placing us under scrutiny that we could ill afford. I had to make a choice.'

'You chose to leave your partner to the enemy.'

'Christopher – that's not his real name, of course – is a professional. I doubt that Colonel Shroff – or his goons – will get anything useful out of him.'

'Every man has his breaking point.'

'As does every woman.'

A silence passed. Persis heard the sound of a brook chattering over rocks.

'Did you kill Sinha?'

'No.'

'Did Christopher?'

'Not to my knowledge.'

'Why should I believe you? Everything about you is a lie.'

'I'm not asking you to believe me.'

Another silence.

'Why did you need Sinha's help? Why wait for a permit? Why not just infiltrate the hills and find Baba Dao yourself? I mean, you seem to have managed it now, anyway.'

'Our orders were to infiltrate with a plausible cover story so that we could move in and out of the area without restriction for an extended period of time. If we had simply entered covertly, sooner or later word would have got back to the Indian authorities – a pair of white Americans in the hills is a difficult secret to keep for any length of time. Shroff would have sent his soldiers after us. Our long-term mission here would have been compromised.'

'And now? Is Baba Dao everything you hoped he would be?'

'We're almost there,' said Florence. 'Perhaps you can judge for yourself.'

They removed the blindfold just before entering the village.

Persis blinked into the late-afternoon light, saw, to her right, the head of a dirt track winding into the jungle. To her left: a collection of vehicles parked on a square of cleared earth on the very outskirts of the settlement – a truck, a jeep, a motorbike, and several bicycles.

The village bloomed out of the trees, a collection of thatched-roof huts scattered around the clearing like birdseed flung by the hand of an untidy Creator. A troop of wild pigs gambolled past her. She saw villagers emerge from the dwellings, or stop mid-conversation to watch them pass. Bare-chested hillmen in black kilts, armed with spear and dao, torsos covered in tattoos. A pair of women squatted by a bubbling cauldron beside a large, central hut; a haunch of meat hung from a hook behind them. An emaciated elder sporting a bear-fur hat decorated with a pair of tusks and what she guessed was a monkey skull pulled a cigarette from his mouth to stare at her with undisguised hostility.

Half-naked children followed the troop's progress. Persis saw a small boy, copper-bellied, holding a bamboo flute, eyes rounded. She wondered if he had ever been out of the hills, had ever seen someone like her before. Then again, there were still men in Bombay who looked at her the same way, the idea of a female police officer as abstract to them as a ghost.

'In here,' said Florence, indicating the hut at which they had arrived.

Persis looked around her escort, at the sombre faces of the men ranged behind the American, faces lit by something she couldn't quite place. A curious sense of hunger.

Fear shivered along her spine. She knew, at a visceral level, that, despite Florence Danvers's cordial demeanour, she was in mortal danger. Baba Dao's actions had made it clear that he held the lives of non-Naga in contempt, particularly those who served the central authorities. In her khaki uniform – torn and tattered as it was – Persis was the living embodiment of everything he stood against.

She searched Florence's face for some sign of what awaited her inside the hut. Baba Dao, perhaps? But the American emanated only a quiet sense of sadness. Perhaps *that* said all that needed to be said.

There was no point in making a run for it. Even if she could evade the Naga, where would she go? Back into the jungle? What would be the point? Fate, the very idea of it, her father had once told her, should be fought against, with every fibre of one's being, right up until the point when fate became observable reality, impeachable and unalterable.

Persis drew herself up, then turned, and ducked into the hut.

She found herself in a high-roofed space, the roof held up by a central wooden beam, its underside coated in soot. Around her, on the walls, were bamboo shields; on the floor: bamboo mats, dyed primary colours. Several woven baskets were ranged to one side of the door. On the other, a bamboo cot, covered by a bearskin.

And in the centre of the room, a man, waiting to greet her.

'Hello, Inspector,' said Oren Rake.

46

The address that Persis had given him for the lab carrying out Mohan Sinha's toxicology analysis took James to the Command Hospital in Alipore.

The hospital was run by the Indian military for the benefit of the army's Eastern Command, catering to both active and ex-service personnel. The place boasted a hundred beds, white-washed corridors smelling of disinfectant, and a crisp sense of its own worth. White-coated doctors whizzed to and fro at the double, trailing cadet medics struggling to keep pace. Fierce-looking nurses sat behind gleaming counters as if they were gun emplacements.

The lab was located in the basement.

James entered to find himself in a small, neatly ordered, and blindingly white space. Heaven's anteroom.

Two men, both relatively youthful and both in lab coats, sat at a desk in one corner eating lunch scooped out of steel tiffins with their fingers. They stopped as he entered and looked at him warily, as if he might be a courier delivering instructions from army HQ ordering them to the front in some blood-soaked theatre of war.

He introduced himself and explained his errand.

The taller of the two men wiped his mouth with a cloth and stood up. He had a puckish aspect, clean-shaven and with amused eyes. The other was rounder, with a shaggy moustache and sloped shoulders. They introduced themselves as Shami and Ghosh. 'Yes, we received the samples,' said Shami. 'But there was no urgent tag accompanying them. And so we set them to one side. We have an enormous backlog, you understand.'

'Have you any idea how many people are murdered in Calcutta every day?' added Ghosh. 'We can barely keep up as it is.'

James frowned. 'You do realise that I'm talking about Mohan Sinha? The man whose killing has been on the front pages for the past few days.'

Ghosh shrugged. 'A body is a body. Once you're dead, who cares?' He shovelled rice into his mouth, messily festooning his moustache.

James gaped at the pair. 'Perhaps I am not being clear. I need that tox analysis. *Now*. As to who cares? *I* care. My commanding officer cares. The prime minister has taken a personal interest in this case. *He* cares. Perhaps I shall ask my CO to inform Delhi that a pair of lab jockeys in Calcutta have decided that the prime minister's wishes really aren't that important. Certainly not as important as sitting around stuffing their faces.'

Ghosh scowled and began to rise from his seat. 'Now, you look here—'

Shami waved a hand at him, cutting him off. 'Very well, sub-inspector. I believe you have quite clarified the situation. Given the circumstances, we would be more than happy to move this to the front of the queue. But the fact remains that no one informed us that this analysis was *that* important. As far as we were told Sinha was murdered by decapitation. The tox screen is irrelevant.' He sighed. 'We get it in the ear as it is, from the doctors at this hospital. As high and mighty as an elephant's bottom just because they carry military rank and we do not. The truth is nobody wants us here. We've been promised our own premises next year, but, until then, what you see is what you get. We're understaffed, overworked, and chronically unappreciated.'

James dipped his head. 'I meant no disrespect. But it really is crucial that I have this analysis before I leave Calcutta.'

'We shall see to it with alacrity,' said Shami. 'But it will take several hours. Perhaps you'd like to wait outside?'

47

For the longest moment all she could do was stand there, a cold wind gusting through her, despite the broiling heat. The sight of the American, in this place, at this instant in time, seemed a howling joke, played upon her by a god with a ribald sense of humour.

'You have questions,' said Rake.

She said nothing. Rake moved to a small bamboo table, picked up an earthenware pot, filled a clay glass, then walked over to her. He held out the offering.

Her instinct was to take it from him and dash it into his face.

The moment passed. She took the glass, gulped a large mouthful, then said, 'I can only assume the opium fields that Zhimomi showed me are yours.'

Rake shrugged. 'I wish he hadn't done that. But the man has become somewhat unreliable of late.'

'Try disillusioned. You're poisoning his people. How did you expect him to react?'

'Poisoning?' He gave an empty laugh. 'You really don't get it, do you? Those opium fields aren't *mine*, Inspector.'

His words broke over her like the sudden heat from a raging fire. 'The tribals,' she breathed.

Rake's eyes glimmered. 'The Naga grow the opium. I sell it for them and take a cut of the profits. They use the money to buy weapons to fight their war. The more weapons they have, the harder – and longer – they fight, and the more the Indian government opposes them. And so they need more weapons. So they grow more opium. It's a virtuous circle.' His expression was one of stifled amusement.

'And the Danvers? How do they fit into your operation?'

'The Danvers, as you have no doubt discovered, are CIA. They came here to support the Naga separatist movement.'

'Why would the CIA do that?'

'The CIA are a law unto themselves, Inspector. Who can truly understand their motives? But think about. It was American Baptists who converted the Naga to Christianity. There are old hawks in Congress who consider the Naga kinsmen, albeit of a duskier hue. And then there is the vast mineral and oil wealth in these hills. An independent Naga state will roll out the welcome mat for those who help them achieve emancipation.'

'Men like you?'

'*Americans* like me. I've been here a long time. I know the terrain. I know the people. I know what can be accomplished here.'

'You would hollow them out. Cheat them of their birthright. You and your masters back in America don't give a damn about these people.'

His eyes flashed. 'I'm a damn sight more sympathetic to them than Nehru's government.'

'Is that why you're helping to ravage them with drugs?'

'The opium is a means to an end. The mantra of all business is to diversify or die. If the Indian government wants to take my mine from me, I have to find another way to make a living.'

Her mind seethed at his obtuseness. She focused elsewhere. 'What is Florence Danvers doing here? In this village.'

'When she realised that her cover was about to be blown she fled. It's not as if she had a choice.'

'You were working together?'

'The Danvers initiated contact when they arrived out here. They wanted me to help expedite the permit from Mohan Sinha. They had a file on me. The CIA is nothing if not thorough. Besides, they couldn't have the Danvers slipping in and out of the jungle without permission, risking capture. They wanted a cover that would maintain its integrity while they established their operation in the hills.'

'That's why you were staying at the Hotel Victoria. That, and the fact that your mining licence was in jeopardy.'

'Yes.'

'And when Sinha didn't play ball, you killed him.'

Rake was already shaking his head. 'I didn't kill Mohan. And it wasn't that he didn't want to play ball. It was simply that his asking price was too high. Mohan wanted a cut of the opium profits. He wouldn't hand over the permits – or help me renew my mining licence – until we reached an agreement.'

She felt a hollowing-out of her stomach. Rake must have sensed her reaction. 'Frogs don't become princes in the real world, Inspector. Most men work for their own profit. If life has taught me anything, it is that.'

'It sounds to me as if you had ample motive to kill Sinha.'

'Mohan was a pragmatist. We would have reached a deal sooner or later. But he enjoyed keeping the Danvers dangling. He wanted to show them who was in charge.'

'He knew they were CIA?'

'He knew. And he was keen to demonstrate that he was no pushover. If the CIA wanted to operate in the hills, they would have to answer to him.'

She considered his words. 'Did Florence or Christopher Danvers kill Sinha?'

He shrugged. 'I can only speak for myself. But if they did, then it was on the orders of the CIA.'

'Why are you helping them?'

'Why do you think?'

The answer was obvious. 'They're paying you.'

A little bow of the head. 'The CIA paid me to keep them safe once they made it out into the hills and to introduce them to tribals actively engaged in the insurrection. Frankly speaking, Mohan's death – and your investigation – has queered the pitch. You've forced Florence to go on the run. That was never part of the plan.'

'Christopher Danvers is in Colonel Shroff's custody. They'll soon know what you've been doing.'

'I highly doubt it. Do you know what Danvers did in the CIA before he took up missionary work? He was an interrogator. There's not a thing they can do to him that he hasn't seen or done himself.'

'Shroff is in the hills. Sooner or later he'll find your opium fields. And then he'll burn your operation to the ground.'

Rake was shaking his head in amusement. 'Shroff is an army man to the core. Thinks he's an Indian version of Patton. Blood and guts. And tanks. But in these hills, on this terrain, against an enemy that can move quickly and unseen through the jungle? He's outgunned and he doesn't even know it. As for the opium fields – we can move sites at the drop of a hat. You should see the Naga in action. They can clear a hillside in a matter of days. And there is no shortage of secluded hills out here.'

A beat as she gripped down hard on her thoughts. 'I found a list of Chinese military ordnance – small arms, mortars, radio sets – in the Danvers's room. I'm guessing that their task was to act as middlemen between the Naga and the Chinese. But why were the Chinese providing arms to the Naga in the first place?'

'The Chinese are hot on the idea of Naga independence. They've been talking about it in Peking for years. Anything to poke Nehru in the eye. Plus, of course, strategically it serves China's long-term territorial ambitions.'

'And here you are, in the middle of it all, a giant spider at the centre of the web. You're playing a dangerous game.'

'Life is dangerous. I thought you would have figured that out back at the mine.'

Her brow furrowed. He cut her off before she could respond. 'No, Inspector, I didn't have anything to do with that rock fall.'

'And the snake in my room?'

He seemed genuinely puzzled. Was it an act? 'If I wanted to kill you, it wouldn't be that subtle.'

'And now? Am I your prisoner?'

'*My* prisoner? No, Inspector. You're Baba Dao's captive. And Baba Dao will decide what to do with you.'

She gaped at him. 'I – I thought *you* were Baba Dao.'

He smiled. 'Whatever gave you that idea?'

48

Having been ushered out of the lab, there seemed little point hanging around the hospital. His brief stint in the army – and the bloody action he had emerged not entirely unscathed from at the Battle of Kohima – had left James with a residue of bad memories and a surfeit of ill feeling towards military rank. Wandering around the hospital made his palms itch. At any moment he expected to come face to face with the sort of chinless, medal-encrusted barbarian who had so distinguished himself during the war, feeding young men into the meat grinder of his own ambition.

But the truth was that the British officers he had served under were nothing but a memory now, having long ago taken leave of the hills, the country, and their own senses. In their wake remained the smell of rotting principles enshrined in a military legacy that men like Colonel Hiten Shroff appeared desperate to live up to.

The thought of Shroff and his heavy-handed tactics in the Naga Hills warmed a slow rage inside him. Following his graduation from the police academy, James had returned to Kohima. Here he had found comfort in the past, in the familiar, enough, at least, to hold at bay the ghosts of war. But he had always known it was a temporary truce. War was like a bad case of syphilis. Once infected it never truly left a man, no matter how far you ran from it and no matter that you lulled yourself into believing that you were cured. The Naga Hills had become a battleground, the death of Mohan Sinha a shot across the bows that would not go unanswered. The ghosts were gathering once more.

And James had, as yet, no idea which side he might eventually end up fighting for.

He found a decent-looking hotel on a bustling Calcuttan thoroughfare not far from the hospital and sat down to a leisurely meal in a restaurant featuring white-clothed tables set with shiny cutlery and single flowers in vases. A waiter in white clicked his heels like a Nazi commandant and presented a menu with gold-inked fleurs-de-lis in the corners.

While his order was being prepared, James walked back to the lobby and asked the receptionist to connect him to the Kohima police station.

Instead of Persis, Constable Binny's grating rasp came on the line. 'She's still out. Come to think of it, I haven't seen her around all day.'

'Did she call in?'

'No. Are you still in Calcutta?'

'Yes.'

'Anything new to report?'

James almost dropped the phone in surprise. In the time he had known Binny, the constable had distinguished himself with his unwavering commitment to avoiding doing any actual work. Investigations came and went and Binny simply grinned – and smoked – his way around them. If malingering had still been an offence, the constable would have been up on charges a dozen times over. James had often wondered just how long Binny had been around. With his boot-leather features, the man reminded him of an old tortoise, slow, measured, and seemingly immortal.

'I'm waiting on the toxicology analysis. We'll soon know if Sinha was drugged by his killer.'

The constable grunted and shut the phone. James stared in astonishment at the receiver, then set it back into its cradle.

Binny. A law unto himself in a place where the *law* often seemed a law unto itself.

He returned to the restaurant and settled into his meal. His mind found its way back to Persis. The woman was a stickler. Unusual for her to be out of touch for so long. Then again, she had always presented herself as the type to sneer at danger.

The case flapped its way across the room and settled on his table.

Mohan Sinha's death had made national headlines. The prime minister himself was awaiting the outcome of the investigation. It was not so far a leap to believe that those responsible for unravelling the mystery might find themselves in line for preferment.

How would he parlay his moment in the sun?

A transfer. That was a given. He hated the idea of leaving his grandmother behind, but his period of emotional convalescence back in the hills was coming to an end. Six years on from the war, it was time to move on.

Where would he go? The mainland, undoubtedly. But where? Calcutta? Delhi? Perhaps even Bombay?

A thought that, once again, returned him to Persis.

All roads seemed to lead to the woman.

And in that moment, sitting there, he resolved to say something. He couldn't let the situation carry on as it was ... It was hardly a crime, was it? Two single people, seeking companionship. Why *shouldn't* they find safe harbour in each other? That they shared a mission, wore the same uniform, should not stand in their way.

Assuming he hadn't misread the situation entirely.

Anxiety pulled up a seat at the table, grinned at him.

What if Persis held no feelings for him whatsoever? He played out the hideousness of rejection ... by his superior officer! How would he ever be able to set foot in the station again?

His soup arrived, the waiter making a convoluted cabaret routine out of serving him.

James waited for him to leave, then picked up his spoon.

In truth, he had lost his appetite.

49

She heard the wooden crossbar fall into place with a *thunk* behind Rake as he left the hut.

Why had they bothered? Did they think she would walk out of the front door and stride confidently through a camp of armed men and into the jungle?

Her emotions roiled. Rake's words had set her afire. She had grasped the edges of the unravelling conspiracy before the American had laid it out for her, but to have her suspicions confirmed gave her little satisfaction. The Danvers had proved to be liars, Rake a ringmaster in a deadly circus.

Anguish tore at her and she found herself gravitating towards the centre of the room, where she stretched out on the bamboo cot and stared sightlessly at the ceiling above. It bothered her less that she found herself once more in mortal danger, but rather that she might be sent spinning into the great abyss without determining the identity of Mohan Sinha's murderer. Rake's denial could not easily be dismissed. The man had no reason to lie, not now. And Florence Danvers's claim that she – and her 'husband' – were also innocent of Sinha's killing . . . Was she willing to accept that at face value?

Where did that leave her investigation? The thought drew a hollow laugh from her. Investigation? She would be lucky to make it through the next day.

She heard the door being fumbled open and twitched on to her elbows.

A Naga woman entered, bearing food. A fistful of rice on a clay plate, together with a steaming earthenware bowl sloshing with a murky broth. Pieces of boiled meat bobbed in the broth. She hoped it was chicken. Or, at least, something that had originally had four legs.

Her first thought was to refuse the food. But then her father's words returned to her. 'You never know where your next meal is coming from, Persis, so take what you can.' A strange sentiment for a man who, since the day of his birth, had been fed three square meals a day by his mother, maid, wife, daughter, and, on those occasions he could stand her presence in the house, his wife's younger sister.

After the woman had left, she sat cross-legged on the floor and ate quickly, a sudden, ravenous hunger lending teeth to her stomach.

Her thoughts drifted back to Bombay, to her father, her cat, Aunt Nussie, and, ultimately, to Archie Blackfinch. She wondered how the Englishman was faring, what he would make of her predicament, had he been capable of conscious thought and not lost within the dark whirlpool of his coma.

She realised that her anger had all but ebbed away. Archie hadn't really lied to her, had he? Yes, he had concealed from her the fact that he was, technically, still married, but his sentiments had not been false. Marriage was more than a piece of paper. It was a connection and once that connection was severed you were estranged in all the ways that mattered. Perhaps Archie had simply told the truth as he saw it. And he had told her that he loved her. That had to be worth something or what was the point?

She heard the crossbar lift once more.

Florence Danvers made her way into the room. 'It's not exactly the Hotel Victoria, but I hope you're comfortable.'

'As comfortable as a condemned woman can be.'

'Nothing is decided.' The words seemed more hopeful than a statement of fact.

Persis snorted. 'I suppose Baba Dao is just going to let me walk out of the jungle?'

Florence sighed. 'Why couldn't you have let it go? The investigation into Sinha's death?'

'Is that how they expect you to do your job in the CIA? By letting things go?'

The woman folded on to the floor. 'In the CIA we understand the risks. We train for them. *You're* a policewoman.'

'I took an oath, the same as you.' Persis shook her head in anger. 'This isn't your country. You have no right to be here.'

'A righteous cause observes no boundaries, Persis.'

'So you're here because the Americans believe in the Naga cause?' Her cynicism could have melted a hole in the floor.

'*I* believe. My brother fought in the Burma campaign. He was killed by the Japanese out in these jungles. Killed fighting for freedom. So, yes, I believe in the right of the Naga to determine their own future. I believe in the basic human right to freedom.'

'You're here because America enjoys playing puppet master. The great chess game of nation states. We Indians have been on the receiving end for centuries. First, it was the British. Now it's China and the USA. When will it ever stop?'

Florence said nothing. An uncomfortable silence passed.

'Are you still denying that you killed Sinha?'

'Neither I nor Christopher had anything to do with his death. Yes, I slept with him on the evening he died – I didn't lie about that – but I didn't kill him. Not that I mourn his passing.' She got to her feet, followed quickly by Persis. 'I truly hope that we can both reach the other side of this,' said the American, and then, as a seeming afterthought, 'In another life, we might have been friends.'

Persis's hand flashed out. Her fingers clutched the woman's arm. Her eyes blazed. 'Are you going to let them kill me?'

The American's expression was one of infinite sadness. 'It's not up to me.'

50

The results of the analysis were waiting for him by the time he returned to the hospital.

He found the two technicians, Shami and Ghosh, in their basement lab, looking more than a little pleased with themselves. 'Blue 88s,' announced Shami.

Something clicked at the back of James's mind, like the coming together of two ball bearings. Blue 88s. He was certain he had come across the term before.

'They were pills used in the war,' continued Shami, 'prescribed to shell-shocked soldiers – mainly Americans – as a form of sedative. The pills employ a mixture of barbiturates, such as sodium amytal, and will induce an extremely deep sleep for up to forty-eight hours, depending on the dosage.'

Now he knew where he had heard the term. In the barracks at Kohima, when he had been fighting alongside an American infantry unit. The Blue 88s were so called because the pills had been blue in colour. He remembered the Americans talking of the men in their unit who had suffered such terrible psychological damage in the war that they wandered around hollow-eyed and lifeless, their minds orbiting some distant planet. They called them the 'rag men'. Not that the brass cared. If you could move, if you could hold a rifle, you were sent back into action. That's when the Blue 88s came in. The assumption was that the drug would drop the men into a sleep so deep it would have a cathartic effect. They'd come out the other side ready, willing, and able to walk back into a barrage of enemy gunfire, a smile on their faces and a song in their hearts.

Which told you everything you needed to know about the mindset of those running the army.

'You're telling me Mohan Sinha was taking these pills?'

'We're telling you these pills were in his system on the night that he died,' said Ghosh. 'Whether he took them voluntarily is anyone's guess.'

James considered this. Might the politician have been using the pills as a form of nightly sedative? He imagined that Sinha had his own anxieties, in a region beset with violence. Perhaps he had become addicted to the pills.

Then again, wasn't it more likely that his killer had simply used the pills to drug him? So that his body might be moved into the bathtub and his head more easily rendered from his shoulders.

The gruesome image returned him to the lab. 'Thank you,' he said. 'You've been most helpful.'

'If you do solve the case,' said Shami, 'do let the prime minister know that we were of assistance.'

'Maybe inveigle us an invite out to Delhi, for tea and samosas?' added Ghosh drily.

James allowed himself a smile. 'I'll be sure to put in a good word.'

An hour later he was in a police jeep borrowed from the Manicktala station, headed north on the highway out of town. With luck and a fair wind he would be back in Kohima in a little over twenty-four hours, thirty at the outside.

His thoughts leaped ahead to how his discovery might impact the case. Did it tell them anything that they hadn't already guessed? If so, how might it help in identifying the killer? Or indeed working out how the killer had carried out the murder and then vanished from a locked room? That remained the most vexing part of the puzzle.

James had never been much of a reader. He supposed that this sort of thing was all the rage among the sort of squares who read mystery stories. Locked rooms and fiendishly clever killers.

Well, he'd like to see a killer clever enough to outrun a bullet.

The thought gave him a grim sense of satisfaction.

Gunning the engine, he roared along the road.

51

The gecko watched her balefully.

She couldn't sleep. Not with that thing staring at her. Or with the grim spectre of Death snuggled up beside her on the bamboo cot. Each time she thought of what the morning might bring, a shot of adrenalin surged through her system.

She checked her watch. It was past three, the darkest part of night. Silence reigned.

She wondered briefly if Rake had posted a guard beyond the door. What did it matter? She couldn't get out that way.

But neither could she simply wait here for the axe to fall. That wasn't in her nature. If life in the police service had taught her anything it was that surrendering was never an option. You fought, and carried the fight to the forces ranged against you, for as long as you could. Or until the road ran out.

She stood and walked to the earthenware water pot. Hefting it, she went to the back of the hut, then poured the water along the base of the wall, on to the earth, wetting about a yard's length. Setting the pot aside, she dropped to her knees, and began churning the resultant mud with her hands. When she had achieved the consistency she was looking for she began smearing the mud over her khaki uniform, beginning with her trousers and working her way up to her half-sleeved dress shirt. Finally, she layered mud along her throat, and then over her cheeks, her brow, and her nose.

As night camouflage went, it probably wouldn't pass muster with the military, but it was the best she could do.

She turned back to the pot, picked it up, pulled her handkerchief from a pocket, wrapped it around the pot, and then, wincing at the small explosion of noise, smashed it on the ground. Picking up a broad, triangular shard, she dropped back to her knees and began using it to scoop earth away from the base of the wall.

Twenty minutes of exertion later, she had dug a wide enough gap under the wall to allow her to wriggle through. She saw the gecko watching her with beady-eyed interest. 'Didn't anyone tell you it's rude to stare?' she muttered.

She turned to the remains of the broken pot, slipped another, smaller shard into her pocket. Lying flat on the ground, she worked her way into the gap. As she wriggled out the other side, she felt her shirt snag, and then rip against the sharpened points of the bamboo stakes making up the hut's wall.

Once outside, she stood and braced herself against the wall.

Night sounds filtered in from the village and the surrounding jungle. The stars above were stencilled in a blue-black sky. The treeline was barely forty yards from the hut, just beyond a pair of smaller huts, shrouded in darkness.

No point hanging around.

She crouched low and moved quickly towards the trees, at any moment expecting a shout from behind her. But none came.

A wave of relief fell on her as she made it to the treeline. The jungle seemed to welcome her with a susurration of noise. The drone of insects. The crackle and slither of things moving through the undergrowth. She ignored the sounds. Her plan did not involve entering the forest in search of a way back to civilisation. That would be foolhardy in the extreme. Her previous jungle adventure had convinced her that if she never saw another tree again it would be too soon.

Staying in the shadows, she ghosted her way around the village perimeter, working her way through an obstacle course of tree trunks, bushes, and prickly creepers until she arrived at the spot where she had entered the village the day before and where she had seen a collection of vehicles parked at the head of a dirt track.

There was only one vehicle still in place. A jeep. It would have to do.

Whispering a prayer to any gods who might be lurking in the vicinity, she dashed from the cover of the treeline. Jerking open the jeep's driver's side door, she slipped inside.

With shaking hands, she searched the dash, then the glovebox. No sign of any keys.

A curse escaped her.

She sat back, her thoughts beating out a panicked rhythm at her temples. The jaws of an invisible trap closed around her. Now was the moment of greatest danger. Succumbing to hopelessness.

She got out of the jeep, swept her gaze around the darkness of the jungle. She could feel beads of sweat on her scalp. The road before her narrowing. But if the choice was between the terrors of the deep forest or waiting here for Baba Dao to pronounce death, it was no choice at all.

A voice exploded into her thoughts. 'Looking for these?'

She whipped around, saw Florence Danvers standing at the rear of the jeep, arm raised, keys dangling from her fingertips.

Persis reacted instinctively. She stepped quickly towards the American, balled a fist and jabbed her in the solar plexus. Florence doubled over, a thick sound mingling pain and astonishment escaping her. Persis grabbed her by the arms and slammed her against the rear of the jeep. She slipped the pottery shard from her pocket, and pushed it against the woman's throat.

'Take it easy, for Christ's sake!' hissed Florence. 'I'm here to help.'

Persis said nothing. Adrenalin surged through her. She looked into the American's face, saw that the woman was breathing heavily. But she didn't seem overly afraid.

'I could have shouted out,' continued Florence. 'But I didn't.'

Still Persis said nothing. The shard remained poised at the woman's neck.

'I knew you wouldn't hang around waiting for the firing squad.'

Persis released a slow breath. 'You were waiting for me to escape.'

'I had a hunch.'

She lowered the shard, stepped back. 'Why?'

'Why am I helping? Let's just say, woman to woman, I don't like the idea of you ending up in a shallow grave out here. Not when all you're guilty of is being a little overzealous in your duty.'

'If I make it back to town, I *will* tell them everything I've learned.'

'I would expect no less.' The American rubbed her throat, then held out the keys. 'Follow the dirt track. It's about thirty minutes to the main road. Turn right and keep going for about an hour. You'll soon figure out where you are.'

Persis took the keys. 'And you?'

'I'll be fine. They need me. And I can hardly show my face in Kohima any more. Frankly speaking, this op is blown. The best I can hope for now is to finish the job and then slip out the back way, into Burma, and then home.'

'By finish the job, you mean help the insurgents get their Chinese arms?'

The American nodded.

'And the fact that you're interfering with the wishes of a sovereign power doesn't bother you? How many Indians will Baba Dao kill with the weapons you put into his hands?'

She gave a brittle smile. 'We all have our duty, don't we, Persis?'

52

He was in desperate need of a shower.

That became apparent as soon as he had parked the jeep outside the Kohima station and wandered in to find Roshan Seth in his office, nursing a whisky as his eyes burned a hole in the copy of *The Statesman* laid out before him. The commander's nose wrinkled as James wandered into his presence. 'Have you been rolling around in a pigsty?'

'I'm sorry,' said the young officer, adding, pointedly, 'I've been on the move for the past three days.'

'Don't you Christians say cleanliness is next to godliness? Well, if this is what passes for cleanliness in your house I'd hate to see you get *really* dirty.' Seth waved him into a seat. Then, on second thought, motioned for him to stay standing. 'No need to ruin a perfectly good chair . . . What have you found?'

He brought Seth up to speed on his findings at the lab. He considered telling him about Maria Fontanelli, but decided to wait until Persis was with them.

'Blue 88s? Catchy name.' Seth tilted back in his seat. Possibly to get away from his junior officer's rank odour. 'It's progress, I suppose. The question now is whether they were Sinha's own pills or whether his killer brought them along for the party.' He waved at the newspaper before him. 'The headlines are getting jauntier by the day.'

James looked down at the newspaper, deciphered the upside-down text. The incendiary double-page focused on Colonel Shroff's deployment into the hills, and his assertion that the insurgency would be done and dusted by the end of the year, Baba Dao in chains, everyone home in time for Christmas.

Where had he heard *that* before? 'Where is Persis?' he asked.

'At the hospital,' said Seth. Registering the sub-inspector's confusion, he continued, 'Ah. Of course, you've been out of the picture. She's just returned from a rather woolly adventure in the woods. Andrews is giving her the once-over in Kohima. I was just on my way to debrief her, as it happens.'

'I'll come with you.'

'Not smelling like that, you won't.'

'Give me half an hour.'

Seth considered the request, then nodded, adding, drily: 'Fine. It's not as if we're in any hurry to solve this case.'

They arrived at the hospital with evening having fallen.

Hurrying through the corridors, James was suddenly conscious of the weight of expectation. In the recent heat of battle he had had little time to step back and examine his own role in a case that had made national headlines. The outcome of his and Persis's investigation would impact not only upon those directly affected by Mohan Sinha's murder, but, in all likelihood, would steer Delhi's approach to the political situation in the region. In a very real sense Sinha's corpse was still pulling at the levers of power in James's hometown.

The thought filled him with a sense of foreboding.

They found Persis in a hospital room with Andrews. Judging by the state of her tattered and muddied uniform, and the various cuts and bruises that decorated her features and the visible sections of her arms, she appeared to have not only been put through the wringer, but mangled inside a washing machine.

Andrews had concluded his examination by lighting a cigarette and now spoke through a cloud of smoke. 'The cavalry is here.

About twenty-four hours too late, as usual.' He glared balefully at Seth. 'Aren't you supposed to be responsible for your officers' welfare? What do you intend to do for an encore? Drop her into a shark tank?'

'Don't let us keep you from your other patients,' replied Seth, coldly.

'I'm fine right where I am. And, in case you've forgotten, you're in *my* hospital.' The doctor lowered himself into a seat and looked belligerently up at the policeman.

Seth seemed to swallow a retort, then turned to Persis, where she sat on the edge of the hospital bed. Slipping a cloth bag from his shoulder, he took out a clean uniform and a revolver, and handed them to her. She checked the weapon, then set it down beside her, nodded her thanks.

'How are you feeling?' Seth asked.

'They say that each brush with death ages you. Right now, I feel about a thousand years old. I think the only reason I'm still alive is out of sheer habit.'

Persis glanced at James. The man seemed tongue-tied, face blanched. Her own thoughts momentarily veered off course. She had the sudden urge to be alone with him.

'Try to keep it that way,' said Seth. 'I'd rather not have your father turn up on my doorstep demanding explanations.'

'If my father turned up here, even Shroff would run for the hills.'

Seth grimaced at the mention of the colonel's name. 'Well, if you're feeling up to it, perhaps you might want to tell me exactly what you've been doing?'

Persis hesitated. The truth was that she was still feeling her way back into the business of being alive. Perhaps it wasn't force of habit that was keeping her that way. Perhaps it was sheer bloody-mindedness. Her body was a mass of aches and pains. Random thoughts rammed into each other in the curdled soup of her brain.

The drive back from the Naga village had taken several hours. At any moment she had expected pursuers to ghost into her rear-view mirror. But none appeared.

Back in Kohima, she had driven to Seth's residence. The man had taken one look at her, bundled her back into the jeep, and driven her straight to the hospital. Here she had been given a cursory once-over, before being assigned a bed. Moments after her head hit the pillow, she had plunged into a deep and formless sleep from which she had only awoken as the sun was setting outside her window. Andrews had then arrived to give her a more thorough examination.

She was still struggling to understand why Florence Danvers had helped her. It seemed improbable that the American had let her go simply to save Persis from certain death. For, in so doing, Danvers had sealed her own fate. She might survive Oren Rake and Baba Dao's displeasure, but once the powers-that-be knew of her true role in the hills, she would leap to the top of Colonel Shroff's Most Wanted list.

Whatever the reason, Persis now found herself reluctant to reveal the woman's role in the events of the past twenty-four hours. She owed Florence Danvers her life. But did that debt stand above her duty as a police officer?

She looked at Seth, waiting expectantly. And, beside him, James Angami. The pair had as much at stake in the outcome of the investigation as anyone else in the region. And wasn't that what it boiled down to, in the end? Policework was about trust. You trusted yourself, your instincts, and your team. You trusted that you were doing the right thing, even when sometimes it was hard to judge where the line should be drawn. The law was immutable. But the people observing the law rarely were.

She began to speak, detailing everything that had happened since she had left Kohima the day before with Adam Zhimomi:

discovering the opium field, the chase into the jungle, the crash, becoming lost in the deep forest, the cave of skulls, and then being found by Florence Danvers.

'So Danvers is CIA,' muttered Seth. 'I wonder if Shroff and his men have managed to get anything out of her husband.'

'He isn't really her husband.'

'No. Well, whoever he is, we're not going to see him again any time soon.'

She continued with her story, detailing the march to the Naga village, the meeting with Oren Rake, her subsequent escape, and Florence Danvers's intercession on her behalf.

'Too little, too late,' muttered Seth. 'The woman is a foreign spy operating in a region under Indian military jurisdiction. She's admitted to arming the insurgency, to working with China against our national interest. If Shroff catches up with her, there's only one way her story ends.'

'Hah,' said Andrews. 'Shroff couldn't catch a fly if he stood in a swamp with his mouth open.'

Seth frowned at him, as if he had forgotten that the doctor was in the room. 'Nothing you hear here may be repeated outside of these walls. This is an extremely delicate situation. American and Chinese involvement in the Naga Hills insurgency would make for all sorts of ugly headlines. And, at this point, all we have is Persis's testimony that any of it is even true.'

Andrews appeared ready to rumble out a protest, but then subsided, choosing instead to plug his cigarette back into his mouth. Possibly to stop himself from saying something others might later regret.

'Are you saying you don't believe me?' said Persis.

'You know that's not what I'm saying,' said Seth irritably. 'But without corroboration, or other tangible evidence of an American-Chinese conspiracy in the hills, all I can do is report what you've found to Delhi and hope they don't give Shroff the go-ahead to flatten everything in a hundred-mile radius.'

'What makes you think Delhi doesn't already know?' said Andrews. 'It's always wheels within wheels with intelligence agencies. Politicians and spies. I'd trust either about as much as I'd trust an intern to perform heart surgery on me.'

A part of her was almost relieved. Seth's position on the matter meant that Florence Danvers would be safe. For now. Perhaps that would give the woman enough time to come to her senses and leave the region. Then again ... Danvers was an enemy agent. Her actions, if unchecked, would lead to Indian deaths. And there was still the possibility that she had killed Mohan Sinha, despite her denials.

James appeared to have read her thoughts. 'Does any of this bring us closer to resolving our case? Do you think Florence Danvers was behind Sinha's death? Or Christopher Danvers? Perhaps even Oren Rake?'

'Why not all three?' said Seth. 'You've already stated that they're working together. If Sinha was holding up the Danvers's permits for a slice of Rake's opium operation, he was pitting himself directly against all three of them. And, of course, Baba Dao. No love lost there, permits or no permits.'

'I'm not sure,' said Persis. 'Florence Danvers denied having killed Sinha. She had no reason to lie, not with me as their prisoner. And Rake had known Sinha, on and off, for two decades. I didn't get the impression that he would have simply turned up one day and cut the man's head off.'

'I think it's time we brought him in for questioning,' said Seth. 'At the very least we have him for illegally imprisoning an officer of the law.'

'Oren Rake knows these hills better than most Naga,' interjected Andrews. 'Good luck finding him.' He lifted himself to his feet. 'From the sounds of it, you haven't really solved very much. Which reaffirms my faith in the state of policing in this country. I have work to do.'

They watched him clump from the room.

'That man is really beginning to try my patience,' muttered Seth. He checked his watch. 'I need to go and make my call. Perhaps I can catch the prime minister just in time to spoil his supper.'

After he had left, James took Andrews's seat.

'There's something else.' He told her about the Blue 88s. 'Sinha was drugged before he was murdered.'

Persis considered his words. 'Which tells us that his killer wasn't certain of being able to subdue him by other means.'

'Sinha was not a strong man,' said James, following the thought to its obvious conclusion. 'Indicating that his killer could have been a—'

'Woman,' finished Persis, adding, grimly: 'Florence Danvers.'

Her thoughts whirled. Had she read the American wrongly?

'Danvers wasn't the only woman there that night,' countered James. And he told her about Sin City, watched as his senior officer's eyes widened with shock.

'Maria Fontanelli is Mohan Sinha's daughter?'

'Illegitimate daughter,' he corrected. 'She came all the way out to the hills to track down the man who betrayed her mother. That's motive.'

A silence settled between them. She became acutely aware of James's closeness, the scent of his soap, the lustre with which his hair shone.

Without warning, he reached out, found her hand where it lay in her lap. Shock moved through her, but she resisted the urge to shake it away. 'You could have died,' he said.

Blood thundered in her ears. She found herself standing, dragging James up with her. They stood barely inches apart. Their eyes met and something passed wordlessly between them. She focused on the planes of his face, his lips, the sheen of sweat along the muscles of his neck. She had the sensation of falling.

The door swung back, breaking them apart. A nurse bustled in, checked Persis's blood pressure, then left again.

Persis gave the sudden awkwardness no chance to gain a hold. She sat back on the bed, turned her thoughts back to the case. As good a place as any to hide from her rampant emotions. James folded his arms, leaned against the wall.

The investigation had sprouted several new heads, like the mythical Hydra. It remained to be seen which would prove to be the right one.

The thought of heads returned her sharply to Mohan Sinha's headless corpse.

She dwelt momentarily on the man's last moments. She imagined him becoming drowsy under the influence of the Blue 88s, perhaps falling to the floor in a stupor. His killer leading him – or dragging him – to the bathtub, to perform the coup de grâce. She superimposed Fontanelli's face on the killer's shadowy form.

How had the woman got into a locked room?

An itch at the back of her brain. She returned to her earlier ghostly reconnaissance of the room, when she had floated above the suite, and thought that she had almost had the answer. The feeling returned. Like a woman moving through fog to the edge of a cliff she knows to be there, she was certain that she was edging ever closer to the truth—

'I didn't mention Fontanelli to Seth.'

She stared at him. He seemed embarrassed. 'It's our case,' he said. 'And Seth strikes me as a political animal.' He tailed off under her gaze.

'Roshan Seth is a man of integrity,' she said stiffly. 'You have no idea what he's been through.'

He coloured. 'I didn't mean to suggest that I didn't trust him.'

'But that's exactly what you implied.'

An uncomfortable silence sauntered into the room, hands in pockets, whistling nonchalantly.

'In the war,' he said, 'trust was something you couldn't always rely on. You trusted your comrades with your life. They trusted you with theirs. But what did that really mean? During the Battle of Kohima, we found ourselves dug into trenches just yards from the enemy. On the second day, I was walking down the line when a volley of grenades came over the top. A friend of mine caught one just yards away from me. He just stood there, grinning stupidly. And then it blew up. It's quite something, being splattered with your friend's bloody remains.' The past glowed in his eyes. 'I've learned not to rely on people.'

She realised that, in the month or so that she had known him, this was the first time he had talked about the war. She knew that two million Indians had fought in the conflict. She herself had served in Bombay's auxiliary women's corps. But she had never been directly involved in the fight. She couldn't imagine what James Angami had been through.

For a brief instant, she imagined herself in that dismal hole up on the Kohima ridge with him, seeing the things he had seen, living the horror of mankind's ultimate credo: death and destruction.

'I think it's time we talked to Maria Fontanelli,' she said.

53

They found the Italian at the Hotel Victoria, taking a late supper in the dining room.

Five minutes later, they were installed in the library, Fontanelli swirling a wine glass in her hand. She stretched out languidly on a sofa, a Chinese gong at her elbow.

James set down the charred photograph on a teak coffee table.

'When I showed you this photograph you claimed you had never seen it before,' said Persis. 'Yet, the woman in the picture is your mother. Mohan Sinha was your father. Which means that you have just become the frontrunner in his murder. Congratulations.'

Fontanelli's elegant features had frozen. Her eyes remained on the photograph. And then she lifted her glass and drained it. She seemed to gather herself. 'Well, there seems no point in denying it. Yes, Mohan Sinha was my father. As much as you can say that about a man who abandoned me before I was born and who I didn't even know existed for the first twenty-seven years of my life.'

'When did you find out?' asked James.

'My mother fell chronically ill a few months ago. She told me the truth, not wanting to take the secret to her grave. Until then I had no idea that I wasn't my father's daughter. I suppose I should have suspected. I've never favoured either of my parents. Not in looks, at any rate.'

'That can't have been easy,' said Persis. 'Finding out the truth.'

The Italian flashed her a bitter look. 'Easy? Try earth-shattering.'

'Is that why you came out here?' said James. 'To track down Sinha?'

'I came here because my mother asked me to. She gave me the photograph, begged me to find him. To tell him that she'd never stopped loving him. Pined after him, all these years. Love of her life. You know how it goes.' Bitterness laced her voice. 'It wasn't easy, finding him. He was out in the Naga Hills district and Westerners were not exactly being made to feel welcome. I came out to Calcutta, joined a paper there, and then petitioned my boss to get me out to the hills. He thought I was crazy. Right up until the insurgency started to heat up and then the region suddenly became interesting. Bombs and bullets. That's what it takes to turn a newsman's head.'

'So you really are a journalist,' said Persis. 'One thing you didn't lie about.'

Fontanelli merely stuck out a belligerent jaw. 'I didn't kill Sinha.'

'But you were in his room that evening,' said James. 'That's how the photograph got there.'

'Yes,' she admitted. 'I went to his room that night. To finally confront him.'

'Why then? Why not when you first arrived in the hills?'

'Because I wanted to observe him for a while. To gauge, up close, what kind of man he was. I found out he was staying at the Hotel Victoria and booked myself a suite. It meant I could be in close proximity to him without raising suspicion. Not that he let me in. He seemed deathly afraid of journalists.'

'And what did you observe?' said Persis. 'While you were sounding him out?'

'He was a vain, foolish man. I have no idea what my mother saw in him. Then again, aren't most fathers, ultimately, disappointments?'

Persis was struck by a brief vision of Sam, frowning at her over the top of his half-moon spectacles, demanding that she set the record straight. She shoved her father to one side, focused. 'What happened that night?'

'I knocked on Sinha's door, told him I wanted to speak to him about a personal matter. He'd just returned from Kohima, looked haggard, but he let me in anyway, led me to his office. I didn't stand on ceremony. I simply laid it out for him. You can imagine his expression when I told him I was his daughter.' Her lips tightened. 'He denied it, at first. And then I showed him the photograph. He seemed to go into a trance. When he finally snapped out of it, he took the photograph, set it alight, and threw it into the ashtray. We both watched it burn. And then something strange happened.' She paused. 'It was as if the burning flame released him from some sort of curse. I saw tears in his eyes. He picked up the photo, blew out the flame, looked at it a second time, then set it down again. He asked me about my mother. I saw something in him I never expected to see. Tenderness.'

'You expect us to believe that he embraced you as his daughter?' James's scepticism clanged sharply from the Chinese gong.

A hollow laugh escaped the Italian. 'No. Because he didn't. In fact, he told me that he would categorically deny any public assertion that I was his daughter. He had a political career to think of, after all. Aspirations of finding his way into Nehru's cabinet. But he didn't want to cut me off, not entirely. Claimed he could see my mother in me. And so he asked for time to think.'

'You came all this way to confront him and then you simply walked away?'

'Believe what you want to,' she said. 'But that's exactly what happened. He was very much alive when I left his room that evening.'

'What time was that?'

'I went to his room at around eight. I was only in there fifteen minutes.' She sighed. 'I didn't kill him. I couldn't have. My mother would never forgive me.'

'Does she know that you found him? That he's dead?'

'Not yet. She's in a hospice. She doesn't need any more bad news.'

'Why are you still here?' asked Persis. 'Why haven't you gone home?'

'You told us not to leave, didn't you?' she snapped, then: 'Besides, I want to know who *did* kill him. And not just because he was my father. I'm a journalist. And this is the biggest story I've ever been this close to.' She stood up. 'Now. If you're not going to arrest me, I'm going to bed. And perhaps another glass of wine.'

James began to protest, but Persis waved him into silence. 'And John Templeton? Do you know anything about *his* death?'

'No. I do not.' She swept them with a cool look, then turned on her heel and stalked from the room.

As the door closed behind her, James burst out, 'You don't believe her, do you?'

'I don't know. But I'm in agreement with her about one thing.'

'What's that?'

'The need for a drink.'

54

She returned to the hotel's dining room, ordered a glass of wine, and a meal to go with it. Grilled lamb.

The place was deserted and she found herself seated alone, James having decided to return to his home in Kohima.

The wine, a red poured from a bottle brought up from the hotel's own cellar, was blunt and heavy, a smack across the chops, rather than the elegant accompaniment to a meat supper that she might have hoped for. She didn't mind. The case had taken hold of her once more, and she found her senses occupied with the complicated business of wrestling it into some semblance of order.

She saw the investigation – its various aspects, suspects, and revelations – as a forest of tall trees. To chart a path through to the far side, she would need to swing from tree to tree, stringing together connections as she leaped. Easier said than done.

The idea of brachiating through a forest veered her thoughts, momentarily, to the troop of capuchins assaulting her balcony with excremental fury each morning. Perhaps Roshan Seth might employ the same gambit when Nehru's myrmidons next called to hold his feet to the fire, flinging excrement at them, while gibbering out his ignorance in full-throated rage.

She focused on the interview with Maria Fontanelli.

Did she believe the woman?

The jury remained out. Just as the verdict remained in the balance when it came to Florence Danvers, her faux husband, Christopher Danvers, and the American mining baron Oren Rake.

And, for that matter, John Templeton. The prevailing theory – now splashed across the national newspapers – was that Sinha's aide had murdered his boss, then taken his own life. Would the latest revelations – the Danvers's involvement with Baba Dao's insurgency, Rake's secret opium racket – serve to alter that conclusion? Would it convince Nehru's man in the hills, Colonel Shroff, that Templeton's presumed guilt might warrant closer investigation?

Probably not. The colonel was a man who thought in straight lines. Blaming the Englishman for Sinha's murder served as the most convenient solution to a thorny problem, particularly if he could claim that Baba Dao had somehow been behind the undertaking. To publicly lay the blame at the feet of the CIA – and, in so doing, the American government – would prise open a particularly smelly kettle of fish, one that even Shroff might balk at. Persis strongly suspected that all those who knew of these recent revelations would soon be rendered mute, either by official decree or threats emanating from the Centre. The prime minister could scarcely allow such an explosive disclosure to gallop around the global countryside unbridled. Catching the Americans with their hands in the till was the sort of political gift premiers could only dream of. Nehru would, no doubt, wish to bend the diplomatic gaffe to his own purposes.

And with Christopher Danvers in custody, she suspected that Shroff would soon be ordered to deliver the necessary proof of America's perfidy with which the Indian prime minister might blackmail his counterpart, Harry S. Truman.

And yet.

She had a strong feeling that something was being missed. A fleck of lint on her mind that defied capture. And she believed this missing piece to be related to Aaron Koza.

How did the young Naga's death, some two decades earlier, tie in with Mohan Sinha's murder? That there *was* a connection now seemed an article of faith to her. She couldn't be certain, of course, but the idea had become a roaring in her ears, drowning out all other conspiracies.

Aaron Koza, who had taken the message of a future independent Naga Hills district to heart, back when Sinha had first been posted to the region. Koza's arrest and subsequent death in police custody. The police had claimed it to be suicide. But their actions in cremating the body before an external investigation might determine otherwise hinted at something altogether darker.

Then again, Koza would not be the first young man to die in a police cell. So why should *this* death reverberate down the years?

What was fact: two decades ago, soon after an official complaint in the wake of Koza's death had been lodged with Mohan Sinha, the man had been whisked back out of the hills and returned to Calcutta. Why?

And then there was the police report of Koza's arrest, pages torn from the file. Who had torn them out? What had they been attempting to conceal?

Similarly, she evaluated the revelation that pills – Blue 88s – had been found in Sinha's system on the night of his death. The pills – army issue – were not exactly easy to come by. Yet, Sinha or his killer had obtained them. How? She considered the problem, and as she did so, another outlandish thought fell into place. Excitement pulsed through her. The more she turned the conjecture over in her mind, the more it made sense.

She walked to reception, and put a call through to the hospital. She asked for Ravi, the young doctor. When he eventually came on the line, she told him what she was looking for.

While she waited for him to get back to her, she returned to the dining room and ordered coffee and a dessert, a banana split served in a bowl large enough to bathe a baby elephant. She pulled her notebook from her pocket, flicked through the pages, seeking out the scribbles she had made while going through the Aaron Koza arrest report. Though critical pages detailing the actual interview had been torn out, one key detail had been left intact, at the very front of the file: Koza's residential address.

She was called back to reception. Ravi had been as good as his word. He had found what she was looking for. The discovery confirmed her suspicions, and with it another part of the solution cemented itself into place.

But before she could follow up, she had another errand to run.

She set down the phone and headed back out of the hotel.

The house was large, by Kohima's standards, a sprawling home perched on the city's outer edge.

Persis parked her jeep, and entered the property via an iron gate fronting a meandering tiled path that zigzagged between a miniature jungle of planters. She arrived at a porch, and an arched front door painted in a striking shade of colonial blue. A bulbous moon, as fat and milky as a pearl, hung off the house's shoulder.

A bespectacled young Naga woman answered the door. 'Yes?' Her tone seemed irritable, setting Persis on the back foot.

'May I ask who lives here?'

'Are you asking as a police officer?'

'Well, yes.' Persis waved a hand over her uniform, as if to indicate the redundancy of the question.

'What is this with regards to?'

'I'm not at liberty to say.'

'You're here to ask questions and you don't know why?'

Persis spoke stiffly. 'Is there an older person in the house?'

'Is that voice meant to intimidate me? If so, it's not working.'

'Catherine. Who is it?' An older woman appeared, dressed in a simple nightgown, greying hair pulled back into a bun.

'It's that famous policewoman. Though I'm not sure if her fame is justified. She doesn't even know why she's here.'

'Hush now. Go on, back to your room.'

The woman mouthed something under her breath, then turned, and went back into the house. The older woman turned to Persis. 'Inspector. How can I help you?'

'May I ask how long you've been living here?'

'That's a strange question.'

'I'm looking for whoever was living in this house twenty years ago when Aaron Koza resided here.'

A light winked out in her eyes. For a moment, Persis thought she might buckle forward into her arms. But then the woman steadied herself. 'Aaron was my son. Why are you here?'

The woman's name was Mary Koza.

She led Persis through the house to a drawing room floored with blue tiles, and lined with teak sideboards heaving with ceramic objects. Mary fell into a broad umber sofa, ushering Persis into the armchair opposite. 'Aaron was adopted. I married young, at sixteen. For the first five years of our marriage, I could not conceive. I began to believe that it was not in God's plan for me to have children of my own. A close aunt suggested adoption. I was hesitant, at first, but my husband was supportive. We went to the orphanage here in Kohima. I fell in love with Aaron at first sight. He was a baby then; an angel. Later, he would prove a blessing. After we adopted him we had five other children, all daughters.' A smile creased her features. 'Two of them have moved to the mainland. Two of them are here, fighting for Naga independence.'

'And the fifth?'

'The youngest. You've already met her. She's smarter than the rest of us put together. She says she wants to be prime minister. And who's to say she won't be?'

'Tell me about Aaron.'

'He was a firebrand, from a young age. Always in trouble; always ready to fight, though half the time he didn't really know what he was fighting for. I suppose he was looking for a cause. Or a cause was looking for him.

'It was later, when he went to college in Calcutta, that he found it.

'As a parent I could tell you that he fell in with the wrong crowd. Or the right crowd. It's hard to know any more. Student radicals voicing the call of the Naga Club, namely, for an independent Naga state after the British might leave. Aaron took the cause to heart. Instead of making a career for himself in Calcutta after graduating, as was his father's wish for him, he returned to Kohima determined to fight. Hah.' Her lips pursed. 'He was a child, with a child's understanding of the world.'

'What happened that night?' said Persis, gently. 'The night that he was killed?'

'Aaron had been making a nuisance of himself. For months, he led a student faction agitating for independence. He was vocal, addressing journalists, printing up leaflets, organising street protests, stirring up trouble. That evening the police came to the house and took him away. For questioning, they said. We never saw him again.' The past flowed from her mouth like the dark tide of a river in flood. Tears welled in the woman's eyes and a chill spread through the room. When she spoke again, light shivered across the dark planes of her face. 'Do you have children?'

'No.'

'Losing a child is like a red-hot coal pressed against the flesh. They say the living hold on to the dead. But sometimes, it's the other way around. More than anything else, it's the not knowing. The police claim Aaron killed himself. I'm his mother and I can tell you that he would never have done such a thing.' Grief gusted from her. 'I feel . . . helpless. To know that the truth is out there, walking right by you each and every day, but refusing to speak. And there is nothing you can do to compel it.'

There was something about these last sentences that struck Persis as odd. But another question was clamouring for attention. 'Do you know who Aaron's birth parents were?'

'Why do you ask?' Her tone had become defensive.

Persis waited her out.

Eventually, the woman shook her head. 'No. We asked at the orphanage, of course, but Aaron's mother had left him there in anonymity.'

'Is there anything else you can tell me about him?'

Mary looked at her with a quality of pain clouding her eyes that Persis could not begin to fathom. 'Why do you care? Why now? Have you any idea how difficult it is for me to sit here and talk about Aaron with a police officer? Frankly, if you were not a woman, I would never have let you in.'

'I cannot claim to understand your grief,' said Persis. 'But I can promise you this. I will do all I can to bring Aaron's killers to justice.'

'Killers? So you don't believe he committed suicide?'

'No. I do not.'

The woman's face seemed to crumple in on itself. Persis suspected that she had waited two decades for such an admission. She held back her questions as Mary Koza wept, shoulders trembling. When she was done, the Naga woman drew herself up, and said, 'How can I help?'

'Can you think of any link between Aaron and Mohan Sinha, back then?'

'Sinha?' Her features contorted in surprise. 'Why do you ask?'

'Two decades ago, Sinha was given authority to liaise with the Naga tribes. A complaint was made by the Naga Club to him following Aaron's death. I don't know precisely how Sinha responded, but someone in authority was clearly displeased with how he handled the situation because a few weeks later he was sent back to Calcutta.'

'Are you suggesting that Sinha's death has something to do with my son's murder all those years ago?'

'I honestly don't know. Frankly speaking, I'm following my instincts.'

The woman was shaking her head. 'Aaron would often speak about Sinha back then. He was disparaging. Called him Delhi's stooge. He actively called for Sinha's attempts to influence the tribes in favour of a future Indian union to be rejected. He was quite vociferous, in private and, occasionally, in public.'

'It sounds as if he went out of his way to make an enemy of Sinha.'

'My son was fearless, Inspector. He spoke his mind. He believed himself invulnerable.' She sighed. 'To answer your question: I don't know of any connection between Aaron and Mohan Sinha – other than the fact that my son denounced him. And, to answer your *unspoken* question, I had nothing to do with Sinha's death. Until this moment I have never connected him with my son's killing. Aaron was murdered in a police cell.'

Persis picked her next words carefully. 'I dug up the police report into Aaron's arrest and death. Vital pages are missing, including the names of the officers who interviewed him. Do you know who they were?'

'No. After Aaron was arrested we were told that he would be questioned and returned and that we were not to come to the station. Later, after we found out he had died and his body had been cremated, we petitioned for the truth. We demanded to know who it was that had been in that cell with him. But we were told the names would not be released in order to protect the officers involved from unwarranted reprisals.'

Persis paused, a previous thought circling back. 'You said something earlier. That the truth is out there, walking right by you each and every day, but refusing to speak. What did you mean by that?'

She grimaced. 'On the night that he was arrested, a policeman came to the house. Just the one. He promised to have Aaron back to us in a few hours. I believed him. That man is still here. In Kohima. That's the reason I haven't left this home. One day, I wish to hear him speak. I wish to hear the truth from his lips.'

Persis hesitated. She considered the woman's words, considered the mutilated report in the stationhouse's old storeroom. Her own half-formed thoughts sharpened to a point. The name, when she presented it, seemed obvious. The policeman who had come to the Koza home all those years ago and taken Aaron Koza away, never to be returned.

'How did you know?' breathed Mary.

They regarded each other, and then Mary stood up, walked to a sideboard, returned with a photograph set inside a small, ceramic frame. 'There's one more thing. We didn't know this at the time, but when he was killed Aaron had been stepping out with a young woman. He had proposed to her. They were going to be married. After his death, we discovered that she was carrying his child. This is his son.'

The hammer blow of astonishment fell on Persis, knocking cobwebs from her skull and shuddering pistons into movement. Gears turned in her mind . . . Finally, in a lightning burst of inspiration, she understood how it had been done, and by who. She returned to Mohan Sinha's suite, followed the murderer in her mind's eye, looked on as the killer planned and executed the murder, understood how the impossibility of the locked room had been achieved.

'This is your grandson?'

'Yes.'

'Tell me about him.'

'There's not much to tell. Aaron met the boy's mother at university, in Calcutta. She was a Naga, but a local to the city. They fell in love. After Aaron's death, she cut herself off from us.'

'Why?'

'Because I blamed her for Aaron's death. At the University of Calcutta, she ran a student forum campaigning for Naga independence. That's where Aaron first became infatuated with the idea.'

'Because of her.'

'Yes. Because of her.' She sighed. 'I tried to make amends. I went to Calcutta. For years, she rebuffed me. But then, a while ago, she relented. I don't know why. She allowed me into her home. She allowed me to meet with my grandson. That's when this picture was taken. It's the only one I have of him.'

'And do you know where he is now?'

'Studying. In Calcutta.'

'And if I were to tell you that that is not where he is?'

Her brow furrowed. 'I don't understand.'

Persis levered herself out of the armchair. 'I will leave you now. But I'll be back to explain everything. Thank you. For your honesty. And your courage.'

'What use is courage, Inspector, when it cannot protect the ones you love?'

55

A policeman in shorts was far from a novelty on the subcontinent. Constables of varying feathers had been modelling the garment since Lord Cornwallis, former Governor of the Calcutta Presidency, had established the first permanent police force in the country back in 1791.

But this was the first time Persis had seen her deputy in half trousers.

James Angami stood in his doorway, staring at her in confusion. He understood, of course, that this wasn't a social call: his senior officer was still in uniform and looked like she meant it. A floating part of his consciousness mused on the fact that he had almost never seen her out of it, wondered what she might look like in a dress or a sari or perhaps even a brightly coloured Naga shawl and kilt. The thought was chased out of his head by Persis's next words. 'Go put on your trousers. We have work to do.'

He listened, with an increasing sense of dislocation, as she explained the reason for her late-night roust. When she had finished, he said: 'Are you certain?'

'As certain as I can be.' She handed him the photograph given to her by Mary Koza.

His eyes rested on the portrait. For a moment, Persis thought he would say more, but in the end he simply nodded, then turned back into his home.

*   *   *

Less than half an hour later, they arrived at the second of the three stops she had mentally pinned on a map since leaving Mary Koza's home.

The residence was small, a roughly built one-storey home on a tiny plot of land on the city's outskirts. As they walked to the entrance, she half expected a chicken to come flying at her out of the darkness.

She watched James knock, then stand back. His sense of apprehension had been apparent from the silence in the jeep as they had driven here from his home. She knew that he still harboured doubts. The forthcoming encounter would determine whether or not those doubts were justified, whether or not she had miscalculated and her conjectures were built on foundations of clay.

For the second time in the hour, a door swung back to reveal a policeman in shorts.

If Constable Joshua Binny was surprised to see his senior officers standing on his doorstep, he managed to conceal it. The man leaned against the doorframe, a cigarette in his mouth, his scrawny shoulders glimmered by light pushing out into the night from the interior of his home.

For an instant, Persis saw their silent diorama from above, three points of a triangle, poised to reform into something else, the design of which would be dictated by Binny's response in the coming moments.

The constable plucked the cigarette from his lips and said: 'Inspector, this is a surprise. Do come inside.' And there was something in the tone of his voice that told her that the man had understood instantly why they were here. A look, in the eyes of those whose time had come to face a reckoning long overdue, that was unmistakeable. She had seen it before. No doubt, she would see it many times again.

They followed him inside.

To her amazement, the tiny home was neatly ordered. She had expected chaos. The obstreperous life of a bachelor. Clothing flung carelessly to all parts. Dirty dishes in the washpot. Chickens roosting atop sideboards.

But there was only serenity, and a radio tuned to soft music, a raga of some description that floated on the edge of recognition.

Binny sank into a wicker chair, indicated a sofa. 'Would you like something to drink?'

'No,' said Persis. She chose to remain standing, as did her deputy. 'Just over an hour ago, I visited Mary Koza at her home. She confirmed my suspicion that you were the man who arrested her son, Aaron, back in 1930. Yet, when I asked you to search for the records of his arrest you failed to mention that. Neither did you mention that his family lived right here in Kohima.'

Binny said nothing.

'That night Aaron Koza died in police custody. His body was cremated without being returned to his family. They were told that he had killed himself. I believe that was a lie. Koza was murdered and the evidence of the crime covered up. Later, a complaint was filed by the Naga Club about the incident. It cost Mohan Sinha his position as overseer of the Naga tribes.'

The constable raised his still-glowing cigarette to his lips. Smoke made a mist around his dark features. Still, he said nothing.

'The record of Koza's interview had been torn out of his arrest report. I presume you were the one who removed it? After I asked you to dig up the file?'

'Yes,' he said, simply.

'Did you do that because Sinha had ordered Aaron to be killed?' She had arrived at the conclusion based on Mary Koza's assertion that her son had made an enemy of Sinha. Aaron's death in custody, Sinha's subsequent removal from the hills district – all seemed to point towards the politician's involvement in Aaron's killing.

A hesitation, and then Binny plunged. 'No, Inspector. It was because the report showed that Aaron Koza had been *interviewed* by Mohan Sinha that night.'

Persis heard a hiss of breath escape James's throat. Shock reverberated through her. *This*, she hadn't guessed. 'Why was Sinha there?'

'My commanding officer at the time called him in. A man named Duleep Pujari. He's dead now.' A beat. 'Sinha had been trying to get a handle on the radicalism that was threatening his attempts to negate the demands of the Naga Club. It was on Sinha's instructions that Koza was arrested. Sinha thought he could frighten the boy. But Koza wouldn't be cowed. Sinha lost his temper. Things got out of hand. He lashed out. He struck Koza. The boy fell over, cracked his head on the stone floor. At first, we thought he would get back to his feet. But he just lay there. It was only when I tried to pull him up that I realised something terrible had happened. Call it mischance, call it bad luck. That single blow had killed him.'

The words, delivered matter-of-factly, were all the more devastating because of it. A young life lost to a moment of madness.

Persis was glad that Mary Koza was not present to hear this. 'And so you covered it up.'

'That was Sinha's decision. What else could he do? If it had come to light that he had killed Koza there would have been riots.'

'You're a Naga. How could you have helped him bury this?' James had spoken. Persis heard the anger trembling beneath his words.

Binny made no attempt to defend himself. She watched him rub the socket of his right eye with the heel of his hand. The man seemed to have aged a decade in the past minutes.

'Did you kill Sinha?' asked Persis.

'No.'

'Do you know who did?'

'No.'

She held up the photograph that Mary Koza had given her. 'Did you know that Aaron Koza had a son? That this is his child?'

Binny blinked rapidly in confusion. 'No. I didn't know. And if that's true, then perhaps you have your killer.'

'Perhaps,' said Persis. 'But, if so, how did he find out that Sinha had killed his father? The only people who knew were in that police cell. So, I ask you, did *you* tell him? Or your colleague, this Duleep Pujari?'

'No. Duleep died a long time ago. And I've never spoken of that night.'

'Then there must have been someone else there. Someone else who knows exactly what happened to Aaron.'

Binny dropped his eyes. Persis knew that she had struck close to the truth. 'Who else was there that night? Who else knew what happened?' For an age it seemed that Binny wouldn't answer.

But Persis had all but worked out the answer before asking the question. 'You had a body on your hands. There was really only one person you could have called.' And she named him.

Binny's shoulders slumped. 'Yes,' he said, simply.

The shock of revelation was muted by the fact that she had guessed correctly. She exchanged glances with James. 'Blue 88s,' she said.

He seemed confused, and then understanding dawned. She explained the call she had made to Ravi, the young doctor, earlier that evening. And with Ravi's answer had come another name, another player in the convoluted plot to murder Mohan Sinha.

But that was for later.

A grim silence crowded into the room. 'So, what now?' said Binny.

'Now we arrest you for complicity in the murder of Aaron Koza. You will give a formal statement to James. Mohan Sinha was a murderer. Koza's family deserve the truth. The people of the hills deserve the truth.'

'Delhi won't like it,' said Binny.

'I think we're past caring what the Centre wants, don't you?'

'Is it worth your career?'

She leaned over him, eyes flashing. 'You lied to preserve *your* career. You allowed a killer to walk free. Was *that* worth it?'

For a brief moment, she thought he might protest; but then his head dropped to his chest, his shoulders sagged, and he fell to weeping, a flood of relief two decades in the coming.

Perhaps this was how it always was, she thought. Men who knew that they had transgressed, long wracked by guilt, but unable to take that final step towards the truth, until they were pushed into the light. And then it all became too much, walls of vanity crumbling, the cold hard mirror of self-revelation forcing the inner man to come to terms with the monster of the past.

Could she sympathise?

On the whole, she thought not.

56

She arrived at the hotel at just after ten.

Pausing a moment at the entrance, she looked up at the white-washed façade, the night sky a satin cloth draped behind it.

It would soon be over. She knew that she now had enough to piece together the exact events of that night. But would it be enough to shake the killer from their lair, to force the truth to be acknowledged? On the way to the hotel, she had gone over the details in her mind, setting each piece into place. Her thoughts roamed back over the search of the hotel premises she had conducted after Sinha's death. Now, with her newfound knowledge, she believed that there was only one place that the murder weapon – together with Sinha's missing head – could possibly have been hidden, evading her searchers. It was simply a matter of access: who had it, and who did not.

She walked into the hotel, found David Keishing and Peter Jadonang at the reception counter. 'I'd like a bottle of wine,' she said.

'Of course, madam,' said the young man, rising from his seat. 'What sort of wine would you like?'

'I'd like to pick one myself. From your cellar. It's for a special occasion.'

His mouth opened, and he glanced at Keishing. The man hesitated, then smiled. 'Of course. Peter, please take the inspector down.'

Minutes later, they were standing inside the wine cellar, racks of bottles to one side, a dozen wine barrels to the other. Persis ignored the bottles, instead turning to examine the enormous barrels. 'Apeni Ao told me that you fill these on the premises.'

'Yes, madam, that is correct.'

Persis looked around the cellar, then walked to the corner of the space, returned with a stepladder. Placing it against the first barrel, she clambered atop it, and examined the curving top of the cask.

'Are you looking for something, madam?'

'Just curious,' muttered Persis.

She clambered down, then repeated the operation with the remaining barrels.

At the tenth barrel, she found it. Her fingers moved over the wooden staves between two hoops at the widest part of the barrel. On one of the staves, approximately a foot in width, she could see two tell-tale grooves scored into the wood, roughly eighteen inches apart along the length of the stave. It was obvious that a section had been cut out and then put back.

'Madam? Can I help you?' She noted a sudden rise in the pitch of the young man's voice.

Ignoring him, she removed her revolver from its holster, then banged with its butt on to the stave. On the third strike, the marked section fell into the barrel.

She peered into the revealed cavity.

As she had suspected, the barrel was only half full. And, floating in the liquid, a dark, spherical shape. The shape rolled around and Mohan Sinha's face turned up to meet her.

Even though she had been expecting it, she was almost shocked into stumbling from the stepladder. She suppressed an instinctive cry of horror, instead focusing her emotions, and then twisting around on the stepladder, leaping back to the cellar's stone floor, and turning the revolver to Peter Jadonang, whose face had taken on the aspect of a stone bust.

'I think it's time that we went to speak with Madam Ao, don't you?'

Back up in the lobby Roshan Seth was waiting for her. 'James called me from the station. He asked me to meet you here.' His eyes fell to the revolver in her hand.

'You're just in time,' she said.

Seth fell in behind her as they made their way to the hotel's dining room where Apeni Ao was sitting at her private table at the rear, hidden behind latticework screens. David Keishing stood beside her. The pair appeared to have been waiting for her.

Persis indicated with her revolver that Peter should move across to stand beside Keishing.

When the youth had done so, she reached into a pocket with her free hand, took out the photograph that Mary Koza had given her and flicked it on to the table. It landed between a glass of water and a carved wooden salt shaker in the shape of a seated monkey.

Ao's eyes fell to the photograph. Her pupils seemed to contract, and then her gaze lifted, returned, once more, to its previous equanimity.

The photograph was that of a young man.

Peter Jadonang.

'Here's what I know,' said Persis. 'Twenty-one years ago, a young Naga named Aaron Koza was arrested. He later died in police custody. The police claimed that he had committed suicide. They cremated his body so that the truth could not be determined. But his family always suspected that the officers who had arrested him had killed him. They were not entirely wrong. The officers in that cell *were* guilty, but only of complicity. The hand that actually killed Aaron was that of Mohan Sinha. Aaron's vociferous calls for a future independent Naga state had undermined Sinha's mandate in the region. Perhaps he didn't mean to kill the boy; but that night his anger boiled over, and the result was Aaron's death. He ordered the killing covered up. But the stink remained and because of it he was subsequently removed from the Naga Hills.

'But what Sinha didn't know was that Aaron had left behind a pregnant young woman, carrying his child. Peter. For the next two decades, the boy was raised by his mother's family, in Calcutta.' She paused. 'Here is where I have to take a leap of faith. The very fact that Peter is here, now, in this hotel, is proof enough that he somehow found out that Mohan Sinha had killed his father, killed Aaron Koza. His actions on the night of Sinha's death tell me that he was intimately involved in the man's murder.'

'No.' The single word, ejected from Ao's lips, resonated with force. 'Peter didn't kill Sinha. I did.'

The youth began to speak, but was cut off by a curt gesture from Ao.

Persis locked eyes with the woman. 'Yes. I was coming to that. The real mystery here was how a killer could have got into a locked room. The answer is *you*.

'On the evening of Sinha's death, you hid inside the dining cart that Peter took up to Sinha's room. You're the only person in this entire plot small enough to fit inside the cart. Peter served Sinha a dish laced with Blue 88s, sedative pills. The powder inside the pills was sprinkled over his food. Perhaps that's why he called down to complain about the seasoning after Peter left his suite.

'Once Sinha succumbed to the drug, you came out from your hiding place, dragged him to the bathtub, and killed him by cutting off his head. Sinha didn't weigh much, and I suspect you're a lot stronger than you look. You then bolted the front door, wrapped Sinha's head and the murder weapon in a cloth, and returned to your hiding place.

'Later, when we burst into the suite, you waited until we had stepped into the bathroom, and slipped out. While we were distracted upstairs, you went down into the cellar, and placed the head and murder weapon into a wine barrel. You had kept the barrel ready, cutting out a section in a single stave of a single barrel.

'Having dumped the head and weapon, you went back to your room and waited for Peter to pretend to wake you and bring you to Sinha's suite. And that was how the locked room illusion was created.' A beat. 'The question is: why? Why would you murder Sinha? Peter's motive, I can understand. But why would *you* embroil yourself in such a plot? Why would you involve Peter? There's only one answer that makes any sense to me.' She waited, hoping the woman would speak, but Ao said nothing.

'Aaron was adopted. Mary Koza was not his real mother. *You* were.' She pointed the revolver at Apeni Ao. 'As a young woman you ventured out of the Naga Hills district. Forty years ago, you returned. You were pregnant. The circumstances of that pregnancy are irrelevant. What matters is that you chose not to raise the child. Instead, you handed him over to an orphanage, right here in Kohima, and then you left the region again. It was from the orphanage that Mary Koza adopted him, raising the child as her own.

'I suspect that you secretly followed Aaron's progress over the years. Because of this, you heard of his death, back in 1930. You must have been devastated, devastated enough to return to Kohima for good. You returned and you built the Hotel Victoria.

'Perhaps, like others, you always suspected that Aaron had been murdered. But you couldn't prove it. And then, two decades later, Mohan Sinha returned to the district. And something happened – you discovered that *Sinha* was responsible for Aaron's death. I don't know exactly how you found out – though I have a good idea. That's when you decided to kill him.' A beat. 'And that's why you invited him to stay at the hotel. You wanted him close. By now you had formed a plan. And you decided to bring Peter into it. Your grandson. Aaron's son. I expect you had found out from Mary Koza about Peter – not directly, but you're a resourceful woman. You approached Peter and told him the truth, swore him to secrecy so that neither Mary nor his own family would be involved. And then you hired him to work at the hotel.' Silence. 'Or perhaps I have it back to front and it was Peter who approached *you*?'

'Peter is innocent,' repeated Ao. 'He has nothing to do with this.'

'I'm afraid you'll have a hard time convincing a jury of that.'

The woman said nothing.

'Why was John Templeton killed? Was it simply to try and put me off the scent?'

Silence.

'I suppose I have you to thank for the snake in my room.'

Ao stirred. 'You were on the way to Mokokchung the following morning. That meant you were on Aaron's trail. And that would eventually have led you to Peter. You became a threat.'

Persis accepted the explanation with a nod. 'One thing I still don't understand. When I interviewed you, you alibied each other. David Keishing confirmed that you and Peter were with him at the time Sinha was killed. Why did David choose to help?'

Keishing twitched. His face was lathered in sweat. He glanced down at Ao, then: 'All I have is this hotel. If you had arrested Madam Ao, what would have become of the Hotel Victoria?'

As pure a motive as any other, Persis supposed. 'There isn't much else to say, except that you are all under arrest for the murder of Mohan Sinha.'

She watched Ao pull a packet of cigarettes from her pocket, light one. 'Do you believe in justice, Inspector? I don't mean the law, but in justice.'

'Murdering a man in cold blood isn't justice.'

'In your world, perhaps. But I grew up in the hills. Don't weep for Mohan Sinha. He deserved everything he got.'

Persis had one final question. 'Why did you prop Sinha's corpse up in the bathtub, then fill the tub?'

Ao's gaze was impenetrable. 'It seemed . . . appropriate.'

57

The woman's words stayed with her as she drove to her final destination of the evening.

A part of her knew that Ao was right. She had felt that same sting often enough herself, hadn't she? Watching evildoers escape the consequences of their actions. In a fair world, fate would intervene, or make an illicit bargain with those equipped to mete out justice. And who was she to say that that was wrong?

Then again, she was a police officer, not a mercenary. To wear the khaki you swore to uphold the law. Not when it suited you, not only when it was easy, but even when every fibre of your being was screaming at you to go against the grain.

It would have been easy to let them go.

But living with such a decision would have been all but impossible.

It was by this same reasoning that she had now arrived at the Kohima hospital.

To make one final, unwelcome arrest.

She found Andrews in his office, filling out paperwork, a glass of whisky by his elbow.

As she saw him sitting there, bent over his desk, she wound back the clock to that day at the bridge, the scramble down to John Templeton's waiting corpse, the cross in Templeton's hand. How had it ended up there? Placed so conveniently to incriminate Christopher Danvers? What had Templeton been doing out at the bridge?

She had known, even then, that something did not sit right. An instinctive distrust of the dramatic gesture, the obvious clue. If her career had taught her anything it was that fate rarely laid the answers in your lap.

Andrews sat back. 'Are you never off duty, Inspector?'

'I could ask the same of you.'

She took the chair opposite him, rummaged in her pocket, then set a small pill bottle on to the desk. 'Blue 88s,' she said. 'Before coming to your office I asked to be taken to your medicine store. I found these in there. Right at the back. Ravi had already confirmed for me that they were there. Apparently, they're rarely prescribed. They were for military use and we're no longer at war.'

'Are you sure about that?' he said, softly. He picked up the bottle, squinted at it. 'And what do you think this proves?'

'It proves that you gave these to Apeni Ao. It proves that you had a hand in the conspiracy to murder Mohan Sinha, that you deliberately dragged your heels over the toxicology analysis. The question I've been asking myself is why? And there's only one answer I can think of.

'You told me that you had been out here, in the Naga Hills district, for a very long time. You were here two decades ago when Aaron Koza was murdered in a police cell by Mohan Sinha. Constable Binny has testified that you were the doctor called out to examine Aaron's body. You saw what Sinha had done, but you were forced to collude in the cover-up. Why did you go along with it?'

His eyes retracted into their sockets. 'I had no choice. I was under orders. Back then, the British army was still in charge here. They were already attempting to quell an initial uprising in the hills. The family suspected Aaron's death had been at the hands of local policemen – but they couldn't prove it. If it had come out that Sinha – a non-Naga – had killed Aaron, a man sent to the hills to undermine Naga calls for independence, all hell would have broken loose. And so I toed the line, Inspector. I did as I was told. Because I was a coward.'

'What changed?'

'Sinha came back. I was his doctor, and I quickly realised that the man had not an ounce of remorse for his actions. He was intent on more murder, subduing the Naga insurgency at all costs. There was a savagery in his eyes, hidden behind a veil of urbanity.'

'*You* told Apeni Ao that it was Sinha who had killed her son. But how did you know Aaron was *Apeni's* son?'

'There's no great mystery to it. I visited the hotel on regular occasion over the years – I am the on-call doctor there. Apeni and I developed a . . . friendship. One day, she revealed her secret to me. Her lost child. The child she had given away, the boy who had grown up in Kohima, and subsequently died in a police cell. I couldn't keep it from her then. I told her what I knew. I begged for her forgiveness. For not coming forward with the truth.'

Another part of the puzzle fell into place. 'And that's when you both hatched out a plan to murder Sinha.'

'It wasn't enough to kill him. Apeni wanted him to die in such a way that it would do justice to Aaron's memory. And, of course, so that suspicion wouldn't fall on her or Peter. Making the murder a locked room case was my idea. I have a weakness for detective novels. But I also hoped that it would make the case effectively unsolvable.'

'How did Peter become involved?'

'Apeni found him, told him the truth. Enlisted him. She had this idea that he needed to be a part of it. It was his father, after all.'

'She willingly put him in the firing line?'

'That's not how she thinks. She's descended from Naga warriors. As is Peter. Vengeance is a warrior's right.'

'By cutting off Sinha's head, you pointed the finger at Naga insurgents. Revolutionaries. Call them what you will. I can't imagine that that's what Aaron would have wanted.'

'On the contrary, Aaron was extremely proud of his Naga ancestry. Nothing would please him more than to see the old legends gaining national prominence once more. If Aaron were alive, he would have flocked to Baba Dao's banner.'

A thought struck her. 'Did you plant the note? In Sinha's desk?'

'We did.'

'Why?'

'The same reason Apeni chose to cut off Sinha's head. We had to make Baba Dao *real*.'

Something in the way he said this, a twist of the lips, set loose another boulder in her thoughts. Apeni Ao's words, uttered seemingly an age ago, returned to her: *And remember this: Baba Dao is more myth than man.*

'He doesn't exist, does he?' she breathed.

Andrews said nothing, then: 'Would you like a cigarette?'

She ignored him.

He reached into his desk. When his hand emerged, it was holding an automatic, pointed at Persis.

A nova of shock erupted inside her. *This* she hadn't foreseen.

'I'm sorry, Inspector, but I must ask you to very slowly take out your revolver and slide it across the desk.' He watched her carefully as she followed his instructions. Picking up the weapon, he thrust it into the pocket of his hospital gown. 'Hats off to you. Quite a feat, working that out. You're almost correct. Baba Dao *is* real, just not in the way you think. He is . . . an invention. Mine and Apeni's.'

'*You're* Baba Dao.' The very idea seemed absurd. 'Why?'

'The tribes are divided. Put them in a room together and they would find fifteen ways to engineer a war with one another. But the true enemy is out there. The mainland. The Centre. Apeni and I understood that the only way to bring the tribes together is to give them a symbol. A symbol that harks back to their ancestors, a symbol greater than the sum of their fears.'

'Why do you care? You're an outsider. A foreigner.'

'That's where you're wrong. I've spent more years out here than I can remember. I fell in love with these hills, these people, long ago. I understand them. Twenty years ago, I understood why they were dreaming of an independent nation. I'm a Scot. I've spent my life dreaming of an independent Scotland.' His eyes gleamed. 'Aaron Koza's death was my Damascus moment. From that instant, I became enjoined to the cause. Men are reinvented by their circumstances, Inspector. And there must be an accounting for outrage.'

'And what of the outrages committed by the British when they were here? Or by Naga insurgents when they murder Indian soldiers?'

'You should have been here during the war. The absurdity of foreign nations fighting over land that belonged to hill-men they had once labelled savages. But the Naga were never the savages. It's simply the nature of empires to seek hegemony over the earth. To justify greed and murder.' He broke off, choked off by his own rising anger. 'The Naga were better as pagans than Christians. We supplanted Gods they could touch and feel with a God that induces them to forget themselves. Baba Dao isn't a bogeyman. He is the embodiment of everything they once believed in.'

A silence. 'Did you kill John Templeton?'

'No, Inspector. You did.' He waited a beat. 'You were pursuing Aaron's death. We had to put you off the scent.'

'And so you murdered an innocent man?'

'Innocents die in every war. It was unfortunate for Templeton that he made the perfect scapegoat. I knew he was besotted by Sinha. It was a simple enough task to get Peter to take a message to him telling him to meet me out on the bridge, telling him to come alone.'

'Why would he trust you?'

'I told him I had information pertaining to Sinha's murder.'

'How did you overpower him?'

'I didn't have to. I asked him to lean over the bridge, to take a look at something below. And then I simply pushed him over.'

'And then you planted Christopher Danvers's cross in his hand.'

'Peter stole Christopher's cross from the Danvers's room. I put it in Templeton's hand.'

'Why? What I mean is, the Danvers were helping broker arms for your insurgency. Why would you point me in their direction?'

'The Danvers needed a short, sharp shock. We're not averse to using the CIA, Inspector, as a means to an end, but we won't allow them to dictate terms to us. These hills don't belong to them. They belong to the Naga. Besides, Florence Danvers is more than capable of handling the Chinese arms deal on her own.'

'Do they know that Baba Dao isn't real? Does Oren Rake know?'

'No. They've never met Baba Dao and they never will. All their dealings with the insurgency are via tribal connections that I – and Apeni – have cultivated over the years.'

She looked at him, a man on the edge of ruin, yet still holding forth like a Tudor king. 'It's over,' she said. 'Apeni has been arrested for Sinha's killing. Oren Rake is on the run. His opium operation will soon become untenable, cutting off finance for your insurgency. The Danvers's attempt to broker arms from China will fail, now that the Centre knows of the CIA's involvement. All that remains is to arrest you. And then Baba Dao's rebellion will truly be ended.'

He rose slowly to his feet. She watched him walk around the desk and loom over her. Fear bloomed at the base of her skull.

'The world isn't as black and white as you think. The Naga *must* fight. For their future and for their past. If the Centre continues to try to compel them, there will be decades of bloodshed.'

'Or perhaps the Naga will simply realise that it is better to be part of a powerful whole than out on their own?'

His brow furrowed. 'Is that really what you believe?'

Did she? She couldn't be sure. But her loyalty lay with the mainland, with the India that she knew, the India that she believed in. The India she had fought so hard for during the bitter years of the struggle to oust the British. A country – or, at least, the vision of one – where all Indians came together, united by common cause. Could she really yield that dream?

'Here's another ending,' said Andrews. 'Perhaps I'll vanish into the jungle and you'll never see me again. And Baba Dao's myth will grow stronger by the day.'

Before she could reply, his arm whirled. The butt of his weapon connected with her temple.

The lights went out.

58

'We weren't entirely wrong,' said Roshan Seth. 'It *was* a Naga who killed him, after all.'

It was the following afternoon and Persis was sitting in the Kohima station with her commanding officer and James Angami. The sweltering heat would have made the denizens of hell reach for a jug of lemonade. As it was, the only cooling on offer came from the stuttering ceiling fan, and the even cooler gaze of Constable Binny's chicken, who had wandered in to fix Persis with a beady glare, as if holding her personally responsible for the loss of its patron.

The morning had been eventful.

Colonel Shroff had arrived at the station as if marching into battle, intent on personally debriefing the investigative team. Persis, head still throbbing from the blow by Andrews, had been in no mood to accommodate him.

'Do you really expect me to believe that Baba Dao is the creation of a foreign doctor and an old woman who runs a hotel?' Shroff's incredulity had been a living thing, strutting around indignantly in Seth's office, hands clasped behind its back. 'Baba Dao is real. He's out there, laughing at us. But not for long. I'll get him soon enough. And when I do I'll parade his body up and down the hills.'

Persis hadn't the energy to rail at the man. She had set everything down in a written report. The report would find its way to those that mattered. Ultimately, Apeni Ao, Peter Jadonang, and

David Keishing would be tried for the murder of Mohan Sinha. And Andrews too, if they ever caught up with him.

She knew, from witnesses, that the doctor, having incapacitated her in his office, had immediately left the hospital. Last seen passing a checkpoint headed into the deep interior, claiming that he was on his way to tend to wounded soldiers. She suspected that the checkpoint guards who had waved him blithely into the night might soon find themselves stretched on a rack with Shroff turning the handle.

She had little doubt that Andrews would evade his pursuers. The doctor had been around the hills for decades, had cultivated Naga friends in every hilltop village. The chances were that he would never be seen again.

She wondered, briefly, at the choices the Scotsman had made, the winding path that had led him to throw his lot in with the Naga. In time, perhaps, he too would vanish into myth, a bedtime legend to frighten children, the white devil haunting the hills.

'What are they going to do to Binny?' asked James.

'That depends on how much of his story they believe,' said Seth. 'He says he never touched Aaron Koza, that it was Sinha who killed him.' He picked up a glass and raised it to his lips. 'Whatever happens with Binny, his days as a policeman are done.'

'And the Danvers?' said James.

'Beyond our remit. We have been instructed to keep our mouths shut on the matter of the CIA's involvement in the insurgency. As far as we're concerned, the Danvers do not, and have never, existed.'

Persis raised an eyebrow. 'Is Oren Rake going to get the same consideration?'

'Rake is dead,' said Seth. 'He was shot by Shroff's soldiers this morning. I received the news just an hour ago.'

The chambers of her skull hummed. She was struck, suddenly, by an image of the American on the night Sinha had been killed, leaning over the balcony at the hotel's rear porch, peering into the jungle with a cigar in hand. His voice returned to her, tumbling through the dark. *The Naga say each star is a warrior fallen in battle. They love a good death here.* Had Rake died a good death? She doubted it.

Her thoughts flashed to Florence Danvers.

She hoped the American had had the good sense to abandon her mission and leave the region. But good sense had been in short supply of late. Perhaps that was what war did. Blew to smithereens any sense of perspective. In a world that made sense Mohan Sinha and Aaron Koza would both still be alive. And Templeton, Andrews, Rake, and Florence and Christopher Danvers would not have been caught up in the madness.

Her thoughts persisted with Florence Danvers, an image of the American hacking her way through the jungle to China to close her arms deal. A part of her wanted to see the woman caught; a greater part of her wished her godspeed and a safe journey home.

'What happens now?' asked James.

'Now?' Seth's eyes might have been the points of twin knives. 'Persis and I are out of the doghouse. It's not beyond the bounds of possibility that our masters might consider a petition to transfer us home. Should we wish it.' His gaze turned to Persis. 'Well, Persis? What say you?'

She looked at him for the longest time, then wearily got to her feet, sweeping up her cap from his desk. 'Let me think about it.'

Back at the Hotel Victoria, she found Maria Fontanelli in the lobby, bags packed and waiting for a driver. Soldiers were conspicuous by their presence, marching around like ants on the warpath. A pair hovered beside her suitcases.

'Are you returning to Italy?' asked Persis.

'Just Calcutta for now. I've been ordered not to leave the country.'

'You realise that he has no *actual* authority over you?'

'Shroff?' She smiled grimly. 'I've dealt with worse. He reminds me of an uncle. A haircut and a pair of trousers and not much in between. He's told me I mustn't write about the case.'

'Why do I have a feeling that you're going to ignore him?'

'What else is a girl to do out here?'

It was Persis's turn to smile. 'How do you feel? I mean, you came out here to find your father. And then he . . . died.'

'He didn't die. He had his head cut off.' A noise dragged the Italian's gaze momentarily to the far side of the lobby where a pair of soldiers had collided with a bust and toppled it to the ground. A military operation was underway to clean up the mess. It seemed to involve a lot of shouting and gesticulating and some pointing of rifles. 'He wasn't my father,' she continued. 'Not in any meaningful sense. I should be grateful, I suppose. Bad enough he abandoned us. Now it turns out he was a murderer.'

'We can't choose our parents.'

'No. We can't at that.' She tipped her hat, then headed off towards the entrance, a brace of lovesick soldiers following in her wake with the suitcases.

Back in her room, Persis considered the days ahead.

Once the turbulence of recent events had settled down, the region would continue to remain in flux. Andrews had been right. The insurgency wouldn't die. It would go on and on until one side or the other yielded. How many lives would be lost in that time?

But then, was that not the great comic opera of history? Men never learned from their mistakes.

The phone rang. She picked it up.

A hoarse silence drifted down the line. And then a voice. Male. British. A voice she knew almost as well as her own, now transmuted into something all but unrecognisable.

'Persis? It's me. Archie.'

She placed a hand on her stomach as if struggling to hold in her own guts. Seconds ticked by.

'Persis? Are you there?'

She swam up from the swamp. 'Yes.'

Another silence, and then, 'Sam tells me you're in the Naga Hills. In the thick of it.'

The world snapped sharply back into focus. 'When did you come out of your coma?'

'To be honest, I'm not entirely sure that I have. Everything seems surreal, blurry. The doctors keep poking and prodding me as if I were a human pincushion. I don't think they expected me to make it back to the land of the living.'

'I knew you would.' The words were choked out of her.

'Is that why you ran away to the other side of the world?'

'I was transferred here. I didn't have a choice.'

'We both know that's a lie.' A silence. She imagined him on his hospital bed, skull bundled in bandages, green eyes flashing. 'In my head, I've apologised a million times. For not telling you the truth from the very beginning. When I came out to India, I severed all connection with England, with my past life. As far as I was concerned, I was alone. My divorce may not have been settled on paper, but my marriage was over. It's as simple as that. And then I met you. Could I have imagined the strength of feeling I would develop for you? And, once I knew that I felt that way, I couldn't bring myself to risk jeopardising what we had. I made a conscious decision not to tell you. That was a mistake. I should have trusted you. I should have trusted myself.'

His words battered at her, a gale howling around her ears. Her knuckles had turned white on the receiver. In that instant, she was back in the Kohima hospital room, looking into James Angami's eyes. That sensation of falling.

'Come back, Persis. Come back to me.'

She felt herself shaking, a trembling that rose inside her until she felt she might shake herself apart. 'How can I?' she said, her voice breaking. 'I will never be any man's mistress.'

'Do you really believe that I think of you that way?' he said, softly. 'No, Persis. Never that.'

She set down the phone, then returned to sit on the bed. She stared sightlessly at the floor, and then, driven by agitation, rose and went to the French windows, flinging open the doors and walking on to the balcony.

Her expression must have been fearsome to behold, because the capuchins, a cluster of smudged shadows in the branches of a tree sprouting from the courtyard below, remained where they were. She saw one reach for his rear end with a cupped paw. Her own hand drifted to her revolver. 'Go ahead,' she heard herself mutter. 'Make my day.'

Something of her intent appeared to communicate itself to the monkey. It turned its back on her and vanished into the tree's upper branches.

She stood there, staring out at the courtyard, the blistering blue of the sky above, the hard white ball of the sun beating pale fire on to the earth below.

What was life anyway but a series of events over which you had only the illusion of control? A rollercoaster ride with no one at the controls, doomed to cycle around endlessly, clinging grimly on until the inevitable crash. In the end it simply boiled down to this: *what could she live with in the pursuit of her own happiness?*

It took a while for the answer to arrive, and when it did, she walked back into the room, picked up the phone, and asked to be connected to Roshan Seth. 'I've thought about what you said.'

'And?'

'And I want to go back. Back to Bombay.'

Author's Note

Although this is a work of fiction, many of the ingredients have been culled from fact:

- The Naga tribes in the eastern jungles of India have a long history of headhunting. The practice was officially banned in 1969, with the last reported cases in the early 1960s.
- American Baptists – and British missionaries – did indeed convert most of the population to Christianity.
- The Naga National Council declared 'independence' on 14 August 1947, one day before India officially became independent from Britain.
- The Naga Hills region became an official Indian state called Nagaland in 1963.
- An insurgency in the region in support of Nagaland's independence has been ongoing till today, with many deaths on both sides, and regular accusations of murder and torture. The Aaron Koza case is fictional, but several similar cases have made headlines in the region over many decades.
- The Battle of Kohima was indeed one of the bloodiest in WW2 and is known as the 'Stalingrad of the East'. Its most famous engagement was the Battle of the Tennis Court.
- The fact that the CIA has been involved in supporting the Naga insurgency has been recorded in official assessments of the region by several sources.

- Opium has been a scourge of the eastern hills of India for a very long time.
- I am indebted to the book *Nagaland* by Jonathan Glancey in helping bring to life Naga history and culture.

Acknowledgements

India is such a vast place that there are endless fascinating stories. As with all the books in this series, *this* story is based on certain hard realities, blending fact and fiction. As a novelist I consider it my job to entertain and inform, striking a balance between truth and fiction. I hope I have managed that.

This book wouldn't be possible without the efforts of many.

So, thank you, firstly, to my editor Jo Dickinson, who has believed in this series - and in Persis - from the beginning, and my agent Euan Thorneycroft at A.M. Heath, who continues, tirelessly, to guide my career.

I would also like to thank the others involved at Hodder, namely, my publicist Alainna Hadjigeorgiou, assistant editor Kate Norman, Alice Morley in marketing, Juliette Winter in production and Dom Gribben in audiobooks. And thank you, once again, to Jack Smyth for another eye-catching cover, perhaps the best of the lot.

Thank you also to the many readers, critics, reviewers, bloggers, book-groupers, booksellers, and word-of-mouth enthusiasts who have helped build this series.

A writer's life can be a lonely one but the idea that there are readers out there, in all corners of the world, enjoying these books always leaves me feeling that I have friends in abundance. Thank you!

READ THE HIGHLY ACCLAIMED
MALABAR HOUSE SERIES

BOOK 1

BOOK 2

BOOK 3

BOOK 4

BOOK 5

BOOK 6

Listen to the MURDER JUNCTION podcast

British crime writers Vaseem Khan and Abir Mukherjee bring to life history's most intriguing murders, both true crime and fictional, in the company of the world's best known crime writers. They make murder . . . fun. Listen in on iTunes, Spotify, Spreaker or your favourite podcast app.

Join Vaseem's Newsletter

You can also keep up to date with Vaseem's work by joining his newsletter. It goes out approximately six times a year and includes:

*Extracts from Vaseem's next book
*Exclusive short stories
*Competitions – win signed copies of books
*News of forthcoming events and signings

You can join the newsletter in just a few seconds at Vaseem's website:

WWW.VASEEMKHAN.COM